Gallant rubbed his brow, gauging the speed of the approaching enemy brig. She was swooping and lifting over the swells, fine on the bow, now no more than three hundred yards away: a beautiful image, the curving canvas gleaming in still power in the sunlight, the bow wave a roaring, frothing white as she bore in.

Two hundred yards. One hundred.

And then suddenly she was there, her bowsprit arrowing past that of *La Bretonne*, the combined speed of the two ships making her rush past like a carriage at full gallop. From her rolling, pitching foredeck a bow gun banged out, and with a hollow, slapping sound a neat round hole appeared in the mizzen spanker, fifteen feet over Gallant's head. Her broadside would follow in but a moment more—

Now. Now!

"Fire as you bear!" Gallant roared.

"Spirited, primary-colored period adventure." —*Kirkus*

THE GALLANT SAGA

IN PERILOUS SEAS

Look for all these Tor books by Victor Suthren

THE BLACK COCKADE
A KING'S RANSOM
IN PERILOUS SEAS

VICTOR SUTHREN

THE GALLANT SAGA

IN PERILOUS SEAS

A TOM DOHERTY ASSOCIATES BOOK

IN PERILOUS SEAS

Copyright © 1983 by Victor Suthren

Reprinted by arrangement with St. Martin's Press

First Tor printing: May 1987

A TOR Book

Published by Tom Doherty Associates, Inc.
49 West 24 Street
New York, N.Y. 10010

ISBN: 0-812-58868-1
CAN. ED.: 0-812-58869-X

Library of Congress Catalog Card Number: 83-26998

Printed in the United States of America

0 9 8 7 6 5 4 3 2 1

For Lindsay

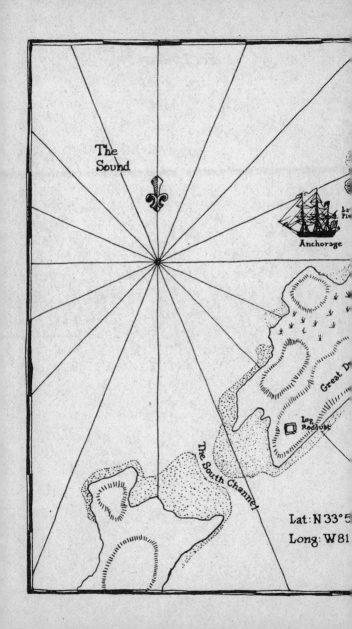

The Sound

Anchorage

Great D[...]

Lo[...]
Redou[...]

The South Channel

Lat: N 33°5[...]

Long: W 81[...]

The Stronghold

The North Channel

Well

Swampy Land

The
Atlantic
Ocean

The Lair of the
Privateer
Jacob TenHaaf
The Carolinas
1747

THE GALLANT SAGA

In PERILOUS SEAS

ONE

Tuesday, the ninth of October, 1747, was ending in a magnificent Antilles sunset of towering, flame-coloured cloud to the westward on the Caribbean horizon. The sun was sinking in golden, bloated glory, turning the sea to a pathway of burning copper. The Pitons du Carbet, the ridge of three high green peaks that formed the spine of the lush French island of Martinique, were turning a deep amber, and the same light washed down the dark slopes to the low white buildings of the capital, Fort Royal, touching the tile and tin rooftops and the spires of the cathedral with the same peach tones. The trade winds, fitful on this western, leeward side of the island, had died and the curls of vapour from the first cool of the evening rose like delicate smoke into the heavy, fragrant air. It was a golden moment, brief and fleeting before the suddenness of the Caribbean night; but from the Governor's residence, set high behind the town on the foothill rise of the Pitons, a pair of eyes was gazing out at the splendour clouded with a preoccupation that had little of the appreciation of nature in it.

1

The Chevalier Jean-François Auguste Grégoire de Blois, Sieur de Valigny, and His Most Christian Majesty Louis XV's Governor-General of the Windward Islands, and thus of Martinique, stood at the great flung-back windows with hands clasped behind his back, the toes of one foot in its elegant, glossy pump idly tapping in rhythm. He was a tall man, with a patrician hooked nose between pale eyes set in a careworn face. There was an elegance to his form and dress, as befitted a senior official of the Marine in the Americas, and against his tasteful stylishness the more prosaic dress of the admirauté clerk who hovered in attendance seemed sombre indeed.

"His vessel. The frigate, *La Bretonne*. Is that her, the one on the right?" said Valigny.

"Yes, m'sieu'," said the clerk, who was called Gignac. "The thirty-six-gunner, off the mouth of the Monsieur." He coughed into a crumpled handkerchief. "Been at anchor for three days. And already driving my assistants insane with his requests for stores and victuals."

Valigny nodded. "Indeed? Read his dossier again."

Gignac sighed, as if with great patience, and opened the leatherbound folio he was carrying. For a few moments he riffled through the pages, and then he coughed and dabbed at the corners of his mouth with the handkerchief.

"Capitaine de frégate Paul François Adhémar Gallant. Chevalier de Saint-Louis. And recently Chevalier de Saint-Lazarus. Native of Louisbourg. Cadetship in the Troupes de la Marine, Louisbourg garrison, 1742, after leaving merchant service. Promoted enseigne, 1743. In 1745 he commanded the corvette *Echo* with dispatches to Toulon. In 1746, in the same vessel, successfully recovered the most significant item in a Royal treasure from the hands of buccaneers. Regrettably lost his vessel in the process," Gignac sniffed.

"Ah, yes. I recall. That gold figurine, hein?"

"Yes, m'sieu'. The King made him a Knight of Saint Lazarus, and he was promoted directly to capitaine de frégate, in command of the new national frigate *La Bretonne*, thirty-six. Took part honourably in the affair of M. de la Jonquière in May of this year, escaping with several of the most valuable merchantmen from the Englishman, Anson."

Valigny pursed his lips. "Interesting. An obvious capacity for initiative. What else?"

"Nothing, m'sieu'. On his return to l'Orient he was charged with the escort of a convoy to the Senegal and was after inbound to the Biscay when *Emeraude* finally found him."

Valigny narrowed his eyes. "Did *La Bretonne* speak any other vessel after *Emeraude*? Any at all?"

Gignac scanned the folio. "Apparently not, Your Excellency. This copy of his report says he spoke no vessel until landfall, at Pointe d'Enfer."

"Hmm. Then he has been without contact with France for some time indeed."

"Yes, m'sieu'. He sailed at the end of April. He was already a month at sea when the *Lima* sailed."

"Very well." Valigny's eyes grew thoughtful again. "There is one possible problem. Is he married?"

"No."

"Betrothed?"

Gignac riffled through the folio papers for a moment. "He was, m'sieu'. To an Englishwoman, an Abigail Collier. She had been named to the Court as a lady-in-waiting in partial reward for capitaine Gallant's last success."

"And?"

"She died suddenly of a fever, m'sieu'. He was with her when it took place." He paused, reading. "There was some question for a time whether he might resign his commission. His grief was great, apparently."

Valigny nodded, his expression thoughtful. "Indeed? A sobering grief, few ties. . . . Perhaps not unwelcome things for our purposes." He turned from the window. "Very well. Send a boat for him."

"Er — I have, m'sieu'. He's been on the terrace for an hour." Gignac dabbed with the handkerchief.

Valigny looked back out the window, at the dark mass of *La Bretonne*, a looming shadow against the copper surface of the evening sea. "And in a foul mood, I'd think. Sometimes, Gignac, you overly anticipate me."

Then, moving toward his nearby desk, he shot his cuffs in a businesslike gesture.

"Have him shown in, Gignac," he said. "I must see if he is the man. The man I need." And as Gignac bowed and turned away, Valigny added under his breath, "And by the Saints, I pray God he is . . ."

Capitaine de frégate Paul Gallant was indeed pacing in steadily mounting irritation across the white-tiled terrace. Under different circumstances he might have enjoyed the view out over the

3

rooftops of the languid capital to the harbour; Gallant's feet were at a level with the clumps of palm and roof peaks that marked the expanse of the town, spread out before him in the deep orange wash of the sunset. There had been a brief, thunderous shower a half-hour earlier, and every colour in the rich, brilliant foliage seemed washed and lustrous. The green masses of the hills and plantation fields running down to the shoreline, the white evenness of the airy, single-storey buildings, and the burnish of the sea below the cloud-hung glory of the sunset, silhouetting the black shapes of the anchored shipping in the harbour, were awe-inspiring.

The mind of Paul Gallant was on other things, however. To begin with, the dying of the usually steady breeze meant the air was now thick and humid, and steaming with heat. Gallant could feel sweat running down his back and arms, cementing his uniform, his best, to him disagreeably and making him yearn for the cool looseness of his well-worn sea clothes. He pried the gilt-laced black tricorn from his head and tugged at his neckcloth, blowing a drop of sweat from his nose.

Gallant was tall, almost six feet in height, and he had the broad-shouldered athletic stance of a soldier in his carriage, his body more slim and angular than thickset. His hair was dark brown, neatly queued with a simple black ribbon, and his face was long, a look of command and authority to the set of the jaw. The dark, intelligent eyes that peered out from below even black brows were edged, however, with lines that spoke of a certain humour and sensitivity as well as the professional squint of the seaman. For all that he was a young man, he carried with him an aura of competence and perceptive self-assurance more commonly seen in older men.

Even in the fading light of the sunset his uniform was a pale swatch of colour against the whitewashed stucco and tile of the residence. Although entitled to the full regalia of an officer in the navy of Louis XV, Gallant preferred the simpler dress of the Compagnies Franches de la Marine, the naval infantry of French vessels and overseas colonies in which he had begun his career. His full-skirted uniform coat of off-white had cuffs and turnbacks of deep blue, and was worn over breeches, waistcoat and hose of the same deep blue. All were fixed and fastened with large brass buttons, and there was a brass button on the three-cornered hat of felted beaver with a silken black cockade that he wore low over his eyes. Low, buckled black pumps and an elegant dress sword on his left hip completed the picture, but at the moment, Gallant loathed it all. The heavy wool of the

4

uniform could keep a man reasonably warm in the bone-numbing chill of an autumn gale in the Biscay; in the tropic heat of Martinique, prized French jewel in the Caribbean, it was a stifling garb of torture.

Gallant tugged again at his neckcloth and blew another drop of sweat away, the maddening repetitiveness of the action stoking his increasingly short temper. And then there was a click of pump heels behind him, and a black servant in pale green livery and powdered dress wig, studied and slow, appeared in the open terrace doors through which Gallant had been shown almost an hour earlier. The man's face bore a horrid, livid scar, as though from a cutlass blade, which cut diagonally across his features from forehead to cheek through one eye. The eye it crossed was clouded with the white glisten of a cataract, a repelling disfigurement. The servant adopted a position of studied elegance, langour mixed with disdain eloquent in his bow.

"If m'sieu' would care for some refreshment—," he began.

"God damn your hide. If I want something, I'll call!"

The servant straightened as if struck. His one good eye flashed for a moment at Gallant. Then, with immense dignity, he retreated into the interior. Gallant regretted the words the instant they were out of his mouth. The servant had only been solicitous.

Pox the regrets, said another, unrepentant part of his mind. He was a King's Officer and he commanded a King's ship. If the Governor wished to keep him cooling his heels in an idiotic show of bureaucratic superiority, room would have to be made for Gallant's temper.

He wiped his forehead with one heavy cuff and stalked to the balustrade, beyond and below which the crowns of the unmoving trees stretched away. Out past the town, beyond the curving seafront of the Place de la Savane, he concentrated on the shapes of the assembled vessels in the anchorage, naval and otherwise. He ran his eye professionally over each dark shape, estimating the power of its sail plan, its seakeeping quality, its guns and weight of broadside. There was the comforting shape of *La Bretonne*, of course, somewhat off to the right, scarcely three cables off the murky mouth of the Monsieur River. Directly before him, in the shimmering copper light of the setting sun, rode a clutch of local craft, sloops and cutters most of them, with one schooner with a New England look to its raked topsail rig. A little to the left rode a portly Indiaman of the Compagnie des Indes. Heavily built, under-rigged—and likely undergunned, with a smug and near-mutinous crew of ill-disciplined layabouts, if Gallant knew Indiamen. But even she might carry eighteen or

5

perhaps twenty guns, eight pounders or larger. Not a broadside to sneeze at.

Gallant tugged a handkerchief from his sleeve cuff and wiped his brow, trying to keep his mind on the ships as a check to his steadily growing annoyance. Further to the left, almost under the peach-tinted stone mass of Fort Saint-Louis, rode the newest addition to the anchorage's collection, the hulking shape of a sixty-gun ship. She was Spanish: the *Nuestra Señora de Lima*. And had the glare of the dying sun not thrown her into shadow, the gilt and red of her hull paint would have challenged the hues of the vegetation around Gallant.

He snorted and resumed his pacing, listening to the echo of his heels off the residence walls. Not that all that Spanish gilt meant the ship would be worth a sous in a fight, he thought. He had seen the *Lima's* captain row by in his gig last evening: by all appearances an arch and arrogant *hidalgo* wreathed in lace and feathers and surrounded by a shoal of slavering sycophants, the supposed officers of the ship. One look at the man, and another at *Lima's* crewmen, and Gallant felt sure the big vessel would suffer the usual Spanish disease: the tendency for individual bravery, real enough, to become group incompetence, and on occasion, cowardice. But it would be a different matter if he could get his hands on a line-of-battle ship like that, but crewed with the likes of *La Bretonne's* sturdy lads.

Gallant found his hand reaching for his waistcoat pocket, to take out a small oval locket on a slender chain. He opened the locket slowly and looked down with a tender expression at the small, beautiful portrait.

Ah, Abigail, he thought. My dear, lost love. Damn the war that kept us apart, when we might have shared those months together. Damn the war that keeps driving me through this misery of hate and killing and never releases me from the thought of you, and what might have been. . . .

"M'sieu'?" the servant intoned unexpectedly from the doorway. "His Excellency admits you. If you'll follow me—"

Gallant looked up sharply, the mask forced swiftly into place over his expression. He slipped the miniature back into his waistcoat and, with a curt nod, strode after the man. They passed into the shadows of the interior, now being lit by servants igniting the great chandeliers which lowered on cords from the ceilings. Within a minute the servant pushed open high, panelled doors into a large room, and stepped back.

"Your Excellency. Capitaine de frégate Gallant," he announced. The blind eye gleamed whitely in the gloom.

With his hat tucked under his arm Gallant went in, his heels

6

ringing on the tiles. Ahead of him across the broad floor a delicate white and gilt chinoiserie desk sat before the exquisite splendour of a Gobelin tapestry. From the ceiling the flickering flames of a crystal chandelier cast a muted glow over the otherwise empty room, matching the last rays of the sun which streamed in a window overlooking the distant anchorage.

Standing behind the little desk, which bore but an inkstand and two neatly ribboned dossiers, was the slim and courtly figure of the Sieur de Valigny. Gallant's eyes took in his gilt-edged elegance of pale grey silk, the white hose above neat grey shoes, the spotless and snowy wig clinging close to his head in smooth waves until ending at the grey silken bow at his neck. The lace at Valigny's wrists and throat seemed fresh and unsoiled, the brow of the patrician face regarding Gallant with a touch of relaxed imperiousness untouched by a drop of moisture. To Gallant, chafing in a dozen places and running with sweat, the tidy calm of Valigny was a final humiliation to be added to the Governor's infuriating silence since *La Bretonne's* arrival three days ago.

Gallant drew himself to his full height and into a position of attention.

"Your humble servant, m'sieu'," he said, as smoothly as he could manage, and inclined in a slight bow.

Valigny gestured sparingly at a small chair before the desk.

"Capitaine. I am delighted," he said, in smooth tones. "Please."

Gallant folded himself into the little chair, hitching his scabbard out of the way. Valigny had seated himself behind the desk and was regarding him intently over steepled fingertips. For a brief moment a waft of air touched Gallant from the doors, heavy with the scent of sodden undergrowth.

"I regret the delay in receiving you, capitaine," said Valigny. "My affairs. You will understand." He smiled lightly.

Gallant kept his face a benign mask. It would do little good to point out that since *La Bretonne's* arrival Gallant had already been launched into an exasperating battle with the arrogant clerks of the local admirauté over every conceivable concern involved in maintaining a King's man-of-war, and which a few direct orders from Valigny might have avoided. The task had also begun of keeping *La Bretonne's* seamen from sliding into the quicksand of sloth, vice and drink Fort Royal offered. The arrival in the Martiniquan fleshpot, it seemed, was proving to be redeemed only by the recovery it afforded from the rigour of the transatlantic passage.

"Of course, m'sieu'," said Gallant.

Valigny tapped the dossier before him with one long and carefully manicured finger.

"Your report is thorough enough. I shall ensure that the portion dealing with the convoy to the Senegal is forwarded to France at the earliest opportunity."

"Thank you, m'sieu'." Gallant's reply was even.

Valigny's eyebrows lifted almost imperceptibly. "Your annoyance is justified, Gallant. I do apologize again for having delayed our interview so long." He leaned forward. "There was, of course, just cause."

Gallant waited for him to continue.

"You've seen the large Spanish vessel in the roads, I should think. The — er —"

"The *Lima*, m'sieu'," said Gallant. "Sixty guns."

"Quite. Have you met her captain? Don Alfonso Castelar?"

"I've not had the honour, m'sieu'. Seen him, but at a distance."

"Ah. Yes." Valigny pursed his lips. "Pity. Thought you might have had a chance to take his professional measure. Reassure me that he's not as worthless as he seems."

This time it was Gallant's eyebrows that lifted.

"Oh, don't look surprised. In this sort of work, my dear Gallant, one learns to judge men quickly and accurately." He smiled thinly. "A condition of survival."

Gallant nodded. In spite of himself he felt his annoyance fading, to be replaced with a rising warmth at the candour Valigny was showing.

"Don Alfonso — the remainder of his elaborate name goes on for nearly a paragraph — is socially, at least, proving to be an incarnation of every possible vice of his nation, with damned few of the virtues. Haven't the ghost of an idea of him as an officer. You may smile, Gallant. You didn't spend last evening at cards with the fellow. Or trying to restrain him from pursuing other less acceptable diversions with every upright planter's wife in the room."

"The Dons have their appetites, I think, m'sieu'."

"Quite. However" — Valigny rose and paced carefully to the windows — "one has more to worry about than keeping some Spanish oaf from mounting one of our panicky matrons on the dinner table, what?"

Gallant controlled his smile. "Of a certainty, m'sieu'."

Valigny's pursed lips marked a return to serious thought, and he looked out over the dying embers of the sunset.

"This damnable war. It's drawing to a close, Gallant. Did

you know that?'' he said, after a moment. "And there is every appearance that we have lost it."

Gallant was silent.

"In this part of the world, the capture of Louisbourg has made trade transshipment virtually an impossibility, hein? I look at that pitiful collection of worm-riven merchantmen and wonder what I'm to tell the planters tomorrow, Gallant. They're being ruined. No bottoms to carry cargoes for France, no trade with the English colonies, insurance underwriting costs near the moon, hardly enough specie in the coffers to keep things ticking along. . ." He paused.

"I can sympathize with your position, m'sieu'," offered Gallant.

Valigny eyed him. "Likely you can. Your record suggests enough damned perceptiveness for that. It may help you to perceive my present greatest concern."

"M'sieu'?"

"There is a twenty-vessel convoy inbound from the Senegal which I've been expecting for weeks. They are mostly armed Indiamen, with bulk cargoes. No damned slaves, thank God. There are several vessels only partly laden, and I've got to get my planters' consignments into them." He paused. "If we don't, the colony is ruined. Simple as that."

"How, sir? If I may ask, that is," said Gallant.

"It means we shall simply have to leave the place to its own devices, Gallant. It and every other withered French flower in these Antilles. The damned English can have them."

Valigny took a deep breath and wiped his brow, which for the first time since Gallant had entered was showing tiny beads of moisture. "Those vessels out there. That Indiaman and the other scows. They'll join the convoy, and as soon as possible I'll order them on to France."

Valigny resumed his seat and fixed an intent look on Gallant. "I am sure you can appreciate what the ruinous cost of this war has done to France, Gallant. The King, unless we find an honourable peace soon, will be little better than a beggar." He paused. "The successful arrival of this convoy in France is a matter of considerable importance for Martinique — and the Royal coffers."

"I understand, m'sieu'," said Gallant. So that was it. Convoy escort. *La Bretonne* would be ordered to take part in the tedious escort of the Indiamen back across the Atlantic. Likely the *Lima* would be involved as well, and with her rate, sixty guns, it would be Gallant's ill luck that this Don Alfonso person undoubtedly would be named Commodore. The prospect of months at sea under reduced sail, maneuvering once again to herd slothful and unwilling merchantmen back into some kind of controllable formation, all the while responding to the sort of maddeningly bothersome and insulting orders Gallant could imagine issuing from *Lima* in an unbroken stream was depressing to Gallant, to say the least. And then there was the question of the damned English. The convoy track would have to pass within striking distance of privateer lairs in the Bermudas, to say nothing of the Leewards. And if the French escaped the notice of the British West Indian Squadron every league closer to the Biscay meant a growing proximity to the standing force the British now maintained in the Western Approaches, making any northern French port a risky goal.

Gallant sighed. Not that the whole arc of sea from the Low Countries to Gibraltar was not alive with the increasingly triumphant vessels of England. Altogether the prospect of preparing *La Bretonne* for such a thankless voyage was a gloomy one. What Béssac, *La Bretonne's* Mate, and the others of her company might say was hard to predict, but the groans of dismay were already ringing loud in his imagination.

"Capitaine? Did you hear what I said?"

Gallant started. "Your pardon, m'sieu'?"

"The voyage, Gallant. You'll likely be the target of any number of British warships. Or privateers, for that matter, hein?" His eyes were boring into Gallant.

"Er — yes. That's to be expected, m'sieu."

"What do you know of the Bermudas?"

Gallant thought for a moment. "Low-lying archipelago with a lot of dangerous reefs, as I recall. Some English settlement." He smiled lightly. "And a prodigious number of privateers and other brigands."

"Precisely. I expect Don Alfonso to set the convoy track within fifty leagues of them. So you'd best be prepared for the worst."

Gallant nodded. With the vessels in the harbour added to the twenty-odd inbound from the Senegal, the convoy would be of fair size. And there would be little use in looking to the Compagnie vessels for self-protection. The lion's share of any defence would have to be made by *Lima* and *La Bretonne*. But two men-of-war alone made a thin line of defence.

"Another escort, sir," said Gallant. "What is the possibility of increasing the escort strength?"

"Eh?" said Valigny. "How?"

"Give me one of those vessels out there. Let me improve her armament, perhaps put gun crews and captains into her. Man her outright if I have to."

"Hmm. I had planned to have you get some of *Lima's* stores. She was overprovisioned at Cartagena —"

"It's a ship I need, m'sieu'. With all respect."

Valigny looked at him carefully. "To give you another fighting vessel, is that it?"

"Yes, m'sieu'."

"Damned difficult . . ." Valigny scratched his chin. "I can't touch any of the Senegalese. The others out there all have their ladings assigned, and I'd have a revolt on my hands if I landed one of those cargoes. Except . . ."

"M'sieu'?"

"The *Diane*. A Compagnie vessel to be sure, hein? But I was to hold her in reserve and use her as a Post vessel to Cayenne. She has a reduced rig, as I believe you seamen call it, but restored it makes her handy, and fast in the bargain, I'm told."

Gallant sat up. "The little Indiaman, moored by the *Lima*? She'd be ideal, m'sieu'. A good gun platform, with that hull."

Valigny thought for a long moment. "And I'd suppose you'd want guns for her?"

"Yes, m'sieu'. She's only mounted the usual reduced battery, by her look. I'd need to get a dozen six- or twelve-pounders into her."

"Indeed? And where would you —?"

"Fort Saint-Louis, m'sieu'. I've already had my gunner go through your ordnance stores there. You've got over twenty guns with truck carriages stored there."

Valigny's eyebrows rose. "Your gunner! My dear Gallant, by doing something like that you seriously run the risk of —" The nobleman broke off, and Gallant saw a faint smile cross his lips. "Oh, the Devil take it. Very well, Gallant. You can have the *Diane*."

"Thank you, m'sieu'."

"But you realize I must make an honest woman of her."

"M'sieu'?"

"Buy her into the navy. Or at least write a promissory note for her. And that may mean she'll be without her officers and men. I cannot press contracted Compagnie des Indes crews, hein?" He leaned forward. "She is also a French vessel, and therefore I place responsibility for her with you as senior French vessel. Even with Don Alfonso in command."

Gallant nodded.

"What I'm telling you, Gallant, is that we'll require you to man her yourself if need be. Officers *and* men."

"We'll manage, m'sieu'."

Valigny pursed his lips. "Yes. Well, we'll see. And now to the last problem I shall present to you. There is a certain remarkably handsome noblewoman whom I've had the pleasure of acting as host to. Have you met her?"

"Ah . . . no, m'sieu'."

"Hmm. By your expression you haven't. Any of the young bucks about here who have light up like rockets when her name is mentioned." Valigny sniffed delicately. "At any rate, she's Marianne de Poitrincourt, Marquise de Bézy. Been with us for about five months now. And a travail it's been, I can tell you. Now she's determined to return to France, and this convoy provides the excuse."

Gallant nodded, listening.

"Came out against all advice to marry the Sieur de Courcelette at Cayenne. Fellow had the indecency to die of the bloody flux before she got here. Damned inconvenient. She's been rather an addition to the social scene, I suppose. But it's been tending her bloody wants and thinking of things to keep her amused *and* wondering when in God's name some adequate and appropriate vessel to ship her home in would put in. Your *La Bretonne*, thank God, scratches that particular itch."

Gallant sat up. "I — I beg your pardon, m'sieu'?"

"Surely your quarters will be adequate," went on Valigny with little apparent notice of the expression on Gallant's face, "although wait until you see Madame's mountain of luggage. Quite extraordinary."

Gallant's voice returned. "With all due respect, m'sieu'. *Lima* is a sixty-gun ship. Her great cabin would be twice the size of ours. If this Castelar fellow is somewhat of an embarrassment he is surely still a Spanish gentleman. Would it not be more in the Marquise's interest to have her make the passage with him?" Inwardly, Gallant was quailing at the prospect of what suddenly opened before his mind's eye: an endless Atlantic convoy with the precious sanctuary of his cabin denied to him and given over to a clutch of women. It was a selfish and childish thought, but it came unbidden and strong, and he had allowed himself to give vent to it.

"Not in my opinion, Gallant," said Valigny, the lines on his face deepening noticeably. "I shall, you see, charge you with the personal responsibility of the safe return of the Marquise to

France. In the extreme event that the convoy is threatened, you will have to see that the lady is not taken. Or suffers anything worse."

Gallant's eyebrows rose. "Forgive me, m'sieu'. But are you saying that — that I must concern myself with this *to the exclusion of the convoy*? An absurd implication, I know, but . . ."

Valigny's pale expression revealed the struggle that was going on within him, between the near-desperate concern he felt for the success of this convoy and his responsibility toward the woman. A responsibility he was about to place, it seemed, without reservation on Gallant's shoulders.

"To the exclusion of the convoy," he said, evenly. "And don't think I don't know what I'm saying, for God's sake. Everything I've said about this convoy holds true. But I charge you to see Her Ladyship completes the journey. I cannot put it more simply." He paused briefly, and took a deep breath.

"There is a reason. She's the favourite cousin of the King."

"Oh, Lord," muttered Gallant.

"Exactly. To lose a member of the Royal household to the British Navy would be enough of a nightmare. Losing her to some loathsome privateer would be unthinkable."

Valigny's observation was something of an understatement, as Gallant realized even before the Governor had finished speaking. Nothing would prolong a losing and useless war more than the vengeful fury of a monarch determined to repay a slur on his immediate family.

"I understand, m'sieu'," said Gallant stonily.

Valigny steepled his fingertips. "There is another, more frightening aspect to this whole thing. Something I merely sense. Perhaps because I don't wish to believe the evidence."

Gallant waited for him to go on.

"I'm not certain, Gallant," he said, quietly. "But for the last week or so I believe someone has been trying to kill her. . . ."

The chamber music began again, concentric little ripples of sound from the *concerto grosso* assemblage of bewigged and sweating musicians clustered in the far corner of the great ballroom. The din of chatter of the hundred-odd guests rose at once to be heard above it, so that the elegant, conversational posturings — the timed pinches of snuff, fluttered fans, hands thrust with a scented handkerchief to the nostrils at the approach

13

of ill vapours or a more ill phrase — were tools of conversation held at the top of one's lungs, rather than graceful, sibilant whisperings. The hall was brilliantly lit by a dozen enormous candelabra which diffused a rich yellow glow over the pale arch of ceiling, down the panelled walls with their swept-back draperies and flung-open rows of glassed doors, to the gleaming parquetry of the ballroom floor, over which the guests flowed and eddied. The enormous skirts of the women's gowns rustled against the white silken hose of the gentlemen as they circled and posed passably in the first steps of a *pavane*, and to an observer watching the more or less graceful swirls of silk, satin, velvet and brocade below the inclining white-wigged heads and the powdered, patched faces, there was not a great deal lost between a soirée in Versailles and the one now taking place in the sweltering heat of the Martiniquan evening. That a few of the gentlemen boasted a provincial corpulence, or that a few of the women were not at all at ease under the layerings of wig, powder, paint, patches and sweat did not lessen the fact, and the Governor could flatter himself that he was hosting an evening's gathering of very commendable sophistication.

Standing to one side of a set of the open doors which led out on the terrace, Paul Gallant shifted his weight to ease the cramps in his feet, which were protesting the long evening in the small black dress pumps he wore. He was in full dress uniform, drenched in sweat, and stood toying with the hilt of his gilt dress hanger while listening with half an ear to the muttered complaints of Théophile-Auguste Béssac, *La Bretonne's* First Lieutenant.

"Christ on a crutch, capitaine. How much longer does this go on?" Béssac's ursine form was rarely out of his stained old seacoat, which he wore even on watch in *La Bretonne*, as religiously as he proclaimed he was the Mate of the vessel, and not some damned naval rank. Gallant had given in to him on the business of the rank: efficiency of operation more than naval formality were what mattered in any event.

But Béssac had lost the struggle with respect to the Governor's soirée. Dragged ashore by Gallant at the express order of Valigny, Béssac had been shoehorned by several grinning hands into the full dress uniform of a frigate's First Lieutenant in the French Navy, making the first time he had ever put it on. It was a resplendent rig of scarlet small clothes under a coat of deep blue, but the shaggy Béssac still managed to suggest a circus animal in costume rather than a carefully turned out naval officer. Gallant was having to cover his own mouth with one gloved hand to restrain his laughter at the Mate's mutterings and humorous discomfort.

14

Béssac tugged at the tight white stock that gripped his neck, his face crinkling in a grimace. "Sweet Jesus. I'm going to die in here. I can see it now."

Gallant laughed silently. "Steady on, mon vieux. We've only been at it four hours. There's still the formal dinner to come."

Béssac's eyes bulged. "A *meal*?" he gasped hoarsely. "You're not serious." He scratched at the taut expanse of his waistcoat, stretched in skinlike elegance across his broad girth. "I couldn't get a grapeseed in there, wearing this!"

"Never mind. There'll be lots to wash it down with. Enjoy yourself, Béssac!" He grinned at the Mate. "Look at the women."

"Women? Hah! If I see another fat cow waddle past in a ton of cheap silk with the topsides of her teats slathered down with flour, I'll —— !" The grizzled Mate's obscenity was ingenious.

Gallant laughed again, glad that he had Béssac with him for the evening. It meant company and diversion from the whirling pressure of thought that had filled his mind since Valigny had given him his orders. And not the least of the worry and concern had been the unexpected — and unwelcome — information that not only was he to struggle through a long and tedious convoy operation across the Atlantic, but that the small and tightly organized spaces of his frigate would become the abode of a noblewoman passenger; a noblewoman who likely would have to be housed in Gallant's own sanctuary of privacy, the great cabin aft, and who likely would be accompanied by a mountain of baggage and a coterie of simpering ladies-in-waiting or servants for whom quarters would have to be found, and who would mean trouble from the moment they set foot on *La Bretonne's* deck. Altogether the thought brought Gallant rapidly to a very grim state of mind, and he turned back to the Mate's muttered ramblings.

But as Gallant's attention focussed again on Béssac the burly Mate stopped talking abruptly and looked over the marine's shoulder with a sober glower in his eyes. Gallant turned to see the elegant figure of the Governor moving toward them, accompanied by two other men. One was tall and very dark, handsome in a heavy-lidded, surly way, and dressed in a theatrically elaborate Spanish Post Captain's dress uniform of scarlet and gilt, heavy at wrist and throat with gathered white lace. One hand was pressing a delicate handkerchief containing a slice of orange to his nostrils, as if to ward off foul vapours, while the other lightly swung a gilt-headed ebony cane.

The other figure was a comparative study in sobriety. Not so tall, but better proportioned, he wore a simple frock coat of dark blue over similar small clothes, with no lace, and only the scabbard of the graceful small sword which hung at his hip, and the well-powdered but conservative wig, suggested that he was in formal dress. And in contrast to the languid disdain that characterized the expression of the Spaniard, this man had strong, steady features and a clear look from wide brown eyes that were fixed with friendly interest on Gallant and Béssac as Valigny began his introductions.

"Ah. The very brine-stained gentlemen we were seeking," said the Governor. "Don Alfonso, allow me to present capitaine de frégate Gallant, of His Most Christian Majesty's ship *La Bretonne*. And this, I take it, is his Second, M. Béssac? Good!"

Gallant inclined in a polite but modest bow, aware out of the corner of his eye that Béssac was attempting to follow his lead, and that Valigny's eyes were on him.

"Your servant, m'sieu'," he said. Then he stiffened, a flush coming unbidden to his cheecks as the Spaniard merely grunted and looked disdainfully away, the handkerchief stifling the beginnings of a yawn.

Valigny saw the flash in Gallant's eyes and turned quickly to the younger man in blue. "And allow me to present, gentlemen, the Master of the Compagnie des Indes vessel *Diane*, M. O'Farrell. M. O'Farrell, as you will gather, is Irish."

The Irishman stepped toward Gallant with a look that at once spoke an apology for the behaviour of the Spaniard and the same friendly interest as before.

"Your servant, M. Gallant. I've heard a great deal about you. A great deal. Your exploits travel ahead of you."

Gallant's eyes, still dark with anger, took in the Irishman's manly, straightforward air, and he found himself smiling in return.

"Thank you, M. O'Farrell. I trust what travels ahead doesn't sound too silly. Such tales often do."

"Not a bit, m'sieu'," said O'Farrell. "And it's damned good to hear some accounts of action and conviction for a change!" His eyes flicked with meaning at Don Alfonso in a quick look Gallant did not miss.

None of this had been lost on the smoothly smiling Valigny. "You'll be delighted to hear, Gallant," he said evenly, "that Don Alfonso has graciously indicated there will be little problem in having *Lima's* extra stores transferred to *La Bretonne*, beyond what they shall require for the Atlantic convoy. Your Purser will be required to purchase them, of course, at a price Don Alfonso will set, but I foresee —"

Gallant met with a steady gaze the thinly veiled look of

contempt in Don Alfonso's eyes, and found himself replying in a low voice, "If Your Excellency will allow, m'sieu', I intend to make *no* use of her stores."

Valigny stared, momentarily at a loss for words until he recovered and said, "I — I beg your pardon?"

Gallant felt a small smile crossing his face as his eyes bored into the Spaniard, who was looking at him with anything but langour now. If Gallant refused to purchase *Lima's* stores and provisions Don Alfonso was not only not going to receive the heavy purse from Valigny's coffers he had undoubtedly been counting on, but would have to account for the unwanted stores somehow, whether by sale or simple discharge. Either way, he was being denied the tidy profit the sale to *La Bretonne* would have brought him.

Take that, you limp-wristed bastard, thought Gallant.

"*Lima* is stored for a Spanish crew, m'sieu'," he said smoothly. "My lads have northern tastes. They're Acadiens, or Bretons and Normands — not Iberians. I've no use for casks of olive oil and twenty tons of garlic buds!"

Don Alfonso rose up to his full height, reminding Gallant of a rooster preparing to crow. His face was darkening ominously.

"I'll load as much produce here as I can obtain, m'sieu'. I've prepared a list my Purser will present to the admirauté clerk tomorrow. I'll pickle as much extra as you allow me to purchase. Extra salt fish I can pay for myself. And I'll want to crate as much livestock as I can." He gave the Spaniard a cool look. "So I'll have no use for his stores or for his storage methods, m'sieu'. I'll rely on my own." He turned to Valigny. "But as to powder and shot, I'll need much. Now, if *Lima* carries nines and eighteens —"

"You scabrous French upstart!" erupted Don Alfonso unexpectedly. "How *dare* you sneer at the provisioning of a vessel of His Most Catholic Majesty! Who in God's name do you think you —!" He stepped forward to within a few inches of Gallant, and as the Spaniard was not a small man his eyes met Gallant's on the same level.

Gallant's voice had an edge in it that Béssac recognized as a warning signal. "I am charged with carrying out *your* support in an arduous voyage. With a vessel *half* the size. His Excellency has had to make that necessary. And to carry out my orders I shall make arrangements as I please."

The Spaniard's lip curled. "I dislike your tone, fellow. And I dislike your insolence," he said in a voice not without real menace. "And little insolent boys need to be taught lessons . . ." His hand crept toward his hanger hilt.

"Gentlemen, please!" interjected O'Farrell.

The instantaneous dislike that Gallant and the Spaniard engendered in each other had shown itself so obvious and so volatile that almost as if by signal Béssac had moved to restrain Gallant, while Valigny and O'Farrell had stepped swiftly in front of Don Alfonso. Around them the shuffling of the sweating dancers through the *pavane* continued, unaware of the little drama by the glassed doors.

Valigny took Don Alfonso's arm in a less hostile than commanding grip and with smooth strength, virtually steered the big Spaniard away, all the while washing a soothing patter of words over him. "But come, capitaine, I have been tardy in seeing you meet all you must meet tonight, hein? There is Madame Le Tonnant, who has been driving my secretary mad with requests she may be at your arm during dinner. A sweet creature, that one! You really must meet her, and if I'm not mistaken I believe that's her on the far side . . ."

O'Farrell watched them go, chuckling. "That Governor's a master. How he can deal with that man I'll never fathom." He grinned at Gallant. "You looked ready to come to blows."

Gallant smiled, shaking his head. "Not quite. There are several stages one must pass through before that. I was only at the first."

"Which is?"

"Active distaste."

O'Farrell laughed. "Well put. I must say the fellow gets under my skin. Can't abide how he keeps his ship, for one thing. With the wind in the right quarter the stench and noise from her is indescribable."

Béssac was beaming affably at the well-set Irishman, obviously liking what he had seen and heard so far. "You're Master of *Diane*, m'sieu'?"

O'Farrell nodded. "And a damned fine little ship she is too."

"We've seen," said Gallant. "How long has she been under licence to the Compagnie?"

"Bit more than two years. She's almost straight off the ways. Seakeeps like a cork. I've been proud to have her."

"What were you in before?"

"Coastal brigs. Before that, a Spanish xebec out of Barcelona. Before that" — his expression darkened — "Ireland."

"I'm sorry to be taking *Diane* from you," said Gallant, quietly. "I can see she means a lot to you."

O'Farrell looked at him with a queer expression. "She does. And you're not taking her from me."

18

Gallant exchanged a quick look with Béssac. "I'm sorry, O'Farrell. But the *Diane* will be bought into the navy as an armed transport. She'll accompany *La Bretonne* and *Lima*, as an additional escort vessel."

"I know, m'sieu'."

"I shall be putting my own crew and officers into her. So you see —"

"But, m'sieu'," interrupted O'Farrell. "That was only to be in the event of *Diane's* complement refusing to go. But only a half-dozen have refused. And none of my — none of the officers."

Gallant pursed his lips.

"I informed the Governor today, m'sieu'. He gave me permission to tell you tonight. It was the main reason for my being here." The Irishman's expression changed. "I beg of you, m'sieu', let me command *Diane* with you! I *know* her and her men. They're a robust, ruffian lot, to be sure, but the *Diane's* their only home. And they know convoy passages. That's why most of 'em wouldn't leave her, even if she was bound for Hell. They'll not fail you. By Christ, nor will I."

Gallant looked into O'Farrell's open, honest eyes. This was something he had not bargained on. But then he was hearing his own words, a short two years ago, pleading in the same way for a rough crew and their knockabout little vessel, the corvette *Echo*. And he had a strange feeling of premonition . . .

"Please, m'sieu'!"

Gallant smiled. He reached out and grasped the Irishman's strong hand in a firm grasp.

"Like all your race, you've a way with words, M. O'Farrell. Very well," he said. "But you'll have to accept the King's Commission. And swear by the Articles."

He glanced at Béssac. "You concur, mon vieux?"

The Mate grunted, scratching at a fleabite. "Did from the first. Sure as Hell we wouldn't have ten men and a dog, hein, to send into *Diane,* let alone a prize crew to get her safely home. But our lads have been talking to some of the *Dianes.* They're prime seamen. And they think a lot of this Irish ruffian, the word is."

Gallant could not restrain a smile. "Then I cannot oppose it, M. O'Farrell. You're bound with us. In the convoy, for better or likely for worse."

The Irishman's teeth flashed. "That was what I hoped for, m'sieu'. Thank you, again."

"You know what it'll mean, hein? Weeks of procuring stores

the admirauté will claim don't exist. Cramming your *Diane* so full you'll be lucky to have your cabin to yourself. And a lot worse. I hope your lads can fight, if they have to.''

''Our duty will be done, m'sieu',' said O'Farrell, with a tone of quiet resolution. ''You'll get gunners and the lot.''

Gallant nodded. There was such an aura of competence radiating from the Irishman that Gallant instinctively sensed O'Farrell would prove equal to the task. That meant another capable officer to handle some of the endless work the preparations for the voyage would demand. And if there was no problem in obtaining stores for *La Bretonne* and *Diane*, that would leave only one major problem to bedevil Gallant's mind.

Marianne de Poitrincourt, Marquise de Bézy.

Béssac was looking at him with a half-smile. ''Hah. You're thinking about that woman again.''

''Does it show?''

The Mate winked at O'Farrell. ''Just a trifle. Your expression's like you just found a toad in your boot.''

Gallant smiled ruefully at the chuckles of the other two. ''Um, yes, well, I've — ah — still to meet the creature. Christ knows what sort of headaches she'll cause us, getting her home. You know about her, do you, O'Farrell?''

''Yes, m'sieu'. The Governor told me.''

''As if there will not be enough difficulty —''

Gallant stopped. At the expression on his face, Béssac and O'Farrell turned to follow his gaze.

''I think you're about to have your questions answered,'' the Irishman murmured.

Moving across the floor toward them, the circling couples pausing to bow and curtsy as they passed, was a beaming Valigny with a striking young woman on his arm. She was not tall, but moved with a smooth elegant grace that the voluminous skirts of her pale yellow gown could not obscure. Her unpowdered auburn hair was piled in a delicate mass of curls atop her head, revealing a slim neck and round white shoulders. The cut of her décolletage was so low that the upper curves of her full breasts were quite revealed. About her throat she wore a yellow ribbon centred with a cameo. But it was her face that riveted Gallant's attention: high cheekbones, a pouting, almost sinful little mouth, a thin and slightly arched nose, and wide-set, enormous green eyes below arched brows, now returning the stares of the three naval officers with an expression that might have been amusement — or contempt. It was difficult to decide which. With her free hand she was handling a gauzy Chinese fan with which she

20

delicately fanned herself as she acknowledged the salutes of the dancers with slight inclines of the head.

"Christ. That's quite a 'creature,' m'sieu'," whispered Béssac in Gallant's ear.

Gallant shifted uncomfortably and tugged at his neckcloth. He was finding it difficult to take his gaze off those approaching green eyes, and the steady look they were giving him now in return was oddly disconcerting.

With Valigny's expression one of insufferable amusement, the couple halted before them.

"Gentlemen," said Valigny.

The three officers bowed.

"My Lady," said Valigny, "I have the honour to present capitaine de frégate Gallant, of His Most Christian Majesty's ship *La Bretonne*. His Second, M. Béssac. And this is capitaine O'Farrell, of the *Diane*." Valigny coughed delicately.

"Gentlemen," said the Marquise. Her voice was low, with a husky tone to it that sent an involuntary shiver up Gallant's spine. The green eyes were fixed on him in a most unnerving way.

"So you are to be my host for this very tedious voyage, are you? I trust, capitaine, that your modest little boat will have appropriate quarters for my two ladies and myself. I *had* planned to travel in some comfort with Don Alfonso and his fine vessel." She pouted lightly, and the green eyes turned on Valigny disapprovingly.

Valigny inclined in an apologetic little bow. "Your Ladyship will recall how unavoidable that regrettable —"

"Yes, yes. All very naval and necessary, I am sure. But so inconvenient."

Gallant found a touch of annoyance rising to replace his initial awe at the noblewoman's beauty. God, *three* women, he thought.

"Your Ladyship will be given every possible accommodation in my vessel," he said, "consistent with the needs of a ship of war."

The delicate eyebrows arched slightly. "Oh? Piqued, are we capitaine? At having to interrupt the manly rigour of your frigate's routine to tend to the needs of a coterie of irritating and baggage-laden women?"

The arrow went straight to the mark. Gallant reddened. "You will have all my ship's company can provide, madame. But it will be —"

"A dangerous voyage, and no place really for a woman," finished the Marquise silkily. She gazed in amusement at Gal-

21

lant over the top of the fan. "But of course. I fully expect it to be somewhat of a challenge."

"It may be more than that, madame," said Gallant, darkly. He was beginning to feel foolish and idiotically pompous.

The Marquise laughed lightly, a liquid, warm sound that tingled the hair on Gallant's neck. "I'm sure it will be, capitaine. As I am equally sure you will be heroically capable in the face of the terrors that await us. I shall try to keep my ladies from swooning too frequently about your decks."

At the expression on Gallant's face Béssac could scarcely get a hand up in time to cover a smirk. O'Farrell coughed and looked diplomatically at the ceiling.

The Marquise turned to Valigny before Gallant could fumble out some form of reply. "But là, M. Valigny! We must greet some of your other guests, Governor. And you will recall I did promise to chat with Don Alfonso."

She extended her hand and flicked the fan open, turning away to sweep the green eyes over the crowd. Gallant and his companions were very obviously dismissed, the interview at an end.

Valigny flicked a glance at Gallant and led the young woman off. "Certainly, My Lady. If you'll excuse me, gentlemen . . ."

The three men watched them go, Gallant's expression such a mixture of annoyance and perplexity that O'Farrell and Béssac could no longer hold back broad amused grins.

"By Saint Patrick, there's a woman of spirit for you," said O'Farrell, admiringly.

"Dear Christ," muttered Gallant. "Just what I need."

"Eh?" said Béssac.

"I was hoping for a quiet spinster I could convince to stay hidden away below decks somewhere. But *this* one. Sweet Jesus!"

Béssac scratched his chin, still grinning. "She—ah—somewhat got the better of you in that broadside, m'sieu'."

O'Farrell was watching the Marquise's retreating back. "That's a handsome woman, no denying."

Gallant grunted. It was not difficult to imagine what the reaction in *La Bretonne* would be when the Marquise de Bézy stepped on her decks. Aside from the strain on his ship's discipline the women would produce, it would be difficult to maintain his own authority if his ship's company saw and heard him being treated with such dismissal. It simply would not do.

"Very well, madame," he said to himself, his eyes on the retiring slim figure and auburn curls. "You win the first pass. But I shall be ready for the second."

"Capitaine?" said Béssac.

"Nothing, Béssac." The marine was relieved to see a servant opening the great doors that led into the dining room. He good-naturedly poked a finger at Béssac's broad midriff and winked at O'Farrell. "Gird up, mon vieux. Now's your chance to pack away a big meal. Better than shipboard slop, hein?"

"Oh, God," moaned the Mate. "I'd almost forgotten."

With the other two men laughing at Béssac's expression, the three joined the throng passing into the dining room.

Under the solicitous guidance of a shoal of liveried waiters, they found themselves steered to their places. O'Farrell was placed between a brace of young women who were soon laughing delightedly at his easy charm. Béssac vanished down a far table where he was sandwiched between a plump planter's wife and the spinster daughter of a dockyard official. Gallant's luck of the draw put him between a kindly looking dowager with an enormous excess of makeup on his left and a thin woman with mournful eyes and smallpox-ravaged skin on his right. Across from him sat a portly, sweat-dappled gentleman of middle age whose position Gallant discovered through some tactful questioning was that of senior admirauté clerk. As the women beside him were ignoring him, Gallant concentrated his attention on the clerk. The worried-looking little man reacted with a brightening of his small, porcine eyes to the flattery of Gallant's attentions. The waiters were serving some form of fire-spiced soup, and Gallant was glad of the chance to dally over it and talk.

"Yes, yes," said the clerk, whose name was Doussault. "I know your requests by heart, capitaine. But the paperwork defeats us all. The plume and the épée, hein? Oh, dear, if I could only convince His Excellency that we need more clerks we should be able to handle urgent and necessary requests such as yours."

Gallant knew a bureaucrat weaselling out of a tight situation when he saw one. "Of course, M. Doussault. No one is more aware of your difficulties than myself. You understand, I'm sure, my natural anxiety over the processing of victualling and stores requisitions. Particularly on a mission of such importance to His Excellency, hein?"

Doussault looked besieged and mopped his brow with a large handkerchief. "Of course, capitaine. We will do our best, I assure you. And then" — and here a strange little leer came over his fat, shining features — "you do have the Lady Marianne to concern you." He gave a little snorting laugh.

23

Gallant ignored the leer and his own surprise. How the Devil did this little toad know of the Marquise's passage with Gallant? He made an attempt at spooning in the hot soup while he chose his words.

"We do indeed. And the crossing to France is such a long distance."

Doussault slurped noisily over his bowl. "It would've been a waste of a fine bit of womanhood, I'd say. Marrying her off to that ancient nobleman at Cayenne. The old fool!"

Gallant's spoon paused in mid-air. "Ancient?"

Doussault towelled his chin with the handkerchief. "The Sieur de Courcelette. A tottering old man with one foot in the grave. And half-blind in the bargain." Doussault abruptly lowered his voice to what he thought was a confidential volume. "He was said to no longer be able to hold his water, if you can believe."

"Deplorable," said Gallant.

"A waste of that young woman." Doussault was setting what he obviously believed to be a heroic set to his jowls. "Just as well he died."

Gallant winked at him. "Better to leave her for rogues like us, eh, M. Doussault?"

Doussault beamed at this camaraderie from the commanding officer of a fighting warship. "Heh, heh. Well, I'm married, capitaine, but a lad likes to keep a roving eye."

"She should be safe enough in *Lima*, I think?" ventured Gallant. He was curious to see just how much Doussault knew.

"But she'll be with you, capitaine. Have you forgotten? His Excellency told me just before dinner."

That was one question answered. "You're quite right, of course."

Doussault snorted. "As well she isn't travelling with the Spaniard. That mountebank would try to besmirch her honour in a trice. A terrible fellow. Terrible!" He sniffed at the steaming plate a sweat-dappled waiter had placed before him. "Ah, boudin creole and calalou! And crabes farais! This'll stir your palate, capitaine!" He paused. "And he'd have been after her dowry somehow, I would even wager."

"Dowry?" Of course. Gallant mentally kicked himself. It was impossible for the wedding of a French noblewoman to not involve a considerable dowry. "Er . . . travelling with her, of course, is it?" he asked mildly.

Doussault leaned over the table, the creases of his fat features folding into a conspiratorial leer. "Half her baggage, capitaine. Half! It's preposterous. His Majesty simply cannot afford it. But then you know all about it, of course."

Gallant took an experimental mouthful from the plate, and as the inside of his mouth exploded into heat he managed to get his wine glass to his lips without unseeming haste.

"To be truthful, M. Doussault . . ." he croaked, and sipped at the wine again. He decided to risk a confidence with Doussault seeing the delight of the man at being spoken to as an equal. "I'm not as privileged as you. I don't even know the value of the dowry."

Doussault glanced at the preoccupied dinner guests to either side and then leaned over the table again. "It's fabulous, capitaine Gallant. An incredible sum."

Gallant made himself adopt a conspiratorial expression. "How much?" he said, raising his wine glass.

"Seven hundred thousand livres. In coin and plate. Think of it! And it's *with* her!"

Gallant just managed to avoid a catastrophic gag on the wine. "Dear Lord!" he whispered.

"Eh, capitaine?"

"Ah . . . nothing. The spices." Gallant felt a chill run up his spine. That was an incredible sum, equal to almost one-tenth of the entire yearly budget of the Ministry of the Marine: colony administration, troops, ship operation and construction, pay and replenishment.

Why in God's name had Valigny not told him?

He glanced along the table to where O'Farrell had the young women obviously hanging on his every word, and then to where Béssac sat, poking at his food and making passable conversation, he presumed, with the fat planter's wife. He was suddenly grateful for them both: an old and tried friend and a new one he somehow sensed would not be found wanting. Christ knew there were enough unanswered questions gathering over this whole affair of the convoy and the Marquise to make him value them.

"But now, as for your self, M. Doussault?" said Gallant, turning back. "You're obviously a gentleman of spirit. What brought you to the King's service in the Antilles?"

Several hours and six courses later the dinner drew to a close, and under the affable direction of Valigny, who led out the Marquise de Bézy on his arm, the throng lurched up from the tables and re-entered the great ballroom. The musicians struck up a minuet, sawing away gamely in the heat, and couples moved into position on the floor. Those whom the enormous meal had rendered incapable of much movement were grateful to sink down on the small settees set about the walls, or hovered by the broad glassed doors leading out to the terrace. The servants had thrown these open, and what slight breeze there was in the black night filtered in through them to the great hall, which lay in a sweaty, amber glow below the flickering candles.

Gallant was momentarily at somewhat of a loss, for the fat planter's wife through some inconceivable stratagem had managed to get Béssac out shambling his way through the minuet; O'Farrell was well into the dance, with one of his pretty dinner partners on his arm, and judging by the blushing laughter of the girl and the Irishman's grace in the dance he was no stranger either to a ballroom floor or the ear of a pretty woman. There was plainly more to O'Farrell than met the eye. After standing about for a moment in ill ease to be sure he was not about to be pounced on for the dance, Gallant eased out through one of the open doors onto the terrace, and the hubbub and music faded almost immediately.

He walked out across the terrace, glad of the inky night and the faint coolness of the breeze. His stomach felt uncomfortably full under his waistcoat, and he took a few deep breaths, as much to settle it as to regulate the complex whirrings of his mind. It surprised him somewhat that the business of the dowry made him deeply uneasy; try as it would, his mind could see no other reason for Valigny's omission other than forgetfulness. Forgetfulness, or else some far more sinister motive, which simply did not match Gallant's gut emotion about Valigny.

He sat down on the edge of the balustrade and stared off toward the few dim lights visible from the town. From a brandy shop, he imagined, came the faint roar of seamen in a drunken song, the shrill laughter of a woman high above it. Gallant had developed a strong respect for the strange premonitions and impulses he sometimes felt, and which he had discovered Béssac on occasion experienced. He respected them, whether they propelled him into unlikely situations, or cautioned him against situations or people. Such a premonition usually manifested itself as a slight prickling of the hair at his neck, and Gallant had learned to recognize the signal. It bothered him that he had it now over the business of the Marquise, but in contrast to past situations it was not directed at anyone, or anything Gallant could pin down.

He shook his head. It annoyed him that his orderly sense of preparation for the convoy, a mental exercise in which he shoehorned his normally impulsive self into an ordered regimen of behaviour, should be clouded by a damnable feeling of free-floating unease. And another part of his mind was scoffing at his disquiet. The Governor was merely forgetful, it said. And you are in any event now forewarned about not only the Marquise herself but of her alarmingly valuable baggage.

Very well, thought Gallant. But the sense of unease was undimmed.

There were some bushes and low shrubs masking a far corner of the terrace from the point where Gallant sat. As there were a few other couples strolling about, he was not conscious for a moment of the voices coming from behind the screen of shrubbery. Gradually, however, he became aware of them: a woman's voice, low and insistent, strangely familiar; and a man's voice, deep and demanding, growing in volume and force. The phrases were clear now, and it would have been impossible for Gallant not to have heard.

"You have my final word, hein?" said the woman's voice. "I wish to hear no more of it! Have the decency to act like a gentleman and stand out of my way."

"You — you cannot end it like that. You cannot brush me away as if I were a — a footman!" The man's voice was thick with emotion and drink.

"Why not, since you persist in acting like one. Please, Alfonso! Let me go! Stop it!"

With a few quick steps Gallant had reached the shrubbery and was past it. Not ten feet from him, Don Alfonso Castelar, weaving unsteadily on his feet, was gripping the shoulders of Marianne de Poitrincourt, Marquise de Bézy, in a hold she was struggling ineffectually to escape. Her small fists beat on the Spaniard's shoulders as he bent her backward over part of the curving balustrade.

"Oh . . . God . . . Alfonso, let me go!" cried the girl.

Gallant was there in three strides. Feeling a cool rage bubbling within him, he siezed Castelar's thick, scarlet-clad arm in a steely grip and bodily flung him around. The Marquise, freed from Castelar's grip, sank back against the balustrade, her breath coming in deep gasps.

"Your pardon, *señor*. But one musn't mistreat ladies, hein?" said Gallant, smoothly.

Castelar stared through the gloom at Gallant with surprise wide in his clouded eyes. Then a deep flush filled his face and his features twisted in a grimace of rage.

"You again! The filthy little French colony rat!" He spat. "How da-dare you. By the Madonna, I'll spill your guts for meddling in this!" With dismaying speed the Spaniard reached behind his neck and from the collar of his coat pulled out a gleaming stiletto. He tossed it lightly from hand to hand, and the blade glistened dully in the faint light.

"Alfonso! No! For God's sake, please!" The girl's voice was horrified, pleading.

"Stay where you are, my dear," said Castelar, inching toward Gallant, his blade centred on Gallant's eyes. "You may watch as I teach this little swi-swine an important lesson!"

Gallant licked his lips, wondering what to do next. The Spaniard was steady enough now, cold and measured. Gallant retreated a pace, then another. His mind began to race. What would he do? How could he parry that evil little blade save by drawing his hanger, which was unthinkable, even in self-defence: Castelar was a senior allied officer and Gallant was in Valigny's own quarters. Somehow he had to —

"Aah!" Castelar lunged, and the blade arrowed for Gallant's throat. But the drink had taken its toll after all, and the Spaniard's speed had been slowed just enough that Gallant saw its first impulse, and was ready for it. Twisting hard to one side, Gallant seized Castelar's knife wrist as the latter lunged in, and with all his strength wrenched it back and down. With a grunt Castelar thumped down on a sprawl on the terrace, Gallant pinning the knife hand with one knee. With cold fury Gallant struck Castelar across the face with a ringing backhanded slap.

"Now we'll just relieve you of your toy," he said. He pried the knife out of Castelar's fingers and slid it in under the sole of his shoe. He pulled up sharply and the steel snapped with a thin crack.

"Christ — my arm — you're breaking it!" moaned the Spaniard, struggling under Gallant's grip.

"Please, capitaine. Release him. Please!" It was the girl, standing above them now, pale and still.

"Very well. But no sudden moves, señor," said Gallant. The anger had vanished now, and Gallant rose, releasing his grip on Castelar. Castelar groaned, rolling over and clutching his arm. He weaved to his knees and then stood unsteadily, his hair dishevelled over his eyes, his free arm rubbing where Gallant's knee had pinned him. Gallant stood with the weight on the balls of his feet, ready to move.

"Now señor. Perhaps an apology to the lady is in order," he said, quietly.

Castelar spat at Gallant's feet. "You'll regret this, you — you —"

"The name is Gallant," said the marine. "Capitaine de frégate Gallant. At your service, at any time or place."

"Gallant. You'll pay. Christ you'll pay!" Castelar backed off a few uncertain steps and lurched away unsteadily toward the ballroom. He shouldered through a small, gathering clutch of guests who had come out onto the balcony, drawn by the noise of the scuffle.

Gallant turned to the Marquise. "Madame, I hope you were not hurt in any way —" he began.

His words were cut off as the Marquise brought her hand up and slapped him with surprising strength across the face. She was trembling with rage.

"How dare you," she hissed. "How *dare* you!"

Gallant stared at her. "I beg your pardon?"

"How dare you interfere! Who do you imagine you are, *capitaine* Gallant?" She spat out the title in a bitter and mocking voice.

"My Lady, he was assaulting —"

The Marquise snorted. "Pah! You will do well to remember who your betters are, capitaine. Don Alfonso Castelar is a Spanish nobleman. And neither his affairs, nor mine, are the concern of an upstart colony boat's boy! Do you follow, capitaine?" The look on the beautiful face was a study in imperious fury.

Gallant felt his facial muscles set as if they were a mesh of steel. He stepped back a pace and bowed in impeccable form.

"Your servant, madame," he said coldly. Then he straightened, looking levelly into the flickering green eyes. "I follow only too well."

The Marquise flushed. With a swish of her skirts she spun on her heel and walked swiftly away, toward the open ballroom doors through the staring onlookers.

Gallant watched her go, noticing out of the corner of his eye that O'Farrell had quietly arrived at his elbow.

"And what on earth was that?" murmured the Irishman.

"A lesson," said Gallant quietly. "Once more."

"M'sieu'?"

"A lesson. On how things may not be what they seem to be. Particularly as concerns arrogant and contemptuous young noblewomen." Gallant's lips set in a tight line.

"Ah. Well," said O'Farrell, looking toward the ballroom doors. "Here comes a squall line, or I'm damned!"

Approaching them, his face the colour of a thundercloud even

29

in the evening's gloom, was Valigny. He stopped in front of Gallant, visibly almost at a loss for words.

"In the name of Christ!" he finally blurted out. "What did you *do* to her, Gallant! The Marquise de Bézy!"

Gallant cleared his throat. "I assisted her in some difficulties with another gentleman. She was less than appreciative." Gallant was amazed at how calm his voice sounded.

"Less than appreciative!" Valigny snorted. "Christ's guts, man, d'you realize what you've done?"

"I don't understand, m'sieu'."

"You know the importance I have placed on your getting the woman safely back to France! Or do you not?"

"I do, m'sieu'."

"Well then, perhaps you can describe to me how you are going to carry out that task with things as they are now? I'd be quite interested to hear!"

"I'm afraid, m'sieu', I still don't —"

Valigny flung his arms wide in an expansive gesture of exasperation. "Whatever your idiotic little display of gallantry was meant to do, it sent her stamping over to me in the middle of the bloody dance floor, her face like all the furies in Hell! And she's told me, capitaine, that she'll be damned if she'll so much as set foot in your ship! She's going to cross in *Lima*, with Castelar! And what in the name of Christ are you going to make of *that*!"

The servant in the green livery, his cataract gleaming whitely in the glow of the guttering candle he was carrying, hurried along a darkened corridor of a far wing of the Governor's residence. Abruptly he halted at a door and, with a look back along the corridor, knocked.

"LeBeau?" said a man's voice from within.

"The same," said the servant.

"Come in."

The servant stepped into a candelabra-lit room, only to stop virtually in his tracks. On the far side of the room a large canopied bed loomed, its mosquito netting and coverlets thrown back. On the side of the bed a woman sat in brownskinned nakedness, toying idly with the feathers that edged an elaborately lace-trimmed cocked hat. As LeBeau stared at her, she flashed him a dark look of contempt and tossed the hat lightly onto a nearby chest. With her skin gleaming like copper in the amber light, she moved languidly back onto the bed and lay against the pillows, her arms crossing protectively over her large, dark-nippled breasts.

From an alcove doorway to one side came the man's voice, and the slosh of water in a washstand bowl.

"Well?" it said thickly.

LeBeau had not dropped his stare from the woman. Her eyes mocking him, she reached her arms over her head and stretched in catlike, sensual grace.

"Someone must have told the frigate captain. The Acadien. About the dowry."

"What? That's not possible."

"He knows! I overheard him talking to the Irishman."

There was another slosh of the water. "I'll gut him, if I ever catch the poltroon who did it. Sacristi, no one was to have known of that!"

"Who knows where he heard. Another servant. A clerk, perhaps," said LeBeau. His eye met the woman's gaze, which was still on him. She ran a pink tongue teasingly along the edge of her lips.

"There hasn't been a chance for me to try again, m'sieu'," said LeBeau, after a moment. "Her guards must suspect something. They've been virtually surrounding her since the last time"

"Except tonight," interjected the voice. "When she might have fallen from the terrace, but for that fellow. Damned ill luck!"

"There may be another chance, m'sieu'. The woman, Zadou, cleans the Marquise's chambers each morning. It would be an easy task to get her to wedge her terrace doors." LeBeau licked his lips. "Then, at night, a little knife is very quick and very quiet . . ."

"No. I've changed my mind. It must look like an accident! Or better still, a — shall we say — fortune of war."

"M'sieu'?"

There was a mirthless chuckle from the alcove. "She's sailing for France in *Lima*! By all that's holy, she's refused to sail in the ship of that upstart colony rat. What d'ye think of that, hein? Hah! in *Lima*!"

LeBeau twitched. "I don't —"

"The Dutch, hein? There'll be an attack on the convoy. And casualties will occur. No mere English agent doing her in to enrage His Most Christian Majesty; a damned Dutch squadron of freebooters!" A cough sounded. "You'll be drafting a letter to the sous-ministre, LeBeau. One that tells him he will have

31

the results he is paying us so handsomely for—and without any need to pretend it was the English!''

''Ver—very well, m'sieu'.''

''And then you'll be off in the chasse-marée. Tell Coulombe to be ready to slip.''

LeBeau swivelled the gaze of his eye off the woman's body. ''To sea? What—?''

''Ten Haaf, you fool! He and the *Java* will have gathered in the other Dutchmen and be waiting, by now, for news like this! Like we've planned. And won't we give 'em something, hein?''

''It's the rendezvous, then? At Isle de la Chatte?''

''Of course, y' one-eyed fool! You'll tell him everything about the convoy, eh? And about the Marquise. Tell him a good deal about the Marquise!'' There was a snort of laughter. ''Jacob Ten Haaf has an appetite for women.''

The woman curled her lips at LeBeau in a mocking smile. As his eye gleamed at her, sweat began to dapple his forehead. She arched her back, cupping her breasts in her hands and shaking them gently, teasing him.

''Well? What else do you need? Find Coulombe and get to sea.''

LeBeau licked his lips. ''Yes. I—I'll leave now. The Governor won't notice my absence for several hours—''

''And suspects nothing! Go, for Christ's sake!''

LeBeau turned toward the door, the candle sputtering its last. The woman smirked at him and slid down under the coverlet.

''M'sieu'—?'' began Lebeau again, by the door.

''What! Damn you, I'll—''

''The frigate captain, m'sieu'! He's meant to escort her home, safe to France! What can we—?''

There was a slosh of water into a bucket. ''Hah! The Dutch'll gut him. Save us any trouble. He'll be no worry,'' The man, stripped to the waist, walked heavily into the room.

''But he's bound to interfere, m'sieu'.''

''Well, then, my craven dear LeBeau, it's quite simple. If he is a bother I'll have to kill him, won't I? And the next time I deal with him I won't be portraying a boorish, drunken fool. . . .''

The smile of Don Alfonso Castelar chilled LeBeau to the bone.

TWO

Théophile Béssac stood braced on the weather side of *La Bretonne's* quarterdeck, his blackened clay pipe clenched firmly in his teeth and his hands thrust deep into his seacoat pockets against the early morning chill off the grey sea. To the east, the cloudless sky was beginning to glow with bands of pink and orange as the sun prepared to lift over the distant lip of the horizon.

Béssac puffed morosely on the tabac and squinted up at the frigate's sails. With the wind out of the southeast, *La Bretonne* was broad on a starboard tack, reaching to the northeast. She worked sluggishly over the white-flecked grey swells under reduced sail, which kept the vessel well below the speed she might otherwise have been making good. As she wallowed along, Béssac was allowing himself a moment of disgruntlement. Reduced sail was always the state of things in convoy escort, with the heavy-laden and blundering merchantmen rarely able to keep up to a warship's best speed; no one knew that better than Béssac. But it still annoyed him that he could not give vent

33

to his highest impulse, which was to set every square inch of canvas possible and drive *La Bretonne* like a wild living thing across the sea. It was what Béssac lived for, and he begrudged the necessities of duty that denied this to him.

But the cause of *La Bretonne's* hobbling was evident enough. Stretching away to leeward, in two long lines following each other like obedient cattle, over twenty sail of heavy-laden and labouring merchantmen rolled and heaved northeastward toward Europe, their hulls low and in some cases almost awash in the long, heavy swell, their canvas stained and worn, with luffings and ripplings here and there in the forest of mast and sail that told of casual helmsmanship and slackness on the quarterdecks. As Béssac watched, the sun abruptly winked over the horizon and lit the topmasts of the merchantmen and his own *La Bretonne* with a warm peach glow that heralded another day of steady wind and brilliant tropic sun.

La Bretonne was well to starboard of the starboard column of the convoy, and was dogging along a half-league astern of the great bulk of the *Lima*, whose stern galleries below her pyramid of sails were beginning to glint in the light of the new sun. O'Farrell's *Diane*, metamorphosed into a speedy picket vessel by the changes and improvements to rig and canvas that Gallant had bullied out of the Martiniquan shipyard, was a white and tan blob on the horizon ahead of the convoy. Don Alfonso Castelar had at least had the sense to realize her speed and O'Farrell's alertness made *Diane* the ideal vessel for the picket role. Béssac envied O'Farrell his task, and grumpily considered that with the passage across the Atlantic only just begun in reality, Don Alfonso obviously was intending to make Gallant's —and hence *La Bretonne's*—passage as slow, monotonous and dispiriting as possible.

Béssac stumped to the rail, knocked the dottle out of his pipe over the side, and stared gloomily down at the hissing wake curling out from the frigate's side. They were now perhaps thirty leagues to the south of the Bermudas, with most of the Atlantic still stretching before them, and already Béssac felt his patience had been stretched to the limit.

"Holà, Béssac! Why so glum? Someone stave in the brandy casks?"

Béssac looked back to see Gallant climb the ladder from the waist to the quarterdeck and grin at him. Béssac adjusted his hat in a rudimentary form of salute.

"Hah? Oh, didn't see you, capitaine. Christ, is it the change of the watch already?"

As if to answer him, *La Bretonne's* bell rang out in a series of clean double strokes from its tabernacle forward, a ship's boy tugging at the clapper line.

"There's your answer. Anything afoot in *Lima*?"

"Nothing, m'sieu'. He just staggers along ahead, there. Damned poor helm and sailhandling, I can tell you."

"Has he hoisted another signal yet?" said Gallant, scratching his neck. "I've been expecting another idiotic damned flag every turn of the glass."

"Not since you went below, m'sieu'. He must have forgotten which one to hoist," Béssac grunted. Castelar had concocted an elaborate and impractical series of gun and flag signals to pass his orders, most of which required minutes of headscratching and much peering through a glass to decipher. Gallant had been controlling his temper with difficulty as Castelar sent missive after missive, ordering *La Bretonne* to take station to leeward, then to windward, now astern of the double line of merchantmen, now ahead — and now to wallow along under reduced sail in *Lima's* wake.

"Just so. But keep a weather eye open. I don't want that featherbrained wart to have a thing to complain of when his report hits the desk of the admirauté."

Béssac grinned. "One would think you don't like the fellow."

"Don't make jokes. What's your course?"

"North a half east, m'sieu'. Fore and main tops'ls, jib and foretopm'st stays'l, and the spanker. The watch exercised the larboard battery—Akiwoya used no cartridge, as per the Don's orders — and I had 'em stone down the foredeck again." He squinted aloft, shading his eyes with one hand. "I've had a new weather brace rove to the foretop yard, and a new mizzen tops'l bowline. The larboard main ratlines, about halfway up, are frayed and ready to give way, says the maintop captain."

Gallant nodded. "All right. Galiot can have his duty 'swain take care of it. Did you sound the casks?"

Béssac said he had. The two men knew there was little really to report. The wind had been holding fair, and *La Bretonne* was running on sea routine smoothly enough. The frigate's two hundred and ten men and boys competently carried out the monotonous regularity of the watch changes, and the hundred other daily tasks that were required. For all their clumsy sailhandling and dogleg wakes the merchantmen were keeping station tolerably well, and Castelar was evidently going to rely on *Diane* as the convoy's lookout for strange sail. There was little else for Gallant and Béssac to do other than coax the frigate along under

35

her reduced canvas and try to keep the edge on ship's discipline as best they could. For danger, when it came, would almost certainly fall upon the convoy with suddenness and swiftness.

"Very well, Béssac," said Gallant, adopting a more formal tone and manner. He locked his hands behind his back in a favourite posture and paced over to the windward side of the quarterdeck. "M. Galiot, your relief, is on deck. Please carry on."

Béssac nodded to the frigate's third officer, a thickset and swarthy man of about thirty who had been fidgeting in the waist for some moments. "Muster your watch, M. Galiot," he said.

"Muster the watch. Aye, m'sieu'," said Galiot briskly. He gave an order to the boatswain of the watch, who had been standing watchfully nearby. In the next minute the shrill piping of the latter's call was echoing through *La Bretonne's* gundecks.

Béssac puffed industriously on his pipe. He wanted to say something to Gallant, but waited so as not to break the sanctity of the commanding officer's privileged realm on the windward side. At last Gallant saw his eyes and paced over.

"Good officer, m'sieu'. Galiot, I mean. They must've trained 'em well in that forty-gunner. He and Saint-Armande both."

Gallant nodded. *La Bretonne* had been unexpectedly deprived of the services of a third and fourth officer at Martinique when the Third, De Riencourt, had fallen deathly ill with Yellow Jack and was still languishing in Fort Royal. The Fourth, a callow youth out of the Toulon squadron who had proven ineffectual and of more bother than use to Gallant, had been knifed to death by a Creole whore in some steamy fleshpot along the Place de la Savane. The admirauté's replacements, both officers stranded in the Antilles after being paroled from warships captured by the English, had proven as competent as the other two had not. Amaury Galiot was powerful and experienced, and a rare product of the lower deck; he had come to his commission "through the hawse," as the expression went. There was little of the gentleman about him, but he was sober, intelligent, concerned for the welfare of the ship and his men, and industrious. Panet de Saint-Armande was a slim aristocrat of twenty with a wan smile and a misleading langour. He had proven quick and effortlessly capable, and in the bargain had struck up a friendship with the rougher-hewn Galiot.

"Eh? Yes," said Gallant. "Or do you have cause for complaint?"

"Sacristi, no, capitaine. They run their parts of ship damned well. More like a bloody convent on the messdeck the way

36

Galiot has the boatswain and his mates prowling about. But the lads like it. A taut ship's a happy ship, hein?''

Gallant grinned at him. "Yes. But why don't you stow all this jabbering and get below, mon vieux? Vaubert will probably have some kind of breakfast waiting for you, if I'm not mistaken." Gallant had seen the officers' servant scuttling about in the great cabin as he made his way on deck.

Béssac's expression brightened as he steadied himself against *La Bretonne's* slow pitching. He spat into the sea to leeward and pocketed the pipe. "By Christ, I shall. The morning watch always makes my stomach growl."

"Good. Then take it below. I can't abide all that rumbling. You sound like a washerwoman's cauldron."

"Aye, m'sieu'," grinned the Mate. He clumped down the waistdeck ladder and vanished in under the halfdeck.

In the waist, Galiot was pacing impatiently back and forth while his petty officer had the watch shuffling into line just abaft the longboat gallows. In a moment they would be told off to their stations and the relieved watchmen would go below, the ordered transition of a warship's routine at sea in orderly function.

There was a thump of leather on the companionway leading up from the gundeck, and the slight form of enseigne Thivierge, *La Bretonne's* Officer of Marines, appeared. He was followed in a moment by his sergeant, a moustachioed zealot named Audy, who immediately upon he arrived on deck thumped his halberd impatiently and barked at the Compagnies Franches fusileers who were clambering up into the sunlight. Within a moment they were steady in two swaying ranks across *La Bretonne's* deck as Audy paced past, inspecting them minutely. Thivierge stood idly by at the rail, examining his watch until he saw a shadow on the deck and looked up to see Gallant above him at the quarterdeck rail.

Thivierge doffed his tricorn elegantly in salute. "By your leave, capitaine. A fine morning."

"Indeed," said Gallant, pleasantly. Thivierge was appallingly young and without experience, but he seemed to control Audy and the roughneck marines well enough. "And what are you about today, M. Thivierge?"

The marine waved his hat at the squad. "Independent musket practice for each man, m'sieu'. But first some volley fire. Five rounds to leeward."

Gallant sucked a tooth. Castelar had ordered no escort vessel to "waste" shot and powder in gun drills. That had been a damned foolish order, for it would be better to have ten rounds in the magazine and a half-trained crew than a hundred rounds and a totally inexperienced one. Particularly if English canvas showed over the horizon. But the marines were Gallant's own responsibility. And he was damned if he was not going to let *them* learn about the stink of gunpowder and the buck of a fusil-grenadier against their shoulder.

"Very well," he said. "Toss out a chip from the bows as a mark. I'll give a gold louis to your first man to hit it."

The marines glanced at one another and hefted their muskets expectantly.

Thivierge beamed. "Thank you, m'sieu'. Sergeant! Send a man to the carpenter. Prime and load as you will!"

As Gallant listened to the familiar clink and rattle of the marines' ramrods he found his eyes rising again to the slowly pitching bulk of the *Lima*. What was *she* doing now? Sitting in splendour in the great cabin while one of her women did her hair? Looking back at *La Bretonne* with those damnably disturbing green eyes? Or was she laughing over morning coffee with the repulsive Castelar smirking at her from across the table? Her face was suddenly floating before his eyes: the high curls of auburn hair, the pale, almost translucent skin and pouting mouth. And those eyes . . .

"Give fire!" barked Audy.

Gallant started as twenty-four levelled muskets thumped, their muzzles licking thin pink lancets of flame even in the brilliant sunshine. As the acrid, blue-white smoke swirled around the marines and then back and up over the quarterdeck around Gallant, a little forest of ball splashes leaped out of the face of a swell to leeward.

"Prime and load!" sang out Audy, and the muskets came down, cradled in the left arm while the right hands uniformly slapped the flaps of the russet cartridge boxes, fingers reaching for the next paper tube.

"Gives one a start, hein?" said Béssac's voice unexpectedly at Gallant's elbow.

Gallant peered at him. "What are you doing on deck?"

"Well," — Béssac winced as Audy's second volley banged out — "to tell you the truth, capitaine, I just couldn't stay down. Couldn't eat, either."

"*You*? Christ on a crutch, Béssac. That's impossible."

Béssac scratched a stubbly chin, looking forward to where Galiot was setting the watchmen to coiling and rehanging the foremast halyards and braces on their pins. "Just one of those feelings. As if there's something happening. Or about to happen."

Gallant's eyes narrowed. He gripped the rail as *La Bretonne* heaved hissing up over a particularly large swell. He was remembering past occurrences of Béssac's "feelings."

"About what?"

"I don't know, hein? Just a tickle at the back of my neck. As if—"

"Deck, there! Deck! Capitaine!"

"You and your bloody feelings," Gallant muttered. He cupped his hands. "Deck, aye?"

"The *Diane*, m'sieu'! Her t'gallants have gone aback! And there's smoke, like as if she's fired a battery o' guns!" The maintopmast lookout's voice was faint.

Gallant spun, looking beyond the convoy to the far horizon where *Diane's* topmasts had been showing. He could see little but a blob of white, the flash of *Diane's* upper canvas. But there was something else in the haze along the skyline, to either side of *Diane*. An odd, moving shape. A sail? Smoke?

"Mind the helm, M. Galiot!" Gallant barked out suddenly. "I'm going aloft!"

The marine sprang down into the waist and clambered up on the rail and then out around the deadeyes of the windward main shrouds. The tarred rope shook under his feet as he scrambled up the narrowing triangle of ratlines, then swung with frightening breathlessness out around the futtock shrouds until he hauled himself, panting, into the maintop. Gallant always preferred to go aloft himself when something had been sighted. It was always best to see for yourself.

The lookout, a wizened elder topman named Portelance, grinned at him in gap-toothed pleasure and knuckled a forelock. Then he extended a long bony finger toward the distant horizon.

"There, m'sieu'. He's come about, hein? Foretops'l aback. I'd say he's tacking. And there's the smoke, downwind. From a ship's guns, m'sieu'!" Portelance's breath was rancid with tobacco.

Gallant tried to control his breathing, his heart pounding in his ears. He wrapped one arm around a topmast shroud and squinted along the line of Portelance's arm.

"Christ's guts," he muttered, after a moment. "You're right!"

Out there in the haze of the horizon line, he could see the tiny shape of *Diane*, broadside to the track of the convoy, heeling to the press of sail O'Farrell had crowded on. And drifting around her, white, billowing and unmistakable in the brilliant sun, clouds of gunsmoke.

But it was what lay to either side of *Diane's* tiny, brave shape that sent shivers up Gallant's spine. Hull-down beyond the little ship, perhaps a half-league further on, Gallant counted the topsails of one, two, three, and finally four ships. Two to the left of *Diane's* pitching shape, and two to the right.

"A squadron, I'm thinkin', capitaine, hein?" said Portelance, over the wind and sea noise. "An' sloops o' war at least, all of 'em. Tackin' hard up toward us, m'sieu'!"

Gallant nodded, his lips a tight line. He flicked a glance at *Lima's* towering shape. No evidence there that Castelar's lookouts had seen what was happening. It was obvious what *Diane* was trying to do. The unknown vessels were hostile, that was certain; likely a damned English squadron looking for just such prey as an underescorted convoy. O'Farrell must have been surprised by them, perhaps blinded by the small squall line that had passed just as dawn was breaking. Whether he had hoisted Castelar's makeshift signal for *Enemy in Sight* was impossible to tell at this distance. So O'Farrell had hardened up to tack back toward the convoy, discharging his batteries as the quickest way to alert *Lima* and *La Bretonne*.

"What are they, Portelance? Can you see any colours? Damned if I can."

Portelance grinned at his captain's unpretentious familiarity. "Catch a flicker now 'n then at the foretruck of that one most to eastward, m'sieu'. Bit o'colour in it."

"English?"

Portelance jetted a thin stream of black tobacco juice into space to leeward through a gap in his yellowed teeth. "Can't rightly say, m'sieu'."

Gallant swore under his breath, squinting at *Lima*. Were the Spanish lookouts blind? There was still no activity on those high-pitched, steep decks, no streaming pennants squealing up signal halyards, no signal guns banging out.

"Well done, Portelance. Keep a sharp eye on those vessels and on *Diane*. I want to know everything they do, the moment they do it. Follow?"

"Aye, m'sieu'. Never fear."

"Good. And for God's sake don't spit that foul stuff on me as I go down." Heedless of risk, Gallant reached out for a backstay and clung to it like a monkey. Shielding his hands with his coat cuffs, he slid dizzyingly down to slam the soles of his shoes hard on the deck. He jammed his hat down on his head and bounded up the quarterdeck ladder.

"Béssac!"

"M'sieu'?"

"*Diane's* tracking back toward us under a press of sail. There's four other vessels astern of her, tacking up for us. She's fired on them."

"*Four*? Sacristi! How far off?"

"Three leagues at the most. No more. Still no movement in *Lima*? No signal?"

Béssac shook his head.

"Damn the man!" Gallant slapped the rail in frustration. For some reason the face of the Marquise was floating before him. He had an image of her, the proud, pouting features white with tension and worry, waiting in her cabin for the first round shot to begin smashing in the stern gallery windows at her. . . .

"Enough of this. Bring the ship to Quarters, if you please, Béssac!"

Béssac's eyes gleamed with a feral flash. "Oui, capitaine!" He padded to the rail and cupped his hands. "Enseigne Thivierge! Your drummer to the quarterdeck, if you please!"

Within a minute the youthful Compagnies Franches drummer, the gilded fleur-de-lis on his blue drum shiny in the sunlight, stood at the waistdeck rail. His face set in a look of frightened determination, he began to beat the chilling and ominous rhythm. Its effect upon *La Bretonne* was electric.

Gallant had divided the ship's company into the classic divisions of topmen, fo'c's'lemen, waisters and afterguard. But he had also had his clerk laboriously copy out detailed Watch and Quarter Bills which Gallant had then had nailed up over each gun in the messdecks. Each man had a task to perform or a position to be in, in any conceivable situation *La Bretonne* might be in. The thump and roll of the drumbeat produced an ordered tumult in the ship as each man scrambled for his post. In an extraordinary way, the ship literally became a single organism through this sudden activity: Gallant's own personality functioned as the mind of the creature, and through the disciplined preparedness of *La Bretonne's* ship's company, he became in minutes the commanding intelligence of a fighting mechanism able to hurl a quarter-ton of iron in deadly broadsides; the creation of a naval organization and its discipline had married with

41

the superb technology of centuries of shipbuilding experience to put in Gallant's hands virtually the most immediate and encompassing power any man of his age could possess.

Thivierge's marines broke into two squads and doubled forward and aft to their posts, the shoe leather thumping up the ladders and drowning out the quieter slap of the bare feet of the running seamen. From below, the offwatchmen poured out on to the frigate's weatherdeck, their hammocks tightly rolled, jamming them into the double row of netting that circled the deck, affording a kind of barricade. At each gun in the batteries, the crews arrived to feverishly cast off the lashings and set up the tackles and tools, the gun captains barking out orders for the removal of tampions and the running back of the guns, ready for loading. Castelar had insisted that, contrary to usual practice, no vessel was to sail with guns loaded. But now the gunner's mates in the magazines behind their felt curtains were handing the cartridges in their leather buckets to the ship's boys, who then monkeyed up the ladders with their charges to the guns, ignoring the marine stationed at the hatchway who had orders to shoot them if they quailed and ran below in the heat of the action. The cartridge, shot and wads were being rammed home in each gun, even now in the smaller nine-pounders of the quarterdeck battery where Gallant and Béssac stood.

The frigate's coxswain, Vignac, arrived at the wheel, muscular and capable, his mate at his heels. He took the course from the departing helmsman and settled his broad hands round the spokes.

"Steady as she goes, Vignac," said Gallant.

"Aye, m'sieu'. Sailhandling soon, m'sieu'?"

"Like as not. Be on your toes if we have to pay off in a hurry."

Vignac nodded, licking his lips. "M'sieu'."

La Bretonne pitched in slow majesty over a swell and buried her bows with a roar as, aloft, the topmen were swinging into position, rigging the great net over the deck that would catch debris from falling from aloft to crush the men below. In a moment they would be passing chains as additional yard lifts, and here and there a man struggled up to the tops with boxes of tools to repair damage that might occur aloft. In the waist and on the foredeck the sailhandlers were dodging nimbly around the gun crews, freeing braces, tacks and sheets, snatching coils off pins and taking off all but the last few turns. They would stand ready to work *La Bretonne* into any point of sailing an order from the quarterdeck would demand.

Within minutes all was still. Béssac glanced at the crews

crouched in ready silence round the guns, aloft at the topmen, and then threw a last look at the swaying line of marines standing behind the waistdeck rail. He wiped his mouth with the back of his hand.

"Ship's at Quarters, m'sieu'." He tugged his watch out of his seacoat pocket and peered at it. "Eight minutes, if you don't count the topmen. Not bad."

Gallant nodded. "Very well. Now all we need is just one sign of life out of Castelar." He cupped his hands. "Foretop, there!"

"M'sieu'?" came the faint reply.

"Any change in that scene there, to nor'ard?"

A pause. "No, m'sieu'. *Diane's* bearing this way, and crowding on sail. 'And four sail, astern of her!"

Gallant scratched his neck. "Four, still. Sweet Jesus. . . ." He squinted forward. *Lima* still showed no activity.

Béssac was pointing at the near line of wallowing merchantmen. "*Those* poor buggers have seen what's up ahead, m'sieu'. Look at the scrambling on their quarterdecks!"

Gallant's smile was humourless. "I'd be scrambling, were I in their position. Christ knows who those ships are. Although O'Farrell's not leaving us much doubt!" His eyes searched *Lima* again, his lips a tight line. The Spaniard's inactivity was incredible, and Gallant found himself fighting back a growing bubble of anger and exasperation. To add a chilling note to that was the thought of the Marquise, over there in a ship that, far from being a protective fortress, was acting in a strange and disquieting way. With a rush Gallant wished with all his heart he had not interfered in that scene on the Governor's balcony. The Marquise could have her affairs with repulsive Spanish noblemen; she would at least have been here in *La Bretonne*, where Gallant could have some sense of protecting her person. What in the name of God was Castelar *doing*?

"D'you think he's forgotten his own signals?" said Béssac, abruptly.

"No. He'd have sense to fire a gun. Even send off a boat. There's something bloody well strange going on. He's acting as if — as if —"

"As if he *knew* those ships were out there," finished Béssac. "As if he —"

Gallant stared at him. "As if he wanted an attack to succeed?" he said slowly.

Béssac stared back, and Gallant knew the grizzled Mate was sharing his same outrageous train of thought. A rapid train of thought of the kind that only took place in the minds of men who had developed a sort of sixth sense about survival: the sniffing out of an enemy before he is at your throat.

"Too crazy to be true?" said Béssac quietly.

"No, mon vieux." And then Gallant was filled with sudden resolve. "But we're not going to chance it!" He stared at *Lima*. *God help her if we're not wrong*.

"Crack on sail, Béssac! I'll have the courses and t'gallants, mizzen tops'l and outer jib! Lively, now!"

"Aye, m'sieu'!" hooted Béssac. It was music to his ears. In an instant he was forward, bellowing at the topmen and sail-handlers. Even without the hands of the gun crews, it was a mere matter of minutes before the sails were dropping with a crack from the great yards, bellying out hard into still, powerful curves. Blocks squealed as sheets and tacks were hauled home, and the mizzen tops'l yard rose up its topmast to the rhythmic hauling that was set to a chanted "Ah-hey-ya! Ah-hey-ya!". As the canvas spread to the wind, *La Bretonne* seemed to rouse herself like a great waterbird from sleep beneath Gallant's feet. The deck canted as she heeled slowly to the press of the new sail, and under the counter the sea roar took on a deeper, more urgent tone. A broad swell lifted her bows as her acceleration grew, and she drove her bows into the succeeding swell with a ringing *c-crunch* and a swirling welter of spray that pattered back over the deck.

Behind Gallant, Vignac spat in satisfaction and grinned wolf-ishly at Gallant as he fastened a firmer grip on the great wheel.

"Christ! That's better! Hein, m'sieu'?"

Gallant gave him a small smile, glancing at the compass card. "Yes, it is. But it'll do us no bloody good if we're all over the sea, will it? Your course is still north, a half east."

Vignac looked sheepish. He was a proud man, proud of the fact that he had been chosen as the best helmsman in *La Bretonne*. "Aye, m'sieu'. Steady on north, a half east."

"And watch the bloody luffs of the tops'ls. This'll be no time to be taken aback!"

Vignac bent to his work, all duty and muscular purpose once again.

La Bretonne heeled steeply as another gust pressed her over. She was rapidly beginning to overhaul the slowly pitching mass of *Lima*, and the guns' crews on the weatherdeck peered over their shoulders at the towering Spaniard.

Béssac's yell carried aft from the waist. "Merchantmen are signalling, m'sieu'! Poor bastards want to know what to do!"

44

Gallant slapped the rail with fury. *Lima* was ignoring the flags fluttering forlornly at the trucks and yardarms of the merchant vessels. What in the Devil was happening in the Spanish ship? *Was* it treachery? Or was Castelar simply unable to decide what to do?

"Tops, there! How far off are they, now? *Diane* and the others?"

"Two leagues at most, capitaine!" came a faint cry. "*Diane's* outrunnin' them! He's bearing right up for the head of the convoy!"

Gallant waved that he had heard. *La Bretonne's* speed was now terrific, and the wind hum in the rigging and the roar of the sea under her bows and counter made it hard tk talk at all.

"Béssac! Hoist Castelar's signal number one! At the fore-truck!"

Béssac stared aft at him, wiping salt spray from his face with one grubby cuff. "But that's just —"

"*Assume Formation*! I know, damn it! But we've got to keep 'em from scattering! Hoist it!"

"Aye, m'sieu'!" Already he was turning away, barking the necessary orders.

Gallant sprang to the binnacle. He peered down at the swinging card, then up at the distant horizon and the line of ships past which they were boiling. *Lima*, with an eerie lack of almost any sign of life, was almost abeam now on the other side. Gallant felt a shiver run up his spine.

"Vignac?"

"M'sieu'?"

"In five — maybe six minutes, we're going to be abreast the starboard column's lead ship. The snow, there. We'll alter course then. I'm going to pay off a bit, cross the bows of the column to intercept *Diane*. And the bastards following her. Follow?"

"Aye, m'sieu'! I'll be ready!"

"Good." Gallant filled his lungs and bellowed. "Béssac!"

"M'sieu'?" The Mate came bounding up the ladder to the quarterdeck. His grizzled face looked flushed with pleasure under its stubble of beard and salt-spray sheen.

"Is Galiot on the gundeck?"

"Aye, m'sieu'. Larboard battery, as per your —"

"Good. Tell him to have Akiwoya double shot every gun. And make sure the captains get the vent covers on, if they haven't already. I don't want wet guns at the wrong moment!"

"M'sieu'."

"And one other thing. The small arms chests are to be brought

45

out of my cabin. Here's the key. I want each gun captain to draw boarding arms for his crew."

"Aye, m'sieu'." Béssac paused, looking over at the nearest merchantman as *La Bretonne* drove past. "The signal did it, m'sieu'! They're holding formation!"

"As well they should, the silly bastards," muttered Gallant. "For now. Let's see what they do when those approaching gentlemen get within gun range. I'm going to alter course as soon as we draw ahead of that leading scow, hein? I want to get out to *Diane* as quickly as we can. If we're going to have to engage those vessels — whatever they are — I want it as far off the formation as possible! That'll help give a fighting chance to —"

"Deck, there! Capitaine!"

La Bretonne heeled to a powerful gust, and she punched with a physical shudder into the back of a green, steeving swell. As the sun rose the strength of the wind was growing with it. Gallant clutched at the spray-wet rail until she steadied, and then cupped his hands. "Deck, aye!"

"I can see their colours, m'sieu'!" It was Portelance, his thin voice cracking in excitement. "They're — damn me, capitaine, they're *Dutchmen*!"

"*What*?"

"Dutchmen, capitaine! Sure as the Virgin's pure! I can see their colours! They're Dutchmen, right enough!"

Béssac was returning up the ladder from the waist. He was gaping open-mouthed at Gallant.

"*Dutchmen*? Jesus! Now what'll *that* portend?"

"For our purposes, Béssac, bloody little!" His lips were a tight line. "The Dutch are English allies, hein?" He stalked up the sloping deck, darkening now as the spray was drenching the holystoned wood, and peered at *Diane's* distant, plunging shape, and the vessels astern of her.

"But what size of ship?" Gallant muttered, under his breath. "Surely that can't be a squadron of men-o'-war?"

"Privateers!" said Béssac, almost in a bark. "Got a feeling for it, capitaine. I'd lay a pinch of a trollop's teat that we're looking at a Dutch privateer squadron!"

Gallant grinned at the Mate's language. "Good in a sense, then, mon vieux. They're not the bloody rosbif navy!" He tugged his own watch out of his waistcoat and peered down at it, spreading his legs for balance again as *La Bretonne* rolled steeply to larboard.

"It'll be almost half a glass before we come down on them,

Béssac," he said, looking up and snapping the watch shut. "Broach a brandy cask. Every lad to have a tasse."

"D'you think it might be a bit soon for the brandy, m'sieu'?" said Béssac, quietly. "Before we see a touch of action?"

Gallant kept his eye on *Diane's* tiny, tossing shape over the bows. *La Bretonne* heeled with a roar to a gust, and he clutched the weather rail.

"One thing always to keep in mind, Béssac," he said. "Never keep a crew at Quarters without doing something with them. The brandy'll make them think of their gullets for a while, eh?"

"Bien sur. À vos ordres, m'sieu'!"

In the next minute the boatswain's mates were disappearing below to the spirit locker, and a round of whispers and winks spread through the waiting gun crews and sailhandlers.

Gallant looked aft past the stern lantern. *Lima* was dropping astern, still devoid of any sign that Castelar was reacting to *Diane's* predicament. A cold chill gripped Gallant's spine as he thought again the fear he had shared with Béssac: that *Lima* would not act. It seemed incredible, still; surely there had to be a far more obvious reason for Castelar's behaviour. Unless . . .

"Béssac?" he called out, still squinting at *Lima*.

"M'sieu'?"

"Hoist Castelar's signal for *Enemy In Sight*. And give him a gun when you do."

A moment later a crimson pennant squealed up to its block as one of *La Bretonne's* foredeck guns thumped out. The smoke rolled away to leeward over the swells, shredded and wisped by the wind.

Gallant took the great brassbound telescope from its leather sheath by the wheel and snapped it open to train it on *Lima*. As the image sharpened into focus he could see in the flattened field of view part of *Lima's* side. Her gunports were closed, and even the weatherdeck guns were still run back. Above the rail, just visible below the curving edge of the Spaniard's main course, was the quarterdeck.

And amidst a group of other figures stood Don Alfonso Castelar, brilliant in scarlet and gilt, with a glass to his eye trained toward *La Bretonne* and beyond to *Diane* and her pursuers.

"Well, I'm buggered," muttered Gallant, lowering the glass. *He knows. He knows what's about to happen. And he isn't going to do a damned thing.*

La Bretonne shuddered down into the back of a white-capped swell, and a mist of spray needled into Gallant's cheeks. He turned to look forward again.

"*Diane's* no more'n half a league off, now, m'sieu'!" Béssac was calling through cupped hands from down in the waist. "And the Dutchmen can't be any more than a half-league behind her!"

Gallant looked critically up at the frigate's sails. *La Bretonne* was well off the wind, although moving strongly. If, instead of putting the helm up and simply running down on *Diane* and the Dutch, he put the helm *down* and brought the frigate on to more of a reach than a run, there would be two advantages: he would have *La Bretonne* at her best turn of speed and he would better the windward gauge he would hold on *Diane* and her pursuers.

"Vignac!" he barked. "What's your ship's head?"

Vignac squinted through a mist of droplets at the binnacle. "North by east, m'sieu'."

"Down helm. Bring her through nor'nor'east and nor'east by north to nor'east! Béssac! Sheets and braces! We'll harden up to a reach, starboard tack!"

Dipping and curtsying with exquisite grace, the blocks squealing aloft and dark ripples thumping across the face of her canvas, *La Bretonne* turned in a deep heel from her quartering run off the wind to a tightly hauled reach. In contrast to most square-rigged vessels, this was *La Bretonne's* fastest point of sailing. As Béssac's sailhandlers made last trims of the lee and weather braces, the frigate began to thunder along with almost frightening power. To an observer she was, with her towering trio of still, curving ivory canvas and graceful, ducklike hull heaving and plunging over the swells that foamed beneath her forefoot, an object of incomparable beauty. It was an irony of war at sea that in their hurry toward destruction and doom in the hail of flying shot, the little ships such as frigates and corvettes displayed their greatest moments of beauty and electric excitement.

Gallant squinted against the glare back at *Lima*, now a black shape amidst the twinkling silver of the dawnward sea. Béssac reappeared at his side, puffing industriously at the ancient clay pipe as he squinted up at the set of the mizzen topsail.

"Damned near ten knots already, capitaine. She flies on this point, by Christ! Almost as good as poor old *Echo*."

Gallant did not answer, and Béssac looked at him sharply. The spray had misted over Gallant's black tricorn until it was covered with tiny droplets twinkling like diadems in the bright sunlight. Gallant's tanned face looked like oiled oak wood.

"What *is* the Spaniard really doing, m'sieu?" muttered Béssac, in a guarded tone. "Were we wrong to think —?"

"Christ on a crutch!" swore Gallant, in exasperation. "I don't know. If it is treachery, I can't think of a reason for it. If he's deliberately ignoring action out of fear . . ."

"That could be. The Dons have done that before."

"Yes," said Gallant. "But in that gard   scuffle I had an odd feeling."

"Eh?"

"That he's not as much the buffoon as he pretends."

Béssac cleared his throat and spat out through the lee mizzen shrouds. "So what choice does that leave us? Hell, we've got the convoy to worry about, the Marquise. Those Dutchmen—"

"Exactly. First things first. We've got to do what we can to protect the convoy. And we'll have to let Castelar play his hand, if he has one, and *then* react." He shook his head. "You'd better hope that he is merely afraid to act. That we're wrong in this weird feeling about him. Any other consequence makes my skin crawl . . ."

Béssac nodded. "All right. But what can we do about —?"

Gallant looked at him. "The Marquise?"

"Yes. Christ, if he's gone turncoat on us . . ." The Mate did not finish.

Gallant looked back at *Lima* with a chill knot suddenly large in his stomach. He made a powerful effort to control a sudden turmoil that had welled up in his thoughts. The beautiful face, the hypnotic green eyes, floated before him, and he felt a distinct pang of pain in his chest.

"God damn him. If Castelar is not a gentleman . . ." he said, hoarsely.

"Deck, there!" It was the foretop captain.

"Deck, aye!"

"*Diane's* gone about, m'sieu'! Starboard tack, steerin' about east nor'east!"

Gallant snatched up the telescope and stepped quickly to the waistdeck rail. In the field *Diane* was so close that he could see the gleam off the wet tan and black hull paint, and the glittering, rainbow-laced garlands of spray she was tossing round her bowsprit. Under a full press of sail, O'Farrell had snapped her round so that she was on a course to intercept *La Bretonne*, moving across the track of the Dutch vessels which, in ordered line abreast, were tacking hard up in her pursuit.

La Bretonne sank her bows into a heavy swell with a thump and a tremor, and as she lifted a cloud of spray dashed back along the deck, wetting afresh exposed faces and hands and painting large dark blotches on the headsails and courses.

Gallant wi ed his dripping face with one cuff and pointed for Béssac's enefit. "Look there, Béssac. Our young Irish bucko saw our cou e change. He's altered to meet us. Exactly what I would have rdered him to do! Good lad!"

"Eh?" said Béssac, his pipe crackling.

"The Dutchmen, hein? They've got to either hold that tack to intercept the convoy, or go about like *Diane* and have to make another board or two to windward."

"So?"

"I'd wager they'll go about soon. If *Diane* can stay upwind out of gun range until we close with him —"

"I'm sorry, capitaine, but I don't —"

"The Dutchmen will tack again, Béssac! They'll all be back on a larboard tack, line abreast. At least some of them. That's when we'll hit them!"

"But there's *four* sail, m'sieu'!"

Gallant's mouth was a thin, hard line. "It'll take them a while to tack again to turn their broadsides toward us. So we try and catch as many of them as we can when they go to the larboard tack. We fall off and run across their bows in succession!"

"*Rake* them?"

"Yes! *Diane* tacks or wears round to follow in our wake, hein? And then we rake every one we can catch at it!"

"Jesus. *All* of them?"

"It's our one, best chance, Béssac. One pass to cripple 'em best as we can. Then we beat up to engage again or dodge out of the way, as needs be. Either way, we distract them from the convoy. And we just hope the convoy keeps formation. *And* that the poor buggers will use every puny gun they carry!"

Béssac's eyes shone with an old, familiar reckless glow. "All right. Sweet Mary! Once again I follow you into the same idiotic death and destruction!" He was looking aloft, stuffing his pipe away.

"We'll need more speed!" he rumbled. "Tops'l braces, there!" He sprang off down the waistdeck ladder, voice at full volume.

"Steer small, Vignac," said Gallant, in a voice suddenly hoarse. "I'll want every knot she can make!"

Vignac nodded, his eyes like agates. "Oui, m'sieu'!"

Gallant squinted ahead at *Diane*, his mind racing. They were closing the gap at frightening speed, and she was no more than a thousand yards away. Tossing and pitching, her ensign rippling in the wind, the little ship was a brave sight.

Béssac was suddenly bellowing at him from the waist, standing near the mainmast timber bitts. "Sloops, three of 'em, capitaine! The biggest, there, to loo'ard, might be a forty-four, by the look of her!"

Gallant nodded, scratching the stubble of his chin. A forty-four. He could make out its hull now: broad, russet in colour, like old varnished wood. Bows on to *La Bretonne*, the Dutch ships were coming up fast, the horizontal tricolour ensigns clear now, snapping in the freshening wind from stern staff and foretruck.

"A forty-four. Jesus!" muttered Gallant. He stalked up to the weather rail, clutching it as he stared at the Dutch. What would they do? If he tacked, and they followed him by a tack to larboard, they still would delay their contact with the hapless convoy by only a half-hour or more, with this wind. He bit a lip. Christ grant the Dutch were greedy, and would bore in for the convoy, ignoring *Diane* and *La Bretonne*. Otherwise . . .

"Deck, there! The Dutch have fired, m'sieu'!"

Gallant snapped his head up. From the right-hand Dutch vessel, a fat brig close to *Diane* in size, a gout of smoke was whipping back over its deck, and now just astern of the plunging *Diane* a thin geyser of spray jetted up. The dull thump of a gun reached Gallant's ears over the sea noise.

Gallant turned to his messenger, a frightened-looking lad of about fifteen who had been dogging his side since the ship went to Quarters, his hair straggling wetly over his face from under a stained wool tuque.

"Pass the word to M. Galiot and M. de Saint-Armande, lad! Off vent covers and out tampions, if they're in. And tell 'em we'll engage within ten minutes! Clear?"

"O — oui, m'sieu'!" said the boy, and was off down the waistdeck ladder in a scampering run.

La Bretonne surged in toward *Diane*, and now Gallant could see the swatch of colour that was a familiar blue coat on the little ship's quarterdeck. *Diane's* wet hull gleamed in the sun as O'Farrell turned off the wind to parallel *La Bretonne's* course. Heeling well over to larboard, their canvas drawing hard and full, the two ships thundered along over the great swells, now only several hundred yards apart.

Gallant could see that *Diane's* gunports were open, like red eyelids, her new batteries of long six- and twelve-pounders thrust out through them. And now, on the quarterdeck, O'Farrell was waving his hat and pointing vigorously back over his quarter at the Dutch. *La Bretonne's* men scanned the figures of the men of *Diane*, in her rigging and along her rail, as sailors do with such intensity when they draw alongside another ship at sea. The imminence of battle put a stronger light in their eyes, however, and as waves and gestures were exchanged little cheers were being raised unbidden here and there in both ships.

51

"Belay that noise!" Béssac was roaring in the waist. "You can cheer when we win! And if!"

Gallant followed O'Farrell's indication. The Dutch appeared to be ignoring them. Still tacking hard up toward the convoy, the ragged line of ships was now no more than a thousand yards or so away. In a moment it would be time to —

There was a thump on the wind and from the windward Dutch vessel, the brig, another gout of smoke shot out, to be shredded by the wind. Another geyser jetted up, perhaps three hundred feet astern of *La Bretonne*.

Fired almost in derision, thought Gallant. He could almost see the thoughts of the Dutchmen: a plum convoy, ripe for plucking, being abandoned by its escort.

Gallant squinted back at the convoy and *Lima*. The Spanish ship had still neither made more sail nor changed station.

It was time to act. Now, when the Dutch were certain the prize was theirs.

Gallant cupped his hands and spread his feet for balance. "O'Farrell!" he roared.

At *Diane's* rail, the Irishman waved his hat.

"I'm going about!" bellowed Gallant, over the sea's thunder. "Going to cross their bows and rake 'em! Follow in my wake!"

Around him, the twenty-odd people who were sharing the quarterdeck with Gallant looked at each other, exchanging glances of anticipation and equally of dread. Gallant could see the Irishman's face; he was grinning widely, waving in vigorous affirmation.

"Good!" The marine jammed his hat down harder on his head and strode back to beside the wheel.

"Steady now, Vignac. We've got to come round smoothly and quickly, if we're to surprise the buggers. Move lively now, y'hear?"

"Aye, m'sieu'!" Vignac spat off to leeward, narrowly missing the gun captain of one of the quarterdeck nine-pounders, who looked evilly at him. Vignac cackled through gap teeth. "You just give the word!"

Béssac was reappearing up the ladder.

"Ready your sailhandlers, Béssac! I'm going about! Tacking, not wearing! As I told you, we'll try to cross the bows of the Dutchmen and rake 'em!"

Béssac abandoned his climb up the ladder and bounded back into the waist, barking over his shoulder. "Ready when you are, capitaine!"

Gallant looked up. Abeam, now, the Dutch stormed on, beat-

52

ing in spray-wreathed menace up toward the line of merchantmen that lay helpless while their craven escort fled away to windward.

A minute more. Then . . .

"Ready about!" Gallant paused for a split-second, gauging the valleys beneath the swells. Then, "Helm a-lee!"

"Helm's a-lee, m'sieu'!" snapped Vignac, and with his wet, muscled torso gleaming like sculpture in the spray-rinsed sunshine, he threw *La Bretonne's* wheel over with a slap of one hamlike paw on the spokes.

THREE

La Bretonne heeled steeply as she swept round to starboard, and as she turned into the wind the howl and roar of the rigging suddenly rose in volume. She was turning toward the sun as well, and the swells over which she lifted and pitched down were suddenly glimmering mountains of moving beaten gold. The spray, jetting up over the catheads in sheets, was flung back over the crouching gunners with painful, stinging force.

"Loose headsails!" barked Gallant, his eyes stinging with salt. Ahead, the jib, jib topsail and foretopm'st stays'l whip-lashed, shivering in the wind with reports like musket shots, their sheets and bowlines writhing like snakes as *La Bretonne's* pitching entered the eye of the wind.

"Raise up tacks and sheets! Lively at the mizzen, damn you!"

There was a thunderous slap overhead as *La Bretonne's* great foretopsail and forecourse went aback, the hull shuddering with the force of it. Under the pressure of the straining canvas the frigate's bows swung slowly off the wind, while aloft the in-credible cacophony of slatting blocks, rippling canvas and creaking timber made Gallant's bellowed orders all but inaudible.

"Now! Haul, mains'l, haul! Cast off that whoreson brace, Marquette! Where in Hades is your mind! Haul, there, you to starboard!"

Plunging and hissing, *La Bretonne* turned well off the wind now, still being driven round by the great power of the backed foremast canvas. Then, abruptly, the main and mizzen canvas bellied out with a *whump* into arched, still curves of power.

Gallant's clothing was sodden, and water was running in a stream from the front cock of his hat. The deck canted steeply beneath his feet and he caught at the binnacle for balance. Out of the corner of his eye he caught Vignac grinning at him.

Gallant watched the swinging compass card. Four points off. Then five, then six.

"Let go and haul!" he cried. "Set that fore tack lively, now! Trim her all sharp, Béssac!"

La Bretonne, her momentum still great, continued her dramatic sweep round, well off the wind now. Gallant would have to check her swing before she fell too far off the course he needed.

"Hard a-lee, Vignac! Catch her!"

"Aye, m'sieu'!"

Gallant peered ahead through another cloud of spray that rose above the frigate's bows. Dead ahead lay the sides of the pitching, spray-wreathed Dutch hulls, all four still beating hard up toward the convoy. And on the starboard quarter, *Diane*, having tacked round with *La Bretonne*, was boiling along with thrilling speed, her gunport lids glistening red, the Bourbon ensigns streaming from her staff and truck in pure white bravery.

"Eight hundred yards off, m'sieu'!" came Béssac's boom from forward.

"Steady as she lies, Vignac!" said Gallant, briskly. His heart was pounding so disturbingly he felt as if it was forcing its way up into his throat. "Your course is," — his eyes flicked to the swinging card — "west by north!"

"West by north. Aye, m'sieu'!"

Gallant cupped his hands, seeing the weatherdeck gun crews crouched at their nine-pounders looking ahead and then at him in wild anticipation. "This tack'll do it, lads! Gun action, starboard, in five minutes! Larboard battery crews, stay at your guns! Pass the word below, there!"

But Béssac was already bending to bellow down the companionway a' Galiot and Saint-Armande, pacing in the gloom behind the batteries of long eighteen-pounders.

Gallant squinted at the Dutch. On this point both *La Bretonne* and *Diane* would cross the bows of at least the first three. If only they held that tack!

On the quarterdeck and in the waist, the gun crews made a few fevered last adjustments. More than several tied their thick neckcloths over their foreheads and ears, to diminish a little the damaging concussions of the guns that they knew were coming.

Gallant's knees were beginning to tremble, and he felt a cold knot of weakness clutching at his lower bowel. It was a familiar feeling, and he had expected it — but that made it no less unpleasant, and he swore luridly under his breath.

The four Dutch vessels, three virtually the size of the *Diane* and the fourth, the russet-hulled frigate which had the look of an English forty-four, were in a rough line abreast, and still they beat resolutely up toward the convoy, bows lifting and plunging with clouds of spray into the rolling blue swells. It was as if *La Bretonne* and *Diane* did not exist. The sun glinted off bright paintwork, off brass and steel, off bands of blue and green trim paint against the yellow wood of the hull planking, and off the vivid colours of the whipping Dutch ensigns. Each ship was flying three or four of the red, white and blue horizontal tricolour. The nearest vessel, the thick-hulled brig, was now less than five hundred yards away, and Gallant could see its gunports were open, the dark muzzles snouting out at a high angle as the brig heeled hard to starboard. *La Bretonne*, roaring down from upwind, would cross the brig's bows in only a matter of minutes. . . .

"Christ! She's tacking!" Vignac blurted out.

"What?" Gallant snapped his head up.

"Capitaine!" Béssac was bellowing from the waist. "She's tacking, capitaine! The brig!"

"Damn!" So much for neatly crossing her bows. But then he was a fool to think the Dutchman, or any seaman with half a wit about him, would have allowed *La Bretonne* to move into a raking position that simply.

The brig's canvas rippled, the slapping audible over the sea noise even at this distance, and then the ship was round, heeling away to leeward as she reached toward the onrushing French ships.

Gallant rubbed his brow, gauging the speed of the approaching brig. She was swooping and lifting over the swells, fine on the bow, now no more than three hundred yards away: a beautiful image, the curving canvas gleaming in still power in the sunlight, the bow wave a roaring, frothing white as she bore in.

"A brave man, that," muttered Gallant to himself.

Two hundred yards. One hundred.

And then suddenly she was there, her bowsprit arrowing past that of *La Bretonne*, the combined speed of the two ships making her rush past like a carriage at full gallop. From her rolling, pitching foredeck a bow gun banged out, and with a hollow, slapping sound a neat round hole appeared in the mizzen spanker, fifteen feet over Gallant's head. Her broadside would follow in but a moment more —

Now. Now!

"Fire as you bear!" Gallant roared.

A split-second after the words had left his mouth a thunderclap of sound engulfed him. Ahead, on the foredeck and in the waist, the linstocks were arcing down to the vents of the long nine-pounders, and one after another the pink lancets of the "huff" jetted up, and they fired with ear-splitting bangs. Twenty-foot-long tongues of pink flame licked out from their muzzles, and the guns lurched back across the deck, straining against their breeching lines. Great, dirty billows of stinking gunsmoke rose up like a wall from the frigate's side and were whipped away by the wind to leeward over the heaving sea face, so that for a moment the brig vanished, enshrouded in the boiling gloom. In an ordered succession working aft, the starboard battery guns fired again and again as each captain saw his gun bear on the plunging shape of the brig — or where it had been before the enormous pall of smoke had shrouded it. The din was terrific, and yet even as his own ears rang with each mind-numbing concussion he could see that the gun crews, responding to the long and arduous training the Master Gunner, Akiwoya, had demanded, working furiously. Leaping with swabs to sponge out the bore, ramming home new cartridge, wad, shot, another wad, then crouching wild-eyed and panting at the tackles. A bark of "Run out!" from the gun captain would make them throw their weight on the lines to roll the ponderous guns, trucks squealing, forward into firing position once more.

The gundeck's eighteen-pounder battery had given its full broadside, so that the smoke was now curling and whipping as high as the mastheads. Beside Gallant, the two starboard nine-pounders on the quarterdeck banged almost simultaneously, the twin flashes lighting the faces of the men on the quarterdeck with an eerie hue for a split-second in the brilliant sunlight.

La Bretonne swept on, rolling and pitching over the beam swells, tendrils of smoke trailing from her guns' muzzles. An enormous cloud of smoke drifted away from her over the sea, and for a moment the brig was still hidden.

Then, abruptly, the messenger, who had rejoined Gallant just before the first gun had barked out, was pointing over the quarter.

"Mother of Jesus! Oh, Jesus, look at that!"

Gallant stared. The vast cloud of smoke swirled on, suddenly past the brig to leave it bathed in a sudden wash of sunlight. It was a shocking sight. A moment before the brig had been a beautiful image of grace and power, swooping in toward *La Bretonne*. Now it lay shattered and broken, so down by the bows that the swells were crashing over the foredeck and streaming from the scuppers. The hull had stopped almost dead in the water, and was slewing round broadside to the swells, rolling with a protesting groan and crunch of broken timber and snapping rigging that was in counterpoint to other sounds: shouts, cries, oaths of anger, screams of agony. The brig's mainmast was down, an enormous black tangle of wrecked spar and cordage fouling the foremast rigging and trailing in a netlike tangle over the leeward side. The foremast and mizzenmast canvas were rippling and thumping, untended now. All along the brig's side horrid, gaping holes in the planking showed where the frigate's fearsome broadside had struck home. Gallant could see that virtually every stern gallery window had been smashed, and now here and there he could see axe blades flash in the sun, hear the shouting as the brig's crew fought to save their vessel.

Gallant steadied himself against the rail as *La Bretonne* rolled beneath him. "For'rard, there! Béssac! Béssac! Any damage?"

Béssac's face was peering up at him from the companionway. "No, capitaine!" he roared. "Not a hit! M. Galiot and M. Saint-Armande report nothing! Hell, she missed us completely!"

Gallant looked back at the stricken brig. *Diane*, plunging along astern, was just drawing abeam of it. Gallant could hear faint cheers coming from her. Cheers for *La Bretonne*.

Gallant shook his head. He and *La Bretonne* had been lucky; the frigate's broadside had obviously created such havoc in the Dutchman that the brig had not been able to get off any rounds that struck home. That was damned unlikely to happen again.

He caught sight of the gun crews around him, staring open-mouthed at the brig's wreckage.

"Stand to, by God!" he roared. "Don't gape at that poor bastard!" He looked up. "The second one's tacked as well! Béssac?"

"Aye, capitaine! I see!"

Gallant swung on Vignac. "Steady as she goes, man. Keep her speed!"

Vignac's eyes were shining. "Aye, m'sieu'!"

La Bretonne heeled to a gust, the sea roaring under her lee rail, and Gallant threw a quick look aloft for shot damage there.

But there was nothing. Not a trace. The brig had got off only that one round before *La Bretonne's* hail of round shot engulfed her.

"Too bloody lucky, I'm thinking!" Gallant found himself muttering.

"Eh, m'sieu'?" Vignac had heard him.

"No matter. Eyes on your steering!"

Gallant stalked wide-legged to the rail, slipping on the wet deck. He had to dodge past the busily working members of the nearby gun crews, stepping over uncoiled tackle falls, gun tools, the leather shot buckets, all the impedimenta of gunnery.

"Béssac! Pass the word below!" He threw a quick glance up at the dipping, inrushing form of the second Dutch vessel, a sloop of war, likely a twenty-gunner, which was moving in on *La Bretonne* with every inch of canvas set. "We'll try to hold the weather gauge on this fellow, hein? Tell Galiot and Saint-Armande! I'm going to try and engage him to starboard, again!"

Gallant's messenger had been staring aft, still in awe of the destruction of the Dutch brig. Suddenly he cried out, and at the same instant there was a muffled, deep boom that came clearly to Gallant's ears over the sea noise.

"She's burning!" the boy blurted out.

Gallant spun to look aft over the counter. The brig was an enormous pyre, hideous orange flames licking like long tongues from the wallowing hull up the black masts, surrounded in a horrid black pall of oily, thick smoke that billowed up and out, to spread in dark shadow over the sea face away downwind. And across that inky pall, *Diane* was passing in brilliant colour, her canvas bone-white and set to perfection, the streaming ensign at her stern staff a square of pure white against the darkness.

"Must've been a fire somewhere, and reached her stores. . . ." Gallant cupped his hands. "Béssac! Hoist a signal at the main, there! Give *Diane* Castelar's signal for *Take Station Ahead Of Me*!"

Béssac was standing spread-legged amidst a group of furiously working seamen who were recoiling lines at the mainmast timber bitts, lurching as the ship moved under them.

"Eh? Why, m'sieu'? He'll," — comprehension crossed his gruff features like a wave — "attack the third one! Bon! À vos ordres, m'sieu'!"

Gallant spun to look forward as *La Bretonne* shouldered into the back of a broad, rolling green swell, lifted over it, and then

59

dropped with a deep shudder that shook the planking under his feet. The second Dutchman was tacking hard up in beautiful form, every sail set to best efficiency, the brilliant Dutch ensign streaming stiff from fore and main trucks. On this point *La Bretonne*, still at almost maximum hull speed, was still too far to windward for the sloop to take the weather gauge. And unless he fell off the wind within a moment or two, *La Bretonne*, barely five hundred yards away now, would cross her bows, raking her as each gun bore. But that would only happen if—

"Tacking, capitaine!" came several simultaneous bellows from aloft and on deck.

"Oh, Lord," Gallant said, through clenched teeth. "I knew he would!"

The sloop was turning into the wind, her long lancelike bowsprit lifting and falling in deceptive grace as she swung. Aloft, her canvas rippled, buckled, filled again, and then went suddenly hard aback on the foremast. The sloop swung on, turning its long tan-coloured flank to *La Bretonne*.

Gallant took in the gaping row of open gunports along the sloop's side, seeing the planking gleam as the sun flashed on the wet wood and paint. Then, swiftly, the sloop was about, setting its foremast canvas quickly and visibly accelerating ahead on the new tack.

"By God, that's a seaman!" said Gallant, under his breath.

The sloop was hardened up into the wind several more points now, and it was clear that on these courses both vessels were racing for a collision point perhaps a thousand yards ahead. The Dutch captain had accepted the lee gauge, and the challenge of a brutal, broadside-to-broadside slugging match, with collision and boarding at the end should neither vessel strike colours under gunfire. Gallant shuddered. It would mean a ghastly toll of death, as it always did; in the hell of flying shot and splinters, men would be carved and smashed into horrid masses of wet, red meat as the ship disintegrated around them. The shrieks and screams of the wounded and mangled would rise to a sickening crescendo.

"Damned if I will!" Within him, Gallant felt a surge of determined anger well up. He looked at the crouching men, waiting breathless and staring at the guns, at the sailhandlers, at Thivierge's young drummer, who was visibly trembling. In a moment that would happen to them, if he let the Dutchman have his way.

Unless . . .

"Helm up! Ten points! Lively, Vignac!"

Vignac stared. "M'sieu'? Did you say —?"

"God damn your eyes!" raged Gallant "*Helm up!*"

Vignac slapped the wheel over, lips a compressed tight line.

"Béssac!" bawled Gallant. "Braces and sheets, quickly! I'm running down, cross her stern!"

He spun back, not waiting to hear the Mate's answering bellow. "Thivierge!"

The marine officer swung to him, sword at the salute.

Gallant pointed aloft, wiping his dripping face with the cuff of the other arm. "Two or three marksmen. Your best shots. In the foretop! Quickly!"

Thivierge's quick bark had three men of the Compagnies Franches leaping for the ratlines, slinging their long muskets across their backs. As they clambered furiously aloft up the shaking shrouds Gallant was cupping his hands at them.

"I'll want the quarterdeck people! Helmsman, officers! And for Christ's sake don't miss!"

He swung to look forward. *La Bretonne's* long bowsprit was swinging now, pointing at the rolling side of the Dutch sloop's hull, now at the stern gallery windows that gleamed briefly like silver wafers in a flash of sunlight, now at the huge, snapping Dutch ensign. Further off the frigate swung, the wind roar lessening in her rigging as it went aft, the squeal and creak of the blocks aloft sounding now as Béssac's sailhandlers hauled in frantic effort on braces and sheets. With her wake a boiling track over the faces of the swells that rolled in under her heaving counter, *La Bretonne* rushed in behind the close-hauled Dutch sloop, arrowing to cross its wake no more than two hundred yards off its stern.

Thivierge was pointing suddenly with his sword. "Look there, capitaine! Lot of movement on his quarterdeck! You've upset him with that turn, hein?"

Gallant nodded, teeth bared in a mirthless smile. It was easy gun range now, but the angle was still wrong. A few minutes more would do it. He glanced quickly at the swinging compass card.

"Steady on that, Vignac! Steer small!" He filled his lungs. "For'rard, there! Gun action, larboard battery, in a minute or more! He saw Béssac, who also had command of the waist weatherdeck guns, repeating the word to the crouching gun captains.

Gallant turned, grasping the arm of his wide-eyed messenger. "Below again with you, lad," he said. "Warn M. de Saint-Armande and M. Galiot that they'll engage in minutes to lar-

61

board. And I want them to try for rudder and rigging, hein? *Rudder and rigging!*''

"O — oui, m'sieu'!" The youth's eyes were wide with fright, and he was visibly trembling.

"Steady, now, boy! Repeat that order!" scowled Gallant. His arm grip on the lad tightened to deliberately painful strength.

"'Engage to starboard in a few moments. Aim for rudder and rigging'."

"Good. Go!" He propelled him toward the ladder.

"Deck, there!" came a cry from the maintop.

Gallant moved to one side to make way for a boy scrambling past with a powder bucket for one of the nine-pounders. "Deck, aye?"

"She's wearing, m'sieu'! Seen 'er helm going up, the helmsman spinning it!"

Gallant swore. He vaulted back to the rail. Now scarcely three hundred yards away, the Dutch vessel, a moment ago tacking hard away in a beautiful position for *La Bretonne* to run past her stern, was turning off the wind. Again the courageous Dutchman was maneuvering for the broadside-to-broadside encounter. But now *La Bretonne's* guns could bear. Was it too late?

Rudder and rigging. The old maxim. It *had* to work this time.

Gallant counted the last few agonizing seconds, forcing himself to wait for the last possible moment. His eyes were locked on the tall, ornamentally carved stern of the Dutch vessel, gleaming in gilt-paint glory in the brilliant sun above the blue and white froth of its wake. *La Bretonne*, the full force of the wind driving her before it, surged on past the swinging stern of the sloop. And now Gallant could see figures moving on the Dutch quarterdeck, in quick and frantic motion, an officer waving a sword and pointing aloft as the sloop's canvas buckled, filled with a *c-crump* audible even at this distance, and then rippled again with dark, thundering waves.

A second more. Then, "Fire!" Gallant barked.

Almost as the word left his mouth it was lost in a rippling crash of licking pink flame and enormous gouts of smoke that erupted from *La Bretonne's* larboard side. The deck shook beneath his feet with the ringing concussions as singly, or in twos or threes, the long eighteen-pound guns thundered out. The enormous wall of smoke billowed up above the rail, borne along with the wind that drove *La Bretonne*, and Gallant ducked and squinted through the stinking, weirdly lit miasma, coughing as the stench and gloom enveloped the quarterdeck. There was a sudden hum in his ears and his cocked hat was snatched roughly from his head, spinning off over the rail to starboard into the cloaking pall.

"Down, capitaine!" called one of the shadowy figures working at a nearby gun. "They've got sharpshooters firing!"

"To hell with them!" Gallant spat. "Quarterdeck battery! D'ye need an invitation? Fire, damn you!"

In front of him, the two larboard quarterdeck nine-pounders banged in unison, their sharp, brutal concussions making Gallant's ears ring. A spatter of water hit Gallant's cheek as one sponger thrust his swab into his water bucket and then swung it round as he leaped forward to swab the bore of his gun.

Still blinded by the smoke, Gallant slapped the rail in exasperation. "God damn this smoke! Where *is* she?" He spun on Vignac. "Keep your eyes aloft, Vignac! Steer by the truck pennant. We'll clear this smoke in a moment!"

The guns ceased firing. All around Gallant, above the noise of the wind, the creak of the rigging, the rush of *La Bretonne's* hull through the sea, the clink and bustle of working gun crews filled his ears. They would be ready for another broadside in scarcely a clock's —

"Deck! Deck, there!" The foretop lookout was shrieking. Even as he cried out, three muskets levelled from the top where he perched, and barked out at the hidden Dutch vessel.

"Deck, aye!"

"Turning broadside to, m'sieu'! Christ, she's lost her rudder! Her sternwork's a bloody shambles! But she's still turning! She's run out her guns, m'sieu'! Starboard battery! She's —"

The youth's voice was lost in a thunderbolt of sound that struck at Gallant and the men around him with stunning physical force. The Dutch sloop, her steering shot away, her stern part of the ship a tangle of shattered timbers, planking and mangled men, had continued on in her turn off the wind. She had turned parallel to *La Bretonne*, rushing on past. And then she emptied her entire starboard battery's broadside into the French vessel in one wild and ragged blast at two hundred yards' distance.

The effect of the howling storm of flying shot on *La Bretonne's* exposed flank was devastating. Before Gallant's aghast stare a ten-foot section of the larboard rail seemed to disintegrate in eerie suspended motion, black, jagged splinters cartwheeling toward and past him in whirling parabolas. The air was suddenly thick with fragments, hanging as if floating in mid-air. Gallant was conscious of rushes and whooshes past his face, of tugs and pulls at his clothing, of a cacophony of breaking and clanging sounds in his ears. Before him, one of the nine-pounder guns reared up as if suddenly maddened and alive, and toppled backward atop the crouching form of its gun captain, who gave a brief, choked-off scream before it smashed the life out of him. A man who a split-second before had been stepping forward with the rammer to drive home the shot and wad in the same gun was tumbling backward, a brilliant scarlet stream running from his mouth as he fell, legs twitching, against the wheel. Vignac kicked him away. The slim rank of Thivierge's marines standing at the waistdeck rail had been swept down as if by an invisible scythe, and now lay in a horrid welter of bloody flesh and shredded uniform cloth on the far side of the quarterdeck. The air in front of Gallant's eyes in that nightmarish instant was filled with a welter of flying splinters, writhing lines, and split-second images of men being pulped and savaged by the hail of flying, invisible shot. A deep ringing, as if from bells, was in his ears, the sonorous chime of the iron gunpieces as the shot struck against them and careened off into the shadows of the ship.

Gallant saw Vignac spin round, a great gash opening in the helmsman's shoulders, and he leaped to the wheel to seize it and prevent it from spinning wildly.

"Stay with it, man! Don't lose her helm!"

Then Vignac was suddenly looking up, his voice cracking in a shriek:

"The yard! The yard! The cro-jack! Christ, it's —!"

Gallant looked up, only to see the huge timber of the cro-jack yard, above on the mizzen, its lifts and lines in a snarled welter whiplashing and coiling in the air, hurtling down toward the quarterdeck with a fearful rending and splitting sound. An unbidden instinct thrust Gallant backward, rolling on the deck, as with a tremendous crash the yard struck home. It had come down squarely on *La Bretonne's* wheel, and Gallant heard a quick, bitten-off shriek as it smashed Vignac into a pulp and splintered the wheel.

Gallant fought to his feet, throwing off a cable that had slapped painfully across his shoulders, coughing uncontrollably in the clinging, pinkish smoke that swirled round the nightmare scene. The air was filled now with shouts and cries, the screams of dying, mangled men, the hoarse, frantic shouts of men trying to keep order, carry on. Among them Gallant could hear Béssac's booming voice.

"Béssac! Béssac!" Gallant cried hoarsely, and staggered over the rubble and wreckage-strewn deck toward the rail.

La Bretonne, out of control, veered in a sharp heel off toward the hidden shape of the Dutch vessel, and suddenly broke clear of the clinging smoke cloud. Aloft, her canvas luffed in rippling booms, cut lines snaking and tangling everywhere, and with the sudden motion of the deck under his feet Gallant lost his footing again and sprawled in a heap against the remains of the waistdeck rail. His head and shoulder impacted against something soft, and with horror he saw that it was the corpse of Thivierge, grotesquely sprawled, face white, one eye glassy and staring, the other eye socket a bloody crater.

Up. Up! With an inchoate growl in his throat, Gallant fought his way back to his feet. He lunged over Thivierge's body toward the rail, looking for the Dutch ship.

The sloop lay three hundred or so yards away, bows on to *La Bretonne* and wallowing in a chaos of unsheeted canvas and wildly swinging mastheads. For the moment she was unable to bring a gun to bear on *La Bretonne*, and by the frantic activity on her decks the Dutch were fighting for control of their vessel.

Gallant swung back to look up the length of the frigate, running his hands quickly through his hair to clear it away from his eyes. His feet slipped on parts of broken gun tools and fragments of line and tackle. Everywhere was a ruin of smashed and over-turned guns and wreckage, with red smears and the grotesque, humped forms of corpses here and there. Everywhere men were struggling out from under wreckage, coils of slack cordage, working savagely with axes and bare hands to free shipmates trapped, to clear away some of the chaos all about them. Their voices rose in hoarse shouts and calls, and mixing with their voices were the cries and sobs of the wounded and the dying.

La Bretonne was rolling hideously on the swells that were coming in abeam now, the wind whistling in the torn rigging, the topsails and t'gallants luffing and rippling noisily aloft, lines that had been shot adrift trailing on the wind far out over the water to leeward. With each roll the ship's timbers and gear groaned loudly, and the slithering crash of loose wreckage and gear added to the horrid din of the voices of the wounded.

There was a sharp, distant sound of gunnery, and behind the billowing shoulder of the forecourse Gallant had a glimpse of *Diane*, tiny and perfect, alongside her Dutch prey, clouds of smoke rising from between the hulls and thin jets of pink flame licking from their sides.

Three men of one of the quarterdeck gun crews stumbled past, carrying the limp, bloody body of a fourth. Gallant stopped them.

"Where are you going, you men?"

"It's Jean-François, m'sieu'! We're taking him below!"

Gallant threw the man a look. "He's dead. Leave him!"

"But, m'sieu'!"

"*Leave him*! You, Jacquard! Get below! Tell M. Galiot we need emergency steering! Tell him to put M. Akiwoya in charge of the batteries. We'll need new tiller ropes and a whipstaff of some sort! Do you follow?"

"O—oui, m'sieu'." The man knuckled a forelock and stumbled away toward the ladder.

The other two men had put down the body and were hunched over it, staring up at Gallant.

"Get up, damn your eyes! Chiasson! Get below to M. de Saint-Armande! He's to send on deck every second man in his gun crews. All he can spare!"

The man nodded, Gallant's words clearing the odd light he had had in his eyes. "M'sieu'," he said, moving away toward the waist.

Gallant spun on the third man, bracing himself as *La Bretonne* rolled sickeningly. There was a horrid chorus of screams and moans, punctuated by the slither and crash of moving and collapsing wreckage. Gallant gritted his teeth and forced the sounds from his mind.

He looked around for his youthful messenger, and then stopped. The youth lay in a bloody heap a few feet from Thivierge's body. *Damn*, thought Gallant. *Must I kill children too*?

He took a deep breath and turned back to the waiting seaman, poking a finger at him. "Right. *You're* my messenger now. Follow me. And for God's sake stay with me!"

Without looking to see if the man was at his heels Gallant sprang to the waistdeck rail, scanning the ruin in the waist below for the burly form of Béssac amongst the figures moving there. A silent prayer formed on his lips . . .

Then he saw him. "Béssac! You're—?"

"All right!" came the booming answer. The Mate picked his way to the foot of the ladder. His hat was gone, and his face was blackened and bloody from a hundred tiny cuts and wounds. "What in Hell's happening now? This is—it's—" He could not finish.

Gallant nodded, looking up. They were now about a league distant from the convoy, which still was holding its formation, far off to windward. And now the Dutch sloop they had fought had a peculiar look to it, and it was only after a moment that Gallant realized it was settling heavily by the stern. The canvas flailed and lashed aloft, untended. But Gallant could make out the crew, working with antlike vigour amidships. They were swaying out the ship's longboat, using the mainyard as a derrick.

"Sinking, by God!" said Gallant, through his teeth.

"What?" said Béssac. "The Dutchman?"

"Must have holed her below the waterline," said Gallant, with grim relish. And then he heard again the screams and moans all about him. *And what a price it cost.*

La Bretonne heeled wildly to leeward, so steeply that Gallant and Béssac had to lunge for the weather rail to keep from slithering down the canting, wreckage-littered deck.

"We've lost the helm, Béssac!" said Gallant, through gritted teeth. "I've ordered up every hand Saint-Armande can spare—"

Béssac shook his head. "He's dead, m'sieu'."

"What?"

"Galiot too. There's no more'n forty men left on their feet down there!"

"Sweet Mother of Christ."

"What of *Diane*?" said Béssac, his voice hoarse.

"There!" Gallant's face was like a thundercloud. "Alongside the third Dutchman. Trading broadsides and looking to board!"

"The convoy? The forty-four?"

"Still on course a moment ago. If we could get some bloody *way* on —" He stopped, staring. "Christ, Béssac!"

"Eh?"

"The Dutch forty-four! It's *ignoring* the convoy!"

Béssac scrambled up beside him. "What's Don Alfonso—?" He stopped as Gallant pointed, and his jaw dropped open.

The *Lima* had turned into the wind, waiting for the Dutch vessel to come up. And had let fly the tops'l sheets, and even as the two incredulous Acadians watched, the great Bourbon ensign dropped from its stern staff.

"Christ on a crutch," whispered Béssac. "He's *struck*!"

Gallant could not speak. He had an image floating before his eyes: an image of a beautiful, pale face below auburn hair, with green eyes widening in terror as Christ knew what cruelty closed in on her . . .

There was a slap of running feet on planking behind them, and Gallant turned to see Chiasson, panting from the run up the companionway. At Gallant's expression the seaman paled, hesitating.

"What *is* it, man!" barked Gallant.

"M. de Saint-Armande and M. Galiot are — they're —"

"Dead. We know. Where's Jacquard?"

"Don't know, m'sieu'. The senior gun captain's trying to put some order in things, m'sieu'. M. Akiwoya's already tending some of the wounded. And there's a lad come up from the orlop who says it's full of water, m'sieu'."

"What?"

"He was screaming that we're sinking, till M. Akiwoya told him to be quiet."

Gallant swung on Béssac. "Bloody luck! Béssac, get another lad or two who know what they're doing and get a report to me on damage down there! And I want it quickly!"

As Béssac scuttled off, Gallant fixed a look on Chiasson. "I'll need ten hands from the gun crews, if they can move. Tell the senior gun captain that. And tell M. Akiwoya he's to continue with his surgeon's duties! There'll be little need for gunnery for the moment!"

He paused for an instant. "Someone's got to do the loblolly, Chiasson. Get the wounded down to him, eh?"

"Oui, m'sieu'. I'll need a half-dozen lads."

"Done. See M. Béssac. And use my cabin for a surgeon's bay. No one's to go below past the gundeck. Tell M. Akiwoya that." His voice hardened. "The dead go out the ports."

"Oui, m'sieu'. Done it before."

Gallant nodded. "All right. Get on with it!"

There was a slap of more feet up the midships companion and Gallant turned to see the smoke-blackened forms of the gun crews lurching up on deck. Not a few were streaming blood from splinter wounds. Their eyes had a dazed look.

Gallant stepped quickly over to them. "Sharp, now, lads! You six on this side, tell M. Béssac you're with Chiasson, there. He's senior hand of a watch, as of now! You others. I need a damned good seaman. Who is the senior man of you?"

A pause. "That'd be me, m'sieu'. Brulé. Gun captain, number six gun, larboard battery." This from a swarthy man with beetling brows and powerful arms who had stepped forward a pace.

"Right. Brulé, you're boatswain, as of this moment. Divide your lads into three groups: foremast and headsails, main, and mizzen party. I want sheets, braces and lifts knotted or spliced, lines reroved — damn me, I want canvas that can *draw*! And quickly!"

Brulé nodded. "Do it best as we can, m'sieu'."

"Good! Then get at it!"

Gallant coughed and spat, looking back at the convoy scene. Still the double column straggled off on its course, as if oblivious to the bloody struggles that had been going on downwind. And now the Dutch forty-four was hove-to, barely a cable off *Lima's* slowly pitching mass. The Spanish vessel lay with her foretop-

68

sail aback, her colours down now from aloft as well. As he squinted, a sick numbness in his chest, Gallant could see a boat leaving the Dutch vessel's side, oar blades glinting in the sun as it lifted over the swells and vanished in the troughs, pulling strongly toward *Lima*.

Gallant cursed silently and spun to look for *Diane*. Drifting far off to leeward, the little vessel was still locked alongside its adversary. But there were figures in *Diane's* rigging, arms waving, and the white Bourbon ensign was rippling from the Dutch ship's ensign staff.

"Good lad!" Gallant muttered. He looked back at *Lima*. It *was* happening, so clearly that it might have been laid out for him in a book. The Dutch were not going for the convoy except as a secondary target. Somehow, somewhere, Castelar had to have made some kind of agreement, some understanding with the Dutch. It was the only answer. Word had by some means been passed northward — to the Bermudas, perhaps? — that the Marquise de Bézy and her dowry were in the convoy. And the Dutch had lain in wait, and had pounced.

Gallant bit his lip. It *was* the only possible answer; otherwise the Dutch forty-four would have grappled with *Lima* with the usual Dutch ferocity or attempted to intercept the hapless convoy. The image of Castelar's face suddenly floated before him, and a taste of bile rose in his throat.

There was a slap of shoe leather behind him, and Gallant turned to see Béssac appear up the waistdeck ladder, exchange a few words with Brulé, and then move quickly aft to him, dodging past several of Brulé's men and the remaining bits of wreckage.

"Good news, capitaine."

"Eh?"

"Hull's tight as a drum. All the lad saw was one of the water butts, stove in by a splinter, and he panicked. But the steering should work, after a fashion. I've rigged a whipstaff on the gun deck. Like a xebec, hein? It's in the forepart of your cabin. Your door's jammed open and if you bellow enough the lad on it can hear you." He scratched his beard stubble. "No binnacle, though. Can't give him a point to steer by."

Gallant felt a rush of relief. "Good man! Is there a man on it?"

"Aye, m'sieu'. Burly lad out of one of the gun crews. She'll answer her helm."

"Sheets? Braces?"

Béssac looked tired. "Knotted and spliced enough to give you the spanker, topsails and headsails, at least. That Brulé's a prime hand. These lads of his are trying to rig a jury on the cro'jack yard. Christ be thanked. There's less damage than—"

Gallant strode to the rail, not listening. He looked sharply down the length of the ship. The last of the wounded were being lowered below to where Akiwoya, the big Master Gunner, was plying his secondary trade as surgeon. As Gallant turned back to the quarterdeck, a clutch of men lifted the last clutter of wreckage from the remains of the cro'jack yard and pushed it over the leeward rail with an enormous splash. In the next moment they were hauling on the jury-rigged lift, swaying the splintered yard out of the way. And now the pathetic remains of Vignac were gone out through a gunport, leaving only a broad scarlet stain on the planking.

He fixed a hard look at the distant *Lima*, a deep anger stirring within him. And over there the last chapter in the morning's grim and bloody story was being written.

He slapped the rail, the force of it making his palm sting. "Not yet. Not yet!" he cried.

Gallant swung to look forward. Béssac and Brulé were waiting now in the waist with the pathetic little knot of remaining healthy seamen, swaying to *La Bretonne's* roll.

"Tiens, Béssac!" Gallant barked over the sea noise and the slatting and rumpling of the canvas overhead. "Sheet in the mizzen spanker! Braces, there, windward and loo'ard! One man on each, if you have to! We'll bring her to the larboard tack, close-hauled!" He cupped his hands toward the open companionway. "Below, there, on the staff! Can you hear?"

The bellow in reply was muffled but very audible indeed. "Aye, capitaine! Matelot Lajoie on the helm!"

"Look out at the wave crest line through the windows of the gallery if you have to, Lajoie! And listen sharp for my orders! We're going on the larboard tack, close-hauled! You'll have to react to my word quickly when I give it!"

"Aye, m'sieu'!"

Gallant looked up. The hands had tailed on to the spanker sheet and, forward, the sheets and braces. All eyes, including Béssac's, were on him.

Gallant threw a last look at the distant *Diane*. *Christ grant you've got enough sense to follow me, O'Farrell*, he thought.

"Now, Lajoie! Down helm! Haul in on that spanker sheet! Lively! Béssac! Let go and haul!"

Slowly, dipping and rolling, *La Bretonne* came to life again after her fearful battering. Blocks squealed aloft, mingling with the rhythmic grunting of the hauling men. The wind began to

70

hum and roar as she turned into it, and with the great press of the taut spanker pushing her ahead and toward the wind, the frigate slowly began to accelerate.

The ship lifted over a swell and thumped down, sending the first cloud of spray, the certain burden of a windward tack, pattering back along her deck.

"Trim all sharp, Béssac! Lajoie, ease her to larboard a touch more! There! Steady on that point, as best you can!"

As the frigate's canvas settled into place, *La Bretonne* heeled slightly and steadily over and began to drive with real speed up and through the swells, glittering rainbows of spray clouds garlanding her bows with each pitch and toss. The sea ahead was a moving mass of shining molten metal, and dead ahead over *La Bretonne's* bowsprit lay the dark shapes of *Lima* and her captor.

Béssac, dripping wet, staggered up the ladder to the quarter-deck and joined Gallant, braced against the chipped and splintered weather rail.

"Just what in Hell *is* it we're going to do, capitaine?" he called, over the building roar of the sea and wind noise.

"I can't let them have died for nothing, Béssac! Galiot, Saint-Armande, poor Vignac, the others. I can't let Castelar have his way! And damned certainly not with *her*!"

Béssac nodded. He was waiting for the plan, the wild scheme that always surfaced in Gallant's mind in such moments.

"Castelar and the damned Dutch!" Gallant went on. "It's what they're doing, don't you see? They're after the Marquise and her dowry, I'm sure of it! They didn't give a trollop's kiss for the convoy!"

Both men stared forward. The trailing vessel of the fleeing convoy was a good two leagues off now.

"It *was* as we thought, back there, I'm sure of it!" said Gallant. He squinted as a cloud of spray needled into them. "Lajoie! Starboard a bit! You'll have us in irons!" He wiped his dripping face and spat over the rail. "But, by Christ, I won't let him have her without a fight!"

Béssac stared at him, aghast. "*Fight*? Christ, capitaine, what with? You've barely enough lads to sail this ship! I couldn't give you two gun crews and still maneuver!"

Gallant shook his head. There was a deadly light in his eyes that chilled Béssac. He had seen it before.

"I don't give a damn for the guns, Béssac. We're going to board *Lima*!"

"Christ. You're joking."

71

"No! *Board* her, man! Maybe we can rally some of Castelar's crew, hein? If we can take her before the Dutch can get the Marquise and her dowry off, rally 'em, turn her guns on the forty-four—"

Béssac wiped his face with his cuff. He staggered a bit as *La Bretonne* pitched up and shuddered down over a huge swell.

"My God," he muttered. "The lads that are left. We'll — we'll be killing the rest of 'em, capitaine! And ourselves!"

Gallant looked at him, eyes like black points of steel. "Béssac, we've *got* to try it! What else? Tail off after the convoy and leave the Marquise to the Dutch and Castelar? What choice do I have, hein?" He shook his head, one fist slowly punching into the other open palm. "No! For Galiot, Vignac, all of 'em — and for us, too. We see this through!" His lips tightened in a white line. *And for her*, said a voice in his mind.

Béssac nodded, slowly. He became once again all resolve and purpose. "All right, mon vieux. You're the whoreson capitaine of this hell ship."

"Bon! Open the small arms chests. Have the lads arm themselves to the bloody teeth. We'll go in," and here he squinted aloft at the wind direction and then at *Lima's* dark shape, "larboard side to. Tell 'em the waisters and topmen are to come with me and board aft. Fo'c'sle and any marines left—"

"Three."

"My God! They'll — board with you, aft."

"If the forty-four fires on us?"

"Ignore it. Press on."

"The gear and lines? She'll foul aloft—"

"Let her. *Let* the yards foul. Put grapnels over and to Hell with everything aloft. I'm going to have Lajoie just run us in alongside, and over the damned rail we go, hein? I don't care if we rip the sticks right out of her!" He peered forward. "You'd better get your weapons issued. We'll be on 'em in fifteen minutes, no more!"

"Aye, m'sieu'!" And he was gone down the ladder.

That is, if Lima doesn't blow us out of the water first herself, said Gallant's mind. *Or that damned Dutchman.*

Gallant braced himself against the rail as *La Bretonne* pitched again, ignoring the needling of spray that drove back into his face. *Lima*, and, a little to the right, the Dutch forty-four, loomed ahead like black ghosts in the eye-straining gleam of the sunlit sea. Now the distance was under a thousand yards, and as *La Bretonne* drew ever closer, there was still no reaction in the movement of either ship.

Gallant looked grimly round the quarterdeck. Where twenty minutes ago it had been crowded with the gun crews and sail-handlers of the afterguard, he was alone. The hastily knotted halyards hung in loose coils on their pins, and the deck was still strewn with small bits of wreckage and stained with dark, bloody smears that glistened scarlet as spray pattered over the deck. With oppressive clarity a terrible picture materialized in Gallant's mind as he stared at the stains. An image of *La Bretonne's* dead, dropping like smashed dolls over the rail and out the gunports, floating and bobbing in the ship's wake like grotesque, abandoned toys. The horrid flotsam of naval war.

Ahead, *Lima* lay tossing, barely three cables off as *La Bretonne* pitched and heeled in toward her. And there, menacing and deadly on the larboard bow, the dark flank of the Dutch forty-four. Within minutes, *La Bretonne* would close with *Lima*. It was time!

"Béssac!" barked Gallant, his voice hoarse. He clutched again at the rail as the frigate heeled before a howling gust. "The arms! Are they issued?"

"Aye, m'sieu'! To the teeth!"

As he reached the waistdeck rail Gallant could see that the Mate had gathered one party of men forward, in the lee of the foremast timber bitts, and the other huddled in the break of the waist. Cutlass blades gleamed in their hands, and more than a few brandished half-pikes. A few pistols and musketoons were being hefted. It was odd and strangely moving to see the frigate's deck, so usually crowded and tidy in the naval way, now almost empty along its marked and scoured length. *La Bretonne*, her sheets and braces lashed, stormed in almost a ghost ship but for the men who crouched in their groups and watched the pale, hatless figure on the quarterdeck. Their white, staring eyes looked shocking in the strained, blackened faces.

Abruptly, a half-dozen pink flashes flickered along the flank of the Dutch forty-four, the deep thump of the reports coming a split-second later. There was a sound in the air like ripping linen, and then a similar number of towering, gleaming white geysers of spray shot up as high as the frigate's foretop in a jetting cluster just off the larboard side.

"Christ's guts! I thought it was too damned easy!" came Béssac's bellow from forward.

"Get down! All of you!" roared Gallant. "Flat on the deck, y'hear? And not a man rises till I order you up!" He cupped his hands to be heard over the wind roar. "Lajoie! Starboard a point! Gently, now!"

73

The two gangs of seamen were sprawled on the deck now, only Béssac still on his feet and staring out over the rail. In *La Bretonne* rushed, and now Gallant could see clearly a tumultuous wave of action beginning to break over the figures visible crowding the decks of *Lima*. The gunports of the big Spanish vessel were fearsomely gaping at him, and Gallant felt a shiver run up his spine. If, as he brought the frigate crashing in alongside, the Spaniard's near battery were to fire—

There was a sudden and sharp sound of wood snapping and popping, and the groan of protesting timbers being subjected to enormous stress. As Gallant stared, *La Bretonne's* foremast suddenly canted forward, the deck buckling, stays and shrouds snapping like bowstrings. The headsails sagged and then ballooned grotesquely as their halyards went slack, and the great foretopsail, and instant before drawing taut and full, was filling and collapsing with sonorous thumps as the yard slewed round, braces and bowlines snapping and writhing round the canvas in a wind-lashed welter.

"Damn!" Gallant sprang to the rail, bellowing over the sea noise as the frigate lifted over a breaking swell and then crashed down in a cloud of spray, a chorus of breaking sounds keening high over the hiss and thunder under the bows. "Hold her, Lajoie! Hold her!"

"Capitaine!" Béssac was running aft, pointing. "The foremast! It's sprung out it's wedges! Christ, it'll go any minute—!"

"What's happened?"

"Those rounds that did for the lads on the gundeck! We must've been hurt far worse below than we—than I—thought! You've got to put her right into the wind! She'll not hold a tack like this!"

Gallant threw a glance ahead, his mind racing. *Lima*, huge and brilliant against the golden sea, was looming a bare five hundred yards away. There were figures everywhere on her deck; moving, shouting, struggling.

Struggling!

"No, Béssac! We're going in! Stand by to board!"

"Christ, capitaine, you'll rip the foremast out of her!"

A serried line of pink flame flashed again along the side of the Dutch forty-four, with billowing clouds of wind-wisped smoke. As the reports struck at *La Bretonne*, much sharper now, the ripping sound of the hurtling shot filled the air. A ball banged into the frigate's side with a splintering crash, just ten feet below where Gallant stood, the heave of the planking with the

74

impact so marked that it staggered Gallant off balance. Another round spooned out a section of midships rail and sent it cartwheeling and splintering against the mainmast timber bitts, inches over the heads of the men lying prone in the waist. Overhead there were several sharp sounds like fists hitting leather, and more ragged, round holes appeared in the spanker and main topsail. Alongside, the rounds that had missed sent jetting silver geysers of water shooting up, hissing and pattering back on *La Bretonne's* deck as she stormed on.

Gallant wiped the spray from his face with a cuff. "Next broadside will kill us, Béssac! We've got to get into the lee of *Lima*! Lajoie!"

"Still here, capitaine! Only, where in Christ's name —?"

"Steady as you lie now! How does she steer?"

"Damned awful lee helm, capitaine! I . . . don't know if I can . . . hold her!"

"You've got to! A clock's tick more! When you feel us strike alongside her, lay aft on deck! Follow me aboard *Lima*!"

"Aye, m'sieu'!"

Lima was huge ahead now, pitching and tossing, a towering shape of red and gilt, her lofty canvas slatting and rippling as she lay hove-to. Her gunports were black, and menacing. And still Gallant could make out struggling knots of men everywhere on her deck.

"Come on, come *on*!" Gallant banged his fist into the rail with frustration, his heart racing wildly in his throat. Lajoie, performing awesome prodigies on the whipstaff, was managing to hold *La Bretonne* on her course. Rolling and slatting, the forward rigging a welter of snarled lines and ballooning canvas, she pressed in through the golden swells toward the hulk of the Spanish vessel.

And then suddenly they were there, rushing in at *Lima's* towering sides like a coach at full gallop, the sea leaping into a cauldron of white froth as the two hulls surged together, the shouts, cries and tumult of the battle on the Spanish decks ringing down over the narrowing space and the crunch and hiss of the sea.

Gallant's heart was pounding so wildly he thought it would burst. A second more. Then —

"Now, Lajoie! Hard a-larboard!"

Swung by the pressure as Lajoie strained breathlessly on the helm, *La Bretonne* swung her quarter in toward *Lima's* gleaming, rolling wall. Overhead there was a snapping and rending cacophony as the frigate's yards caught and enmeshed themselves in *Lima's* lower yards. The two hulls impacted with a shudder that threw Gallant to his knees, a horrid groaning filling the air as the ships ground together. The sound of the deadly struggle in *Lima* filled Gallant's ears now, and above the voices and the clash of steel several pistol shots rang out.

Gallant scrambled to his feet. Dodging out of the way of a collapsing topmast shroud, he scooped up a seaman's cutlass where he had seen it lying in the quarterdeck scuppers. He sprang for the rail, conscious out of the corner of his eye that the men in the waist were tumbling up the quarterdeck ladder after him, and that forward, Béssac's men, cheering and shouting incoherently, were leaping for *Lima's* side with their cutlasses in their teeth like desperadoes. Grapnels arced through the air, and as one hooked in *Lima's* forechains Gallant heard a brief scream as one of Béssac's men lost his footing and fell into the heaving, frothy abyss between the two hulls.

Gallant thrust his cutlass behind him down the neck of his coat, teetering on the rail for a split-second. Then, with a wild effort, he launched himself across the yawning gulf. He grunted in pain as he banged down against *Lima's* red planking, pain shooting from knees and elbows. He clung, panting for a moment, before clutching at the battens and then struggling, like a squirrel on a brick wall, up toward the entry port high above at *Lima's* rail. Below and beside him he could hear the rest of *La Bretonne's* men leaping across, oaths and curses on their lips as they struck the ship's side. Gallant struggled up, sick with fear that he would lose his grip on the slick, wet wood and drop to be ground to death between the groaning, working hulls.

Then, in the next instant, he was at the port, pulling himself through, stumbling and falling to his knees, gazing wildly round and clawing for the cutlass behind his neck. Gunsmoke drifted in a stinking mist across the deck. In it, the scene was a wild mêlée of struggling bodies everywhere, the grim noise of a desperate hand-to-hand fight punctuated by cries and screams, the ring of steel and the thump of bodies on the broad deck. For a moment Gallant was utterly confused, seeing Spaniard struggling with Spaniard. Then, in a break in the tumult, he saw the pale faces of Dutchmen, all with odd red ribbons laced on their hats or dangling from stocking caps. And many of the Spaniards wore the same ribbons. It was suddenly clear. The remaining loyal crewmen of *Lima* were locked in a desperate last struggle for their ship with the Dutch boarders from the forty-four and the Spanish hands who had gone over to them.

Gallant swung round, coughing in the smoke. Forward, he could see Béssac and his men tumbling over the rail.

"*La Bretonne*!" Gallant bawled. "At 'em, lads! Strike at the red ribbons! *Come on*!" He waved the cutlass over his head and lunged toward the nearest knot of fighting men.

He was suddenly bodied into by two swarthy, thick-set Spanish seamen, one with a battered red ribbon tied to the tail of his long stocking cap. Hands locked round each other's throats, they fought in grim silence. Gallant seized the shoulder of the beribboned man and spun him round with such force that he lost his grip on the other man, who sprawled off-balance into the scuppers. With a grunt Gallant swung the guard of his cutlass in a roundhouse swing into the astonished Spaniard's jaw, and the man went down like a tree.

Gallant lunged on, to see only at the last split-second a heavy-bodied seaman with ruddy features and wide, staring blue eyes beneath a tattered, uncocked hat, lunging at him with a half-pike. Gallant twisted, and the point of the pike passed under his armpit. The Dutchman bodied into him, dropped the pike, and wrapped apelike, brawny arms round Gallant. With a horrid, toothless grin and eyes crinkled into little porcine glints he pinned Gallant's arms to his side and bore down with a spine-crushing hug of appalling strength.

A red haze began to close over Gallant's eyes and he felt a wild bubble of rage well up in his throat. With savage effort he butted the Dutchman in the face with his forehead, the blow sending his own ears ringing. The Dutchman grunted, staggering back and releasing Gallant, a perplexed expression on his face as a scarlet jet of blood shot from the nostrils of his broken nose.

His breath heaving, Gallant planted his feet and put all his weight behind a deep straight thrust with the cutlass. The blade sank to the guard in the Dutchman's stomach, and he screamed, clawing at Gallant's hand. Gallant yanked it out violently, with a little unbidden cry of revulsion, and the Dutchman toppled past him to the deck.

A blurred image passed swiftly in front of Gallant's eyes, and then he was knocked sprawling to the deck by a wild-eyed Spaniard with a ribbon gleaming in the cockade loop of his hat. As Gallant stared, the breath knocked from his lungs, the man levelled a huge, bell-mouthed musketoon at him, discoloured

77

teeth bared in a mirthless grin. But in the next instant one of *La Bretonne's* men was driving his bayonet into the Spaniard's belly, and he was collapsing back with a shriek, the musketoon clattering to the deck.

Gallant struggled to his feet and fought his way through the wild brawl, striking out almost blindly with fist and blade, hearing deafening screams in his ears, conscious only of pain in his wrist when the blade struck home through cloth or gristle, then reeling as a glancing blow to his head briefly stopped his progress aft.

He glimpsed the quarterdeck ladder through the smoke and struggling shapes, and then in the next second a Spaniard was running at him, cutlass brandished high, from under the halfdeck. Gallant parried the blow with fierce strength before giving the man a cut across the face that sent him reeling back under the halfdeck, clawing at his eyes. As the man stumbled back, he shouldered into three figures, and was thrust away into the shadows.

Gallant stared. One of the three was a tall, red-haired Dutchman, all in blood-spattered green velvet, a huge, scarlet-ribboned cocked hat pulled low over hard, glittering eyes. Small braided pigtails hung from his temples, with little bells on them, and he was carrying a heavy, dragoonlike sword that was stained scarlet from tip to guard.

But it was the two figures with the Dutchman that sent a violent shock through Gallant.

Eyes wide with horror in the pale, beautiful face, seeing Gallant now with shock, and another flicker of a strange, indescribable emotion, was the figure of Marianne de Poitrincourt, Marquise de Bézy, a scarlet cloak and hood carelessly thrown about her over her petticoats. And holding her in an iron grip, propelling her roughly toward the entry port on the far side of *Lima's* deck, a scarlet ribbon gleaming over the cockade of his cocked hat, was Don Alfonso Castelar.

"Castelar!" Gallant bellowed. He saw the Spaniard turn, glaring, seeing him with a flare of shock and malice in his hot, dark eyes. A savage fury took hold of Gallant, and he lunged in, the cutlass lifted. "You traitorous bastard!" he roared.

"No! Oh, God, no!" It was the Marquise's voice, in frantic pleading.

And then Gallant saw the pistol in Castelar's hand. He was watching, almost as he lunged in, the pink flash that suddenly sprang from it, impossibly bright in the morning sunshine. He heard the report, loud and deafening. He heard the Marquise scream, high and piercing, and saw with astounding clarity the green eyes fixed on him with horror and the other strange, inexplicable emotion.

But then he was turning, staggering back, the open entry port gaping behind him, the three faces white and staring at him, the Marquise's mouth still open in her scream. And then he was falling, falling, and a warm soft darkness was closing around him. He fell and fell, and he wanted the darkness to close over him before he struck the water so far, far below. Which it did.

FOUR

The snow was falling, thick and swirling, drifting down into the grey evening light around the dark masses of spruce and pine, to settle in the already deeply snow-covered gloom beneath. Along the narrow snowshoe trail that wound through the trees toward the distant fortress town of Louisbourg, Paul Gallant strode, his snowshoes squeaking and sinking with a satisfying crunch. His breath curled in white clouds round his head in the frigid air, floating behind him like a wake, and beyond the sound of his snowshoes he heard nothing but his own breathing. The Cape Breton forest was still and cold in the depths of an unusually icy winter, and all day during a fruitless hunt Gallant had seen no sign of life, no track of moose or deer. Only the blue flash and raucous bray of a solitary blue jay had disturbed the impenetrable northern silence, when Gallant had paused at noon to gnaw on a strip of salt pork and gaze down the brilliant white expanse of the snowclad, frozen river of the Miré.

Gallant hefted his musket to his other shoulder, careful not to miss the long, swinging rhythm of the snowshoe march. He wore a tuque, blue and pointed in the Montréal style, and indeed all that he wore marked him more like a Canadian habitant than an Isle Royale garrison officer: a white blue-trimmed blanket coat, with a peculiar upright pointed hood; a broad woven sash in brilliant arrowhead pattern, knotted on the left side, into which a tomahawk was thrust; large fur gauntlets, and blue woolen leggings rising in Indian fashion from his moccasins to above his knees. On his back swung a bulky hunting pack, and slung from his shoulder was his powder horn and shot pouch for the long Tule musket. He increased his pace, a glow of anticipation warming within him. In a few moments he would see the firelit windows of the first few outlying cabanes of the habitants-pescheurs round this end of the kidney-shaped harbour, and then it was but a half-hour's trek to the Dauphin Gate, where he —

But something was odd. Ahead, now, on the trail, was the buxom figure of Jeannette Rodrigue. Sweet Christ, was she not cold, dressed in nothing but a billowing chemise and a little white cap? And she was running toward him now, her black hair floating out behind her, so long, so dark; an inky river over the white snow.

Now she was beside him. No, above him. Why was he lying down? Had he fallen? She was bending over, touching his forehead, the chemise falling away from the beautiful fullness of her breasts, her eyes full of warm concern.

She was calling him. "Gallant," she said. "Capitaine. Capitaine."

But that was absurd. He was but an enseigne. . . .

"Capitaine? Capitaine, can you hear me?" The voice of Jeannette deepened ludicrously. "Capitaine?"

Gallant opened his eyes. Above him he could see a mast, the curving face of a sunlit sail. Rigging, lines. And under him it was not snow, but planking. The hard deck of a ship.

And peering down with intent concern as he knelt over Gallant, the person of Richard O'Farrell.

"Richard!" croaked Gallant, hoarsely. His head was roaring with noise and pain. "What in the name of God —?"

"Steady, capitaine. You're safe. In *Diane*. You've taken a hell of a blow to your head, there. No, don't touch that bandage. You'll bleed like a stuck pig."

Gallant tried to sit up, but the pain in his head welled up so fiercely that he fell back to the deck even before O'Farrell's hands pressed him back. He became aware that he was dripping wet, and the sodden chill set his body trembling uncontrollably. His mouth was dry, and tasted as if he had been sucking on a copper rivet.

"Here. Drink this." O'Farrell lifted him and pressed a tin cup to Gallant's lips. Brandy, hot and stinging, burned down the marine's gullet, and he coughed, tears coming to his eyes.

Gallant put his hand over his eyes as a brief surge of nausea overcame the glow of the brandy. "Aboard *Diane*?" he whispered. "Then you—"

"Found you in the water. Dead unconscious, but with an arm over a broken sweep and kicking a bit to keep afloat. Christ knows how. Didn't know it *was* you for all the blood and whatever till my boat's crew picked you up." He grinned. "You Acadians are tough nuts to kill, capitaine."

"*La Bretonne*! Béssac and the others. And *Lima*! What—?"

O'Farrell frowned. "In a moment. I'm having you taken below." He stood, his voice rising in volume. "Quickly with that pallet, there! I want him below and out of these clothes!"

Gallant felt himself being lifted abruptly and placed gently down on a thin palliasse. Then he was lifted, and many hands eased him below down the little ship's cramped midships companionway until, after many dodges and juggling in the gloom of the passageway, he was in O'Farrell's tiny cabin, being lowered into a box bunk, watching the flickering sunlight reflect from the sea through the stern lights on to the low beams and deckhead above.

He sank back, glad of the comfort of the small pillow. His eyes closed, and an enormous fatigue took hold of him. He barely felt the dripping uniform being stripped off, the rough woolen blanket being tucked around his shivering nakedness. He tried to beat back the roaring in his head, but it grew again, blotting out the voices, the voices he wanted so much to hear if only he did not need to sleep so very, very much. . . .

"He's asleep, M. Béssac. Thank God for that. It's what he needs, now," said O'Farrell's voice.

Béssac! *Thank Christ. He was alive, at least. But the others*?

"Aye, m'sieu'," said the Mate's voice, deep with concern. "He'll need it all. I—I don't know how I'm going to tell him."

Tell him? *Tell me what*?

"In good time. Keep me informed, every watch, on his condition, will you?"

Tell me what? said Gallant's mind, in rising anxiety. And then

82

the darkness returned again, a warm and comfortable oblivion. And he slept.

Marianne de Poitrincourt, Marquise de Bézy, put a hand to her throat as the crash of struggling bodies fell against the cabin door. She shrank back in the small, dim space, her widening eyes reflecting the single flickering flame of the small lantern that hung from the deckhead of the Dutch forty-four gun vessel. Quailing on her knees against Marianne's legs, her servant Lisette uttered another wail and buried her face in the noblewoman's skirts.

"Christ save me! Oh, My Lady, save me from them! Oh, please!"

Marianne's full lips were tightened into a tense line. "Hush, Lisette!" she said sharply. Her heart was beating so rapidly that she felt she would faint in the next moment. There was a tremor in her voice she could not control.

"Stand up, now. Beside me. Hold on to my hand!"

The girl's sobs increased as the tumult of the struggle continued in the passageway. "They're — they're going to do the same to us as — as they did to Marie! They are! Oh, God, please!"

Marianne passed a hand across her eyes. As she and her two women servants had been carried aboard the Dutch vessel, Castelar and the fearsome Dutchman in green velvet had thrust them toward the companionway leading below through a mob of jeering, roaring seamen, whom Marianne remembered only as a horrid sea of braying, gaping faces, savage and repulsive. They had been calling for the women to be given to them. And then, at the last moment before Marianne and Lisette had been taken down the steep companion, the Marquise's other woman, a dark-haired Basque girl named Marie, had been pulled away by Castelar and pushed screaming into the clutch of men.

Marianne shuddered. She had had a last, nightmarish image of the hysterical, pleading girl being held spread-eagled over a hatch cover while hands tore at her clothing, raucous laughter and a deeper, chilling sound coming from the men's throats as the first of them was pulling at his breeches front, pressing in to mount her.

"No. Oh, sweet lady of my prayers, no!" whispered Marianne.

83

"Wh — what, My Lady?" The terror-stricken Lisette had turned her round, pretty face up to her mistress. She was shaking with sobs, and tears had streaked across her powdered cheeks. Strands of hair wisped across her eyes in pathetic abandon.

"Come!" said Marianne, putting as hard a tone into her voice as she could. "Up, up!"

Lisette stood. She was shorter than the Marquise, no more than nineteen or twenty years of age. Her torn chemise that hung from her shoulders did not obscure her rounded, full figure, and her long, dark hair tumbled down her back in waves. With the shudder of a small child that has been crying too long, she clung to her mistress, sobbing anew as, outside the cabin door, a savage oath rang out, followed by the clash of steel on steel.

Marianne felt a tremor go unchecked through her own body, in spite of her fierce determination to remain brave, as there was a fearful crash of bodies against the door once more. There was a brief and cutting shriek of agony that trailed into a liquid bubbling, and then the thump of a slack body being thrust aside.

With a sharp bang that made Lisette cry out, the cabin door slammed open. Marianne could not control her own sharp intake of breath as a figure stepped from the gloom of the passageway into the cabin. Against her, Lisette trembled, wailing anew, and Marianne shrank back against the small shelf bunk behind her.

Sword in hand, Don Alfonso Castelar directed a long, slow smile at her. "Ah. My Lady."

Marianne stared at him, her eyes wide and glowing deerlike with fright and anger. Castelar's gaze had a ckld and frightening intensity. Across the front of his coat and waistcoat there was a dark splattering of blood, and from the tip of his hanger a bright, scarlet drip fell on the toes of his glossy shoes.

"You!" Marianne hissed. "Coward! Traitor! May God strike you, Alfonso! You —!"

Castelar pursed his lips. "Dear me. Must you be so disapproving, my dear?" he said in velvet tones. "You might be a trifle more grateful. I've just saved you from a most unpleasant rape. For the time being, at least. These Dutch have such appetites. . . ."

"How can you do this, Alfonso?" burst out the girl, shaking with fury. "I am of the King's family! The Royal household of France! And you —!"

"Are a rogue. Oh, indeed, my dear. You needn't go on with

an outraged litany of my evils. I'm quite aware of them. And do tell that creature to stop sniffling so repulsively."

The girl's eyes met the Spaniard's with level hatred. "She is afraid, Alfonso. Afraid that you are about to have us killed. Or worse," she said evenly. "What have you done with Marie?"

Castelar shrugged. "A misfortune. She—ah—expired in the arms of love, might one say?"

Marianne stared at him, a cold, trembling rage building through her. "You . . . swine," she managed to whisper. "You disgusting. . . ." She could not go on, and lowered her head, hugging the sobbing Lisette to her.

Castelar smirked. He pulled a lace-edged handkerchief from one cuff and began idly wiping the bloody blade.

"My appetites, should you care to know, my dear, are for something more lasting than your undoubted charms. Or those of your wretched girl there."

"How gallant of you," said Marianne, raising her eyes again to him. "Where does a pig learn such manners?"

Castelar's smirk faded. "You would be wise to be a shade more courteous to me," he said, in a low and menacing tone. "These Dutchmen will obey orders—and some, like the fool in the passageway, will not. But they all fear my dear colleague capitaine Ten Haaf, who *does* listen to me. So mark your tongue. I do not have necessarily any interest in preserving your virginity —or your life."

Marianne lifted her chin, her features a pale and icy mask. "What do you intend to do with us?"

Castelar's smirk returned. "An interesting game we hope to play, my dear. With you. And of course your maid. Bait for larger fish, shall we say?"

"You have the dowry. What more do you need of me? Why did you not leave me —?" Marianne broke off, feeling the resolve begin to crack. Willing back the panic and the tears, she forced the stony mask back into place once more. "What sort of game, Alfonso? Or need I ask," she said bitterly.

Castelar paced over to her and thrust Lisette roughly aside, ignoring the girl's wail as she collapsed against the bulkhead. He lifted Marianne's chin with one hand, and she met his cold, dark gaze as evenly as she could.

"Why, *money*, my dear! You're worth a shipload of gold louis to His Majesty, I'd think." He smiled thinly. "And I'd think he'd be happy to pay for your return."

Marianne snapped her head away, refusing to meet his gaze any longer. Her heart was drumming in her ears, and behind her back she clenched her fists, willing back the faint that threatened to overcome her. With a shudder she felt his hands drop and cup her breasts lightly.

"You—abomination!" she spat, turning on him again, thrusting his hands away. "A gentleman of Spain. Holding a noblewoman to ransom from her own King!" Her eyes flashed with fury. "You have no honour at all, do you, Alfonso? Not a trace!"

"Spare me sneers at my honour, Marianne. They leave me unmoved."

"Evidently. On your knees before your betters is where you belong." She smiled mockingly at him. "Where capitaine Gallant put you!"

Castelar's eyes blazed, and he seized her by the shoulders in a painful grip. His hanger, which he had thrust under his arm, clattered to the floor.

"Witch!" he snarled. "You try my patience too far!"

Her lips curled in a little mocking smile again. "Touched a nerve, did we, Alfonso?" she said acidly.

"You fool!" hissed Castelar. "I could have had you torn to shreds by those animals on deck a hundred times by now! My mission has been to dispose of you as easily and as profitably as possible! Mind your civility to me or—!"

"What? What did you say?" Marianne's face was stricken. "Your mission? *Your orders*?"

"Touched a nerve, have we?" repeated Castelar, in a cold, mocking sneer.

"You—you were *ordered* to have me killed?" she whispered.

"Of course. Therefore mind your gratitude that I have decided to use you a shade more profitably. Press me too far and I may decide otherwise!"

"Who, Alfonso? For God's sake, who wishes me dead?"

Castelar released her roughly and scooped up the hanger. He paced back to the door and then turned to look back at her, his face half-hidden in the shadows save for the mocking smile.

"Your ignorant little mind does not conceive of itself as having enemies, does it? Or indeed how this very venal world works."

"Who? Please tell me. I—I must know." Marianne's voice and expression had become quiet, almost pleading.

"In good time. But in the meantime, remember that your life," and his eyes travelled down her body, "—and your health—depend on me. And if you wish to keep both away from the attentions of m'sieu' Ten Haaf and his lusty gentlemen you'll have to consider—shall we say—a price."

Her face hardened again. "Ah, yes," she whispered. "The price. And what is it you have in mind, Alfonso?" He had stepped forward a pace, bringing his face into the light, and she flushed when she saw his gaze was locked on her breasts. Her hand came up protectively of its own accord to her throat.

"I think you know," he said smoothly. "And in my own time, my arrogant, imperious Marquise, I shall collect it!"

And without waiting for her answer he stepped out and thrust the cabin door shut behind him.

Paul Gallant awoke with a start. He stared up at the heavy beams of the low deckhead above, and at a slowly swinging lantern that hung there, trying for a moment to recall where he was. Then in a flash it was all back in his memory, and he reached gingerly up to touch the linen bandage that was bound round his head. There was a dry stiffness to it over the wound, but there was no pain as he touched it.

He sat up, throwing back the coarse blanket that had covered him. He was naked save for his shirt, and had been lying in a box bunk to one side of a small, cramped stern cabin. It was the captain's quarters in *Diane*, Gallant knew. And the usual occupant of the bunk was *Diane's* master, Richard O'Farrell.

Gallant felt lightheaded and woozy, and he blinked to clear his vision. Out through the stern lights he could see a brilliant flash of blue and white sea, and a foam-flecked wake trailing away to the blue horizon below wheeling gulls. The ship moved and creaked beneath him, and from above there came the sound of rigging being handled, the clump of footfalls and a voice raised in sharp command.

He ran his fingers through his hair and fingered the stubble on his chin. He felt dismayingly weak, but he was thankful that the pain and roaring had gone from his head, and he was ravenously hungry.

As if on cue the cabin door opened, and the blue-clad figure of Richard O'Farrell stepped through. The Irishman stopped in surprise when he saw Gallant sitting on the edge of the bunk, a surprise that faded immediately into a pleased grin.

"Well!" he said. "About time, by the Virgin. We'd about given you up for lost."

Gallant grinned back. His skin felt leathery, *like a lizard*, he thought, and he scratched self-consciously again at the stubble on his chin.

"How long have I been asleep?" he croaked.

"Asleep? More like poleaxed. About two days, now."

"*What?*"

"Like a proper log, you were. Fever at first, but that went. We poured some soup into you. Didn't even wake up for that." The grin widened. "Even managed to get you out to the seat of ease on the gallery, there, without so much as an eyelid flickering."

Gallant shook his head. "Two days. Sweet Mother." He touched the bandage lightly.

"Gently with that," said O'Farrell. "That black gunner of yours will put some damned hex on me if you mess with his bandage."

"Akiwoya? Then he survived, then." The sea battle was coming back into his memory now. The convoy and the attacking Dutch. The boarding party. And the bright pink flash of the pistol. . . .

"Yes," said O'Farrell. His face had fallen sombre, and he sat down heavily in a small ladderback chair beside the cabin door.

"There was Béssac, too. I remember him. Here, when you brought me down."

"Yes."

Gallant looked keenly at the Irishman. "You'd better give me the whole story, Richard. Where's *La Bretonne?*"

O'Farrell looked at his shoes tips for a moment, and then back at Gallant. "Gone. Burnt by the Dutch," he said simply.

Gallant closed his eyes and took a deep breath. "Christ save me," he breathed. "Why?"

"She'd sprung the main mast and was taking water below the waterline. She was down by the bows. After they—after your attack they just cut her adrift and set her afire."

"They took nothing out of her?" Gallant's voice was barely above a whisper.

"No. They—she was gone in fifteen minutes. Went up like a torch."

Gallant stared out at the heaving, froth-white wake. A gull was hovering out beyond the stern lights, his head on its fat neck canting this way and that, his beady eyes hopeful for something edible in the churning wake.

"The convoy. What—?"

"Ahead of us. Still on a course of nor'nor'east. Two columns, and not a peep of complaint about my shepherding, either. The

Dutch attack frightened them silly. *Diane's* about three cables astern of the starboard-hand column, if you're wondering why you can't see anything out the stern lights."

The next question Gallant almost dared not ask. "My men, Richard. What about my men?"

"Well, we found you right off when we came up. I stayed out of gun range of the *Java*—"

"The *Java*?"

"The Dutch forty-four."

"Go on."

"Out of gun range until she cast *La Bretonne* adrift and had set her on fire. She stood off due westward then. Didn't pay any attention to the convoy, which was damned surprising, I can tell you. Or to me. Acted as if he'd found what he wanted."

"He had," murmured Gallant. "The scheming bastard. What about *Lima*?"

"Fell in astern of the *Java*. Seems half the Spaniards were waiting for the whoreson Dutch to arrive in the first place. Went over to 'em when the squareheads attacked."

Gallant nodded. "I know. We boarded them as it was happening. Castelar was with the scheme from the start. He and some hellish-looking Dutchman were taking the Marquise out of *Lima* when I got aboard"—he winced glumly—"and got this."

O'Farrell's expression became a studied mixture of concern and anger. "When we came up, we could see what was going on, right enough. They were . . . heaving the loyal Spaniards over the side. And your lads as well. It took us a good twenty minutes to beat up to them . . ." He trailed off.

Gallant stared at him. "Castelar would know most of them wouldn't be able to swim," he murmured. "So he *drowned* them? Is that what you're saying, Richard?"

O'Farrell nodded. "Yes."

"How many?"

"We—we came up and found about twelve still alive. Mostly those that had something to cling to. Like your sweep. The rest. . . . Well, the sharks had started to come in, and—"

"How many *La Bretonne* men, Richard!" Gallant was shaking.

The Irishman met his gaze. "Your Mate, Béssac," he said, quietly. "The big gunner."

"Akiwoya."

"Yes. And one other. A seaman, named Brulé."

Gallant's face was ashen. "Three men? *Three*?"

O'Farrell nodded. He looked down and began to fiddle with the cockade of his hat.

"Three men," whispered Gallant. "Oh, dear Jesus."

"I'm sorry, capitaine. I am, truly," said O'Farrell quietly.

For a moment Gallant could not answer. A black cloud seemed to well up out of nowhere around him, and he closed his eyes against it, waiting till the ache and pain that gripped his heart passed. It was several minutes before he looked up at O'Farrell again, with a look of such focussed, controlled anger in his dark eyes that the Irishman felt an involuntary shiver pass up his spine.

"I'm going to kill him, Richard," said Gallant, tonelessly. "He and the Dutchman both. Before God, I swear it!"

O'Farrell looked at him for a long moment, and then resumed fidgeting with the hat.

"The — ah — Marquise. Do you think she —?"

"She's with them. Castelar was taking her off *Lima* when I boarded."

"Her women too?"

Gallant shrugged. "Qui sait." He smiled without humour. "Castelar's pistol ball got in the way of my finding out."

"That whoreson Spaniard!" blurted out O'Farrell suddenly. "Christ knows what he'll do to her, poor creature!"

Gallant stood. He saw his clothing hung at the bottom of the bunk and reached for his hose and breeches, hauling them on gently, conserving his strength.

"I have a feeling she'll be all right for the present, Richard. He's after something else. Some kind of bigger game."

"Why do you say that? — Your shoes are under the bunk."

Gallant reached for them and slipped them on. "Because of what he's gambled, hein? The man's no fool. And he's forfeited his career, his social standing, his honour, the lot, by doing this. Either he's mad, or —"

"Or?"

"—Or he's involved in something like a plot or plan. Béssac and I had a feeling about this. As if he's following orders or directions. Or else merely hoping for some kind of pot of doubloons at the other end."

"The Marquise'd be no use for that dead, then," said O'Farrell. He watched with some concern as Gallant gingerly pulled on his waistcoat. "Are you —?"

"I'm fine, Richard. But you're right, or at least I pray you are. Unless his task had been to kill her, or have her killed."

"What?"

"In which case, when I boarded he'd have been putting a knife into her instead of getting her off into a boat." He shook his head. "No. He wants — or needs — her alive. At least until he can let someone know who might care he has her. And her bloody great dowry, I'd imagine, although *that's* probably gone into the Dutchmen's sea chests. Their end of the bargain, so to speak."

O'Farrell stared at him. "Holy Mother. You've deduced all that, have you?"

Gallant smiled lightly. "Simply stands to reason, Richard."

"Um. There's one other possibility. Nasty one at that."

"Oh?" said Gallant.

"Castelar may be keeping her as a toy for his cabin bunk. She's a handsome woman, as you'll recall."

In spite of himself Gallant shivered. He thrust an arm into the sleeve of his off-white coat, settling it on his shoulders before fixing that intent, furious expression on O'Farrell once more.

"He may," he said levelly. "And all the more reason, Richard, why I intend to kill him." Then his expression altered with the humorous lift of one corner of his mouth. "Are you sitting on my hat?"

"Eh? No. It's there, on that hook. Above the musketoon rack. But how will you go after him? You've no ship save little *Diane* here. And there's the convoy to concern you, if you don't mind me reminding you of that."

Gallant lifted the hat off the hook and dropped it on the bunk. He reached behind his neck and deftly retied the black ribbon of his queue.

"What about that prize you took?" he said. "The little sloop. As we were coming up on *Lima*."

O'Farrell's expression fell. "Not possible. Her hull was holed in a dozen places at the waterline. Foremast was split to the hounds and the mizzen would have gone by the board if you'd set a handkerchief on it. The hull was hogged badly, after the fight; she must've sprung the keelson. All of it irreparable, at any rate."

"Damn!" Gallant pursed his lips, fingering the bandage again. "All right. What are you doing with her?"

"It's done. I got off her stores — all I could use, at any rate. Then I clapped her hands into irons in the cable tier — there weren't too many left alive, I'm afraid — and put four round shot into her. She went down like a stone."

Gallant managed a grin. "So much for your first prize, hein?

91

Then it's just *Diane* we have left.'' He steadied himself as the little ship heeled to a gust. ''Don't misunderstand me, Richard. She's your ship, not mine.''

''But you're right. She is all we have left,'' said the Irishman. He stood up, returning the grin, if a trifle ruefully. ''I'll send word to the galley. You must want something to eat.''

Gallant nodded, setting his hat on gently over the bandage. ''You're damned right. Not that I haven't food enough for thought. Such as where Castelar and the Dutchmen have sailed off to with the Marquise!''

O'Farrell paused by the door. ''That's the least of our problems, m'sicu'',' he said.

''Eh? How so?''

''When we fished out you and your three lads, we got some of the Spaniards, too. The lot with red ribbons in their hats, as well as some of the other—''

''The loyal ones.''

'' — The other loyal ones.'' He sucked a tooth. ''But we got a Dutchman, too. Must've fallen overboard in the fight.''

''Ah.''

''Well, not precisely a Dutchman. An Englishman, actually, who was with them.''

''So much the better,'' said Gallant. ''I don't speak Dutch. Where is the swine?''

''In the cable tier with the rest of 'em,'' said O'Farrell, jerking a thumb downwards. ''He should be as slimy as an eel when we pull him out of there.'' He stepped into the passageway, leaning to one side as *Diane* heeled. ''Do you want to see him now?''

Gallant stepped through the doorway and paused, waiting for a momentary lightheadedness to fade. ''No. Not yet. I've got to talk to Béssac and Akiwoya. And poor Brulé. I've got to hear it from them how it happened.''

O'Farrell settled his own hat on his head as he paused at the foot of the companion. ''Right. And you'll get below here again when the lad brings a meal from the galley for you.''

Gallant nodded. ''Yes, I shall. But first let me get up on your quarterdeck, Richard. I've a good deal of fog in my brain to clear away!''

Ten minutes later Gallant was standing in the waist of the ship, feet braced against her motion, looking with a scarcely concealable emotion into the faces of the three men who stood with him, their own expressions sombre and dark. He looked in turn into the eyes of Akiwoya, the huge gunner, and then Brulé, down whose sturdy and reliable-looking features a tear was coursing. And then Béssac; gruff and ursine as ever, hatless, but still in the battered seacoat, and gripping his hand with steely power.

"Capitaine," said Béssac hoarsely. "Thank God you're all right. I — we — that is. . . ."

Gallant grinned through misty eyes at him. "It's all right, mon vieux. It's good that you three at least survived. Tell me what happened."

Akiwoya had balled one huge fist and was slowly punching it into the palm of his other hand.

"We fought well, capitaine," the African said. "Had them almost beaten on the foredeck. But there were too many of them. And when the lads saw you go down, over the side, they — well, they lost heart."

"You couldn't have asked for braver men, m'sieu'!" put in Brulé. "But there were just too many of them."

Gallant nodded. "Go on."

"After you fell, I took a pike butt in the guts and blacked out," said Béssac. "Woke up to find Aki here and the others pressed up against the break of the quarterdeck with their hands up."

"They got us from behind," put in the African. "Climbed out the foremost gunports and then up on deck."

"And then, quick as a snake, the Dons made sail to follow the Dutch forty-four. The *Java*, she is. She'd already hardened up to a windward tack, starboard. Bore off due west," said the Mate.

Akiwoya spat off to leeward and wiped his mouth with the back of his hand. "That's when they put us over the side, m'sieu'. Living or dead, wounded or not. Except most of the loyal Spaniards. Them they knifed or ran a cutlass through before putting them over."

Gallant's lips were a tight line. "And our lads —?"

Béssac shook his head. "Hardly a man of 'em could swim, capitaine! Peste! Me and Brulé tried to keep some hanging on to bits of things that had fallen over the side. But it was no use. And we never even saw you until M. O'Farrell fished you out."

Akiwoya's fist made a hard, leathery sound. "And by then the sharks had come," he said bitterly. "They got everyone else. Except us."

There was no sound for a moment other than the rush of the sea past the ship's side and the hum of the wind in the mainmast rigging. The watchmen on deck were silent, as if *Diane's* ship's company felt the grief and loss of the four men standing silently by the rail, and kept their distance.

"We're going to repay them. For all of it," said Gallant, after a moment. "You have my word on that, mes amis. My word!"

The three men looked silently at him, and then nodded slowly, as if pledging themselves to the same oath.

There was a polite cough behind Gallant, and he turned to look up at O'Farrell, peering down at them from the quarterdeck rail.

"There's a meal to split a duke's britches in my cabin waiting for you, M. Gallant. If you'd care —?"

"Thank you, Richard. I shall in a moment. But first —"

O'Farrell gave him a lopsided smile. "I know. The prisoner, hein?"

"The prisoner."

The Irishman nodded. He cupped his hands to bellow forward. "Master at arms! Ho, there, Vaillancourt! Bring the prisoner before M. Gallant!"

A burly-looking petty officer with a wicked black cudgel gripped in one meaty fist appeared up the companionway, propelling ahead of him a dirty and dishevelled figure laden with wrist irons and chains. He was thrust along until pulled to a stop several feet in front of Gallant and the others.

Gallant's eyes were hard as he looked the man up and down, forcing his own sense of hunger and faintness to the back of his mind. The prisoner was thin and stooped slightly, his wiry ratlike body covered in the too-large folds of a tar-smeared, fullskirted seacoat of green wool that had long since lost most of its large brass buttons. A scarf knotted round his thin neck and tattered, sagging hose stuffed into mould-whitened shoes were completed by a red stocking cap from which the man's long, greasy locks of unqueued hair escaped limply. His eyes were bright and ferretlike, and below a long, thin nose his lips were split in a small, sneering grin over bad yellow teeth. The stubble of several days' growth mottled his small chin.

Gallant thought over his English vocabulary for a moment, quelling a deeper and unexpected impulse to draw back his fist and bury it in the man's mocking face.

"What is your name, fellow?" he said.

"Why, bless 'ee fer a Christian gennulmun t'ask, mongsewer. Miller'd be the monicker. Jack Miller, and true as snuff, too. But Dusty Miller to me mates. An' who might yew be, then, by way of askin' —"

"Watch what you say, Miller. I'm not interested in insolence from bilge filth like you."

Miller's eyes crinkled to small hard points, and he bared the horrid teeth in a gust of whistling laughter. "There, now, yew just lay a course for Dusty t' steer, yer honner, an' I'll point my stem at —"

"Shut your mouth. You were part of *Java's* crew?"

The man cocked his head to one side. "That's as may be, say I, as dependin' on where I put me mark to th' Articles, and —"

Gallant spun on his heel. "M'sieu' O'Farrell!" he barked.

"Aye, capitaine?" answered the Irishman, pacing forward to the rail of the quarterdeck that overlooked the waist.

Gallant pointed aloft. "I'll have a line to that yardarm end, there! With a running bowline! And I'd be obliged if you'd have your watchmen tail on to the fall directly it's rigged!"

"Aye, capitaine!" cried O'Farrell. In the next instant he was bellowing orders forward.

Miller was staring at Gallant as the marine turned back, his eyes lit with a hard glitter.

"N — now, avast, say I. Wait 'alf a turn on that, there, yer honner —," began the Englishman.

"You see that line, Miller? Look hard at it. You'll be choking your guts out at the end of it in five minutes. Slowly!"

Miller licked his lips, a beading of sweat showing on his brow. "Yew've no right —!"

"*Right*? Hah!" Gallant snorted. "Have you ever seen a man strangle to death, Miller? He kicks a lot, you know. Particularly frantic as he's lifted, inch by inch off the deck. His neck starts to stretch, and it'll stretch a lot before it breaks, like dry wood snapping. But his eyes bulge out as his breath is cut off, hein? At first his face gets red, and then redder —"

"Fer th' love o' mercy, yer honner —!"

"— But then as it gets worse, he begins to turn black. Sometimes he soils himself, too, all the while writhing and trying to scream up there, *feeling* all of it, wanting to breathe just a little, but the rope stops all that, garotting him, even though he won't be dead for a long time yet."

"Wait!" Miller's brow was beaded with fine droplets of sweat, and he was breathing shallowly through his teeth, like a man about to be sick. He licked his lips, looking up at the yardarm and fidgeting. "Wha — what is it ye want t'know, like?"

"Where is she bound, Miller? The *Java*. And who's her master? In the green velvet." Gallant's eyes bore like augers into Miller.

95

"She was t'be bound in to our stronghold. Now, that's true as duff. *Java*, her'n what prizes we took."

"Stronghold? Where?"

Miller wiped his mouth. "In th' Carolinas, zur. A snug cove amidst the dune islands, there. Ye'd fare no better as a proper berth, what with guns, and stockade, and water sweet as air, and never a King's man to twig to yer whereabouts nor how ye takes yer ease —"

"Where in the Carolinas, Miller?"

Miller balked. "Well, zur, it bein' so hidden, like —"

"Keep that line to hand, M. O'Farrell!" barked Gallant over his shoulder.

"Wait! Hell's fire, zur, I be no Pilot!"

"*Where*?"

Miller paused, trembling. He could not meet Gallant's hard gaze, and dropped his head, looking miserably at the planking.

"She lies near thirty-three degrees, fifty minutes north. I — I can shew ye on a chart. Like a long beach, wiv dunes, when ye see it from seaward, like. There's a north channel, an' a south 'un, an' a smart anchorage in behind."

Gallant stepped closer to the man.

"If you're *lying*, Miller —!" he hissed.

"Christ lumme, zur, it's the truth!"

Gallant paused for a moment, deliberately staring into the eyes of the trembling Englishman until he forced the latter to drop his gaze.

"All right, Miller. You'll show me on a chart. Lead me false and I'll see you gutted and over the side. Who was your captain?"

"Ten Haaf. Jacob Ten Haaf, zur. A Texel man, and a rum lad, he is. Ship's company's half Dutchmen an' half good Britons, like m'self. Ne'er under a better sea capting, I'd take my davy of it! Why, he —"

But Gallant was not listening. "Vaillancourt!" he barked. "Throw him back with the other rats. I'll need him later!"

Gallant turned away, ignoring Miller's last babbles, and moved to the quarterdeck ladder. A brief wave of lightheadedness made him pause at its foot, and O'Farrell's face appeared over the rail above, lined with concern.

"Are you all right, capitaine? Would you like —?"

"Nothing but a word to your servant, Richard, that I'll have that meal. And I'll trouble you to leave the deck to your first officer and join me."

"I'd be delighted," said the Irishman, and in a few moments

joined him at the head of the companion leading below. "But by your expression you seem to be thinking about—"

"A voyage," said Gallant, ducking down the steep ladder. "That we're going to make to the Carolinas. Or at any rate, that *I* shall make."

O'Farrell paused in the gloom at the foot of the companion, looking at him. "I beg your pardon?" His mind flicked to the long line of vessels ahead in the convoy. "I'm afraid I don't understand."

Gallant looked warmly at the Irishman, putting a hand on his shoulder. "You will, Richard. I have an engagement with a lady, one might say, that I must not miss. And now I know where I shall find her." The marine smiled. "And if you'd let me get to that damned meal before I fall in a faint at your feet, I'll tell you *how* we're going to do it!"

The forty-four gun ship *Java*, its dark hull a looming black mass against the moonlit sea, worked westward under reduced night canvas, the only outward sign of life being the golden light from the stern lantern and the candle glow from within the lights of the great stern cabin. The glow came from the silver Spanish candelabra set in the centre of the broad table that occupied the centre of the cabin. It cast its flickering light over the intent, flushed faces of Jacob Ten Haaf and Don Alfonso Castelar, who sat hunched, fixing each other with cold stares across the welter of trenchers and wine cups on the table.

Ten Haaf suddenly lay back in his chair, curling his lip in a belligerent alcoholic sneer. His hat was off, and the matted mass of his red hair hung down over his eyes, shading their wine-reddened glint.

"Devil take you for a slimy bastard, Castelar!" slurred the Dutchman, in a peculiar accent that mixed Dutch intonation with English dialect. "No one keeps a wench t'hisself in this ship! Share an' share alike, ay? I'll be no gap stopper, an' let ye pleasure yerself with that rum piece y'have there, while me lads make do with smash an' plum duff!" He drew a wicked-looking dagger from his belt and tossed it on the table, leaning forward over it with his fingers spread on the wine-streaked wood for emphasis. "She's fer *all*, Castelar. Now ye mark that!"

Castelar's eyes were brittle, black points in the flickering orange light. For a moment there was no sound but the dull roar of the sea under the counter, and the creak of timbers and rigging as *Java* rolled slowly.

"I'll mark only one thing, Ten Haaf," said the Spaniard, evenly. "I made it possible for you and that leprous filth you call a crew to pick up this prize. And we had a covenant. The woman's money was yours, outright! And the woman was mine." He paused. "Now, you'll hold to that," he said, "or by the Madonna I'll see you in Hell!"

Ten Haaf leered, wiping his mouth with the back of his hand. "So that's how ye set yer canvas, ay? Well, you lay to this. All's mine that I takes, under a letter o' marque! You'd know I mind what old Bill Duthy did, out o' Charles Town, him and his sweet *Mercury*. Why, he got alongside a French sloop, th' *Angelica*, ay? Now, she were a spruce ship; smart as a carrot new scraped. And a Frenchie in Martinique put 'im on to *her* —"

"Get to your point," interjected Castelar, tersely.

" — The point being' that old Bill, why, he took *all* rights to th' *Angelica*, and a fine cargo, and a lass or two what was aboard, and with no truck o' rights to some rum-togged swell, that's as merely gave 'im a course t' steer —"

Castelar was out of his chair and across the table in a movement so quick the Dutchman was unaware of what was happening until, with a crash, he had been smashed back off his chair to the deck, with one of Castelar's hands in a steely grip at his throat and the other holding a shining, slim-bladed knife at his windpipe. Castelar's face was inches from Ten Haaf's, and the Dutchman's eyes widened in a strange mixture of anger and terror.

"Now, you mark this, you slime-gutted bastard!" said Castelar, in a low and chilling tone through clenched teeth. "I've made you a rich man by all this. You and that whoreson crew. And I'll make you richer still, if I don't cut your damned throat first! And that'll need the woman alive and not torn to pieces by you or your damned dogs!"

"Christ's sake — can't breathe —," gagged Ten Haaf, his face darkening.

"D'ye understand, Dutchman!" roared Castelar. "Richer still! But the woman stays *mine*!"

Ten Haaf struggled for a moment. His eyes met Castelar's and he nodded.

Castelar rose, the knife vanishing into its sheath behind his neck. He turned his back on the Dutchman who had rolled over and was wobbling to his feet, face ashen, and slumped into his chair again. He clutched at a tankard and drained it as Ten Haaf regained his own chair.

"Drink up!" barked Castelar, abruptly. A thin line of wine ran down his chin from one corner of his mouth. "Madre, Ten Haaf, you'll have a *hundred* women the likes of the Marquise, there, when we're through! And wealthy beyond count! Now, you think on that!"

The Dutchman scratched himself and swigged heavily from the tankard that Castelar refilled and thrust across at him. His eyes were little pale glints through his matted hair as he stared at the Spaniard over the rim.

"All right," he said. "Ye can have the woman. But I an' the lads will hold ye to yer word. You may lay to that."

Castelar said nothing, but took a deep swill from a wine bottle. And if he perceived the look of murderous intent that crept into Ten Haaf's eyes he gave no sign.

Diane lay hove-to against the steady trade wind, the first blush of dawn from the cloudless eastern sky painting her gathered canvas in apricot tones. The sea was a gunmetal grey, not yet its deep, crystal blue. Away to leeward the convoy lay a league off, working away to the northeast under reduced night canvas. *Diane* was pitching in the long, stippled swells with easy grace, and alongside her a longboat rode, tied on at the lee forechains.

The boat was rigged with two masts and twin lugsails that lay brailed up against their uneven yards, the boat moving as if anxious to be off. Several men were working quickly in the boat, stowing away the small chests and bags that a half-dozen men at *Diane's* rail were swaying down to them. The boat was already crowded with other stores, and in the bows a small one-pounder swivel gun had been mounted, the pin of its yoke dropped into a recess in the head of the boat's towing strongback.

Standing at *Diane's* rail as well, his hands clasped behind his back as he supervised the loading operation, was Richard O'Farrell. The Irishman stopped an irritated pacing when he saw the tall figure of Gallant appear up the companion and move to join him. But O'Farrell continued shaking his head and muttering in exasperation.

Gallant grinned at his friend as he arrived at the rail and gave a quick appraising glance at the work going on below.

"Good, Richard. Almost all stowed?"

"Yes. Look here," said O'Farrell. "You won't listen to

common sense, will you, capitaine? You're determined to do this? A damned fool venture if ever I heard of one."

Gallant laughed. "You've said that before, my friend. You might at least come up with some original abuse."

O'Farrell caught his eye and could not maintain the pose. He snorted with laughter. "All right. Have it your way. But I'd like you to explain what in Hell you're hoping to achieve again. Either I didn't hear you first time around or else I'm refusing to admit I heard it!"

"All right. Look here." Gallant squatted on the deck, pulling a folded chart from an oiled pouch that had been in his coat pocket. He spread the yellowed, watermarked paper on the planking, and tapped a point on it.

"We're about here, hein?" said the marine. "One hundred leagues off the Carolinas, or thereabouts. And with that sight yesterday, about latitude thirty degrees north."

"Or thereabouts. Hmpf. I still don't see —"

"The privateers' lair, Richard. You'll recall what Miller said. A dune island, channels at north and south ends leading to a lagoon behind? And hardly a day's sail to northward along the shore, above Charles Town?"

"Yes."

"And the seaward mark was a height of land. And didn't he mutter something about 'astern o' the Bull'?"

"After you threatened to stretch his craven neck again, he did," said O'Farrell. "Made no sense to me. Not enough for a landfall, or whatever."

Gallant smiled lightly. "Ah, but it *is*, Richard. Look again, over here," he said, bending closer to the chart. "This is an English chart of the Carolina coast. Christ knows how accurate it is, but it's got lots of detail. And some of Miller's babblings tally with it."

"Oh? Where'd you get —"

"The chart?" said Gallant. "Part of this folio the Sieur de Valigny slipped me before I left. Didn't know it'd be *this* useful. It was in my uniform coat pocket all the time." He sniffed. "But look how it jibes with Miller's drivel."

"Eh?"

"Here, for instance. Look at this island, northward along the coast from Charles Town. The one that looks like a lozenge."

O'Farrell leaned forward. "I'll be damned. Bulls Island."

"Right. And what's that mark on the nor'east point?"

"Sand Hill. 'The highest part of land on the coast'." He looked up at Gallant. "You think *that's* Miller's rathole?"

Gallant nodded. "The area, at any rate. I'd wager on it. Look here. To the north, a large bay, hein? But southwest, along the coast, Bulls Island tails off to a point. And there's another island. That one, marked Capers Isle. And a shallow lagoon behind."

"Yes. Still —"

"But in the channel, here. Between Capers and Bulls. What's that?"

O'Farrell squinted again. "A small islet. Pen scratching, which I presume means hillocks."

"Or dunes."

"Or dunes. And narrow channels at either end." He looked up. "I see what you mean."

Gallant nodded. "'Astern o' the Bull'; a channel at either end, leading in to a lagoon; a day's sail northeast from Charles Town." He stood up. "I think it all fits, Richard."

O'Farrell shook his head as he rose. "Christ's guts. It still seems a damned slim premise, capitaine."

"Agreed," said Gallant, folding away the chart into its cover. "But it's the one thing I have to work on. And therefore it's a premise I'll follow."

O'Farrell stared out at the distant vessels of the convoy for a moment.

"Very well. I'm to assume escort of the convoy," he recited. "It is to proceed under reduced sail by a northerly track, to avoid Bermudamen, before striking nor'east for France."

"Good. And my report goes —"

"Into the hands of M. le Comte de Maurepas. And none other."

"I'll be counting on you to do just that, Richard," said Gallant.

"And you're determined to try this damned silly small-boat voyage?"

"No less," said Gallant.

O'Farrell shook his head, looking sombrely at Gallant and then at the three men standing a few feet away. "But I find it most melancholy to think of losing a capitaine, and a friend, on so fruitless an endeavour."

Gallant smiled warmly at the discomfited Irishman, and laid a hand on his shoulder.

"Thank you for that, Richard. But don't give up hope before the effort. I don't intend that it should be fruitless." He flicked his eyes to the three waiting men. "All right, lads. Below and into the other clothing. It's time." And before O'Farrell could say more Gallant was gone down the companionway.

Within twenty minutes the marine and his three companions

had returned on deck, each man hefting a small canvas bag of personal belongings. The change in the appearance of all four, but in particular in Gallant, was striking. In place of his Compagnies Franches off-white and blue uniform, the marine was barefoot, and clad in stained and ragged canvas trousers which were held at his waist by a knotted piece of line. A patched, loosesleeved checked shirt, casually held at the throat by a red bandanna, was complemented by a tattered straw hat with a ludicrous drooping brim that left Gallant's face in shadow. The other three men were clad in similar ruffians' dress, and grinned at O'Farrell as the latter stared at Gallant with a look of some amazement.

"What in the name of God —?" began the Irishman.

"Bits and pieces from *Diane's* slops," grinned Gallant. "And a few from our friend Miller. These are his pantaloons." Gallant hitched up the greasy trousers. "Hope to Christ I don't catch some loathsome disease from the damned things."

He leaned over the rail and tossed his bag expertly into the sternsheets of the boat.

"Right, Béssac. You and the lads into the boat. Below, there! Secure that stowage and scramble up here, unless you want to come along!"

The hands who had been working in the boat swarmed up the side and over the rail. Akiwoya, Béssac and Brulé exchanged a few jocular insults with them before throwing their legs over the rail and vanishing down the battens. Once in the boat, stepping agilely in bare feet from thwart to thwart, they busied themselves in stowing the seabags away and laying a familiarizing hand on the coils and pins of each sheet and halyard.

The senior hand of the working party knuckled a forelock to Gallant.

"Stow'd just as you ordered, m'sieu'. And I struck in the swivel's shot cask forward, there, by the strongback." He smirked. "You look like a Martiniquan *gommier* fisherman, m'sieu'."

"Smell like one, too, I'll warrant," said Gallant. "Thank you, Dionne. Good work."

The marine swung to O'Farrell, a firm set to his mouth. "Time to go, Richard." He held out a strong brown hand which the Irishman grasped firmly. "Give us a prayer or two. And for God's sake get the convoy through as best you can."

O'Farrell nodded. "I will. Sorry there's no side party to pipe you off."

Gallant grinned and slung a leg over the rail. "I'll take you to task about that in my next report. If I ever write one." He gave O'Farrell a long, straight look. "Watch your helm, there, Irishman."

"And you," said O'Farrell, his voice suddenly hoarse. He gave Gallant a court-perfect salute. But before he had straightened from the slight bow Gallant was gone over the side, and the Irishman moved to stare down over the side as Gallant's figure monkeyed down the battens and leaped lightly into the boat.

The marine braced himself in the sternsheets, steadying the tiller between his knees after swinging it from side to side as a precaution. He looked round the boat carefully, threw a last look at O'Farrell's concerned face high above, and then cleared his throat.

"Have a care in the boat!" said Gallant, sharply. "Cast off the after line, there! Aki, hoist the fores'l. Mind those sheets. Don't let her fill to quickly." He looked up and ahead. "Cast off, for'rard!"

The canting yard of the foresail and its rumpling canvas squealed up the foremast to the African's rhythmic hauling. The wind, curling round *Diane's* bulk into the lee, pushed at the sail's face, and the boat began to foot along *Diane's* side. Gallant steadied the tiller with a prehensile foot and gathered up the mainsail sheets, holding them while Béssac swiftly hauled in and coiled the stern line. Gallant handed the sheets to the Mate and then nodded to Brulé, who sat waiting on the thwart that acted as the mainmast strongback.

"Right, Brulé. Hoist the main."

As the mainsail rose to join its twin on the foremast, the longboat footed out past *Diane's* bow into the full force of the wind and sea. Abruptly it lay over in a steep heel as Brulé hauled in the mainsail sheets and then joined the scramble to the weather rail as the boat lifted and plunged swiftly through the wavelets on the whitecapped swell faces.

Gallant bared his teeth as a dappling of spray wisped back over the longboat, tart on his lips. He glanced at the card of the little compass and pushed the tiller over lightly, letting the plunging boat fall off slightly to more of a run before the wind.

"Ease the sheets. Set the fores'l to starboard, Aki. Let her run wing and wing."

"Oui, m'sieu'," grunted the African. With quick strength he brailed up the broad sail, thrust the foot of its yard round the other side of the mast, and then let the sail fill with a resounding thump on its new side. The boat was soon dead off the wind, and lifting and surfing with exhilarating speed down the blue-backed swells, pausing in the troughs and then shooting ahead again with the next stippled, mountainous rise of water under the transom. The four men grinned at each other, stirred by the rapid progress of the craft, and settled themselves into individual nests amongst the casks and bags. They squinted up at the boat's sails, the twitching lines of reef points, or astern at the rapidly dwindling form of *Diane*, so relatively motionless when seen from their moving, hurrying viewpoint.

"She's making sail, m'sieu'" said Béssac, following Gallant's look astern. "That's the last we'll see of her."

Gallant did not answer, watching as dark ripples played over the *Diane's* topsails, and her hull swung slowly off the wind. In a few moments she was standing off to the northeast, toward the distant sail pyramids of the convoy, and Gallant could see small figures scrambling aloft and out along the ship's upper yards.

"No fear of canvas, O'Farrell," said Gallant. "He's setting t'gallants. Good lad." He looked at Béssac. "He's got a damned hard voyage ahead of him, mon vieux."

Béssac had dug out his blackened pipe and was hunting for his flint striker. His ancient seacoat was of such disreputable appearance that Gallant had allowed him to keep it, and the Mate had packed its pockets to overflowing with "necessaries." All of which were now getting in the way of finding the striker. At length he fished it out and struck up an odorous conflagration in the pipe.

"Peut-être. But if anyone'll get 'em to France, he will. Less'n the pox gets 'em all. You made a good choice letting him and that *Diane* sail with us."

Gallant smiled grimly. "If I hadn't we'd be shark meat by now. Christ, how Fate works. I'll never . . ." He trailed off, lost in a last look at *Diane*. Then he turned and took a fresh grip on the long bar of the tiller, bracing one foot against a thwart, letting himself enjoy the steady effort to keep the hurrying boat from broaching and turning turtle before the great swells.

"All right, lads," he said. "We've got a good two or three days ahead of us in this cockleshell to get through. If we're lucky. And it'll take good humour from us all. Now who's for some biscuit and brandy?"

As the day wore on, a manner of work and movement settled over the little boat. Gallant established a watch routine that had he and Akiwoya spelling Béssac and Brulé on a watch-and-watch basis. The boat was cramped with the various chests, small hogsheads and seabags Gallant had ordered put in, but as the craft footed westward over the sea the men stowed things about until they each had made some kind of nook to call their own. The small mortar and the cask of gunpowder were wedged in firmly abaft the foremast. But they were merely the beginning of the list of equipment. There was a sizable tool chest, and a sailbag with spare canvas; several oilskinned breadbags, chock-full of rock-hard biscuit; a good-sized water butt and an equal one of brandy; an oiled canvas case that contained five muskets; and a chest with cartridge boxes, shot, and flints. There were several other casks of unnamed supplies Gallant had seen put in, a small boxed boat compass, and a flat oilskin folio containing several large scale charts, one of which, as noon approached, Gallant was examining across one knee, steadying the tiller under his armpit.

Béssac took a few pulls at the mainsheet, cleated it down with a slip knot, and leaned back. He looked in satisfaction at the full, arched sails and the glittering blue swells over which the boat pushed steadily.

"Sacristi. There's something to be said about sailing a small boat, hein? No damned big ship wallowing round in the sea."

From forward, where Akiwoya sat with his back against the mainmast foot oiling a long-barrelled pistol, came a snort.

"Hah! You tell me that if we run into a real squall line, Théo. We wouldn't last a minute. Loaded with all this gear. Christ, barely six pouces from waterline to gunwale." He flashed even white teeth at Gallant. "Not that it isn't all necessary, eh, m'sieu'?"

Gallant grinned back at him. "Every bit."

Béssac scratched his head and reset his hat low over his eyes. "It is a hell of a lot, capitaine. What's in those other two little casks, there?"

"In a minute," said Gallant. He squinted at the chart a last quick moment. Then, "Tend the sheets, there! Fores'l gybe to larboard!"

Gallant leaned into the tiller bar, swinging the boat off a point or two to a new heading, his eyes flicking down to the rocking compass card. Béssac and Brulé tightened up the sheets as the sturdy craft began heeling slightly in a broad reach. The loose-footed foresail had come across in a quick welter of ripples and writhing sheets until it filled with a thump on the larboard side.

"The casks?" resumed Gallant. "Nothing really. Powder."

"Powder? Those?" Béssac's eyes widened. "Sweet Jesus. That's enough to blow the stern off the poor old *La Bretonne*!"

Then he caught Gallant's look. "What *is* it you want to try with that damned stuff?"

Gallant grinned at him and gnawed at a biscuit. "Whatever I can, mon vieux."

"Splendid plan. Now what in Hell —?"

"Steady, mon ami," laughed the marine. "Firstly, to get us alive to a landfall on the Carolinas. Secondly, to try and find Miller's bloody little island before some rosbifs, or Miller's shipmates, find us."

"What then? Hell, if the *Java's* in there, you can't exactly pull smartly in like a regatta launch and threaten to blow him out of the water unless he hands over the Marquise, hein?"

Gallant settled his tattered straw hat over his eyes. "No," he said, after a moment. "But a man can die from a bee sting as much as from a cougar bite, Béssac."

Béssac gaped at him. "And that means exactly what?"

"Think about it for a moment. It's a Micmac saying."

Béssac thought. "Jesus," he breathed, after a moment. "If it is the right island, and the *Java's* there, you're going to *attack* it?"

Gallant spread his feet on the floorboards. He leaned his weight against the pressure of the tiller as the boat foamed with a roar down the back of a steep swell, the sails crumpling and filling as the wind died momentarily in the trough.

"Of course I am, Béssac!" he called, over the sea's roar. "What other plan could I possibly have?"

FIVE

His Britannic Majesty's Ship *Saracen*, forty-four guns, under
the command of Captain Sir Aubrey Cathcart, moved through
the deep ochre light of the open ocean sunset in tall, majestic
dignity. Away to the west, the sun was sinking in an eye-straining
orgy of red and yellow behind the low line of humped purple
that marked the American coast. Her flaxen sails turned almost
copper by the exquisite light, *Saracen* was working to the
northeastward, the gentle dusk breeze filling the frigate's canvas just enough to keep the water gurgling under her forefoot as
she passed over the glimmering sea face. The sunlight touched
the ship's tan side, the black waterline wale, and glinted dully
from the gilt of her stern gallery. It caught in the hawk-visaged
image of the robed Bedouin that rode below the long arm of the
bowsprit, fierce brown eyes above a black beard staring un-
blinkingly at the grey line of the northern horizon. And it was
throwing into bronze relief now the stern features of the Royal
Navy officer who paced the windward side of *Saracen's* quarterdeck, lost in thought.

Sir Aubrey George William Augustus Cathcart had his route

carefully delineated. He would halt his forward process a pace from the top of the ladder which led down off the quarterdeck to the waist, turn on the heel of his black pumps and stump back up the sloping deck, passing just inboard of the six-pounder guns snugged down in their tackles and breeching lines. Then he would be drawing abeam of the binnacle, and *Saracen's* oaken-and-brass double wheel, with its helmsman, and the clutch of figures around him: the Officer of the Watch, the Fourth, Jeremy Poynting; the Sailing Master, Winton; the Sailing Master's messenger, and the Officer of the Watch's messenger; the boatswain's mate of the watch, idly swinging his starter and waiting for an order from Winton; and a ship's boy, about to turn the glass and sound *Saracen's* bell, but terrified to do so lest he disturb Cathcart's imposing march. A few paces beyond and Cathcart was approaching the summit of the slope, fetching up against the transom rail above which curled the huge Red Ensign on its tall staff, its colour lit now as well by the glow from the great stern lantern on its arm out from the transom head. Here he would pause, glower for an instant at the flickering flame behind the milky glass of the lantern, and then begin pacing back down hill toward the waist. It was regular and predictable, and it was a ritual carried out each day by its performer during the First Dog Watch. Woe betided the unfortunate midshipman or, for that matter, the lieutenant who trod the sacrosanct weather side of the quarterdeck when the captain paced it. And even greater woe betided the individual who dared invade the hallowed realm of Cathcart's thoughts except under the most pressing circumstances.

Just to leeward (he would have said "loo'ard") of the clutch of men near the wheel stood *Saracen's* First Lieutenant, in the tall and angular form of Sebastien Rye. Although his captain was resplendent in the evening light in a full-skirted scarlet coat that would have done justice to a Vice-Admiral, Rye was a far more sombre figure in a brown frock coat, similar small clothes, and an unlaced cocked hat. He was thin and small-shouldered, with the look of haggard worry that was common to many first lieutenants. He was short-tempered, now, because he had missed his supper while supervising a gun exercise and now wanted the Master to reduce sail. But knowing Cathcart as he did, he was obliged to await the opportunity of catching the captain's eye rather than barging in on his train of thought.

Finally the opportunity arose, and a dark, beady eye was fixed on Rye.

"Eh? Well?," said Cathcart, pausing in mid-pace.

"Permission to shorten sail, sir. For the night."

Cathcart looked aloft. "Damned little wind in any event, what? Very well."

"Thank you, sir," said Rye. He coughed lightly and nodded to Winton. "Carry on, Mr. Winton. Take in the t'gallants and jibs. Then she'll carry what?"

"Foretopm'st stays'l and tops'ls, zur."

"Just so. Carry on."

"Aye aye, zur," growled Winton, a weatherbeaten older man with a shock of curly white hair escaping from under his Dreadnought cap. "Spanker as well, zur, oi'd think."

"Yes." Rye gestured to the waiting boatswain, who was whispering to one of Winton's mates who had come up. "Pipe *Hands Aloft*, Wellburn."

As the men erupted from the companionways and swarmed up ratlines to lay out along *Saracen's* yards or cluster at the pin rails, Rye paced over to where Cathcart stood, staring up at the topmen. Cathcart had his hands locked behind his back and his lips pursed, a long-recognized pose of disapproval.

"Fore t'gallant clew'n," muttered Cathcart. "Sloppy work, sir. See the man is told."

Rye touched his hat. "Aye, aye, sir." He paused, held by the sudden darkening look of preoccupation that had clouded Cathcart's features. Behind him he could hear Winton, who had overheard Cathcart's remark, bellowing up at the unfortunate culprit aloft.

"Anything — wrong, sir?" said Rye, quietly. "If I may ask?"

Cathcart's eyes flicked to Rye's. "All that evident, is it?"

"Quite, sir."

Cathcart made a small, humourless smile. "Not bloody surprising, I suppose. Well, you should know. It's our orders, Mr. Rye. Or should I say, *my* orders."

"How d'ye mean, sir?"

"Damned humiliating, is what! *Saracen's* a forty-four gun ship, sir. Not a bloody revenue cutter!"

Rye's expression was patient. He looked aloft where, high above their heads, men were laid out over the mizzen topsail yard, their feet on the slack footropes, pressing their bellies against the yard while they clutched at the canvas, gathering it into a mass along the yard and quickly passing the gaskets, small lengths of line, round the yard and the sail to secure the sail in place. Forward, the foretopmen had already finished taking in the topgallant and were sliding in simian abandon down backstays to the deck, hooting in good-natured derision at the slower workers on the main and mizzen until silenced by a bark from Winton.

"It's the responsibility of Vice-Admiral Townsend, eh?" went on Cathcart abruptly, as Rye knew he would. "Ever since that damned Louisbourg venture he's obsessed with cozening the bloody colonials."

"In what way, sir?"

"Why, a smuggling matter, Mr. Rye! But the damnedest bit of tomfoolery . . ."

Rye looked baffled.

"Still not an answer, is it," said Cathcart, gruffly. "Ah well, pardon me, Mr. Rye. I've been too preoccupied. And it's damned melancholy." He paused. "Mr. Poynting!"

"S — sir?" said the Officer of the Watch, blanching.

"Have the helmsman watch his duty. She's luffing like a doxie's petticoats, sir!" Cathcart turned back to Rye. "It's the town merchants in Charles Town, this time. Got the ear of the Admiral. Seems they've got a lucrative trade with the damned Frogs in the West Indies."

"Is that not illegal, sir?"

"How refreshingly naive, Mr. Rye. Of course it is. And equally certain are the profits accruing to the merchants' pockets from the trade. The problem this particular time seems to be with a clutch of fat burgers facing unexpected losses."

Cathcart smiled at Rye's uncomprehending expression. "The trade in sugar, rum, and God knows what else out o' the Froggy islands — Martinique, the lot — is, or was, a steady source of income. They were taking in a half-dozen cargoes a week from Cayenne alone — and turning a handsome profit. But now the trade's been cut into. More'n just due to the confounded war. And they're damned angry about it, what?"

Rye stared. "D'ye mean to say they complained to the Admiral that an illegal trade was *stopped*?"

"To the Governor, to be precise. Not stopped, but interfered with."

"By whom?"

Cathcart tugged at his neckcloth. "There appears to be a problem with privateers, eh? Always a clutch of 'em out of the Yankee ports, and this war's produced thousands. Fair number sailing out o' Charles Town, with a lot of these burgers having shares in their prizes. But they've had a 'gentleman's agreement,' so to speak: one that left certain French hulls trading in to the Carolinas untouched. Given the blighters free pratique."

"And now, sir?"

"Simple, Mr. Rye. Someone's been picking off the protected vessels. One of 'em, a brig, showed up at the Boston Prize Court. Taken in the letter of the law. And incidentally thereby causing the concerned gentlemen in Charles Town to lose a fat purse each."

Rye watched as a ship's boy scuttled past, knuckling a forelock, to turn the glass and then strike three bells on *Saracen's* great bell, in two quick rings and then a third.

"In other words, sir, there's a privateer under a legitimate letter of marque, unaware of this — ah — agreement —"

"Taking the ships involved. So it appears. And there even appears to be a suspect, or suspects, if one can use the term."

Rye's eyebrows rose.

"A Dutchman," said Cathcart. "Name of Ten Haaf. Put out from the Low Countries with a catchall squadron and his flag in an old East Indiaman. Been operating under proper letters of marque from Bermuda till three months ago, then vanished." He coughed. "And the time he vanished, the — inconvenient — captures began. In addition, the man who brought the brig into Boston admitted acting as an agent for the fellow."

Rye thought for a moment. "So we are to do something about this fellow Ten Haaf —"

"To protect the interests of influential men in the Carolinas who have the ear of the Governor, and hence the Admiral. Exactly, Mr. Rye."

Rye said nothing. He had long ago ceased being surprised by the realities of wealth and greed in the world. More acute was his interest in what Cathcart was planning to do.

As if in reply, Cathcart said, "We've been ordered to patrol the approaches to the Carolinas and make an attempt to interdict Captain Ten Haaf's activities. The Admiral is perplexed by the seeming lack of a base for the fellow, since he abandoned the Bermudas. There may be a possibility he is operating out of some kind of personal harbour anywhere from Hatteras to the Floridas. Certainly any known port would allow the Governor to put an end to his indiscretions immediately."

Rye thought for a moment. "If we can apprehend the Dutchman and his little squadron — I presume it is little, isn't it, sir? — or find his harbour for that matter. What is it you have authority to do, sir?"

Cathcart smiled, his dark eyes hard points of light. "Inform him of certain vessels 'under protection.' Determine the legality of his enterprise. Verify his letters of marque, and that sort of thing."

"And if he objects?"

Cathcart's look was cool. "Put him out of business if need be, Mr. Rye. Put him out of business."

Rye nodded, a sober look on his features.

"Don't be too put off, Mr. Rye," said Cathcart. "The world is certainly not just and seldom honourable. But His Majesty's interests — and our own — may still be served in doing what we are told. However dubious that may seem. Or how distasteful."

Rye looked at him, squaring his shoulders. "Yes, sir," he said, accepting the closure of discussion. "Presumably, sir, you'll wish —"

"Deck, there!"

By the helm, Poynting cupped his hands. "Deck, aye?"

The foretop lookout's voice rang down, the clear high tones of a boy barely into manhood.

"A sail, sir! Starboard bow, broad! A skiff or some kind o' ship's boat, sir!"

Poynting was bellowing up again. "Where away, d'ye say?"

"Starboard bow, sir. Lugsail rig, fore n' main, like a ship's boat!"

Poynting looked inquiringly at Cathcart, who was peering off in the appropriate direction.

"Captain, zur? Foretop lookout reports —"

"I heard, Mr. Poynting. Bring her into the wind. I'll speak that boat. And I'll trouble you to have the gunner put a shot cross her bows from the fore chase."

"Aye, aye, sir," said Poynting, his youthful face a mirror of eagerness. "Mr. Winton. Bring her into the wind if you please. Messenger? Call the gunner at once."

Winton's foghorn tones were rolling across the deck in seconds. "Sheets and braces there, lively now! Mind that stays'l sheet! That sheave's jammed!" He paused. "Ready about, zur!" he bellowed back to Poynting.

Poynting licked his lips. "Down helm!" he ordered. Then, "Helm's a-lee!"

Saracen turned with ponderous grace into the wind, and her broad foretopsail thumped gently as it went aback, pressing against the foremast to slow the frigate's progress through the sea.

Rye paced over to join Cathcart, who was leaning on the rail, staring out at the small white speck of the boat, visible now on the gloomy eastern horizon.

"Odd to see a boat this far offshore, sir."

"Hmmm? Yes. Could be anything, of course. Derelicts from

a sinking. Prisoners sent in by the Frogs. Some bloody fool onshore fisherman blown out and trying to work home.''

"But he might be more."

Cathcart pursed his lips. "No point in speculating on thin air, Mr. Rye. I simply want to have a look at every thing in my corner of the ocean, what?

"Indeed, sir," said Rye.

Paul Gallant stirred in his nest in the bottom of the boat as Akiwoya's toe dug into his ribs. The marine had wedged himself down between two biscuitbags and a powder cask and had drawn a salt-whitened bit of tarpaulin over him, and he floundered for a moment before managing to sit up.

"Wake up, capitaine!" the African was saying. "Sweet Mother of God. There's a new fish in the sea."

"Eh? What?" Gallant rubbed his face, feeling the grit of salt, and jammed his straw hat over his eyes. He struggled up on a thwart, ducking under the curving foot of the mainsail. "Damn it, Aki, I've hardly slept for more than five —" He stopped as his eyes followed the African's pointing finger.

"Christ. A man-o'-war," breathed Gallant.

"Thought you'd need to know," said Akiwoya. "Shall I —?"

"No. I'll take the helm. Scramble forward and rouse up Brulé. Béssac?"

"Awake, capitaine," rumbled the Mate, from the shadow of the foresail. He had been lying in its shade along the gunwale, his great seacoat drawn round him like a blanket. Now he was sitting up, scratching a thatched head and peering into the western horizon at the dark mass of a ship, distantly outlined against the orange and ochre riot of the sunset.

"What in Hell is *that*?" said the Mate.

Gallant squinted, shifting his grip on the tiller to hold the boat a little more before the slight breeze. As the boat rose to the top of the next long, smooth swell he sucked a tooth. "Sacristi!" he muttered.

"What?" Béssac was looking at him, as Akiwoya and a groggy-looking Brulé peered forward.

"English," said Gallant, in an even voice. "Frigate, by the looks of her. Too big for a twenty-four. Looks like one of their forty-fours."

Béssac stood up, arm clutched at the mainmast for support, and shaded his eyes. "You're right," he said, after a minute.

113

"I'd say he's seen us." He sat down, swivelling to look at Gallant. "What are we going to do? Hell, nightfall's not half a glass away. Turn and tack away from her! She'd never come up to us by nightfa—"

As Béssac had begun his last sentence a pink flash had winked in the bows of the black silhouette. Now a thump stopped the words in his mouth. An instant later, there was a slap, not unlike, Gallant thought, a report of a beaver tail on a pond surface. A geyser of hissing spray shot towering into the air barely a hundred yards ahead of the boat.

Gallant shook his head. "No warning shot. He wants us to let fly our sheets. So he can send a boat over."

Béssac looked anxiously at him. "You're not going to, are you? Christ, capitaine, you let the bastard English take us, and you'll *never* see that woman again—!"

Another pink flash had shown in the English vessel's dark mass, and this time there was a frightening sound, like ripping linen. With a ringing slap another shot struck the top of a swell not twenty feet off the boat's bow, and the awesome jet of water and spray that leaped thirty feet above the four staring men fell in a hissing rain back over them, drenching them.

Gallant wiped his dripping face and spat. "Bloody rosbif luck! The bastards have the range already. So much for tacking smartly away for nightfall! Aki! Let fly the fores'l sheet! Béssac, the main! I'm rounding up!"

"But—!" began the Mate.

"*Do it*!" Gallant thrust the tiller hard over, and with her canvas rippling loosely above her, the boat swung into the wind and lay tossing gently. Gallant sheeted in the main again to keep slight way on, and then slumped back against the transom.

"She's lowering a boat," said Béssac, looking over his shoulder. "Oh, God. Capitaine, I don't want to die in a British prison hulk! That cell in Louisbourg was enough for me. You'd better think of something, or—!" He stopped, as Gallant's mouth curved up in the slightest of smiles. "Or have you already?"

Gallant kept his eyes on the small shape of the boat that had pushed off from the distant frigate and was now oaring industriously toward them, like some enormous black water beetle on a copper sea.

"It's a slim idea," he said. "But have you ever been to Portugal?"

Forty minutes later Gallant was standing on *Saracen's* quarterdeck, holding his tattered straw hat in his hand and looking with what he hoped was an affable and somewhat simple expression into the hard eyes of Sir Aubrey Cathcart. Behind the marine, Béssac, Akiwoya and Brulé stood shifting their weight from one foot to another and eyeing uneasily the two British marine sentries in brick red coats and mitre caps who flanked them. The Englishmen's bayonets were fixed and they were cradling the heavy Brown Bess muskets with an air of practiced ease. Alongside *Saracen* Gallant's boat rode, hooked on at the frigate's forechains while several seamen and marines poked through the contents of the craft.

"Let me rephrase that," said Cathcart, pursing his lips as his eyes bored into Gallant's. "Your ship was the *Dom João*? An Azorean whalecatcher?"

Gallant nodded his head vigorously, baring his teeth and running the rim of his hat through his hands.

"*Si, capitano!* It was terrible. The *Dom João*, she was a xebec, yes? The whale was so big! *Senhor*, he struck us in the bows — once, twice! Then the water, she began —"

"Just a moment. What was your course? Your destination?"

"*Senhor*? Gallant's voice faded, and his eyes glazed over stupidly.

Cathcart's toe tapped in irritation. "Oh, for God's sake! Where were you going in that damned boat?"

Gallant's teeth flashed again in breathy comprehension. "Ah! *Si*! That way, *senhor*!" He pointed to the dim purple line of the American coast. "A landfall, *senhor*? We were only a day's sail eastward when the whale, she catch us. So, to the west I take the boat, and my poor *niños* here —"

"What of the rest of your crew? Your captain?"

Gallant shrugged and hung his head. "*Nada*. It was so quick, enh? The others, they took the other boats. These are my crew. So I take some things we need. The *capitano*, *Senhor* de Fora, he is gone already in another boat. Then the wind, she hits, and after I see nothing. *Nada*. So I try for America —"

"Your captain and the other crew are dead?" said Cathcart, sharply.

Gallant shrugged and looked down, fidgeting with his hat.

Cathcart was about to speak when *Saracen's* Officer of Marines, an elegant lieutenant with a pale, aquiline face, stepped briskly up, saluted, and then whispered a few sentences into Cathcart's ear. As Gallant watched, working at keeping the earnest and stupid expression on his face, he felt his heart begin to pound like a hammer within his rib cage. His knees began to tremble slightly. If the English looked carefully in the boat and put two and two together. . . .

115

Cathcart's voice abruptly broke the tension. "Thank you, Lieutenant. Carry on."

"Sir," said the marine. He saluted languidly once more with a slight lift of his hat and moved away.

"Well, then," said Cathcart, looking back at Gallant, and briefly at the three men behind him. "*Senhor . . .*"

"Pessoa, *capitano*. João Pessoa. At your—"

"Yes, yes, I'm sure. Mr. Pessoa, you've had a great misfortune indeed. The loss of one's ship is a tragedy every seamen can understand. You have my sympathies."

Gallant gaped, not entirely in counterfeit. "Er — '*Brigado, senhor*! Thank you."

"Mr. Rye!" barked Cathcart.

"Sir?" said Rye, who had been standing nearby.

out These gentlemen are castaways of the sea. They deserve assistance at the very least. See that a cask of good Jamaica rum is put into their boat. And show them where they are on the chart, if you please. They are but a short sail from the coast, where I am sure they will find charity and shelter. We must help them all we can."

Rye stared for a moment, first at Cathcart and then at Gallant and his companions.

"Come, come, Mr. Rye! What are you hesitating about, what? Do carry on!"

Rye recovered and saluted. "'Sir." He moved away, speaking to Poynting.

Cathcart had proffered his hand to Gallant, who gaped at it for a moment before sticking forward a paw in an inept clutch in reply.

"And we'll bid you good luck and good day, sir!" beamed Cathcart. "I'd give you passage, of course, but I've m'duty to consider, eh? But you're damn near a gun shot off the coast, and there'll be good Christian charity for you ashore, nay doubt."

Gallant bobbed his head, grinning. "You are too kind, *senhor*! We are but poor sailors —"

"Pah!" said Cathcart, good-naturedly. "We're all the same lot, under the cloth, eh? Come. I'll see you to your boat. And remember to drink the health of His Majesty with that rum, what? Blast this confounded war!"

"Th — thank you again, *senhor*," managed Gallant, after a quick glance at Béssac's uncomprehending stare. With the marine guards clumping behind, the men followed Cathcart to the rail.

Some twenty minutes later Cathcart stood with Sebastien Rye on *Saracen's* quarterdeck, looking off to the west where Gallant's boat, footing along well in the breeze that was rising now, was dwindling against the dark line of the coast. There was activity at the helm and aloft in *Saracen* as Poynting was endeavouring, not a little nervously, to take the ship off the wind and resume her northeastward track.

"If you'll pardon me, sir —," began Rye.

"Yes, Mr. Rye?"

"That fellow in his boat. Did you actually *believe* his story, sir?"

"It seemed plausible enough," said Cathcart, mildly.

"But Simpson's lads went through the boat, sir. Did he tell you what they found?"

"He summarized it quite thoroughly."

"But then, sir, don't you think they were anything *but* Azorean whalers? At the absolute minimum they were up to no good—"

Cathcart turned abruptly on his heel. "You're quite right, Mr. Rye. And that is why I'd be pleased if you would now have the launch swayed over and a picked boat's crew put into it. You pick 'em, sir. And I would suggest you have Lieutenant Simpson provide you with a picket of marines. Full field pack and breadbags for 'em, I should think. And see that the hands are armed, and have a good quantity of biscuit."

Rye swallowed. "An — inshore party, sir?"

Cathcart smiled. "Of course. I quite agree with you, you know. That fellow's not up to something in His Majesty's interest. And I have an odd feeling that he might lead us to—well, perhaps something not unrelated to our present duty, what?"

"You mean the privateers."

Cathcart shrugged. "Who can say about such things. But I have this deuced odd feeling. And I want you to find out if it is a feeling I should have ignored."

"Ah. You mean, sir, *I'm*—"

"Indeed, Mr. Rye. You'll command the launch. Take her in, but keep our fellow Pessoa—such an unlikely monicker, b'God! Sounds like a seaman's bad joke—in sight. He'll not reach the coast before dawn. Fly no colours and he'll think you a fisherman or whatever."

"And then, sir?" Rye felt a queer mixture of dread and expectation welling up within him, and he fidgeted with a waistcoat button.

"You'll have a choice. If he makes for a legitimate harbour, see that he reaches shelter, and the notice of the authorities and return out to me. I shall follow you inshore, visible from masthead height, if the wind favours it. If he is a solitary lawbreaker bent on mischief, deal with him on the spot as your resources allow. And if—'' he paused.

"Sir?"

" — And if he leads you to what appears to be bigger game than you can handle, Mr. Rye, stand out briskly for me as well. Or if you cannot, light three fires in a line. And I'll bring *Saracen* in.''

"Aye aye, sir!" said Rye. His eyes were alight, and in the next instant he had turned away, bellowing in the same breath for Winton, Poynting and Lieutenant Simpson.

And as the tumult began to grow on *Saracen's* decks and below, Aubrey Cathcart leaned on the rail and looked at the distant, tiny shape of Gallant's boat.

"We'll see, our Portugee whaler, if you are what you say you are," he breathed. "Or," he added, with a narrowing of his eyes, "if you are what *I* think you are!"

Marianne de Poitrincourt, Marquise de Bézy, awoke with her hand at her throat, struggling out of a terrifying dream in which she had been held down by sweating, foul-breathed seamen and slowly suffocated by a maniacally laughing Alfonso Castelar. She sat up in the darkness in the narrow box bunk, her heart thudding against her ribs, and tried to slow her breathing.

On the deck beside her, curled on a rough pallet, Lisette stirred and sat up.

"What is it, madame? Are you ill?"

Marianne hugged her knees and pressed her forehead against them, fighting for self-control from the quick clutch of panic. It was always worse just after awakening.

"No. It — it's all right, Lisette. I'm fine."

The servant girl drew her rough blanket around her and huddled close to the side of her mistress' bunk. "There's — something strange," she said, eyes white in the gloom of the small cabin.

Marianne raised her head. "It's the ship," she said. "It's not rolling. Or creaking or groaning."

"Are we anchored?" said Lisette.

"I don't think so. It's just not—moving so much." Marianne shivered and pushed back her hair. "Gentle Mother, I'm hungry!" she murmured through clenched teeth.

Lisette was rummaging under the bunk. "There's some of that hard bread left."

"The biscuit? Pah! I've cracked enough teeth on those. I'll not eat another crumb of it." She kicked at the blankets in sudden anger, looking round her with loathing at the small cramped cabin. "Damn Castelar!"

There was a knock on the low door of the cabin that froze both women. Lisette whimpered and drew closer to her mistress.

The knock repeated itself, more urgently.

"Wh — who is it?" said Marianne, her heart in her throat.

"My name is LeBeau, madame. Please. Do not alarmed."

Marianne's heart bounded for an instant at the sound of the French voice. But then her lips tightened.

"Go away. Leave us alone!"

"Please, madame!" The voice was less threatening than pleading. "Let me in. I mean you no harm, by the Virgin!"

Even as she fought to control her trembling, the noblewoman realized that whoever was out there could easily have kicked the flimsy door aside to get in.

"Go away!" she repeated. "Don Castelar will kill you!"

"Please, madame! If I'm found out here —!"

With every instinct in her screaming against it, Marianne rose off the bunk and lifted the latch, shrinking back into the shadows with the moaning Lisette as a man's figure pushed into the cabin. He shut the door quickly behind him.

"*You!*" gasped the Marquise. She stared at the black face with its single, gleaming eye and the hideous scar coursing down through the middle of the white orb of the cataract.

"You know me, then."

Marianne's eyes were stony. "What is it you want!"

"Please believe me, madame. I mean you no harm. But if you want to live . . ." He paused, listening at the door.

"Live? Wh — what do you mean?"

LeBeau's lips curled in a mirthless smile. "Do you think, madame, that Don Alfonso Castelar is interested in the slightest in saving your life? Hein? When he is through with you . . ." He shrugged.

Marianne felt Lisette trembling against her side. "You still have not said," she spat out, "what it is you want. Or is it *your* particular pleasure to torment helpless women?"

LeBeau's eye flashed in the dark. "You must not be a fool, madame. Please listen to what I have to tell you. Even for but a moment."

Something in the man's tone made Marianne hesitate. "What choice do I have?" she said, holding Lisette close to her side.

"Exactly!" LeBeau put an ear once more to the cabin door

and listened intently for a moment. Then he was turning back, licking his lips and wringing his hands in what might have been excitement or anxiety. But there was no mistaking the chilling note in his voice.

"We are coming to anchor, madame. And the greatest danger for you is here!"

"Where are we?"

"On the coast of the Carolinas. An island. The stronghold of the Dutch pig, Ten Haaf. He has a stockade ashore." LeBeau licked his lips. "And Castelar is already planning what to do with you. The Dutchman and his dogs are ready to fight over your dowry gold. Christ save us, what a fortune!"

Marianne was pale. "Get to your point," she whispered.

LeBeau leaned forward, menacingly. "But that isn't all Don Alfonso's promised the Dutch, hein? Nor all he wants. He's told 'em they'll have more. And he'll get it by selling you back to His Majesty."

"How nicely you put it."

"And for God knows how many livres. You'll write a letter for him, he plans. And then a fast chasse-marée will take it to the Antilles, and it'll go on to France."

"But — that may take months!"

LeBeau shrugged. "It's the gold or your life, hein? Except—"

Marianne's chin lifted. "The money will be paid."

"—Except that you'll die in any event, madame," said LeBeau smoothly.

The girl's hand went to her throat. "Wh — what do you mean?" she managed.

"That is my purpose here, madame. To warn you. Don Alfonso intends to hold you alive and well only until he has obtained the payment — of whatever kind — he wants." The man snorted. "Then you and your girl are thrown to the Dutchman's fo'c'sle dogs. And *they'll* slit your white throat for you — after they're through." He sucked a tooth. "They take their time. Your other girl didn't die for some time. . . ."

Against Marianne's side Lisette began to cry quietly. Such a pall of horror had fallen over Marianne's mind that she could bring herself to speak only with great difficulty.

"You — can't be right. He wouldn't —"

"Of course he would, madame," said LeBeau. "I heard him giving the orders to Ten Haaf. You're not to survive."

For a moment, Marianne's will and courage failed, and she sank back against the bulkhead, her eyes suddenly filling with tears.

"Oh, God. Oh, dear God!" she whispered.

"I'm not lying, madame," said LeBeau. His one eye was fixed on her with an odd expression.

"Wh — why are you telling me this?" said the girl, after a moment.

In an unexpected move LeBeau sank abruptly to one knee and lifted the hem of the noblewoman's ragged skirts to his lips.

"I am not a — a murderer of women, madame. A brigand, yes. It was an act of folly to obey Don Alfonso, and I admit my greed, may the Holy Mother forgive me for it. But I cannot abide the killing. I cannot deny my conscience, or my true loyalty. God forgive me for forgetting it! And this heinous scheme . . ." He seemed unable to finish.

Marianne stared down at him. "And you — you would help me? Help us?"

LeBeau's scarred face turned up, the one shining eye alight. "I am your servant, madame. With all my heart. And my life, if need be."

The noblewoman's eyebrows lifted imperceptibly. "And in return . . .?"

"Nothing. Only, if we may escape the grasp of these people, your gracious intercession on my behalf. For mercy and forgiveness from the King's justice!"

Marianne took a deep trembling breath. Her mind raced with questions, doubts, and a part that rang with warning. . . .

"Then we accept you as our servant, LeBeau," she said, in a quiet voice. "But what can you suggest for us?" She looked briefly into Lisette's pale, tear-streaked face. "Is there any escape from this — horror?"

LeBeau rose to his feet and reached up one of his full-cuffed coat sleeves. From it he pulled two gleaming, needle-bladed Italian *stiletti* and handed them to Marianne.

"Here," he said, dropping his voice to a hoarse whisper. "Take these! Hide them on your person. At least they are a beginning. If one of the bastard Dutchmen comes for you, you can at least . . ." He did not finish.

Marianne held the slim weapons against her breasts, shivering as the cold steel touched her flesh. "It is a beginning, LeBeau. Thank you."

LeBeau licked his lips. "I know not what next we can do, madame. But I will watch, and listen. A chance of some kind may come to pass before long. A boat, perhaps, to steal to the mainland. God knows. But you have my word I will fight for your safety and escape!"

121

The girl looked at him, the murmurs of suspicion still loud in her mind. "Is there anything else you hope to gain by this, LeBeau?"

The man lowered his head. "You have heard my reasons, madame. I wish to be free of this villainy. And not be abandoned by you to His Majesty's revenge."

Marianne nodded after a moment. "You have our word, LeBeau," she said. "Thank the Holy Mother that you have been returned to your duty."

LeBeau's eye glistened suddenly with moisture. "I shall not fail you," he said hoarsely.

In the next instant he was gone, the cabin door clicking shut softly behind him.

Beside Marianne, Lisette was weeping bitterly. "Oh, madame! We are lost! We —!"

"Hush, girl!" admonished the noblewoman. "We are lost only when we cannot draw another breath, hein? And now there is hope. And an ally!"

"But — but can we trust that man?"

Marianne looked down at the two weapons in her hands and then pressed them against her breasts again. In her heart she felt a wild and unreasoning bubble of hope forming.

"What choice do we have, Lisette?" she breathed.

Outside in the passageway, Félix LeBeau listened with an ear pressed against the thin wood of the cabin door. When after a few moments he turned and padded away noiselessly, his face was wreathed in a dark smile of satisfaction and triumph.

Paul Gallant stirred uneasily under the sodden scrap of crumpled tarpaulin, then sat up on one elbow as a sudden heave and dip of the boat awakened him. His neck hurt where it had been pressing against a biscuitbag, and his knees were locked uncomfortably round the long case containing the muskets. His clothes were damp, and there was a taste of salt on his lips.

The little boat was pitching and rolling along with a steady roar in a welter of foam and spray, and at first Gallant thought he had awakened in the dead of night. Then he saw the faint, dark outline of the masts against the paler sky, and the curved face of the mainsail. Dawn was near.

He struggled up and looked aft. Béssac, hatless, was braced in magisterial dignity in the sternsheets, feet thrust against the thwart before him, the thick tiller bar in a vicelike grip as he fought the boat along on its downwind rush.

The Mate grunted when he saw Gallant sit up, and spat manfully off into the sea.

"Hah! About bloody time. Wind freshening, no one to take in a reef or lend a hand on the tiller. *And* my guts growling for a biscuit or some wine."

Gallant grinned in the gloom. "Your course is still westward, isn't it? Haven't turned us around, have you?"

"Hilarious, capitaine. Look ahead and you'll get your answer."

Gallant swivelled, ducking to look ahead past the face of the curving foresail and the pitching stempost. On the barely visible horizon, a vague line where black water met an almost equally dark sky, there was an irregularity. A low, humped mass that stretched away to either side. And, before it, the white flash of a long line of surf.

Surf!

"The coast! Christ, Béssac, we're not a half-league off!" He scrambled out of the welter of canvas and worked his way aft, thumping down in the stern beside Béssac.

Gallant ran his fingers through his hair, squinting ahead at the land mass. Béssac was controlling the boat's rush ahead of the following sea and wind well. He had taken all but a few turns off the fore and main sheets, and now kept the falls pinned down with one broad bare foot, ready to cast them off at the first sign of real disaster. But he was steering masterfully, keeping the stern dead into the wind and avoiding the fatal turn that would broach the boat and tumble it sideways in the rolling swells. At the speed they were making, they would be on the breakers within an hour.

"Bloody close," said the marine. He stared at Béssac. "How long *were* you going to wait before waking me, anyway?"

Béssac's laugh rang out above the sea roar. "Just about to kick Aki there and get 'im to wake you. That's God's truth, m'sieu'."

Gallant shook his head. "A likely story. You're never a lad to let go of a tiller until it's pried out of your fingers! Aki? Holà, there!"

From his burrow between the second and third thwarts of the boat the big African grunted.

"How a matelot gets any sleep with all that quarterdeck jabber going on, I'd like to know," he muttered.

"Save the abuse, mon vieux. The coast's ahead!" said Béssac.

"Eh? What?" Suddenly awake, the African sat up, squinting forward. Then he saw the line of surf. "Sweet Christ!" he murmured.

Gallant peered at the dark coast, ignoring the hunger pangs in his stomach. It came to him that although he felt certain they were near Ten Haaf's island refuge, there was the possibility that some unforeseen current, a stronger tidal ebb or flow than usual — a host of things — might have put them leagues to the north or south of where the island as described by Miller should be. Even a two- or three-knot alongshore current could have put them a day or two of hard windward sailing away up the coast.

He put the thought into the back of his mind. It would not be long before he would be able to make out some distinguishing marks. And in any event they were going to be hard against that surf within an hour or two at the most.

"Ho, Brulé!" Gallant called. "Rouse up, you sea rat! Get into some of that biscuit and wine for us!"

Forward, a shaggy-headed Brulé had appeared out from his shelter at the foremast foot and was pawing his way through the welter of boat stores toward the biscuit supply.

"Black as a privy pit!" muttered the man. "Where'n Hades are we, capitaine?"

Gallant caught one of the rock-hard biscuits Brulé tossed to him and dipped it in the hissing seawater for a moment to soften it. He gnawed at the white, plasterish substance and shook his head.

"No idea as yet, mon vieux," he said over the sea noise. "Dead off the Dutchman's island, is what I hope. Tell you when I can see some kind of landmark."

Brulé nodded, then was abruptly all attentiveness as his eyes went past Béssac and Gallant to look out astern.

"Well, capitaine, I can see something else we might want to worry about." He pointed. "There's a boat astern!"

"What?"

Gallant spun to look, toward the pink glow of the eastern horizon. He waited, bracing himself against the gunwale, until the boat rose to the top of one of the huge, overtaking swells.

"There!" said Brulé. "Look now!"

Briefly appearing against the dark hills of whitecapped moving water, Gallant saw it: a small, dark shape against the brightening horizon. A boat, like a ship's launch, with two sails winging out like their own.

"Damn!" said Gallant, sinking back on the thwart.

"What is he?" said Béssac, hauling vigorously on the tiller bar as the boat foamed down the face of a swell. "Could you see —?"

"Nothing. No. Could be anything," said Gallant, biting his lip. "Fisherman, maybe. A lugger, blown offshore. Or —"

"Or a boat from that damned rosbif frigate that stopped us," broke in Akiwoya, his cheek full of biscuit. "Hotfooting it after us with a swivel loaded with canister and a squad of those hellish English marines."

Forward in the boat, Brulé stopped coiling the foresail halyard and hung it on its pin. "Sweet Mary," he breathed. "You think, maybe?"

Gallant braced himself for another look as an onrushing swell lifted the boat's stern. His face took on a look of puzzlement. "Damned if I can tell. She's lug-rigged, like us, hein?"

"Ship's boat rig, for certain," muttered Akiwoya.

" — And she looks full of people." The marine looked at Béssac. "Could it be? D'ye think the rosbifs weren't fooled by that Portuguese nonsense?"

Béssac snorted, leaning into his effort on the tiller. "Hah! His lads were poking through our kit from stem to gudgeon while you were into the buffoonery on the quarterdeck, capitaine. I wouldn't bet a Dutch guinea we got away with it!"

Gallant's face was grim in the growing light. He took a deep swig from the fat wine bottle Brulé passed to him, passed it to Akiwoya, and wiped his mouth with the back of his hand.

"You're right. Christ knows I'm a fool to think we did. Then we've got a Royal Navy hound on our tails."

Akiwoya took a crunching bite out of a biscuit. "And a prison hulk waiting somewhere?" he asked of no one in particular. For a moment none of the other three could muster an answering comment.

Then Gallant was digging at his watch in a pouch round his neck, and scrabbling into one of the nearby bags for the chart folio. He was soon squinting at the dog-eared and stained document, glancing at his watch, and then standing up to peer ahead at the shadowed coastline.

"That Englishman's a good two leagues astern," he said briskly, after a moment. "We're damn near on the coast. Maybe a quarter-league off. If somewhere *there* is Ten Haaf's island — and we can find one or the other bloody channels before we run on that surf —"

"But what'll that do, capitaine?" interrupted Béssac. "Ma-

125

donna, we're supposed to *surprise* the buggering Dutch. But if we foam into that lagoon or anchorage or whatever at six knots with big smiles on our faces, we'll be dead before we can brail up the bloody sails! And you won't need to worry about a rosbif boat astern then!''

Gallant nodded. Béssac was right. Miller had said the anchorage was a death trap. It was to the seaward side that the only chance lay of landing on the island safely. But then how likely would it be for the Dutch not to have lookouts on watch to seaward? If that *was* Ten Haaf's lair ahead then they could already be in the glass of some Dutchman's ''bring 'em near,'' and the game was as good as up.

Then his eyes fell to the little chart. Unless . . .

The rough drawing of the island Gallant had made after listening to Miller's babblings showed an almost impossible foreshore: long, dune-backed straight beaches, pounded by that boat-smashing surf he could glimpse far ahead. The north channel, if Miller had not lied, snaked in at a slight angle from the sea into the lagoon, but offered no quick shelter along its length. And, once in it, any boat was almost smack atop the stronghold, whatever sort of fortified hellhole *that* might be.

But the *south* channel . . .

''Look here, Béssac! Aki, come aft and take the helm! Quickly!''

The Mate grunted with relief as the African's strong grip closed on the tiller bar, and he clambered over to beside Gallant, staring at the sketch.

''Look there, hein?'' Gallant's voice was tinged with excitement. ''The south channel. There's a little double bay, a cove, about half way in. It's shallow water, and goes into swampland, but if we make it into the channel and then come hard about before we cross into the lagoon, we can put in there! Marshes mean reeds, and that means shelter. And with the Englishman's distance behind us, he'll think we've gone on through to the lagoon, if we can hide the boat well enough. Christ, it's a chance!''

Béssac poked a finger at the southern tip of the oblong island. ''But it stands to reason the Dutchies'll have lookouts there. Christ, we'd be under musket shot before we put a foot ashore. And if we get caught under fire wallowing around in some damned *swamp*, capitaine —!''

''I know, mon vieux. But there's always a chance.''

''Eh?''

''A chance there'll be no lookouts.''

"And we'd just run into that channel and vanish before the eyes of our friends astern."

"Exactly. Why not?"

Béssac scratched his thatched mane. "Damned long shot to me, capitaine."

Gallant grinned at him. He knew when the Mate had been won over.

"All right," said the Mate. "What now?"

Gallant had pulled a small telescope from its oiled bag, and was handing it to Béssac.

"Get forward. Brace yourself up against the mast and scan that coast for the island, for the channels. Miller said there was some sort of log redoubt on the hillock overlooking the south channel."

"I still say they'll have lookouts. . . ." Béssac was already making his ungainly way forward, ducking under the fore and main sheets. As he levered himself up on the thwart that formed the foremast's strongback, the Mate swore loudly enough for Gallant to hear as the boat pitched up on a breaking swell.

"What, mon vieux?" bellowed Gallant. "We're on the surf line already?"

"Damned near! Aki, keep a bloody straight course, will you? She's rolling like the Devil!"

"Hang on, Théo," grinned the African. "Every finger a fishhook, hein?"

"Go to Hell."

Gallant squinted forward, rising in a half-crouch from the stern sheets after a moment or two had passed with no utterance from Béssac.

"Christ, Béssac," he called. "Don't go mute on us! What d'ye make out?"

Béssac was peering ahead with the small glass, which must have been difficult to do with the roll and pitch of the hurrying little craft over the overtaking swells.

"Bloody Hell," said the Mate.

"What?"

"Hell with Bloody before it. Christ, capitaine, can't a man think out loud?"

In spite of his rising anxiousness Gallant found himself exchanging a grin with Akiwoya.

Then the Mate hooted. "Ha! Look at that!"

Gallant sprang up, only to slump awkwardly back again as a wrench of the boat tossed him off balance. "Damn your eyes, Béssac, what —?"

"Either the Holy Mother's had a hand on the tiller, or you're the best pilot since Christ was a pup!"

"Eh?"

"Your island's damn near dead ahead! There's a clear break in the shoreline! Well, maybe a bit more off the starboard bow, peut-être."

"The Hell you say. Certain?" Gallant had to bellow as a huge swell broke under the craft, tumbling white surf roaring at either gunwale.

"It's just like you said! There's a — yes, a channel to the right! Straight in, and I can see open water behind. A long, sandy islet, hein? Big dune hills behind that damned surf! Jesus, we're getting too close to that —!"

Gallant swore. "Can you see the redoubt? Or a blockhouse? Anything? Look at the left-hand end!"

"No — wait — yes! On a dune top, hein? Looks like — Christ, Aki, hold her steady! — like a small low stockade, or something!"

"On the left hand! You're certain?"

"I — yes! And there's a channel or inlet, there, just past it! Can't see the lagoon —"

"That's because there's a turn to the channel, like Miller said!" said Gallant. "Well, I'm damned," he murmured. Then he raised his voice again. "Any sign of life? Smoke? Figures moving?"

There was a pause as Béssac peered into the little glass. The boat rolled its corkscrew way over another overtaking swell, and as it settled back, Brulé emerged from under a thwart with a grim expression, holding a sodden biscuitbag.

"We'd better find a shore damned soon, capitaine," said the man. "We've lost one of the bungs, and th' plankings working loose!"

"What?"

"Or aren't your feet wet, capitaine?"

Gallant looked down, seeing for the first time the water sloshing over the floorboards.

"Oh, Christ," he said.

Akiwoya was muttering something in his native African speech as he hauled with grim strength on the tiller. "Brulé's right, capitaine!" he burst out in French. "I can feel her starting to wallow!"

Gallant plunged along the row of thwarts forward, reaching down between the casks and bales. The water was already up to his wrist. He straightened, bracing against the main mast as the boat see-sawed on the back of a hissing swell.

"Béssac, how far off are we?"

"Much less'n half a league, capitaine! There's no surf line off the mouth of the channel; dark water there! That's fine on the larboard!"

Water sloshed around Gallant's feet. "Right! Béssac, you pilot Aki into a bearing dead on that channel mouth! Aki, you can't let her broach, whatever you do! But you've got to steer her right in! Compris?"

The African nodded, his lips set in effort.

"Brulé?"

"M'sieu'?"

"Help me!" barked Gallant. "Let's get this all overboard! All but the musket case, the bag with the cartridge boxes—that one, there! — and this water butt!"

Brulé stared. "E — everything?" he cried, over the sudden roar of a breaking swell.

"Yes! Come on!" Gallant seized a powder barrel, muscled it to the gunwale, and thrust it over. For a moment it was tumbled in the rush of foam that almost buried the boat, and then sank away.

"Quickly! Quickly!" Working with furious energy, Gallant and Brulé grappled with the stores, and the casks, bales and bags, wrestling them to the gunwale and forcing them over. The boat was riding so low now that the breaking crest of a swell towered above them as it swept past, drenching them with spray. Every few moments both men had to pause for rest, gasping with strain.

From his perch against the main mast Béssac was bellowing his course corrections to Akiwoya. "Larboard a span! Again! Damn it, Aki, hold her on that! We'll be forced on to the bloody beaches if you don't!"

"All — very well — for you to talk!" puffed the African, whose muscles shone like oiled wood in the gathering morning light. "You're not trying — to steer this pig!"

Brulé's breath was coming in gasps, as he levered a last heavy cask over the side. "That's — damned near it — all capitaine! What —?"

Gallant tossed a wooden bucket at him. "Here! Bail as much as you can! I've got the muskets and the cartridge bags wedged back here in the stern sheets! Leave that last water butt, there. Now *bail*!"

The marine had seized another bucket. Straddling the thwarts, the mainsail sheet rasping against his back through his sodden

129

shirt, Gallant scooped up buckets of water and flung them over the side with furious energy. Forward, Brulé was doing the same, and the two men dug at the shin-high water, bracing as best they could against the pitch and roll of the boat. They ignored the white, roaring chaos of the breaking swells that erupted every few seconds along either gunwale, drenching them with spray. Scoop, throw; scoop, throw; Gallant's eyes began to sting with sweat, and his knuckles were streaming blood now where he had barked them on the floorboards.

"Getting lower, capitaine!" called Brulé. "I — oh, Sweet Mother of Jesus!"

"What?"

Brulé swore luridly. "It's a whole bloody strake that's gone adrift, m'sieu'! The water's pouring in! We'll never save her!"

"Don't stop bailing!" cried Gallant. "We've got to keep her afloat till we can ground her! Béssac!"

"Capitaine?"

"Where in Hell —?"

"Just a gunshot off now, capitaine!" bellowed the Mate over the roar of the sea. "Can you look? Aki! Starboard a point!"

Gallant braced himself and looked up, wiping sweat and spray off his face with one dripping sleeve. The salt stung as it bit into open splits on his lips. The little boat was heaving in long, glissando runs as the black swells hissed in from astern, swept under and on ahead. But in the now-golden morning light that flooded across the sea from astern, turning it to a prairie of beaten copper, Gallant caught a glimpse of the dark shore ahead, frighteningly close as the boat lifted momentarily on a swell crest. In a quick glance he took in a low, humped coastline stretching away to either side, the flash of white sand making a line of dune hills behind the smashing tumble of the surf. Almost dead ahead there was a sharp break in the pattern of dune and roaring breakers, a shadowy entrance beyond which there was a glimpse of calm water, stretching away to a murky inner shore. Far to the right, another such gap was visible. And joining them, very close now, was the form of a long, low island, smashed along its foreshore by the vicious surf, with rolling dune hills topped with wind-rippled grass and the gnarled forms of palmetto.

And on the left-hand endmost rise, overlooking the beach and the inlet, a low and angular shape.

"Bloody Hell. Like you said. The redoubt!"

"Aye, capitaine! It's Miller's island, sure!"

Gallant swung to Akiwoya, off balance as the craft lurched awkwardly down the back of a sleek-shouldered, inrushing swell.

130

"Get us in that channel, Aki! Can you?"

"It's — damned hard, capitaine! She's getting heavier all the — time!"

Béssac was still calling out directions. But now the shore was so close upon them that Akiwoya could see it clearly, even when the boat sank into the deep wave troughs. And to all their ears a chilling sound was carrying now, over the whistle of the wind and the boil of the sea beside them: the deep boom of a thunderous surf against those hard, flat beaches.

In the boat rushed. The gap of dark water yawned ahead, and Béssac gripped the foremast as Akiwoya tried to wrestle the wallowing hull back on course for it. Gallant and Brulé still bailed with wild effort, as the water now rose almost to their knees.

And then, as if in a kind of suspended motion, the boat abruptly tilted back at a frightening angle, and slid into a cavernous trough, where the air was suddenly still. The motion sent a chill up Gallant's spine. He fell back against the main mast foot, staring aft past Akiwoya.

"Dear God!" he murmured.

Towering preposterously high above the little boat, its black, curving wall lifting and arching over them like black glass, an enormous wave was bearing down on them. Its cap was a ripple of breaking white, ripped by the wind into spindrift until the mighty mass of water looked like a smoking volcano. Up, up it reared, and above Gallant the boat's sails lolled uselessly as the wind died in the shadow of the giant. The boat was waiting, as if resigned, for the wave to strike.

Gallant found his tongue. "Hang on!" he barked. "Aki, hold her dead before it! Brulé! Béssac! Wrap yourselves around something and hang —!"

The air was filled with a dull roar, unlike anything Gallant had ever heard before. There was a mist-filled wind rushing through his hair, and a great shadow fell over him. He had grasped the edge of the thwart before him, and now under him he felt the boat begin to lift from the stern. Slowly at first, but then in a building rush, lifting higher and higher until Akiwoya's feet lost their place and he was hanging for a split-second in mid-air, brawny arms locked round the tiller bar, eyes locked on Gallant's with a kind of wild horror in them.

And then Gallant was lifted, tossed, falling through a dark, thrumming void of space, until with a thunderclap the enormous black mass of the wave smashed down, and he was caught and pummelled in utter helplessness by a churning, savage river of inky chaos, feeling himself driven down, down, his ears ringing, lights flashing in his head. His lungs began to scream for air, but he could not control his arms or legs as a hundred hands thrust and tore at them. And then the black roaring rose in his own head, and overcame him.

SIX

Lieutenant Sebastien Rye gripped the gunwale and pressed his hat down over his eyes with his free hand. He still felt a chill lingering between his shoulder blades from the damp air of the night on the sea, and shivered under his broad boat cloak. Ahead in the launch, the marines and seamen were chafing their hands together to warm them and looking about as the light grew. Beside Rye, the burly petty officer who gripped the tiller bar muttered and spat into the sea.

"Pardon?" said Rye, over the sea noise.

"'Twere nuffin, zur," said the petty officer. "This 'ere launch takes these swells right well 'nough, zur. But I had a mind that th' wee boat ahead's in a pickle.''

Rye nodded. *Saracen's* launch was a heavy, broad-beamed seaboat, rigged with a stiff standing lug rig on fore and main, working sturdily ahead of the onrushing swells and the almost gale force of the morning wind. The seamen in the boat had been thankful for the quiet night sail, slumped against each other's shoulders for whatever little sleep they could snatch; they were

133

grinning at each other now with the returning light and the rising sea and wind strength. Less certain of it all were the marines, hunkered on their midships thwarts like a rain-sodden congregation of bishops in their mitre caps, hugging their muskets to themselves and muttering. With a dozen seamen and an equal number of marines in the launch, there was room to move about, but not enough for any man's real comfort. Rye was noticing now the pale faces of several of the marines, who were shivering in spite of their woolen brick-red coats. They had not had the relief for aching muscles and sore buttocks the seamen's work had given the latter.

"Sergeant Hewitt?" said Rye.

"Sir?"

"Biscuit and rum issue for your lads. And make it a double tot, all round."

"Aye, aye, sir," beamed the marine sergeant. "Thank you, sir."

Rye nodded. "Petty Officer Prince? I'll take the helm. Get a biscuit and rum issue out to your lads. Double as well."

Prince grinned at him. "Thankee, zur. Break the mornin' chill, that will."

"Yes. When you're done, pick two reliable helmsmen. I'll want 'em watch on, watch off. Send the first aft here to relieve me when he's had his tot."

"Aye, aye, zur. All right, lads. Up spirits!" Prince barked at several hands, who enthusiastically got into the work of passing out the biscuit and thrusting a spigot into the bunghole of the small rum cask. There was a stir of anticipation among the crowded men, and tin cups clinked as they were fished out of breadbags and seamen's bags. Rye noted with satisfaction the brightening expressions on the men's faces. Their preoccupation would give him time to scan ahead and contemplate what his plan of action was going to be.

Not that the slightest thing had occurred to him, he thought in some dismay.

"Mason and Hardwick. Ease the fore and main sheets. Let 'em wing out to the knot in this wind," he said.

Ahead in the boat, two older hands set down their tin cups and turned to easing out the straining sheets. Winging out to either side, the tan-coloured lugsails were driving the heavy launch at close to its maximum possible hull speed. There was no cause for worry yet from the growing swells, and it had not yet become difficult to swing the tiller bar so as to keep the craft carefully stern on to wind and sea as it boiled along. But by the look of things, that might change in an hour or so, in spite of the clear sky which was overhead.

Beside him, Prince tossed back the last of his rum with a grunt of satisfaction and stuffed his cup back into his seabag.

"Puts th' world t' rights, ye might say, zur. Thankee agin."

"Glad to hear it," said Rye, briskly. "Then while you're in such good form, take this glass of mine, will you? And where's your relief helmsman?"

"'Ere 'e comes now, zur," said Prince, as a sturdy-looking seaman with a shock of blond, sun-bleached hair clambered aft over the thwarts, stepping over men who bantered with him good-naturedly.

"Carr, zur," said Prince. "Prime hand."

"Good," said Rye, nodding as Carr knuckled his forelock to him. "Here, Carr. Firm grip, now. For God's sake don't let her broach." Rye pointed to the swinging card of the little box boat compass that sat in the sternsheets beside him. "As far as you can, your course is due west. All right?"

Carr, whose tanned brown arms under his rolled sleeves were as heavily-muscled as some legs Rye had seen, nodded, sliding into place and wrapping powerful fingers around the tiller bar.

"Aye, aye, sir. Due west it is, sir."

"Very good," said Rye. "Got the glass, Mr. Prince? Good. Follow me forward. I want to see what we're getting ourselves into."

A few minutes later Rye was standing with his feet spread wide for balance on the foremast strongback, and his back pressed against the mast itself. He took off his hat, handed it to Prince, and accepted the long telescope from him.

"Ah," he said, after peering through the glass for a moment.

"Zur?" said Prince.

"The coast ahead. There's some islands off the inner shore. Surf along the fronts of 'em. And I've got our little Portuguese friend in sight."

"Still standin' in for shore, zur?"

"Yes. Bloody great swells, inshore, there. The bottom must shallow quickly. He's heading for a low sand dune island, almost dead ahead. Looks like a channel leading in on the right. Ah. How interesting."

"Wot's that, zur?" said the patient Prince.

"Hard to tell from this distance off. But there's some kind of low fortification or remains of a structure on the left end of that islet. And some kind of a bay or cove to the left of that. A channel, perhaps? Christ, look at that surf!" He lowered his glass and

135

stepped carefully down to the floorboards. "Here. See for yourself."

Prince clambered up heavily, the canvas kilt which he wore over his breeches rippling like a sail in the wind. He braced himself and raised the telescope.

"Aye, zur. I have it now. It's a small gun position or summat like that. It's — Fair Christ!"

Rye looked up at him sharply. "What is it?"

Prince lowered the glass. "The Portuguee boat, zur! She was dippin' in and out o' the troughs. And then I saw her dip below one that even hid 'er sails, zur. And she didn't come up!"

"What?"

"She's broached, zur!" said Prince. He stared again through the glass. "Gone. Nothin' at all!"

Rye flung his hat into the floorboards and clambered heedlessly up beside Prince. "Give me that thing."

In the flat field of the telescope the rolling, slick backs of the swells were clear as they swept in to the white spray mist that drifted above the terrible surf, a surf that thundered against the dune landscape's shore with awesome strength. But of the image of the small boat that brief moments ago had been sinking into each dark valley only to reappear again, sailing strongly on for the shore, there was no sign.

"Good God," said Rye. "You're right." He lowered the glass, his mind already trying to reorganize its priorities.

"Wot're we t'do now, zur?" said Prince, over the hiss of the sea along the launch's flank. "It were he we was meant t'follow. But if he's foundered —"

Rye was silent for a moment. He thought of the more than twenty men at his back and the sudden death that appeared to have overcome the men ahead, almost as they watched. There was a chill running down his spine.

"He was bearing in for that island, Prince. It seemed to be important to him. There's nothing else he could have been heading for on this damned coast, unless . . ." He did not finish.

"There's a lot o' lagoons an' such behind them dunes, zur, by th' look of it. Could be he was bearin' in t' find summat behind them. Like in the lagoons."

"A sheltered anchorage? Or something on the mainland coast?"

"Aye, zur. There's no shelter otherwise. Naught but beaches and the bloody surf. Christ, you'd break a boat's back on *that*. Even this old girl."

Rye had swung up the glass again. "I *can* see what appears to be an open channel leading in. On the right hand of that island ahead.''

"So you said afore, zur. D'ye think we should go fir it, zur?''

Rye stepped down. He found the abrupt disappearance of their quarry had left him shaken and disturbed far more than he realized. His knees were trembling, and he hoped Prince would not see that his hands were as well.

He held on to the foremast for balance and looked astern at the sea and sky. The sun was up, now, over the horizon, and the sea, the launch's sails and the men's faces were lit with a brilliant orange glow. The sky was cloudless, but out of it the wind was building steadily, and if the launch was to keep from suffering the fate of that wretched boat ahead . . .

Action, his mind cried. Action!

"That's where we're bound, Mr. Prince!" He began clambering aft toward the stern after scooping up his hat, tossing the boat cloak back over his shoulders. "I'll have a double reef in the fore and the main, if you please! Look sharp, Carr. I'll want you to put us into the wind in a moment. For God's sake listen for my order.''

"Heading inshore, sir? For the inlet mouth?'' said Carr, forgetting for a moment his station.

Rye nodded, letting the impertinence pass. "Yes.. In to the lagoon. By the channel to the right of the island ahead. The boat we were chasing appears to have foundered in the swells ahead—''

"Jesus!'' muttered Carr.

"—So you'll have to mind your helm bloody well! And you'll stay on helm all the way in.''

Carr licked his lips and tightened his grip on the tiller bar. "Aye, sir. Thank you, sir.''

"Never mind the thanks. I'll give you fifty lashes if we end up dead.''

Carr grinned at him. "Never fear, sir!''

Rye looked forward. Prince had detailed off seamen who were looking aft expectantly, clustering and ready to undertake the reefing of the two straining lugsails. It would mean swinging the broad craft into the wind, picking a moment of relative calm between the great copper-coloured swells so that the tremendous pressure of the wind would be eased. The halyards would be slacked off, and the sails, rippling like gunshots in the wind, would be gathered from the foot, the dangling lines of the reef points tied under the gather, and the sails, reduced in size, once more hoisted to their full tension aloft.

Rye watched, judging his moment, looking over his shoulder. If he turned the craft broadside on in a wrong moment, it would all be over in an instant.

Far out to sea, a hand-span along the horizon from the blazing sun, Rye glimpsed a peach-coloured triangular shape. It was *Saracen*, standing in as Cathcart had said he would, the sun making the ship's sails translucent and glowing. . . .

Now!

"Ready about!" Rye bellowed. Then, "Helm a-lee!"

"Helm a-lee, sir!" called Carr in answer. And with a smooth, powerful pull of his arms he swung the launch into her turn into the wind.

Fifteen minutes later the launch was bowling along toward the shore once more, rolling and corkscrewing over the great swells. But with the bunched reefs in her taut sails the motion of the launch was less tender, and Rye noted with satisfaction the easy rise of the stern to the frightening onrush of the swells, and the way the sea-kindly hull felt once more underfoot.

Prince was grinning as he slumped down beside Carr in the sternsheets and looked across at Rye. "Proper bird on the wing with this wind, zur. Them reefs've done it."

Rye grunted. He was peering ahead, looking as the launch rose on each wave to see that Carr was holding them on course for the inlet mouth.

"That's a strange coast," he said, almost to himself. "Wish I'd brought a bloody pertinent chart. Dune islands, all of 'em. Low and humped. Grass and bloody scrub on top. And a lagoon behind. Swampy in places, I'd wager. Where would you hide there? And *what* would you hide there?"

Prince was pointing. "Look now, at the top o' this swell, zur. That's a fair size channel. Be loike you c'd take a ship through it, if ye had a wind!" he called, over the sea noise. "Like this'n!"

"Yes, you could. We'll be seeing damned soon enough!" yelled back Rye. "Watch your helm, Carr. We're coming up on the inlet mouth. I *don't* want us in the bloody surf on either side!"

The great swells were lifting and thrusting the stolid craft forward, their building strength inshore sending it tobogganing down each face with a roar of spray and lather along each flank. The seamen grinned and hooted; but the marines, land creatures in their inner souls, had swivelled in their places and were peering ahead anxiously at the low sandy shoreline, the savage surf and the dark gap in it toward which they sped. It was close, now, so close that Rye scrambled to his feet to watch for an

138

ominous change in the water colour that would mean shallows.

"Steady as you lie!" he said tersely to Carr. "No, don't watch that surf on the beaches! Keep your eye on that black water ahead, in the gap!"

And then suddenly the boat was abreast of the great breakers that were crashing in on the beaches to either side of the gap, so close that the men could see the grass atop the dune hills glisten wet with spray as it shook in the wind, and were deafened by the roar of the surf. Their faces wet with the spray mist that now shrouded the launch, they stared at the sides of the inlet as the launch, still pressed by the full force of the wind and the spent strength of the swell, surged into the gap. So quick was the passage through the gap that Rye and the others merely stared as the high, duned shoreline sped past them, and then in the next few minutes the launch was sliding into the opening of a broad lagoon, a calm, breeze-darkened expanse that stretched away to a low, wooded mainland. To the right, the lagoon stretched away behind a chain of low islands and sand spits, awash and circled over by clouds of sea birds.

But to the left . . .

"Christ on a crutch!" blurted out Prince.

High on a sandy bluff that overlooked the lagoon, a sturdy log stockade stood, the roof of at least one building visible within its serrated log walls. It was a true fortification, with readily discernible bastions at the corners, and a steep sand slope leading down and away from the foot of the walls. A slender flagstaff rose above the walls, and from it, floating in the vagaries of the wind in the lee of the island, an enormous Dutch ensign set a flash of banded colour against the clear morning blue sky.

"Jesus, it's a Dutchie fort!" Carr cried. "An' look at those bloody *ships*!"

Riding at anchor in the calm waters of the lagoon, their shapes dark against the twinkling light of the sun on the wavelets, three ships rode. Two were smaller vessels, the size of twenty-gun sloops, with Dutch ensigns curling gently from their stern staffs.

But anchored further into the lagoon roads, huge and unexpected, was the towering form of a line-of-battle ship, red and gilt colour brilliant on her sides, the canvas clewed neatly up to her lofty yards, and the pale clean beauty of the Bourbon ensign drifting in slow majesty above her canting stern.

"Good God!" said Rye. "A Spaniard! A sixty-gunner, at least!"

But before he was able to say anything further, there was a sharp report from the direction of the fort that snapped every head in the launch around. From the nearmost bastion a white gout of smoke was spilling down over the sand below. In the next instant the air was filled with the familiar sound like ripping linen, and then with a ringing slap, a geyser from the fall of the shot jetted up a dozen yards ahead of the launch.

Rye spun on Carr as the spray from the shot pattered back over the launch. "Carr! Hard a-larboard! Handsomely, now! Mason and Hardwick, haul in the sheets! Gybe the fores'l as she comes in! We'll set 'em on the larboard tack!" He snapped round to Prince. "Get our colours up, Petty Officer Prince! Main truck halyard! Now!"

The small block was squealing within seconds as Prince frantically hauled up the red British Ensign to stream out brilliantly in the still-firm breeze.

The launch swung, and in the instant its bow dipped round, a second gun banged in an embrasure of the fort, and another round impacted into the lagoon with a hissing column of water barely a stone's throw ahead of the launch.

"Damn them! Can't they see the colours, the fools?" Rye raged. "Starboard your helm, Carr! Ten points! Tend those sheets, there!"

The launch fell off the wind, moving toward the middle of the lagoon. As it turned a third sharp report of a gun sounded from the fort. And this time, there was a sharp slap overhead, and the mainsail twitched and shook as a ragged hole the size of a man's head appeared in it just below the yard.

Rye swore as he saw the geyser sent up by the shot's fall hiss down. "Bastards! They *know* we're English! Christ, they must be Cathcart's bloody privateers, Prince! It's out of *here* that the sons of bitches do their—!"

A brilliant pink flash winked in the corner of his eye, and he turned to see a cloud of heavy white smoke puff out from an upper deck gunport of the huge Spanish vessel, looming in the middle of the lagoon. A split-second before the ear-numbing thud of a heavy ship's gun reached them, a huge finger of spray leaped into the air no more than twenty yards off the launch's side.

"The Don, sir!" bellowed a seaman from forward. "He's firin' on us!"

"God damn. That's enough of this!" Rye snarled. "Ready about!"

Prince was instantly all action. "Ready, zur!"

"Helm a-lee!" cried Rye. "Lively with those sheets, lads! We're getting out of this!"

With Carr performing prodigies at the helm, the forty-foot

bulk of the launch swung round in a great arc, as shot geysers, long hissing fingers of spray, leaped up in almost continuous succession all around. The thump of the guns in the small fort, which were firing at almost half-minute intervals, was dwarfed now by the pink flash and slam of the Spanish vessel's guns, which were sending great clouds of smoke rolling across the lagoon surface. Rye estimated there was a least half a gundeck battery banging away at them.

But now the launch was around, and the sails filled with a crump on the new tack as the stem came to face the inlet mouth through which they had passed only moments before.

"Now! Steady as she lies, Carr! But keep her drawing and full! Don't lose her way! Haul in sharp, there, fore and main sheets!" Rye ducked instinctively as a round shot slapped into the water barely ten feet away, the collapsing jet of water splattering like a cloudburst over the huddled men on the thwarts.

"Down, all hands!" barked Rye. "Sit on the floorboards!"

Rye squinted ahead, his heart thudding against his ribs. The launch was pointing well, wallowing along with its skirts up for the narrow sleeve of the inlet. It would not be long before they would be partially screened by the dune hills from fire from the fort. Rye hoped against hope that somehow he would be able to make it through the narrow sleeve of the opening in one or two boards. With luck he might, if the launch's lugsails would let him point up enough.

But God, the *swells* . . . !

"Down, zur!" roared Prince suddenly.

In unthinking response Rye flattened himself in the stern sheets. There was a deep, bumblebee hum in the air, a sharp cracking sound, and the fore and main masts of the launch shook with the force of an impact. Several gaping new rents appeared by magic in the faces of the close-hauled sails. As Rye stared, the shots hit ahead of the launch, skipping once, twice, before burying themselves with a tremendous splash.

And then, in the next half-instant, the launch's masts canted, and then toppled over the larboard side in a snarl of stays, halyards and crumpling canvas. The launch slewed, its progress through the water slowing almost in a jerk.

Rye was on his feet in an instant, barking orders. "Forward, there! Mason, and that lot with you! Clear away the fore mast! Axe it over the side! Sergeant Hewitt have your lads help clear away the main! Quickly, now! Prince?"

"Zur!"

"We'll ship oars, if you please. Have your lads get 'em into the crutches!"

Beside Rye, Carr was swearing. "Christ, what a hopper-arsed do—!"

"Silence in the boat!" called Rye. "Eyes aft! Out your oars!"

As two more terrific geysers shot up beside the boat, the long sweeps reached out, gripped by the seamen and marines jostling each other on the crowded thwarts. The axes were flashing amidships and forward, and then the snarled wreckage of the launch's masts were thrust over the side by many pairs of willing hands.

Rye looked up. The entrance of the channel was just ahead, and already the launch was beginning to pitch lightly in the first of the swells. He felt the wind building against his face, heard the surf roaring to either side of the inlet mouth, and looked beyond it to the dark rolling sea outside. There lay safety. But could they make it?

He swallowed. "Now, lads! Give way together!"

The long blades of the sweeps swept forward and dug in with a will. For the first few strokes they thrashed unevenly, until with Rye's voice hammering at them the marines and seamen achieved a kind of rhythm. The launch began to move forward again, toward the open sea, the pitching increasing as they neared the inlet mouth.

Rye looked wildly up at the dune hills sliding by, hoping against the sight of musketmen that might appear along their crest. The launch was in the narrow sleeve of the channel now, slipping quickly toward the open water. But here they were totally vulnerable, and if a company of musketmen rose from behind those hills they would die like fish shot in a barrel.

"Pull, you bully lads!" Rye chanted. "Ah, pull! It'll be Nancy Dawson when we're clear! *Pull*!"

The men grinned through their sweating effort at the promise of rum, and threw themselves with guttural grunts into the rowing. Around them now was the roar and drifting mist of the surf that flanked the inlet mouth. They were seconds away from the first of the great rollers. A gust of wind lifted Rye's hat and set it spinning into the lathered water astern.

In the next instant, the launch punched with a heavy *c-crunch* into the first toppling swell, and the spray rained back over the oarsmen, making them grimace and curse as they wrestled with the sweeps. They knew now, from Rye's voice and the tumult around them, that this was the moment when they had to clear the beach line, the boat-killing shallows, and get clear into open deeper water. They pulled now by standing up and then falling back to the wet, slippery thwarts, hauling the sweeps with every ounce of their body weight. With Rye roaring at them, they pulled for what seemed an eternity, until they suddenly noticed that the swells into which the launch was shouldering were not capped by breaking crowns so often, and that as they shook the sweat from their eyes they could see the island shore and the back of the killing surf receding over Rye's shoulders, now a good quarter-mile astern. They knew they had escaped a perilous moment, but their discipline held through the fatigue and the relief, and on they rowed, still listening to the rhythm of Rye's voice, waiting with aching arms and backs for the order to rest, seemingly never to come until —

"Way enough! Rest on your oars!" cried Rye. "Well done, lads. Well done. Mr. Prince?"

"Aye, zur?"

"Spell 'em off at the sweeps. Watch and watch. Ship enough sweeps only to keep two men on, two off, on each sweep. Lively, now. Having come this far we don't want to broach."

"Aye, aye, zur!" said Prince. He spat into the sea and stood up, counting off men with his fingers. "Heads up, lads! Must do this quickly! Harris, Fredericks, Van Damm, Jones. Stroke oar. Welch, Fitzroy, Clapper, Hughes. Second stroke. . . ."

Rye sat down, staring over his shoulder at the dune island. It was an oddly unnerving sight, for now there was no evidence at all of the fort, or the anchorage. It was completely hidden from seaward.

"Watch your helm, Carr," he said quietly. "She'll lose her momentum in the next swell or two. Scull with the damned rudder if you have to until they get their first stroke in."

Carr was sweating. "Tryin' to, sir. But —"

"Out oars!" Prince boomed. "Give way together!"

The sweeps dug in, and the launch rose and thumped down over a swell. Carr bared his teeth.

"Steerageway, sir!"

"Very good," said Rye, calmly. "Well done, Petty Officer Prince. Sergeant Hewitt? Crawl out from under those sweeps and see to the spirits. A tot to the offwatch lads, and see that the rowers get their tot directly they're relieved."

"'Sir!" boomed Hewitt, who was at one of the midship sweeps, and who had lost his mitre cap.

"I'll shift 'em about every fifty strokes, zur," said Prince. "Unless you —"

"Good. Just keep her way on, Mr. Prince. That is what I care about most. And see you get a proper tot yourself."

Prince's expression spoke of admiration. "I will, zur. Thankēe agin, zur."

But Rye was peering ahead to the horizon. Below the blazing sun, now well up into the sky, a band of golden light shone from the boiling sea, along which he looked to the distant shape, the suddenly achingly beautiful shape, of His Britannic Majesty's Ship *Saracen* running in. Rye squinted at her for a long moment, and then turned to peer back at the receding island, wreathed in the mist of the surf that beat against it.

"By God," he muttered. "We'll see what Sir Aubrey has to say about you, my fine Dutch lads. You and your bloody Spanish ally. And I hope his answer will be *Saracen's* broadside!"

Paul Gallant opened his eyes slowly. He was conscious at first of nothing but the hard, wet sand under his cheek and the stiff and awkward position his body seemed to be in. To his ears came the frighteningly loud and near roar-hiss of the surf, and he felt seawater rush up the sand round his legs to his waist, then sucking back again, drawing away the sand from around his toes.

He lifted his head, wincing at the pain in his neck. He was lying on a beach, in the dark, smooth sand where the water shot up in flat pans of wavelets at the end of the breakers' reach. The sun was burning into the middle of his back. Ahead of him, the dry sand of the upper beach rose into the grass-tufted dune hills he had been watching from the boat, stretching way to the right. To the left another high dune hill rose.

And no more than twenty feet from him in the wet sand was another slumped form that rolled over and spat feebly as another wave's last fingers of foam slathered over his legs and bumped a broken piece of planking against him.

"Béssac!" Gallant croaked. He got to his knees and then forced himself to stand, dizzy and lightheaded. His face and hands were caked with dried salt, and his lips were cracked and dry. He ran his hands through the stiff, matted strands of his hair and moved unsteadily over to drop beside the Mate. His tongue felt swollen, and he had a raging thirst.

"Béssac!" he said again, lifting the shaggy, salt-grimed head. "Come on, old fellow. I heard you groan. Are you with me?"

The Mate's eyes, red-rimmed and clouded, opened, and he peered up at Gallant in momentary confusion. "I — who in Hell are — capitaine! The boat!"

Gallant looked up at the roaring thunder of the green and white surf, at the dark fragments of wood that swirled in the water or

144

lay scattered along the beach. "Gone. Nothing but bits of it left. Can you stand?"

Béssac sat up. "Oh, Christ," he muttered. "I — haven't an unbruised spot anywhere. Jesus, my *back* —!"

Gallant gripped his arm. "What? Can't you —?"

Béssac shook his head. "Hell, capitaine, I'm not dead, hein? Just help me get up. . . ."

Gallant lifted the burly Mate bodily to his feet and held him until he saw a clearer look come into Béssac's eyes.

"You should see yourself," said Gallant, hoarsely. "You look like you've been burned alive."

Béssac managed a grin. "You're no winning sight yourself, capitaine. Are you —?"

"Hurt? No. But damned sore, I can tell you." He looked round, up the beach. "I can't see Aki or Brulé anywhere. You haven't seen them?"

Béssac grunted. "Last thing I remember," he said over the roar of the surf, "is going arse-over-sternsheets out of the boat and a lot of black water falling on me. Then you were shaking me."

Gallant looked at the huge rollers booming in. "Oh, Lord," he said, watching one break, "d'ye think they've been —?"

"Capitaine! Capitaine!"

Gallant swung round, almost losing his balance in the soft footing of the sand. From between two low dunes the dark figure of Akiwoya, his shirt and breeches hanging about him in tatters, was waving at them, and then running across the sand toward them.

"Aki!" breathed Gallant. "Thank Christ! But where's —?"

Akiwoya halted in front of them, blowing like a draught horse. One eye was almost puffed shut, and a livid welt showed on his forehead above it. He pointed back to the dunes.

"He's in there, in the grass, capitaine! Still unconscious. I came round no more'n a few minutes ago. Saw you there and figured I'd best get you off the beach. I carried Brulé in there and was coming back for you."

"Good man," said Gallant. "And you're right. If there are any eyes watching anywhere, we'd better get off this beach." His voice was stronger now. "Our boat. Is there anything left? Or are these bits of wreckage all there is?"

Akiwoya shook his head. He had opened his mouth to say something when he stopped, staring over Gallant's and Béssac's shoulders.

"Look, capitaine!" he gasped.

Gallant turned, his own eyes widening in surprise. Perhaps a thousand yards from them down the beach, toward the northeast end of the island, a boat had suddenly appeared, issuing from the channel at that end of the island. At any event that was where Gallant's mind assumed it had come from. It was a large craft, white-hulled, with a naval bulkiness to it. And it was pushing strongly out to sea, lifting and shouldering into the swells gamely, propelled by long sweeps worked by the men in uniform that crowded the craft. As Gallant stared, the sweep blades flashed in the sun, and distantly he could hear a strong voice calling the stroke. In English.

"Bloody astounding," Béssac was saying. "Damn me, isn't that the craft that was sailing after us?"

"No time now to talk about it," said Gallant. "Get to cover in those dunes, before we're seen! Come on!"

In a shambling run Gallant led the other two off toward the shelter of the dunes. Their sore limbs creaking and protesting, they ran, kicking the sand ahead of them, until they fell sweaty and puffing into the lee of the closest dune.

"Dear God," gasped Béssac. "I'm too old for this. Christ, I feel like I've been beaten with chains!"

Gallant managed a smile. "You just thank your stars you didn't break anything, you old walrus." He turned to Akiwoya. "Where's Brulé?"

"Just round there," said the African, lifting himself to his feet again. His muscled black torso was caked with salt and sand, and his swollen eye was now almost completely shut. "I'll go and see how he is."

As Akiwoya moved off, Gallant gripped Béssac on the shoulder. "Stay here, mon vieux. Catch your breath. I'm going to look at that boat again. From up there." He jerked his thumb toward the top of the dune.

With a huge effort Béssac rolled his burly form to his feet and grinned crookedly at Gallant. "Hell, capitaine, I'm not dead. Although Christ knows I feel like it. We'll go together."

Gallant grinned at him. "Bon. Come on."

Digging hands and toes into the sliding, treacherous sand, Gallant clawed his way up the steep slope of the dune, until he gained the crest. It was covered with clusters of long, knee-high grass through which the wind was whistling. Gallant lay hidden in it, and from where he lay he could see the beach and the surf below him, and the shore stretching away northeastward. And he could see out to sea, where, a good quarter-mile off now, the boat was lifting and plunging over the swells, her sweep blades still lifting and falling with admirable precision.

Béssac thumped down beside him, wheezing, and Gallant pointed out to sea.

"That's where he's going," he said. "Home to Mother."

Béssac squinted against the glitter of the sea. "By the Magdalene. A ship!"

"And I'd wager you a plug of that foul Minas Basin tabac you cherish so much that she's the Britisher who stopped us yesterday!"

Béssac stared at him. "You think? Then that boat's one of hers — maybe the one that was after us, like you said."

Gallant nodded, rubbing his stiff and aching neck. "I'd bet on it."

Béssac squinted at the boat, biting his lip in thought. "You're right. Hell, they're pulling like a naval crew. But they were under sail coming in, weren't they?"

Gallant nodded. "I think we lay on that beach longer than we think, Béssac. I feel like I lay there for days, for that matter. Anything could have happened. They might have —"

There was a scuffle of sand behind them, and Akiwoya thumped down, his face grim. He looked at Gallant wordlessly for a moment, then looked down.

"Brulé?" said Gallant quietly.

"It — it must have been his neck. He — never woke up."

Gallant was silent for a long moment. The three men shared a look that said what they could not with their voices. It was another death; another death to accept as best each could, and then get on with things.

"The — boat, capitaine?" said Akiwoya presently. "Is it the one we were being followed by?"

"I think so."

"There was something going on when I came to on the beach, m'sieu'. Before I — pulled Brulé up or came looking for you."

"Which was?" said Gallant.

"Guns. Naval guns. About fifteen or twenty rounds. At least twelve-pounders by the crack, if my gunner's ear can tell me anything."

Gallant sat up. "Where?"

"Inland, m'sieu'. Over these dunes. No more'n a long gun shot, I'd say. I thought it was the bloody surf, at first."

Gallant's mind ticked over. He swung to look at the British launch, now well out to sea. "By God. Perhaps *that's* why they're not under sail!"

"Eh?" said Béssac.

"You think maybe —?" began Akiwoya.

"I think perhaps our pursuer came inshore here to see what

147

happened to us. And when he couldn't find us, he went on into the sound, or lagoon."

Béssac's eyebrows rose. "And met Miller's old messmates?"

"What? The Dutch?" said Akiwoya.

Gallant's eyes were alight. "I'd wager you a few sous that he did. Or stirred up Castelar, who might not have received English guests too well!"

Béssac scratched his stubble. "Wonderful news. The bloody privateers and the Spaniard maybe just over the hill, and all we've got is the string holding up our breeches. God, I could use a drink!"

Akiwoya lifted his head as if he had remembered something. "We've got a little luck with us, Théo. I found one thing from the boat."

"What?" Gallant looked keenly at him.

"Or maybe I should say that it found me. As I went in when the boat turned turtle, something hit me in the chest and I grabbed for it. Woke up on the beach still holding it."

"What was it, for God's sake!" rasped Béssac.

Akiwoya grinned. "The smaller water butt. Had just enough air in it not to sink. There's at least a half-full supply of water in it."

"That's something, at least," said Gallant.

The marine looked back out at the dwindling shape of the launch and the distant form of the British warship. He had a disturbing feeling that, in an onrushing way, time was of the real essence. If the British had run into some trouble in the lagoon, one could be certain their bulldog aggressiveness would bring them back. And if over those dunes lay the Dutch, then there also might be Castelar.

And Marianne de Poitrincourt, Marquise de Bézy.

"Come on, lads. Let's get some of that water. And then we'll try to decide just what in Hell three unarmed ragged castaways are going to do next!" His face sobered. "But first, we do something for poor Brulé," he said quietly.

Béssac scratched his cheek. "I wonder if he ever thought a Godforsaken islet like this would be his last—" He did not finish.

An hour later Gallant, Béssac and Akiwoya stood looking down at the low mound they had heaped up with their hands in the lee of a dune. They looked mutely at each other, aware they had done all they could.

"All right," said Gallant. "Let's be off."

With Gallant leading, the three men began trudging up the face of the line of dune hills that hid whatever lay inland on the island. The dunes were high and steep, almost fifty feet above the beach, and it was evident that only the long grasses and the tangled masses of old palmetto root here and there had kept the sea wind from blowing away the line of sand hills. A few gulls circled above them, their plaintive cries sounding over the omniscient boom of the surf. It took fifteen minutes of plodding up through hot sand that sucked at their feet and filled in round their ankles until they approached the crest of the dunes. Béssac, momentarily in the lead, was the first to reach the top. As he did so he froze in his tracks, and then with a muffled exclamation of surprise sank to a squat, gaping inland.

"What is it, mon vieux?" said Gallant, puffing up next. It had been his turn to carry the unwieldy water butt, and he was sweating from the effort. Then as he came up to the crest line, standing knee-deep in the waving grass, he too stopped and crouched.

"Mother of God!" he muttered.

"Something to see, I gather?" breathed Akiwoya, while he struggled up. Then he was on the crest and dropping into a crouch as well. "Jesus," he said simply.

From where the three men crouched in the grass atop the line of the great dune hills, an unexpected panorama stretched out before them in the late burning sun. Immediately before them, the dune hills dwindled into a stretch of low, swampy land of tall reeds and grass, clumps of palmetto and pine and open stretches of marshy water. Along to the right, or northeast, the dune hills stretched to the channel that led in to the lagoon from the open sea; the channel that, Gallant surmised, the English boat had entered. The island, however, was shaped like a thin triangle, with an apex jutting out into the lagoon that had high ground, sandy and grass-covered like the dunes atop which Gallant and his companions now were. But instead of simply dune grass, the crest of the high ground was taken up by a sturdy log fortification: a square, ramparted structure with bastions at each of the four corners, out of whose embrasures the black snouts of guns could be seen protruding; there appeared to be an inner yard with the roof of one and possibly more buildings showing, and a slim flagpole rising from within the yard, with the striped Dutch ensign floating lazily out in the breeze. From the high double gates of the fort, a dusty track wound down through the sand to a low cove which was obviously a boat landing place. To one side of the track, a squat wellhouse sat.

But it was to the calm breeze-ruffled waters of the lagoon that Gallant's eyes were drawn.

"Look there, Béssac!" he burst out. "Damn me, I *knew* I was right!"

149

Riding at anchor were the smaller shapes of two Dutch warships, the sloops that had struck the convoy. And, further into the roads, there rode the hulking red and gilt mass of the *Lima*, vessel of Don Alfonso Castelar.

Béssac gaped. "The *Lima*! Jesus, m'sieu'. She's *there*! But the *Java's* not. I wonder where—?"

Gallant nodded slowly. So Castelar was what he had seemed to be. Was he there in the *Lima*, gloating over his share of the dowry money?

Or was he gloating over the face and body of Marianne de Poitrincourt?

Gallant felt a strange red haze form at the sides of his vision. His lips became a tight line as he stared at the *Lima*.

Béssac was speaking quietly. "There must be something we can do, hein, capitaine? Christ, if that Spanish bastard's got her all to himself—"

Akiwoya cut in. "M'sieu'? What's that? Over to the left."

Gallant followed the African's pointing finger.

Béssac grunted. "Looks like that log pile we could see coming in, capitaine. On the endmost dune hill."

On the last of the great dune hills along to their left, overlooking the broad southwest channel leading into the lagoon, the low and boxy-looking mass of dark timbers was visible. From this point of view it seemed in disarray, as if the remains of a tumbledown building.

"Come on," said Gallant, suddenly. "We need a place to wiggle into until we have a plan. That might be it."

Keeping carefully on the seaward slope of the dune hills, the three men slogged through the sand toward the distant structure, until some fifteen minutes later they were crouched behind one wall of the structure, looking down at the beach and the channel it overlooked.

"A gun position, hein?" said Gallant. "To control the channel."

Béssac slapped the old logs. "Not too substantial any more, I'd say." Then he paused. "Christ. You don't suppose there's anyone *in* the damn thing, do you?" he whispered.

"One way to find out," murmured Gallant. "Leave the water, Aki. We'll come back for it."

Carefully picking his finger and toe holds, Gallant pulled himself up the low wall of horizontal logs and peered over the top. To the left, snouting out through a crude embrasure that overlooked the channel, a large gun, by its look possibly an eighteen-pounder, lay buried up to its trunnions in sand. A few broken casks, odds and ends of weathered lumber, and a tumble-down pile of rusting round shot completed the contents of the little redoubt.

"Hmph," said Béssac, peering over the wall. "They must be pretty sure of themselves to let this place get to this state." He levered a leg over and dropped inside to stand beside Gallant.

"Yes," said the marine. "Unless it was here *before* them. And they've left it untouched so as not to raise suspicions from passing eyes out to sea there." He walked round the gun, brushing sand off the top.

"Look at that cypher. English, Charles the Second."

Akiwoya was giving the gun a professional look. "This piece hasn't been fired in years, m'sieu'. Rust and scale in the bore and vent. Carriage wood's rotten."

Gallant nodded. "Good. That means we're likely safe enough here for the moment. Aki, you'd better get that water butt in. We'll bury it in the sand to keep it cool. Christ knows how long it's got to last." He looked round. "What's that over there? Some kind of sally-port?"

Grinning, Akiwoya vanished through a small opening low in one wall and soon reappeared, thrusting the small cask ahead of him before he clambered through.

"Good way out there, m'sieu'. Fetches you right out behind the dune away from the seaward face or the channel."

"Might prove handy. But get the water buried. Béssac? Have a look round for anything we could use to dig with, would you?"

Béssac grunted. "Hope I find something to eat. I could use a little bit of that Governor's feast in Martinique about now."

Gallant leaned on the redoubt wall, studying the distant fort and the anchorage. Below the line of the dune hills which led down the island's seaward face from the redoubt, there was the marshy land they had seen before. Two smaller dune hillocks projected out of the marshy land on the lagoon side, however; they might make it possible for men on foot to approach the boat landing area more easily.

His eyes narrowed as he watched the anchorage. Something must have happened, indeed; the waters between the ships and the shore were being plied by several ship's boats, and there was some kind of activity going on in the fortification. But, he reassured himself, there was nothing that looked like preparations for putting to sea.

At least, not yet.

His eyes sought out the looming shape of *Lima*, brilliantly lit now by the overhanging sun.

Be there, Marianne, he heard his mind say. Be there, and be ready when I come for you. . . .

"Capitaine! Look!"

Gallant turned to see a grinning Béssac unearth a crate from the sand in one corner of the redoubt. The Mate brushed the top clear of sand, and Akiwoya had appeared in the next minute with a heavy piece of palmetto. With one powerful stroke the African cracked the boards on the crate's top.

Béssac reached fingers in through the split, and his eyes widened in pleasure. "Well, I'm damned!" he said.

Prying off several more planks, he reached in again, to draw out a huge, grease-covered cutlass, an awkward weapon of ancient design with a broad, straight blade and a basketwork hilt.

"Cutlasses!" cried Akiwoya, dropping the palmetto. In the next instant he had pulled two more from the crate, and tossed one to Gallant.

Gallant caught the weapon expertly, feeling its heaviness. With a strip of cloth from his tattered shirt he wiped as much of the grease from the cutlass as possible, and then swung it experimentally round his head. The broad blade hummed through the air.

"Christ, what a weapon!" murmured Gallant. "Damned near twice as heavy as my old hanger!"

Béssac was whacking away at an imaginary enemy with a wild, boyish grin on his grizzled features. "Hah! Here's luck for you, capitaine! Eh? Bring on the bloody Dutchies!"

Gallant grinned, and got a wink from Akiwoya, who was hefting his own weapon with a pleased look on his face. Wrapping both his hands round the grip of the weapon, Gallant let the blade rest against his shoulder, and turned to gaze back at the fort and the anchored ships. His eyes sought out *Lima*, and narrowed as he stared at her.

Please God, you'll be in her, Marianne, he thought. Not in the *Java*, and gone forever from me. Please God, you'll be there!

Jacob Ten Haaf stood behind the small table which, along with a single chair, was the only furniture in the main room of one of the principal buildings within the fort overlooking the lagoon. He was flanked by two menacing individuals in outlandish clothing who were cradling heavy naval cutlasses against their chests. Outside, voices were calling out over the tumult of gear being moved about, the rumble of gun trucks on rampart carriages and a general excited hubbub. But of all this Ten Haaf seemed momentarily oblivious. He was trembling with rage, his pale blue eyes hard pinpricks of steel, and his voice was thick as he roared at the hatless figure of Félix LeBeau who stood before the table. It was dark in the room, and the light from the one small window in the rear wall glistened in the sweat forming on LeBeau's forehead.

"Yew! Ye dimwitted, one-eyed stinkin' privy rat!" snarled the Dutchman. "Why did ye do it? What in the name o' black Hell got into yer head to pass an order for the guns o' this fort t' fire on that boat? Eh? Answer me, or by Christ, I'll—!"

LeBeau fidgeted miserably with the edge of his hat. "I am zorry," he quailed, in heavily accented English. "I t'ought, wid you gone to de ships, dat you would 'ave given de order to shoot—"

"Shoot? You silly buggerin' Frog, don't yew know we's meant t' be *allies* o' the friggin' English? Ay?"

"Oui, but—," began the miserable LeBeau.

"But, Hell! Christ save me! I should've known any damned toady of that damned Spaniard'd do fer us! Ye bloody sapskull, sure's Hell there's a man-o'-war out there, waitin' fer that boat t' pull back! And what a tidy tale *that* Jack Ketch'll have fer his capting, ay? About a bloody Spanish man-o'-war *and* a Dutch fort that fired on an English boat, even *with* 'er colours showin'!" Ten Haaf drew a heavy Sea Service pistol from his belt, and hooked his thumb over the cock. From his murderous expression he was seconds away from putting a ball into the trembling LeBeau.

The latter saw the look in Ten Haaf's eyes and fell on his knees, arms wide. "Please m'sieu'! Don't zhoot me! Before Christ, I meant not'ing but good, hein? Please—!"

Ten Haaf turned to one of his companions. "Take the bastard out an' cut his black throat!" he said viciously.

"No! Wait!" LeBeau shrank back against the wall as the two privateers came round the table toward him. "I can get you somet'ing! Somet'ing you want! Wait!"

"Enh?" said Ten Haaf, pausing at the doorway.

"The woman! The Marquise de Bézy! I—I can get her for you! God's Trut', I swear!"

Ten Haaf turned back in, and the two men who had been closing in on LeBeau stopped, looking at him.

"What of that bitch?" snorted the Dutchman. "Precious bloody good it'd do t' think of rogerin' women when our backsides are about t' be blown off by the damned British, sure's I'm a dog in a doublet!"

LeBeau was streaming with sweat. He stayed on his knees, one eye bright and shining in the gloom. "I wasn't t'inking of dere bodies, m'sieu'! Dey are in *Lima* now, hein?"

"Aye. And that bastard Castelar keeps 'em below decks under lock n' key. Come, y' damnable — !"

LeBeau spread his hands, baring his teeth in a fierce grin. "I only propose *business* for us, m'sieu'! For a common profit!'

Ten Haaf's eyes narrowed. He moved slowly back to the desk, toying with the pistol, weaving it about with slow deliberation until it finally came to rest centred on LeBeau's chest.

"Profit?" he said, pursing his lips. "Yew'd best explain."

LeBeau licked his lips. "The — the women are in *Lima*, and under guard, true enough, m'sieu'. But I know how to get at dem."

"Enh?"

"And get dem out of de ship, m'sieu'. Wid no one knowing!"

"Christ's guts!" Ten Haaf rose from the chair, his pale eyes aflame. "Yew can do that?"

LeBeau nodded. "Bien oui. If — if I had a small boat, an' some 'elp from a few of your men, I could get dem out of *Lima* —"

"Why? What for?" said Ten Haaf suddenly.

"De Hinglish will come in, hein? An' de firs' target dey will 'ave will be *Lima*."

"Mayhap. Or not," said Ten Haaf.

"But unless 'e can fight 'is way out of 'ere, Don Alfonso will 'ave to surrender to de rosbifs, An' *dey* will take de women from 'im!"

"Go on," said Ten Haaf. The pistol had not moved.

LeBeau wiped his streaming forehead with a large lace handkerchief. "So if you, m'sieu', got your 'ands on de women — an' maybe had one of de sloops 'ere ready to make quick sail an' escape, instead of fighting it out —"

"While our bastard Castelar trades broadsides with the poxy English — !" interjected Ten Haaf.

" — You might escape to sea! Wid de women. And *dat* would mean *you* could hold dem for payment from de French King, enh? Not Castelar! And 'is Majesty King Louis will pay *anyt'ing* to get de Marquise back!"

Ten Haaf's eyes narrowed. "Get her back? He can wait till Hell freezes fer that!"

"B — but de money — !"

"Oh, aye! We'll get the money for the bitch, all right. Yew may lay t' that!" Ten Haaf stood up abruptly from his seat on the edge of the table and began pacing the room, tapping his cheek with the pistol barrel in thought. "All right. Yew'll *do* yer picklockin', an' we'll get the bitch here ashore. *An'* take one o' the sloops, an' let Castelar rot on a British gibbet!"

Then he turned, and the expression on his face was cold.

"And what is it *yew* want fer this, ay?"

LeBeau swallowed. "T'ree — t'ree t'ousand Louis. In gold. From de woman's dowry. An' a small boat."

"Three thou — !" Ten Haaf roared. "Christ, who d'ye think ye are, demandin' Judas gold!"

"Pl — please don' call it dat."

"The likes o' that!" The Dutchman paused. And then a mirthless smile crossed his face.

"All right, then, yew can have yer gold. An' yer boat."

"Thank you, m'sieu'! You won't regret — !" grovelled LeBeau.

Ten Haaf was around the table and had seized LeBeau's coat in a vicelike grip, shutting off his throat with a dry rattle.

"But yew mark this, y' one-eyed weasel!" he growled in a tone that made LeBeau's skin scrawl. "Yew give *any* orders t' my lads whilst I ain't abouts, and I'll cut yer guts out! Clear?"

LeBeau nodded. "Please . . . you're choking . . . !" His face twisted in a rictus of fear and pain.

"Ay," grinned Ten Haaf, savouring LeBeau's agony. "Yew'll do yer job, an' get the women t'me, fair an' seamanlike, ay? Yew do that, an' yew'll have yer gold an' yer boat. But yew cross Jacob Ten Haaf, an' I'll *carve* yew. Just enough so's it'll take ye *days* t' die. Ye gather, y' black Froggy bastard? *Days!*"

LeBeau nodded, frantic. His hands clawed at Ten Haaf's sleeves, and his knees began to buckle.

And then in the next instant Ten Haaf had thrown him like a rag doll into a corner, where he lay, slumped and wheezing, near unconsciousness.

"That's fine, jus' fine," said Ten Haaf. He moved toward the door, slipping the pistol into his belt. "Now yew plan t' get the wench, an' yew plan it for today. An' yew'll come and tell old Jacob everythin' yew'll do, ay? An' quick like?"

In the corner LeBeau struggled to speak. "O — oui, m'sieu'. I — hear. . . . " he croaked.

And as he looked at the face of Jacob Ten Haaf, distorted with a leer that was an equal mixture of lust and sadistic cruelty, he felt a bitter taste rising in the back of his throat.

"I hear," he whispered.

"Deck, there!" The foretop lookout in His Britannic Majesty's ship *Saracen* was calling down at the top of his lungs over the roar of wind and sea.

Below on the quarterdeck Jeremy Poynting finished penning a final note in his rough log and sent the midshipman carrying it scampering away. He pushed his hat to the back of his head and looked up.

"Deck, aye?"

"Boat, sir! On the starboard bow! Pullin' out from shore! Looks like the launch, sir!"

"Very good." Poynting looked round the quarterdeck with an odd feeling of regret. With Rye gone he had been, in effect, *Saracen*'s First Lieutenant. And it had all gone well, he told himself. A night watch, and a day one, with nary a problem in either. There was very little to it all, really; just a little common sense, good luck, and —

"*Mister Poynting*!" Cathcart's voice rang like a cathedral bell from the top of the after companionway.

"S — sir?" said Poynting. He had started, rabbitlike, at the sound of the captain's bellow.

"Come here, if you please, Mr. Poynting," said Cathcart, with menacing smoothness.

Poynting touched his hat nervously as he halted before Cathcart. "Yessir?"

Cathcart pursed his lips and studied the foretops'l leech. "Mr. Poynting, the foretop lookout has just made a most significant sighting, which, doing his duty, he has called down to you. It is, oddly enough, a bit of information I have been most anxious to obtain."

Poynting's brief moment of cocky self-confidence began to collapse, as he sensed what was coming.

"Yes, sir. I know. I'm — I'm sorry, sir."

"But I stood at the top of the companionway there, waiting, hopeful — dare I say expectant? — that you would send word for me. Instead I seemed to have surprised you in some form of meditative trance. Or were you reciting classics mentally? Reviewing Euclid? Composing sonnets, perhaps?"

"No, sir."

"Ah. Dreaming deeds of naval glory, what?"

"I — no, sir."

"At any rate, you weren't in the process of sending for me." Poynting's shoulders sagged. "No, sir."

Cathcart tapped a toe. "Indeed. Well, Mr. Poynting, I hope that in future you *will* come to me. When even so much as a bloody chamber pot floats into view. Do I make myself *perfectly* clear?"

"Aye, aye, sir," said the miserable Poynting.

"Very well. Now will you kindly bring *Saracen* into the wind? I really do not wish to run down our own launch."

"'Sir,'" said Poynting, whose face was now the colour of a marine's jacket. He lifted his hat and skittered away, shrieking for Winton, the Master.

Twenty-five minutes later, *Saracen* lay hove-to against the easterly wind, lifting and falling gently. The canvas was clewed up, all but the foretopsail, which lay aback on the mast. The ship waited patiently for the pitching launch and her straining oarsmen to come up.

In the launch, Rye was prodding on the exhausted men.

"No mor'n a few minutes now, lads! Alongside in a clock's tick, we are! There's her lee now! Stroke, buckos! And again! Stroke! Stroke!"

Grunting with effort, the marines and seamen at the sweeps hauled and recovered, hauled and recovered, now almost in a daze of exhaustion. The launch lifted and plunged ahead with painful slowness, and Rye's throat, taut with hoarseness, tightened with an odd sense of emotion as he drew the craft nearer to *Saracen's* welcoming bulk. Only a few strokes more . . .

Then the warship's tarry side was towering like an oaken wall above them, and they were sheltered from the wind and the full force of the swells, moving in now under the shadow of the ship's masts and sails that blotted out the sun, and Rye was making his dry, sunburnt lips move in the needed orders.

"Way enough! Rest on 'em, lads! Now, boat your oars! Roundly, now! We're going alongside!"

There was a good deal of thumping and banging in the launch as the heavy sweeps, dripping wet and awkward, were muscled inboard and dropped on the thwarts. Here and there men cursed as knuckles were skinned and elbows struck.

"Lively with our painter, bows!" Prince was bellowing now. And from overhead orders were ringing down, Cathcart's voice predominant. Lines snaked down, and fresh hands monkeyed down them to pass the lines that the launch's exhausted crew could barely grasp.

"Hold her at the forechains, there!" Cathcart was calling. "Mr. Rye! Please join me on deck here!"

Rye looked up at the heaving line of wooden battens on *Saracen's* side, rolling up and down three or four feet as he watched. "Aye, aye, sir," he said, barely in a whisper.

With a last reservoir of energy he leaped for the battens and clung to them for a moment until he gathered himself and made the long, toes-and-fingers climb to the rail. Willing hands reached down and helped him over, in a sort of controlled fall, until he was staring about him at the enormous expanse of the ship's deck.

And into the perceptive gaze of Sir Aubrey Cathcart.

"Sir," said Rye, and then remembered he had no hat to touch.

"Good God, Rye. You look as if you've been staring into a farrier's forge. Are you all right?"

"Ah — yes, sir. But my lads are exhausted. It was a hell of a row."

Cathcart nodded. "Quite. Very well. We'll get 'em below, give 'em a night in. Mr. Poynting?" he suddenly bellowed.

"Sir!" yelped Poynting from the foredeck ladder.

"Get that launch swayed aboard directly. I want to be underway as soon as possible! And call me when it's done!"

He turned back to Rye. "Come with me."

Below in the cool shadow of his great cabin, Cathcart motioned Rye into an armchair before a desk on which was spread out a chart of the Carolinas. As Rye sank with a sigh into the chair, Cathcart tossed his hat onto the broad leather settee under the stern lights and opened a small spirit locker hung on one bulkhead. He filled two glasses from a decanter and handed one to Rye.

"A good French brandy. Warm you to your toes. Cheers." He sat down heavily in another chair behind the desk and sipped at his own brandy, eyeing Rye over the glass.

Rye closed his eyes as the brandy burned its way down into his innards. It seemed to cut like a knife through all the fatigue and tension, and he felt little tight knots of muscle relax across his shoulders.

"God. That *is* good. Thank you, sir."

Cathcart waved a hand. "Must use the damned stuff up somehow, what?" He paused for a moment. "Perhaps you'd best give me your report. What in God's name has happened to the launch, to begin with?"

Rye hiccuped. "Sticks — shot out of her, sir. Damned lucky I didn't lose some of the lads. Or get bloody well sunk."

"What? *Shot* out? By whom?" Cathcart sat up.

Rye sipped at the brandy, savouring its soothing heat. Overhead there was much barking of orders and squealing of blocks as the launch was swayed inboard on the mainyard.

"I'll swear it's your Dutchman, sir. The privateer? I think we've found his home port, all right." He coughed. "I was hot after that Portugee — or whatever — all night. The sea was fierce just after dawn. He was a half-league ahead of me, running

158

straight in for that island—there," he said, pointing a finger of his free hand at the chart.

Cathcart followed the finger with his eyes. "Between Bulls Island and Capers Island. Hasn't a name."

Rye snorted. "But it's bloody well got tenants, I can tell you."

"Go on."

"The Portugee must have broached and sunk. God knows what actually happened, but the bastard simply disappeared, while he was still well off the island. There are channels, both ends, and I chose to pass into the sound, or lagoon, by the north one. Damned near thing, what with the surf and all. The lads did well. Prince deserves his name."

"You're spilling your brandy. No, don't worry about it, for God's sake. Go on."

Rye ran his fingers through his hair. "We got into the lagoon and I damned near went over the side with surprise. There's a bloody *fort* overlooking the lagoon — right about here — and two Dutch ships, sloops I'd think, anchored just off the fort. There was a Dutch ensign flying over the place."

Cathcart's expression was intent. "Indeed."

"There was something else. A big sixty-four, or thereabouts. Spanish. *And* still flying her colours."

Cathcart stood up. "A Spanish sixty-four? Anchored *with* the Dutch?"

"Yes, sir. And the bastard opened up with half his gun deck battery at us."

"Predictable, at least," said Cathcart, calmly.

Rye's expression darkened. "But so did the bloody Dutch in the fort, sir! Even *after* I showed our colours!" He drained the last of the brandy. "I came about and tacked like a madman for the inlet mouth. Almost made it through when they got the damned masts. Had to pull for it. Bloody tedious, I can tell you." He stared at the empty glass.

"I'll get you more of that in a minute. So the Dutch *and* the Spaniard fired on you?"

"Yes. Colours visible notwithstanding."

"Indicating either the fort was in the possession of the Spanish, and had left the Dutch ensign up; or the *Dutch* were in command, and weren't interested in our snooping about?"

Rye nodded. "I'd agree with that, sir. Or else some Spanish bastard's in league with the Dutch."

"Mmm. Hardly likely. Still —" Cathcart moved to the spirit locker. "Did you notice anything else?"

"Between ducking the damned shot? Good anchorage. Land-

159

ing beach below the fort. Swampy terrain inland, from what I could see. No settlement on the mainland side of the lagoon. Looks like a fever-ridden mass of palmetto, or whatever. It's all quite the hideyhole, as the hands would say.''

Cathcart refilled Rye's glass and his own, and then set the decanter down on the chart. The light from the great stern windows shone through the decanter, casting a blood-and-orange circle of light on the line of the Carolina coast, and the island on which Cathcart now had his finger pressed.

"It's a serious business, firing on a boat from one of His Majesty's ships of war. That alone justifies some action," said Cathcart carefully. "But I have a deuced odd feeling, Mr. Rye, that you may have found the quarry we were seeking."

He straightened, a flicker of new purpose glinting in his eyes. "We'll go in there, by God. We'll go in, by this southern channel, if the wind permits. And a leadsman lashed into the chains. God grant it's bloody deep enough. We'll go in as soon as it's practical, Mr. Rye. Time is of the essence, now that they — whoever they are — know we are here!"

"Once in there, sir?"

Cathcart smiled thinly. "Why, we'll sink their bloody ships. Or make prizes of 'em. And that includes the sixty-four."

Rye paused with the glass at his lips. "And the fort, sir?"

"No half-measures, Mr. Rye. Only get one chance, likely enough. Pound it to rubble with our guns, then put the marines ashore." Cathcart paused with his own glass at his lips. "Do you agree, Mr. Rye?"

"No half-measures, sir," said Rye. And he drained the brandy in one fierce, burning swallow.

SEVEN

Don Alfonso Castelar slammed a lace-framed fist down on the broad table in *Lima's* great cabin, a murderous glint in his eyes. He stared with barely concealed fury into the recoiling faces of the Spaniards who stood, hats in hand, at the far side of the table.

"God damn your leprous disloyal black hearts!" he snarled. "You'll do as I say, or by the Virgin, I'll have ye all at a yardarm! D'ye hear?"

One seaman shuffled his feet. "*Si, señor*. But— "

"No excuses!" roared Castelar, sending the seamen back another pace. "Look, you dim-witted cretins! There is damned certainly a British warship backing and filling out there, champing at the bit to get in here at us! You'll *obey*, now, if you value your flea-bitten skins, or you can stand hat in hand and grovel in front of an *ingles* landing party! Or die under their guns!"

One man cleared his throat nervously, his fingers knotting in the soiled red ribbon on his hat. "Wh— what is it you want us to do, *señor*?"

Castelar leaned on the table, pressing his big fists into its surface.

"*You*," he said, his eyes arrowing into one man, "will take two men with good eyesight and get to the highest line of dunes facing seaward. The whoreson Dutch have no lookouts out there, the fools, and you'll carry my word to that bastard Ten Haaf that, by Christ's guts, he'd better get lookouts up there with you. *And* stand to his bloody guns, if he wants to save his fort—and his filthy Dutch neck!"

"And—then, *señor*?"

"You're likely to see a British vessel. A warship. I want to know *where* he is. How far off. Standing in or waiting. I want to know how big the bastard is. Guns, rate, the lot. And if he's got boats in the water. And when you see him—and I'll have your guts cut out if you don't remember what I have to know—you'll get back to me as fast as your scrawny legs can carry you!"

"*Si, señor!*" the man nodded, wide-eyed.

"Now get clear of my cabin!" roared Castelar.

The man ducked away out the door, and Castelar swung on the other men.

"Garcia. Sanchez. I want *Lima* ready for sea. I don't give a damn if you man her with ten men and a dog! She's to be ready for gun action. And I want her for the next ebb of the tide!"

The two men glanced at each other, their faces paling. The one named Garcia spread his hands. "*Madre mia!* That's—that's too soon, *señor!*" Garcia saw the naked menace in Castelar's eyes. "It . . . it'll mean leaving some of the stores, *señor*. I've only a third of the water butts we need, and with only ten experienced hands in each watch I still haven't finished the work aloft. *Madre, señor*, it's taken me two days to reeve new foretop and t'gallant braces, and I've got barely enough hands for that, let alone securing the gun batteries for sea! Why, I—"

Castelar abruptly drew his long, heavy hanger and threw it with a metallic ring on the table.

"Garcia. I've never taken you for a dog-brained fool. When I say that you will have *Lima* ready for sea for the next tide, then that is what you will do, enh?"

Garcia's fear of Castelar was plainly visible as he repeated nervously: "It—it'll mean leaving some of the stores, but . . ."

"By all means," said Castelar. He was toying with the grip of the hanger, watching the fear in Garcia's face. "Do what you need to. But you'll have *Lima* ready to ride out on that ebb, the wind willing, or I'll gut you where you stand! Clear, Garcia?"

162

Garcia's eyes were white. "S — si, señor. She will be! I swear on my mother's grave!"

"Then get out!'

The two men lowered their heads and moved out of the door quickly. But as they pushed through the opening, Castelar saw a figure in green standing in the passageway.

"LeBeau!" barked the Spaniard. "Where in Christ have you been!"

LeBeau stepped into the cabin, pausing by the door. His one eye glistened in the gloom. "Ashore, m'sieu'. With the Dutchman, Ten Haaf. He — he was organizing the defences of the fort. Says he'd try and sail out of here, but he thinks the British will be in on us with the next flood, that boat getting away as it did."

Castelar put down the hanger and stumped over to a bulkhead rack that held a wine bottle and several glasses. He pried a decanter of brandy from a hidden pocket behind the wine bottle, pulled the cork with his teeth, and took a long, gulping draught. He coughed, spitting into a corner of the cabin, and wiped his mouth on one great cuff.

"The fool! Firing at that damned boat! By the Virgin, they likely could've had the English row into land! Taken 'em without turning a hair!"

"He's frightened, m'sieu'. Says he feels it in his bones that there's a line-of-battle Englishman waiting out there. He's posting lookouts to seaward—"

"Which any fool should have done from the start!"

"But he's done something else, m'sieu'. Something I thought you should know about. It worries me," said LeBeau, approaching the table. He had taken off his hat, and his forehead was dotted with beads of sweat.

"Enh?"

"Colours, m'sieu'. *English* colours. He's had 'em dug out and hidden near his flagstaff. Didn't think I'd seen it."

"What?" Castelar's eyes narrowed. "But what—?" A strange curl appeared at the edges of his mouth. "The pig-faced bastard! He means to *betray* me! Go over to the English!"

"M'sieu'?" LeBeau's face was a study in obedient concern.

"By Christ, the bastard's going to raise English colours if the British attack us in here! He'll save his own skin—!"

"And turn on *us*, m'sieu'?" said LeBeau, with a shocked expression.

Castelar snorted. "I'd not put it past the swine! Christ's guts, if I had my hands around his neck . . . !"

163

LeBeau pulled at his neckcloth. Overhead, he could hear feet pounding about *Lima's* decks, and shouted orders were ringing down the companionway.

"What is it you plan to do, m'sieu'?" he said, his voice somewhat hoarse.

Castelar hefted the hanger once more and then sheathed it with a quick, violent motion. He strode to the stern lights, the skirts of his great red coat swinging, his boots ringing on the canvas-covered cabin planking. He stared ashore at the little fort, hands on hips, rocking a little on his toes.

"Sailing, by God! I'll outwit that Dutch squarehead *and* the whoreson English both! I've got the woman and that wench of hers locked in my sleeping cabin," he said, his fingers touching at a waistcoat pocket. "I've got the bloody dowry still aboard and all still mine! And on the next ebb, by God, I'll take *Lima* out of here and show my arse to 'em all! Ten Haaf can rot on a bloody English gibbet, for all I care!"

"Can you ready *Lima* in time, m'sieu'?" said LeBeau, approaching quietly. "I had thought—"

"Yes! With this wind, we'll have the anchor catted up inside two hours and be beating out through that north channel! And I'll take that wide-eyed French bitch somewhere the King'll pay his guts to get her back from! Madre, they'll not hear the last of me—!"

With a sharp, splintering crash, LeBeau brought the chair he had been holding over his head down with all his strength on Castelar's tall frame, grunting with the effort. Castelar wavered, turned slightly to one side, and then sat down in an ungainly sprawl as his legs gave way. As he collapsed back, a scarlet line of blood began to run from his nose and the corner of his mouth.

Trembling, his breath coming in gasps, LeBeau was on his knees in an instant, scrabbling at Castelar's waistcoat pocket. Then the small key was in his hands, and he stumbled over the Spaniard's form toward the door and out into the passageway, lurching toward the small door for which the key was intended. He thrust the key in, wrenched it round, and threw his weight against the door, pushing it open.

Marianne sat on the edge of the bunk, clad only in her long white shift. Her hair hung, long and glowing in the lantern light. Behind her, Lisette knelt on the bunk, brushing her mistress' hair.

The noblewoman stared wordlessly at LeBeau, her eyes widening in fright. And then in a question.

164

"Now, madame!" croaked Lebeau. "I have a small boat! You must come this instant!"

And his eye gleamed as he saw the light of hope flicker into flame in the girl's eyes.

Paul Gallant stirred in the shadowed corner of the log redoubt where he had been dozing. A hand was rocking him, shaking him awake gently.

"Capitaine?" said Béssac.

Gallant sat up, shaking his head to clear it. "All right, mon vieux. God, how long did I sleep? My neck feels like I've been hung."

The Mate grinned as he squatted in the sand. "You should see yourself. An escaped galley slave looks better."

Gallant snorted, tapping the Mate on the chest just enough to topple him off balance backward.

"Lack of respect to a senior officer. You disappoint me, Béssac," he said, with an answering grin.

Béssac rolled to his feet, jabbing a thumb over his shoulder. "You'd better have a look. That Englishman's standing in, straight for the south channel here."

"Ah." Gallant rose and strode over to the splintery log wall where Akiwoya stood, peering out to sea. He followed the African's gaze.

"He's making to come right in, m'sieu," said Akiwoya. "Barely a gun shot off the channel mouth and he hasn't clewed up a stitch of sail, 'cept his courses. And you can see leadsmen in the chains if you watch. The sun's glinting off the wet leads as they swing."

Gallant narrowed his eyes. Standing in for the mouth of the channel that lay below their perch in the ruins, the English frigate was a brave and formidable sight as it forged in toward the shore. The flaxen sails gleamed like old bone in the brilliant sun, and as the ship lifted and pitched gently in slow rhythm, overhauling her curling white bow wave with a roar that Gallant could hear even at this distance, there were more streaming English battle ensigns rising to the fore and main trucks to join the huge one streaming in a bright, brave swatch of red from the ensign staff.

"God, look at that!" breathed Gallant. "Trust the damned rosbifs. Guns run out. Courses clewed up. Battle ensigns hoisted.

165

And bloody leadsmen in the chains. No lurking about at long range. He's going right in!''

Akiwoya looked over his shoulder, westward. ''He'll have an upwind gauge if he gets into the lagoon, m'sieu'. Christ, he'll be on that bastard Castelar before the bugger knows what hit him. Sixty guns or not!''

Gallant sucked a tooth. ''There's still the batteries in the Dutch sloops. And the fort's guns.''

The African grinned. ''But the rosbif's using *surprise*, hein? Like you did, off Nova Scotia that time. Remember, in Baie Mahone?''

Gallant grinned. ''Yes. I remember.'' Then his expression sobered. ''Christ. We've got to move in *now*! Mari — the Marquise is down there somewhere. If she's locked below somewhere in that damned *Lima* — !''

''May be that she's not, capitaine,'' called out Béssac at the far wall. ''Unless my eyes are getting too old, I'm looking at women in a boat!''

''*What*?'' In a sprint, his bare feet licking up sand as he ran, Gallant was across to beside the Mate, following his pointing finger.

''Just there, a hair to starboard of the smaller Dutch sloop. See it? Pullin' in for the landing place? Maybe I'm wrong, but . . .''

Gallant shielded his eyes with his hand, squinting hard against the glare. And then he felt his heart leap against his chest.

There was one figure, rowing a small skiff in desperate energy. A man's figure. And in the sternsheets, their figures small and slight, the shape of two women.

''Jesus. It's *her*!'' breathed Gallant. ''Someone's taken her out of *Lima*!''

''Look there, capitaine. In *Lima*! There's men working up aloft. I can see hands out on some of the yards. She's getting ready to sail, for God's sake!''

Akiwoya had joined them, and he and the Mate were pointing out other signs of frantic activity that had suddenly materialized ashore, in the ships and now on the ramparts of the small fort. It was clear some kind of panic was gripping those tiny human figures below.

''Hah! The buggers *know* Johnny Bull's coming in after 'em, I'll warrant!'' snorted Béssac, and spat into the sand.

But Gallant's eyes were locked on the hurrying skiff that swung into the crowded beach of the landing place, in amongst the other hauled-up ship's boats. The oarsman leaped up, pulling the two women roughly from the craft, and then pushed them ahead of him in a half-walk, half-run up the pathway on the shallow hill leading to the fort, where they mingled with the labouring seamen who were struggling up toward the gate with powder barrels across their shoulders.

Gallant ran to the log wall that overhung the channel. The English frigate was almost below them now, storming in imposing majesty into the narrow passage. From where he stood Gallant could hear the hiss of her bow wave, the creak of blocks and gear, even the faint cries of the leadsmen in their chains.

And, hunched motionless round their weatherdeck guns, Gallant could see the figures of the English gun crews, the captains holding linstocks at the ready.

"All Hell's going to break loose down there in two minutes, lads!" Gallant cried. "And she's in the bloody middle of it! *Come on!*"

Scooping up his ancient cutlass and thrusting it into the back of his belt, Gallant put a hand on the redoubt logs and scrambled up, to vault over and down in a knee-jarring drop to the sandy slope that led away down toward the fort. In the next instant Béssac and Akiwoya had followed, puffing and blowing as they kept pace with the marine down the long slope.

"Christ . . . they're bound to see us —" puffed Béssac.

"What if they do, hein? They'll have too much to worry about to bother us, mon vieux! This way!"

Ahead of them now was the beginning of a low marshy area that divided the dune hills to seaward from the low rise overlooking the lagoon on which the fort stood. It was treacherous, sodden soil, matted with grass and weed, a waving, shoulder-high valley of dark green reeds. With only the briefest pause to look for the best entry, Gallant plunged into it.

Their breath coming in gasps, Béssac and Akiwoya swung in behind him, ducking and weaving to keep up with the marine's tall figure as he crashed ahead into the swampland. For what seemed like an eternity the men slithered and crashed through the dense growth, feeling the heat of the sun now hot on their backs, spitting and snorting as clouds of insects rose to hum about their faces and torment them. The only sounds became their own laboured breathing and the splash and squelch of their bare feet as they fought their way deeper.

Then, abruptly, Gallant was motionless, crouching, signalling frantically with his hands for the others to stop and get down.

"What in Hell —!" began Béssac, to be silenced by a sharp gesture from Gallant.

Then they heard it. Splashing footfalls, more than one man, crossing from the left toward their front, and getting closer. Voices raised in conversation, in curses and queer cackling laughter. Spanish voices.

Gallant slowly drew the cutlass from his waistbelt, and with a nod to each other Béssac and Akiwoya did the same. Béssac's breath was tight in his chest, and he hefted the ancient, rusty weapon nervously, feeling his knees ache from the squat, conscious even more of the insect hum about his head, of the muddy slime between his toes, of the wet seeping up through the seat of his ragged breeches and the way his heart seemed to be pounding in his throat. And now the footfalls were almost upon them . . .

"Now!" cried Gallant, and dove ahead into the reeds, his voice raised in a roar, his cutlass held high.

Eyes wide, Béssac plunged after him, hearing Akiwoya bounding along beside him. And then suddenly he was bodying into a thickset Spanish seaman, his broad hat festooned with red ribbons, a musket slung on his shoulder. The Spaniard gabbled in terror and fell back, clawing at the musket. Béssac felt the muscles of his right arm bunch, and the ancient brown blade was hissing down to sink with a horrid thunk in the Spaniard's neck where it joined his shoulders. The man screamed, his mouth a pink hole in a matted black beard, and fell forward with a splash at Béssac's feet, a spray of blood and water spattering the Mate's breeches. Béssac stared down at him, until suddenly he was conscious of Gallant in front of him. The marine's dark eyes were glittering with a savage light, and he was pointing his own cutless blade at the man at Béssac's feet. Gallant's cutlass was scarlet from tip to guard, and blood dripped from it in large drops that went pat, pat on the back of the man Béssac had killed.

"His musket, Béssac! Quickly! And the horn and shot pouch! Before the powder's wetted!"

Béssac shook himself and bent to heave the body over, lifting the long flintlock out of the bloody murk below it.

"It's never easy, is it, mon vieux?" said Gallant unexpectedly, his voice quiet.

Béssac stared at him, grateful. "No. Never."

Akiwoya was wiping his cutlass blade on a handful of reeds. There was a deep, bloody cut on the ebony muscles of his upper arm.

"Are you all right?" said Gallant, eyeing the cut. He put his cutlass into his belt and ripped a piece of material from the shirt of the dead man at his feet, binding Akiwoya's arm with quick, expert motions.

168

"Yes, capitaine. Hell, I've had worse at sea. How many were there?" The African was breathing heavily.

"You got your man?" said Gallant.

"Yes."

"Four, then. Béssac got his. I felled one. Another, a boy by the looks of him, got away."

"You mean you let him get away. I saw," said Akiwoya. And then, before Gallant could answer, "I would've done the same, capitaine. There has to be a limit somewhere."

Béssac was wiping the musket lock with a piece of the Spaniard's shirt. "Powder's dry, capitaine. That gives us one."

"Two," said Akiwoya. "Mine had a pistol."

Gallant was still fighting to settle his breathing. He looked down at the bloated shapes that lay at their feet and shivered involuntarily. "All right, let's not waste any more time. That boy'll speak to someone, somewhere. Put on these hats with the ribbons. Aki, you get the shot and powder flask for that pistol. The cutlass'll do me." He peered at the African. "Sure you can manage with that arm?"

Akiwoya nodded. "A land crab hurts more, capitaine. And I've been bitten by lots of those."

"Right, then. Ready, Théo? Let's —"

There was an ear-splitting bang from somewhere off to their left, the concussion of a heavy gun, followed in the next seconds by the reports of more. The air was filled with the characteristic sound of ripping linen passing overhead amidst the thunderous blasts.

"Naval guns!" shouted Akiwoya. "The rosbif's into the lagoon!"

Gallant was counting. "Nine . . . ten . . . eleven. . . . Jesus! A full battery broadside! That'll stir up Castelar and his damned Dutch!" He swung round, thrusting the cutlass back in his belt. "Allons-y!"

The marine pushed off into the reeds, Akiwoya at his heels. With a last look at the bodies, Béssac slung the musket, pushed the horn and shot pouch round to a comfortable position, and squelched after them.

The bang of the English guns made talk impossible, and they stumbled and splashed on blindly, following Gallant's lead. But now, from far ahead, they could hear other sounds above their own heavy breathing and the slap-splash of their feet. Shouting voices, in Dutch and Spanish. And in the next second, a ragged blast from several light-calibre guns.

"Bronze guns!" puffed Akiwoya. "Sixes, or maybe nines!

169

Wager those're the rampart guns of the fort!'' The concussions were very near, and the voices were rising in volume.

And then Gallant was sprawling almost flat in the ankle-deep water, as ahead the reed wall ended as if harvested to that point. As Béssac and Akiwoya squelched in to sprawl alongside him, he was pointing wordlessly ahead.

''Christ. We're *there*!'' breathed Béssac. ''Look at all those—''

''*Down*!'' hissed Gallant.

There was a deep hum in the air, and then, fifteen feet in front of the three men, a muddy jet of earth and water shot up with a slap, pattering gobbets of muck over them as it fell back.

''Christ, that was close!'' said Akiwoya, through clenched teeth. ''We've got to get to some cover, capitaine!''

Gallant nodded, staring out through the concealing curtain of reeds. Directly ahead of them the sandy ground was open, rising slightly to the shallow defile in which a footpath led up from the landing place, a hundred yards to the left. In the anchorage, the vast bulk of the *Lima* loomed, and with it the shapes of the two Dutch sloops. From all three ships there was coming the sporadic flicker and thump of gunfire, off to the left beyond Gallant's line of sight at the English vessel. Between the anchored ships several small boats were pulling with frantic energy through the drifting clouds of gunsmoke that hung low over the water, and on deck and aloft in each ship Gallant could see men making feverish preparations, as if for making sail. It was clear: *Lima* and her consorts were likely going to try and get under way, perhaps to escape, or to get to the open sea where their overwhelming broadside weight would tell on the Englishman.

At the landing place, a half-dozen ship's boats were hauled up on the sand, and in the shallows, a slim skiff rigged with a headsail and a spritsail main like a Yankee fishing craft rode, held by her lines in shallow water just beyond the point of being aground. At least a half-dozen men were offloading several of the boats, hefting barrels and chests on to their shoulders and struggling up through the ankle-deep sand of the pathway toward the rough log palisade of the fort. They worked under the shouted abuse of several bigger, villainous men who swung rope starters with oaths and curses each time a round shot from the English ship struck the water with a frighteningly huge geyser, or thumped into the ground with a spray of sand and earth. A small wellhouse sat part way up the slope to the fort, and then beyond it was the fort itself, a sturdy log redoubt on a rise above which a Dutch ensign floated, wreathed in the smoke from the small guns that

170

banged out sharply every few minutes from the rough gun embrasures cut in the logs.

Gallant watched as the men struggling with the stores vanished in the ajar gates of the fort, to reappear in a moment empty-handed and stumble down the path for another load, ducking away from the blows and shrieks of the overseers.

"Béssac! Musket slung? Aki, stuff that pistol in your belt! We'll make for that nearest boat!" He ducked, wincing as a shot howled inches overhead, to strike the boat he had been indicating. The boat slewed round on the beach, splinters flying in a deadly cloud from its shattered stem. Several men working beside it cried out and fell, and one man stumbled off toward the reeds for several steps, hands pressed to a blood-covered face, before he fell, his legs twitching.

"Dear Jesus," murmured Béssac.

"The *next* boat, then!" said Gallant, grimly. "Pick up something and carry it toward the fort. Come on!"

And before Akiwoya or the Mate could move, Gallant had gone, sprinting ahead to duck under cover of the boat's side for a moment, and then rising, to shamble with the expertly mimicked gait of an exhausted man to the next boat where he clutched a small powder cask and hefted it to his shoulder.

"Come on, mon vieux," said Béssac to the African, as a cloud of concealing gunsmoke swirled momentarily round them. "Can't let our lad do it all himself!" In a low crouch Béssac ran past the body of the dead man, worked to the next boat, paused while a drift of spray from a shot geyser pattered like a cloudburst over him, and then was staggering after Gallant with a bulky bale in his arms. And beside him, his beribboned hat pulled low over his eyes, Akiwoya lurched, a heavy cask on his shoulder. The African cursed as the wood bit into his skin.

"Jesus! A *brandy* cask!" he gasped. "Of all the bloody luck!"

"Trust you to pick something to drink, you silly bastard," puffed Béssac. "Come on. We're losing the capitaine!"

The wild-eyed overseers, oblivious to all but the plunging shot and the swirling clouds of reeking gunsmoke, gave the three men barely a glance as they lurched past. The path was steep, and all three were breathing heavily as they approached the gates. Ahead, a gun snouting out through an embrasure in the crude bastion off to their left suddenly fired, the ear-splitting bang deafening them momentarily. As the smoke swirled down the slope, enveloping them, Béssac reached out, clutching at Gallant's shoulder, feeling the steel-hard muscles there tense with effort.

"What if she's not here, capitaine!" he cried. "What if she's not in the fort!"

Gallant's eyes swung to him, gleaming in the gloom of the acrid smoke. "Then I'll find her, Théo! Even if she's in Hell, *I'll find her*!"

They staggered on. But now ahead the gates were abruptly looming open before them, a musket-armed sentry waving them in.

"Come on, come on, y' bloody greasers!" he was whining in a broad English dialect. "Get along! Shew a bloody leg!"

"Well, I'm buggered!" muttered Béssac to Akiwoya through his teeth. "Shot at by one lot of rosbifs and yelled at by one of 'cm on the other side. Don't they know who in Hell they're *supposed* to fight?"

Then they were inside the fort, stumbling across a sandy parade area, murky with smoke. Figures darted past them, gun crews running with powder and tools for their wall guns, others seemingly aimless in their panic. As Gallant swung round, peering through the haze, he could see several squat, cabin-like buildings of rough log planks and shingles. And a great mound of the casks and bales carried up from the boats.

"Follow me!" Gallant hissed. He lurched over to the jumble of casks, ducking away from a hurrying blow from a privateer's starter, and dropped his cask. Then, as soon as he saw Akiwoya's and Béssac's hands were free, he suddenly pitched full-length on the sand, shrieking and clawing at his belly.

"What the bloody Hell —!" began the privateer.

Béssac was at Gallant's side in an instant, passing his arm round his shoulder, lifting him to his feet. "Splinter, *señor*! It heet 'eem by de boat, dam' hard!"

"Get 'im out o' th' way!" snarled the privateer. "You! Blackface! Give 'im a hand!" This last to a crouching, wide-eyed and fearful-looking Akiwoya.

Both men bobbed their heads obsequiously, clutched at Gallant, and began dragging him away, Gallant still bellowing in what seemed to be appalling pain. All around them the smoke from the guns eddied like fog, and their heads rang with the sharp concussions.

Then in the next instant there was an unearthly howl overhead, and with a terrific impact a shot struck the pile of casks. There was a brilliant pink flash, a gust of hot air and a roar, and the privateer guard and several other men who had been struggling past, laden with cartridges for the guns were struck down as if by a great hand. The concussion bowled over Gallant and his

172

two companions, and they went sprawling uncontrollably into the shadow of one of the low, rough buildings. A black cloud seemed to hover above the ground in the centre of the fort, turning day almost to night.

Béssac scrambled to his feet, his ears ringing, and dragged Gallant round the corner of the cabin. Here in the narrow space between the cabin's wall and the palisade, away from the action, they were momentarily out of sight.

Akiwoya slumped in beside them on the sand, holding one ear.

"God, what a blast!" he said, shaking his head.

"What in Hell *was* it?" said Gallant, sitting up. "Sounded to me like —"

"A mortar shell. Or could've been that a shot touched off something in those casks," said Akiwoya.

Gallant rose to a crouch, peering round the corner of the cabin. The pall of smoke within the stockade was so dense still that the brilliant sunlight of the day was still a murky twilight in which the flash of the guns and the glow of several fires burning somewhere were diffused in an eerie light. The distant thunder of the frigate's guns was mingling with the roar not only of the *Lima's* guns, but of the Dutch sloops, punctuated by the sharp, painful bangs of the fort's guns. Over all this the shouts, curses and orders of the privateers, and the screams and moans of men cut down or mangled by the plunging shot and splinters was a cacophony of noise that beat in on Gallant's mind, making it almost impossible to think.

"What now, capitaine?" yelled Akiwoya in his ear.

Gallant shook himself into action and thought. He rose to his feet, drawing the heavy cutlass. "Ready your weapons. We've got to find her before this gets much worse. The bloody English are pressing in for a kill. But then what else would you expect of 'em, hein? Quickly, now!"

Hands trembling but swift, Béssac and Akiwoya primed and loaded the musket and the pistol, set them at half-cock, saw that their cutlasses slid easily in their belts, and nodded.

"Ready, capitaine!"

Gallant was crouching at the corner of the cabin, "Right! We go along the fronts of each of these buildings. Kick in the damned doors if we have to. Stay behind me!"

Ducking as a shot thwacked into the palisade a few feet overhead, pattering them with bark fragments, the three men dodged around the corner of the cabin to the front. There were no windows. With a quick look around, Gallant motioned

173

Akiwoya and Béssac to either side of the door. Then, with a grunt, he kicked in the door and sprang inside.

Almost in the next instant he was back out again. "Ship and carpenter's stores!" he barked, shaking his head. "Move to the next!"

At a sprint Gallant crossed the narrow gap that separated the first cabin from the next, a more substantial structure with an overhanging porch and two rough windows flanking a central door. Several heavily armed privateers were crouched in the shelter of the building, and they stared wide-eyed at Gallant as he approached, seeing the ribbons on his hat.

"Who in Christ's name be *you* — ?" began one man.

"No time! There's a landing! The English have got a party ashore, down by the boats! They'll cut us off from the ships, sure!" yelled Gallant, in English.

"What?" Several men scrambled to their feet.

"The *Lima* sent us ashore to warn you! We can't hold 'em ourselves! If you don't get some lads down there — !"

One heavy-set privateersman spit a stream of tobacco juice and hefted his musket. "Come on, you lads! No ships means a British gibbet sure, ay?" He jabbed a finger at Gallant. "Yew tell 'is Lordship Ten Haaf we've gone to th' landin' place! Clear?"

"Aye!" said Gallant, the hair on his neck rising. "Where — ?"

Another squirt of tobacco juice. "In there. Playin' with 'is toys. Disturb 'im at yer own peril, mate. Come on, lads!"

The privateersmen moved away at a run, and Gallant watched them go, motioning Akiwoya and Béssac to approach.

"Aki! Stay at the far corner and sing out if any of the bastards approach the building. Théo, stay by the door. Back me up if I need it!"

Béssac nodded. Gallant waited until the Mate was braced against the wall to one side of the doorway, musket at the ready, and Akiwoya crouched at the corner.

Then, as the flash of a gun blast flickered over the scene like the sudden glare of lightning, Gallant kicked the heavy door open and sprang inside, blade at the ready.

"Oh God. Oh dear God!" he cried.

The interior of the cabin, a rough log structure with a packed, sandy floor, was lit by the flickering light of several lanterns set in a rough circle on the floor. To one side, the figure of a woman lay hunched, shaking with sobs, clutching at her torn clothing, her white back bare and lined with horrid scarlet welts, as if

174

from a lashing. From a beam overhead a rope was strung, and into the cruelly tight noose the rope end formed, the slim white hands of Marianne de Poitrincourt were thrust, so that she was stretched up on tiptoe. Her thick, auburn hair hung in curls down her back, and her face was thrown back, eyes closed, the streaks of tears showing on her dust-smudged cheeks. Her clothing had been ripped down to her hips, and her slim torso, the heavy, pink-nippled roundness of the beautiful breasts contrasting with the slim grace of her shoulders and waist, shone like firelit ivory.

Circling her, lightly swinging a massive cat-o'-nine-tails, was a sweating and bare-chested Jacob Ten Haaf, huge in the sullen light. His face lost its leer of enjoyment as he turned to face Gallant, the red hair shaggy and matted, the pale blue eyes, opening for a moment in surprise, narrowing into glints of steel.

"Who are you?" Ten Haaf hissed. "Get out! Get — !"

An unspeakable emotion took hold of Gallant, controlling him as if a dark and savage creature that dwelt unknown to him within his spirit had suddenly risen like a nightmare to life. A red rage closed round his eyes, and with an eerie animal howl he launched into a dead run across the floor. The cutlass clattered to the dust, forgotten.

In the next instant he was upon Ten Haaf, lowering his shoulder and driving it with savage force into the huge Dutchman's midsection, hearing his explosive grunt as the two bodies thudded against the far wall of the cabin.

"You — filthy — bloody — bastard — !" Gallant's voice was so constricted by emotion that it came out in a strangled growl. Gallant began to drive his fists into Ten Haaf's body, the powerful blows impacting like the slap of leather into the Dutchman's belly.

But Ten Haaf was not about to fall. His fist came out of nowhere, impacting against Gallant's temple with a force that put a black screen across the marine's eyes. And then a knee came up, thumping hard and accurate into Gallant's groin.

An appalling pain coursed through Gallant's body, and he staggered back, falling to one knee, feeling the retch in his throat. Ten Haaf loomed over him, and began lashing him viciously across the head and shoulders with the cat.

Instinctively, Gallant fell forward and caught Ten Haaf around the knees. With a desperate strength he twisted, and the Dutchman fell heavily to the floor. In an instant, willing back the nausea, Gallant was on him, driving his fists with wild, sobbing effort into the man's face, hearing Ten Haaf grunt, feeling gristle and bone snap as the Dutchman's nose broke and scarlet blood jetted out over Gallant's fist. But then another whistling blow came out of nowhere, driving Gallant back tumbling dazed on the floor, the grit and sweat tasting in his mouth, and Ten Haaf was rolling, scrambling to his feet, reaching into a corner.

And in his hand a heavy British cutlass appeared. He moved toward the weaving, exhausted Gallant.

"I remember you!" said Ten Haaf, a cold, curling smile on his lips, the blood running scarlet over his mouth and streaking his chest. "The Frenchman. The bastard who attacked us in the *Lima*."

Gallant shook his head, trying to clear it, scrambling backward as Ten Haaf circled in.

The cutlass point centred on Gallant's chest. "Thought we'd done for you then. But I see not. Then I'll have t' do it, ay? Carefully, this time. Aye, carefully!"

And he sprang.

But Gallant was rolling, the Dutchman's cutlass thudding with his grunt into the earth where Gallant's head had been. And Gallant was rising to his feet, looking round wildly.

- "Capitaine!" cried Béssac from the door. And the ancient, heavy cutlass was arcing through the air, and Gallant caught it, spinning to face Ten Haaf.

"All the more sport, then!" boomed the Dutchman. And he lunged in, aiming a wild blow at Gallant's head. Gallant parried the blow with both hands, the steel ringing and sparks flying in the smoky gloom.

Ten Haaf pressed in. Sweat gleamed amidst the blood on his muscular chest, and his eyes were tiny blue pinpoints of madness below the wild thatch of red hair. A fixed smile twisted his lips as again and again he swung blows at Gallant which jarred the marine to the bone. Around the room, past the slowly-turning naked beauty of Marianne the men fought, their grunting breath and the ring of the steel sounding above the detonations outside.

"And now — you meddling little Frog — !" said Ten Haaf, pressing in. "I — shall — kill — you!" And he aimed a huge downward blow that was meant to cleave Gallant from crown to navel.

But a quick impulse in Gallant's brain thrust him away, twisting, so that the blow fell on empty space, and Ten Haaf toppled forward on his toes with its force, momentarily off balance.

And as the Dutchman's arms came down, Gallant planted his

feet, and with every ounce of his remaining strength swung a back-handed blow with both hands. The ancient blade hummed as it swung, and it struck Ten Haaf cleanly at the throat. The shaggy head lifted as if on a puppet string into the air for a split-second, and then thumped to the ground. The headless torso, blood pulsing from the stump of the neck, staggered forward a pace, and then collapsed in an obscene welter of twitching arms and legs.

His breath coming in burning gasps, Gallant turned toward Marianne. He could see that she was crying, her breasts shaking with her sobs, and abruptly Gallant's own eyes were filling with tears, his heart full of bittersweet pain. With a cry he cut the loathsome rope with the bloody cutlass blade, and then dropped the weapon to catch Marianne as she fell. He sank with her, cradling her in his arms, her skin white against his own tanned and dirty body. Her head fell against his chest, her hair cascading round his shoulders, and he felt her tears hot and warm on his chest.

"It's done. It's done," he murmured, his lips caressing her hair. "It's done. . . ."

And then Béssac was standing over him, and out of the corner of his eye he could see Akiwoya wrapping something gently round Lisette's small form and lifting her effortlessly in his arms, like a child.

"Capitaine?" said the Mate. "We — must move. We could be discovered at any moment —"

Gallant nodded. Around him the sounds of the bombardment and the guns suddenly were clear again. He stood up, lifting the half-naked girl with him. Gently he lifted her shift top, sliding it over her arms and bosom, tying it behind her neck.

She clung to him, her eyes still wild and uncertain. "Paul?" she whispered. "It's — it's you, isn't it? How di — where did you come from? How could you have found us? I —"

Gallant caught her as her knees gave way, holding her against him.

"Questions later, ma petite. We have much to do yet! Aki? Can you carry that girl?"

The African nodded. "Easy. She's so slight. That swine Ten Haaf — !"

"Lisette?" cried Marianne. "Is she — alive? Oh, God, what he did to her — !" Her shoulders shook with her sobs.

Gallant's face was grim. "She's alive, Marianne. And we'll all stay that if we move! Béssac?"

The Mate, watchful at the door, looked back, wincing as a shot splinter thwacked into the door inches from his head. "Clear, capitaine!"

"All right. Let's go! Aki, you remember, at the beach? That sprits'l skiff?"

The African nodded, holding Lisette close as he turned. "You're right. It'd be almost the only chance. Either that or we hope to live through this and be prisoners of the English, hein?"

"Bugger that, mon vieux! Allons!" said Gallant. Pressing Marianne close to his side, he moved to the door beside Béssac, paused, and then with him ducked out into the smoky parade ground, running in a shambling crouch for the cover of the next building. In the next instant Akiwoya, with Lisette, had joined them, panting heavily.

They crouched against the building as Gallant thought rapidly on the next move. He felt Marianne's hand tighten on his.

"Paul!" she whispered, in his ear. "The gate's still wide open. The guards are gone! Couldn't we — ?"

Béssac had overheard. "She's right, capitaine! Hell, look at all the panic in here! If we just head straight through it —"

"With you escorting us —," interjected Akiwoya.

"Like a guard with prisoners!" finished Gallant. "Right! Ready with that musket, Théo? Now!"

The little party rose from their crouch and began moving purposefully toward the gate. Béssac, cradling his musket in both hands, roughly thrust them along, scowling and cursing. The men who ran past, the gunners at the fort's guns, all ignored them as amidst the tumult of dust, smoke, explosions and shrill voices they passed out through the fort gates and stumbled down the thick sand of the footpath.

"Quickly, now!" cried Gallant, dragging them into a lurching run down the slope. "Théo! Can you see that damned boat? The spritsail skiff?"

Béssac loped ahead, squinting down at the clutch of boats on the beach, now largely abandoned. In the anchorage the *Lima* and the two Dutch ships were wreathed in smoke, cannonading at the English frigate, which they could see now, a tan and white shape in the centre of the lagoon, bracketed by shot splashes and hung round with its own smoke. One of the Dutch ships was burning in the after part of its hull, and as flames licked up round its mizzen mast screams and shouts were echoing across the water amidst the thunder of the guns.

"It's still there! I can see it. I — Jesus!"

"What?"

"There's someone wading out to board her! Look, there! Carrying something!"

As they stumbled along all of them now could see. A small shape at this distance, it was the figure of a man, hatless, wading hip-deep out to the boat, heaving over its side a small chest and then trying to clamber in. A man dressed all in pale green.

"Get him, Béssac!" cried Gallant. "The musket! *Get him!*"

Béssac lumbered ahead, unslinging the musket. It was a long shot for the smoothbore weapon. Almost too long.

"Hail Mary, full of grace . . . " Béssac began to mutter. He knelt, carefully wiped the frizzen and the edge of his flint with his thumb, checked to see that the pan was full, and raised the musket, sighting on the struggling figure.

"Hurry, Théo! For God's sake — !"

The musket bucked against Béssac's shoulder, and he saw a jet of water spit up five feet away from the man.

"Again, Théo!" cried Gallant. "Run ahead and try again! You've got to get him!"

Béssac rose and jogged ahead of the others, awkwardly loading the musket as he ran, until once again he was sinking down, peering along the gleaming barrel. The man was aboard the skiff now; he had shaken out the brail that had kept the spritsail gathered against the mast, and as he hauled in the sheets, working with furious energy, the sleek little boat tugged at her lines.

"Shoot, Théo!"

Béssac took a deep breath, let it halfway out, and squeezed the trigger. The pan flashed in his face and the long weapon fired with its characteristic deep *ftoom*.

In the skiff, the figure leapt up, clutching his head in his hands. He spun round, and toppled backwards into the bottom of the craft, out of sight. With its sail filling, but still tied to the shore, the skiff fetched up against its lines and swung into the wind, the spritsail luffing and the sheet writhing like a trapped snake.

"Run for it!" barked Gallant. "Come on!"

Slipping and sliding the last few steps down the footpath, Gallant held Marianne's slim form close against him as they ran across the narrow beach to the water's edge. Behind them, Béssac was helping Akiwoya, who was holding the small, limp form of Lisette close to his chest like a sleeping child. The din of the guns filled the air as they splashed into the water, floundering out toward the swinging, impatient skiff. They crouched for an instant as a round shot slapped into the water a hundred yards along the shore, the huge geyser drifting spray over them as it hissed down. Then they were struggling out again.

179

"Hold me, Paul! — I can't — !" gasped Marianne.

"Just a few yards further! Hang on round my neck! Just a few yards!"

There was a peculiar zinging sound, and a foot in front of Gallant a musket ball struck the water.

"The bastards must've found Ten Haaf, capitaine!" boomed Béssac. "That's from the ramparts, behind us!"

"Forget it! Get into the boat!" Gallant rasped, scooping up Marianne as with a cry she fell beside him in the thigh-deep water. They were all coughing now as clouds of acrid smoke swirled like stinging mist round them.

Then, suddenly, they were at the skiff, and Gallant reached up to grasp the gunwale. With his left arm he lifted Marianne bodily until she could grip, and then heaved himself up and over, sprawling into the rocking little craft. He reached over and grasped Marianne's arms, hauling her aboard, letting her fall against him as he fell back.

Then she gave a small cry of horror, one hand over her mouth, turning away from the sight in the sternsheets to press her face against Gallant's chest.

The figure Béssac had shot lay sprawled on its back under the tiller, staring at them with one glazed eye. The man was black, in a rumpled suit of green servant's livery, and he had a vivid scar crossing his face that offset the glistening white cataract of one eye. The mouth was open in a soundless shriek, the face drawn back in a rictus of surprise and agony. Béssac's musket ball had entered the back of his head and exited through the front, and the middle of the man's forehead was a horrid scarlet crater touched with grey-white flecks of brain and bone.

"Mother of God," breathed Gallant. "I know him! Christ, he was a bloody servant at Martinique! He's — !"

"His — name was LeBeau," said Marianne, against his chest. Her frame shook with a shudder "He was with Castelar. He . . . said he wanted to rescue us. He got us ashore to the fort, saying he was going to — to get a boat. That he'd take us to safety, somewhere." She had to force the words out. "But he gave us to that — thing. Ten Haaf. The one you—" She turned away, unable to finish.

His face grim, Gallant eased Marianne down into the floorboards. Then he rose, and with a few quick motions grasped the corpse and pitched it into the sea. It bobbed to the surface, the dead eye staring sightlessly up at the dark clouds of smoke drifting overhead.

Alongside, Béssac's hands gripped the gunwale, and Gallant

leaned over to help as, together with Akiwoya, the Mate gently lifted Lisette up to where Gallant could gather her aboard. Marianne held out her arms, enfolding the moaning and trembling girl like a child as Gallant lowered her into the noblewoman's embrace.

Marianne's hand came away from Lisette's shift wet with blood. Her eyes met Gallant's, a heartrending pain alight in their green depths.

"I'm glad you killed him," she said evenly. And then tears overwhelmed her, and she rocked the girl with infinite tenderness, crooning to her.

Gallant took a deep, shaking breath, and looked up in time to see and hear another round shot strike with a hiss and splash nearby. The little craft rocked heavily as Akiwoya and Béssac hauled themselved, sodden and awkward, into the boat.

"Quickly, lads! Théo, cut away that bow line! Aki, free those fouled sheets! Set the main to larboard!"

Scrambling forward over the thwarts, Béssac parted the line holding the skiff with a swipe of his cutlass blade. The wind caught the broad spritsail, pressing it out against the restraint of the sheet, and as Gallant swung the tiller the skiff accelerated almost immediately, heeling lightly as it swept through the smoke. The shoreline of the landing place was slipping away behind them, and now they were below the fort, with *Lima* and the other ships momentarily lost in the dense clouds off to larboard.

Gallant sat up on the windward side, a wild bubble of hope in his chest as he felt the little craft increase its speed and the reassuring pressure of the water against the rudder, hearing the slap of the bows through the wavelets.

"Haul in the sheet a trifle, Aki! Good! Théo! Can you clear away that headsail? Get it hoisted?"

Béssac was rummaging in the bows. "Soon's I clip these sister hooks on the sheet, capitaine!"

"Good! Quickly as you can!" Gallant winced as a sharp report sounded from one of the fort's guns above them, and a howl sounded seemingly inches above their heads. The fort was shrouded in dense palls of smoke, but even with that Gallant could see great gaping holes in the log palisades, torn by the British shot. And in the smoke a lurid, flickering glow from behind the walls told of a fire raging somewhere within.

He swung on the seat to look in the other direction. The burning Dutch sloop was a huge, roaring pyre now, its upperworks burnt away, the tarry wood of the hull sending licking tongues

181

of flame curling slowly up under a black cloud that mingled with the gunsmoke to drift in a swirl slowly westward across the lagoon, partly obscuring the tan and white shape of the English frigate.

Béssac was pointing. "The Englishman's coming about, capitaine! Going to tack back toward the channel mouth and give 'em the other batteries, by God!"

Gallant nodded. "Not as if he hasn't done enough damage. God, you'd think *he* was the bloody sixty-four!"

"Capitaine! Look there!" Akiwoya called. "At the fort!"

Gallant swivelled back. The fort had abruptly ceased firing, and from within the ramparts the flames were leaping higher, adding more oily smoke to the pall. The figures of men were streaming down from the gates, some swerving off to plunge into the reed swamp, others crowding toward the boats in the landing place.

"Sacristi!" said the African. "If we hadn't got to this boat when we did . . ."

"Simple, mon ami," said Gallant, grimly. "We'd be dead!" He spat into the water. "Look under the sail, there. Where'n Hell does the north channel mouth lie?"

Béssac heard and bellowed from forward. "Fine off the starboard bow! Hold this and we can make it through in one, maybe two tacks if the wind isn't too foul in the channel!"

Gallant nodded. His mouth felt dry, and he had a sudden overpowering desire for a mouthful of rich, stinging brandy. Behind them now was the damned smoke, the noise, the killing. He was not sure what he was going to do if they made it to the open sea; there were some chests and a small water butt in the boat. LeBeau had perhaps been intending to escape with it, and that might mean there were some provisions aboard. Whatever the next few days would hold, they would have a chance if he could elude the English, perhaps try and work south for a French, or even Spanish harbour — it was all so much a chance, so uncertain. But there *was* a chance!

Gallant's eyes fell to Marianne.

"How is she?" he asked gently.

"She woke for a moment, but she's asleep again. I want to do something for her back, but I daren't move her. I — thought she'd never stop crying." She shook her hair back out of her eyes and looked up at him, and in her pale dishevelled beauty his heart went out to her in a fierce surge.

"He beat her. Terribly. It was — unspeakable."

Gallant nodded, silent. He drank in the look of her eyes, the lift of her chin, the exquisiteness of her face. So different now from the mocking, imperious beauty in Valigny's ballroom at Fort Royal. And so infinitely more compelling.

"I thank God I found you," he said, after a moment.

She looked up at him. "Oh, Paul. I could not believe there could be such horror. I — I prayed I would die under his lash." Her eyes swung out over the grey water, her hands stroking the sleeping Lisette's hair. "When the door opened, and I heard your voice, I —" her eyes sought his again "— I knew it was you. Ragged breeches, dusty face and all. I knew. I — I couldn't believe it."

Gallant was silent, listening to the rush of the boat, the dull boom and detonations astern.

Her expression was hesitant, open. "I am sorry I said such hateful things to you at Martinique. If you can believe I — I had already sensed the kind of man you are. And what that meant — what it means — to me. But a foolish pride is a terrible burden. And I am burdened in abundance." She paused, and the green eyes gazed deep into his own, sending the familiar chill down his spine once more. "Will you forgive me?" she said quietly.

Gallant looked for a moment ahead, and then back into her eyes. "There was — there is — nothing to forgive."

"Please," she said. "It — it's important. Say that you do." She was looking at him with an entrancing light in her eyes. A light he had never seen before, that puzzled and at the same time stirred a joy of recognition within him.

"For God's sake, Marianne. Of course I do."

She closed her eyes, as if released, and let out a long sigh. "Good," she whispered. "I —"

"Capitaine!" blurted out Akiwoya, who had been staring aft. "Look! The *Lima*!"

Gallant swivelled and stared. For an instant he could see nothing. The pall of smoke from the burning fort and the Dutch sloop lay like a grey-black wall across virtually the entire lagoon, an impenetrable mass behind which nothing could be seen except the occasional flicker of a tongue of flame. Nothing, except —

"My God!" murmured Gallant.

Like a towering wraith materializing in awesome power, the great hulk of the *Lima* nosed out through the smoke wall. Aloft, every inch of canvas was set and straining, braced round hard as she tacked for the mouth of the northern channel. Beneath her bows a building wave foamed and glistened, and the red and gilt of her paintwork gleamed like blood laced with gold as she swept clear of the smoke.

The Spanish ship's bowsprit pointing like a finger at the little skiff, *Lima* surged toward them. As Gallant stared, a tiny figure in red moved forward to the bows of the great ship and stood motionless, watching the skiff, a sliver of brilliant colour against the dark cloud mass astern.

"Oh, dear Mary," whispered Marianne, and put a hand over her mouth.

"Christ, capitaine, he's *pursuing* us!" cried Béssac. Then he squinted. "Who in Hell's that on her foredeck?" His eyes widened. "Holy Mother. That's — !"

Gallant nodded. "Exactly, mon vieux. Don Alfonso Castelar!" he said grimly.

The marine swung round, looking ahead, biting his lip. The skiff was slipping now into the mouth of the channel. To the right, the island shore and its tall dune hills were sliding quickly by. The other shore was no more than a gun shot away. If he could tack the skiff —

"Ready about!" he barked. "Marianne, watch your head as the foot of the sail comes across! Aki? Stand by the headsail! Ready with those sheets, Théo?"

"Oui, capitaine!"

Gallant waited for the moment, his heart pounding like a hammer in his chest. On *Lima* came, tacking strongly toward the channel entrance, well clear of the mass of smoke. Behind, the fort was fully ablaze now, great billows of flame curling up into black clouds. And then in the next instant a muffled explosion boomed out, debris and wreckage lifting in high arcs clear of the smoke to splash into the lagoon water. Flaming bits cartwheeled into the sky, one huge bit striking with a hiss of steam beside *Lima's* hurrying hulk.

"Blew the fort magazine, capitaine!" said Akiwoya. "Christ, the Englishman's done for 'em, hein?"

"They have a habit of being thorough, Aki!" said Gallant, through tight lips. He was looking ahead, then aloft. It was time.

"Right! Helm's a-lee! Get her round, lads!"

Dipping into the wind, the skiff turned nimbly on its keel, as with much hauling and squealing of blocks Akiwoya and Béssac set the craft's canvas for the larboard tack. The boat footed ahead immediately, and as Gallant peered ahead he could see the open sea through the channel. On this tack the skiff might pass straight through without a touch to the tiller. And now she lifted her bows to the first remnants of swells that had survived their roll through the narrow passage.

"The swell, capitaine!" grinned Akiwoya. "Good, hein?"

Gallant was staring back at *Lima*, and he nodded, preoccupied.

The skiff sped on, pitching and tossing through the narrow channel, and the sandy shores slipped by rapidly. Now, from ahead, they could hear the roar of the surf along the seaward beaches to either side of the channel mouth. In but a few minutes they would be clear of the passage and punching out into those swells. The skiff seemed able and had proved handy so far. But what was he going to do when they reached the open sea? Either he could turn —

"She's firing, capitaine!" barked Béssac.

Before Gallant could react, his ears were punched by the deep thump of a naval gun. He spun round in time to see a grey gout of smoke spill down round *Lima's* stem and be ripped away by the wind.

"Where will — ?" Gallant began, murmuring to himself.

No more than ten feet from the skiff, there was a frightening, ear-cracking sound, as if a broad hand had slapped down flat on the surface of the water. An enormous upjet of green water and white foam shot up as high as a ship's mast, towering over the hurrying little skiff, and then collapsed over the craft in a stinging cloudburst of spray that drenched Gallant and the others to the skin.

In the skiff, Lisette cried out as the cold salt water struck, stinging in the frightful weals on her back. She clutched at Marianne, who pressed her close, trying to shield her with her own body.

"Bow chaser!" spat Akiwoya, his face dripping. "A bloody eighteen-pounder, for God's sake! He'll smash us with that thing!"

Gallant looked wildly ahead. The open sea was only a few hundred yards away. On the little skiff sped, and once out there, said his mind . . .

This time he saw the livid pink flash in *Lima's* bows, the smoke curling back and away around the tightly braced forecourse, the figures of the gun crews hunched and hurrying on the deck. All were working feverishly, serving the two long guns that bore forward past the big vessel's bowsprit.

All but one. The figure in red, standing with arms folded, motionless and watchful.

You bastard, thought Gallant. You're waiting to see us die.

There was a howl in the air, so close it seemed the skiff's spritsail buckled momentarily as its wind was torn away from its surface. Some forty yards ahead there was another slap, another towering column of water jetting majestically up, only to collapse back in a welter of splash and foam through which the skiff danced, her sails blotched with spray now, her sleek white hull gleaming.

"Haul in a touch, lads! A shade more! Good!" Gallant was milking the last ounce of speed out of the little craft. The inlet mouth to the open sea was fifty yards ahead. Now thirty. Now ten.

And then they were pitching over a dark, unbroken swell, the wind suddenly fiercer and veering slightly to one side, the surf to either side a roaring sullen mass of white and dark green below a hanging spray-mist that swirled round the plunging little skiff like pale smoke. They were out!

"He's fired again!" cried Akiwoya.

"Ease the main and heads'l! Right out!" Gallant thrust the tiller hard over. "Béssac! Hike out to wind'rd when we get these swells beam on!" The skiff swung off the wind, reaching along the surfline, and as the building rollers bore in it rolled heavily, causing Béssac to curse as he clambered over the gunwale to pull it back.

Astern, in the place where the skiff would have been had Gallant not turned, a third gleaming geyser jetted up, the thump of the gun reaching their ears as the geyser hissed back into the sea.

Marianne sat up, staring astern and then swinging to look at Gallant, her eyes wide. "That would have killed us!" she cried, her hair streaked and wisped by the wind and spray. "Can you keep dodging like that?"

"Not like this too bloody long!" bellowed Béssac, who was lying on his stomach along the gunwale, half in and half out of the wildly rolling skiff. "She'll broach in a minute, capitaine!"

"Right! We'll turn into 'em again!" Gallant wiped his streaming face with one hand. "Close haul, lads! Larboard tack!"

With the turn the boat righted itself, pitching again bows-on into the rollers, wreathed in glittering garlands of spray as it punched out toward the open water. Béssac fell with a thump onto the floorboards, sodden and cursing.

"Peste! I'm too bloody old for this! The next time you suggest some voyage to the ends of the earth, I'm damned if I'll sign on!"

Gallant managed a grin at the Mate before turning back to Marianne.

"Our only chance is to use our small size!" he said, over the wind and sea noise. "Keep as far ahead or away from him as we can!"

Gallant looked back at *Lima*. The ship's hull was hidden by the land as it passed through the channel. But Castelar had judged his tack correctly. Braced as hard round as the yards would go, staysails drawing between fore and main masts, the ship was surging huge and magnificent out toward the open sea. In a few minutes it would leave the shoal waters, out where Castelar would have more options in his pursuit of the skiff. At most, thought Gallant, he had until that moment to decide how to save their lives.

"Capitaine?" called Akiwoya. "Wouldn't it be better to head inshore? Get into shallow water, where he couldn't follow? Find refuge in a cove?"

Gallant shook his head. "He wouldn't turn back, Aki!" he shouted. "He knows that Englishman back there will be after him after he's finished with the bloody Dutch! He wouldn't want to be caught on a lee shore by the rosbifs!"

"Then why not — ?"

"Look at the angles ashore, there, Aki! If we turn off to loo'ard, he can open up his tack and still cut us off before we can reach shoaling water! We *had* to come out this far because we would've broached turning beam-on to those swells inshore! We've got no choice now but to try to keep ahead of 'em and dodge his shot! That means holding out to seaward!"

"Jesus, capitaine!" began Béssac. "That'll put us —"

Marianne had been easing the semi-conscious Lisette into as comfortable a position as possible on the floorboards of the wet, pitching craft. With her tattered shift drawn about her, she had risen to her knees and was looking ahead out to sea, the long auburn tresses whipped back by the wind. And now she was pointing.

"Paul?" she said, with an intensity that stopped Béssac in mid-sentence. "Paul, there's something out there."

"Enh?" Gallant swung round, following her point over the tossing bows, past the taut face of the spritsail. For a moment he scanned fruitlessly. "Where? I don't —"

Then he saw it. A white square, low on the horizon, dead ahead of them.

"A ship," he said. "Hull down."

"Who might it be, Paul?" asked the girl.

Gallant threw a quick look at *Lima*, now forcing out into the open water, rollers smashing in twinkling clouds against its stem.

"Don't know. Can't see its colours. God, it was *your* eyesight that saw it. Can you make out anything?"

The girl put up a hand to shade her eyes. She was silent for a long moment.

"White. White, at the top of the biggest mast."

Akiwoya gaped. "Sacristi. Can she *see* that?"

Gallant's heart began to beat rapidly against his chest, and he felt the muscles of his legs begin to tremble.

"Are you sure, ma petite?" he said, deliberately controlling his voice. "*Are you sure you see white?*"

"Yes. Look, Paul. Surely you can see it too?"

Gallant steadied the tiller against his knee and rose, squinting to let his eyes reach for the shape.

And then his heart bounded.

"White. A full-rigged ship. And green at the foretruck. Sweet Mother of God — !"

"She's French!" cried Marianne. "Or Spanish?"

"Either," said Gallant. "Christ, if it could be — !"

"Capitaine!" cried Akiwoya. "*Lima's* turning toward us! She's — damn, she's fired again!"

Cursing, Gallant clutched at the tiller. "Helm's a-lee! Back the heads'l, Aki! Get us round!" He flung his weight against the tiller and the skiff lifted, plunged, lifted again, and then was round on the new tack, leaping over the stippled swells as the spritsail filled with a crack.

A hiss and slap sounded in their ears, and twenty yards off to larboard another geyser shot up. As the boom of the gun reached their ears Gallant swung to look at *Lima*. The big vessel was close-hauled on the larboard tack, heeling strongly to the wind, the pennant at its mizzentruck streaming out like an arrow to leeward. The sea foamed whitely under its forefoot, and in ponderous majesty the great red and gilt hull drove out into the open sea, the black, gaping mouths of the chaser gunports ominous and frightening below the cloud of curved, still sails.

"The bastard!" spat Gallant. "He'll get us before the turn of the glass, footing along like that!"

"Capitaine?" called Béssac, coiling the sheets. "That ship out there! If you stand up you can see her hull. Christ, I'm not sure, but — !"

"But *what*, Théo?"

Akiwoya's face had a strange expression. "You — you'd better see for yourself, capitaine!"

Gallant stood again, bracing the tiller with his leg. The skiff lifted high on the back of a cresting swell for a moment. A moment that was enough.

"Oh, Jesus. Sweet Saviour," breathed Gallant.

"P — Paul? What is it?" said Marianne, her face anxious.

"Capitaine, are you all right?" Béssac was saying.

Gallant shook his head, suddenly aware that his eyes were filling with tears. He coughed and laughed all at once.

"It's the *Diane*!"

"What?" Béssac gasped. "Then I wasn't wrong!"

"It's Richard O'Farrell, and the *Diane*!" repeated Gallant, feeling his legs shaking, a bubble of wild joy rising in his throat.

And then Béssac had launched himself across the thwarts and was hugging Akiwoya, pounding the African's back with his huge fists, hooting and laughing. And the gunner was responding in kind.

"Is that — was that the other ship? In the convoy escort?" Marianne was asking. Her voice was breathless, tinged with disbelief.

Gallant could not control a bubble of laughter. "Yes! It *is* the *Diane*! God, look at her come! Christ in Heaven, I can't believe — !"

Marianne and the other two men were bracing themselves to stand, heedless of the skiff's violent motion. And now all of them were waving their arms and shouting at the top of their lungs.

Now hull-up over the horizon, *Diane* was a clear and exquisite image against the cloudless azure sky. The unmistakable black and tan hull gleamed in the brilliant sunshine, lifting and falling in slow, rhythmic grace as it overhauled the dark blue swells. Below the bows a broad white wave foamed, and aloft, the back-lit arches of snow-white canvas rose in perfect pyramids of still grace and power, their glowing faces criss-crossed by the shadows of the rigging. High at the trucks, the Bourbon Ensign streamed out in clean purity from the main, while at the fore a green burgee curled and whipped forward over the face of the fore t'gallant sail. And now, at the stern, Gallant could glimpse the huge colour on the ensign staff curling over the quarterdeck.

Then, as Gallant stared, a pink flash showed along *Diane's* side, a ball of white smoke puffed out over the sea face, and the thump of the report reached their ears.

"She's seen us! She's seen us! Sacristi, capitaine, *look* at her! I've never seen anything so — !" Béssac was almost beside himself.

Gallant swung to look aft. *Lima* had come about, and was tacking off to the east-nor'east. For the moment they were free of her guns, unless those rows of gunport lids opened. But when she turned again . . .

"*Diane's* gone aback, m'sieu'!" cried Akiwoya. "She's waiting for us!"

EIGHT

Gallant squinted forward. The little ship was turning into the wind, swinging in slow majesty, dark ripples crossing the faces of her sails, until with a thump like a gun the foremast canvas went hard aback, and she waited, serene and impossibly beautiful, for the skiff.

"Sheet in, lads!" cried Gallant, his voice suddenly hoarse, a lump of emotion so strong in his throat that he could barely speak. "Let's not keep her waiting!"

The skiff lunged forward, bobbing over the swells, the eyes of the three men and one woman fixed on the shape of the *Diane* as if it were a shoreline and they exhausted swimmers. Marianne lifted the stirring Lisette into an embrace, holding the servant girl close to her bosom, murmuring "Ça va, ça va," with such tenderness that Gallant, watchful, felt the sudden blur of tears in his eyes once more.

And then, almost before he was ready, the skiff was entering the shadow of *Diane's* mass. The sounds of sea and hull, of slatting blocks and creaking rigging, of voices raised in command, of his own voice ordering Béssac to fend off, Akiwoya

190

to make ready a line to heave, both to cast off the skiff's halyards, all blended in Gallant's ears. In the next moment they were alongside the oaken wall of the ship, high and solid, inexpressibly beautiful, and men were clambering down the battens to the skiff, lifting Lisette with gentle strength up the side to the deck, looking at Gallant and the others with wide grins, shouts of welcome echoing down from above.

Now Gallant was lifting Marianne to the battens, and she was scrambling up, legs flashing below her shift to the appreciative winks and grins of the watching seamen, and Gallant himself was leaping for the battens, closing his eyes in thankfulness and joy at the feel, the good, tarry solidity of the wood. And he was at the rail, and over, on to wide, clean decking, and before him, tall and steadfast in his blue seacoat, the wide eyes full of relief and welcome, was the form of Richard O'Farrell.

"Richard!" burst out Gallant. In the next instant he was gripping the Irishman in a steely hug, feeling his friend's arms around his shoulders, seizing him with equal strength.

All around them was tumult, as Marianne, her tattered shift billowing round her, alternately hugged the bearish forms of Akiwoya and Béssac, who were being pummelled on the back and shoulders by a mob of laughing seamen. For a moment in the hubbub it was impossible to speak. But for that moment no speech was necessary.

Finally Gallant was able to hold the Irishman at arm's length, grinning uncontrollably at the answering joy in O'Farrell's face.

"How — where did you — ?" began Gallant, and then laughed, unable to finish.

"The convoy, Paul! After we left you, sailing off in that cockleshell boat, we shaped course for France as you directed."

"Yes, but why are you — ?"

"A French squadron! No more'n leaving you hull-down, we sighted the topsails of a huge squadron, about twenty sail, overhauling us from astern. By Saint Patrick, I thought the jig was up, sure they were English. But, Hell, they were *ours*! French, blown northward by a gale from their usual track out o' Martinique! Blind luck, I'll tell you!"

"My God. Who was it?"

"M. le Duc d'Argennes. With six second-rates, ten fifth-rates, and a clutch of others. Damned glad I was to see him, I'll tell you. One of his ships was carrying the Sieur de Valigny." He coughed. "Under arrest."

Gallant stared. "Enh? Why?"

"He was removed from office. Accused of trafficking with rosbif merchants in the Carolinas. No wonder he wanted you in this business, Paul! You were to lend a pretence that he was doing something to protect the girl, hein?'' Richard grinned as he looked at Marianne. ''My stars, she looks a little different than in Martinique, enh? Where'n God's name did you track her down? Hell, I though I'd be looking for you for *months*—!''

''Wait a minute. You said *pretence*.''

''Exactly,'' O'Farrell nodded. ''Valigny was tied up in a scheme with the sous-ministre of the Marine. The old Comte de Maurepas didn't know a thing about it, apparently. They were setting up the girl to be killed by the Dutch. Prolong the war, because the King'd be beside himself with rage if something happened to her. And keep their pockets filling with the illegal trade into the Carolinas and Floridas. *You* weren't supposed to do anything except botch things and hopefully even get killed. And Valigny knew about bloody Castelar. *Was* he in on it with the Dutch?''

''*Is*, you mean!'' Gallant threw a quick look at the distant *Lima*, his lips a tight line. ''I'll tell you sometime. But I can't believe that Valigny—!''

''M. d'Argennes gave me the whole story before he sent me on my way rejoicing to see if you were still among the living. The King, apparently, is beside himself with anxiety over the girl. There's been Hell to pay in Versailles over the whole thing!''

A seaman was at Gallant's shoulder, pushing a crust of bread and a bowl of dark wine into his hands. Ravenous, Gallant bit into the bread, eyes waiting for O'Farrell to go on.

''Valigny knew Castelar was in the pay of the sous-ministre from the start. Someone must have given him away. To keep it looking good, Castelar was unaware that Valigny was somehow directing the whole bloody plot—''

''LeBeau,'' muttered Gallant, through a mouthful of wine-sodden bread.

''Enh? But the main aim was to do away with the girl.'' O'Farrell glanced again at Marianne, who was hugging a blushing Béssac. ''It seems you interrupted that!''

''The bastard,'' said Gallant, pausing to take a huge swig of the bitter wine, ''was going to sell her back to the King, or some such. She told me that much, at least. Christ, Richard, what she's been through I hate to think! You saw what happened to her servant girl. Speaking of that, what—?''

''The lads took her below, to my cabin. I've got an old bosun who can cure like a grandmother looking at her.''

''Good. Sweet Jesus, Richard, you wouldn't believe what kind of an animal that Dutchman—''

"Deck, there!" From high aloft in *Diane's* maintop, a lookout was calling down, his cry hushing the excited babble on deck.

O'Farrell cupped his hands. "Deck, aye?"

"The big Spanish vessel, m'sieu'! She's come about! Tacking dead for us, m'sieu'!"

Together Gallant and O'Farrell stepped to the rail, Gallant tossing off the last of the wine and dropping the bowl on the deck.

"Jesus!" began O'Farrell. "Look at him. He's —!"

"Coming back to finish the job, Richard!" said Gallant, his face grim. He narrowed his eyes. *Lima* had swung round to the larboard tack, its enormous bowsprit pointed like an arrow toward the *Diane*. No more than a half-league away, the Spanish vessel already looked huge in comparison to *Diane's* lighter, smaller size. As Gallant watched, he could see sudden activity, the shapes of seamen moving up on shrouds and out on yards, small ratlike forms.

"Clewin' up his courses, m'sieu'!" came the lookout's cry. "Like as if for action!"

The man was right. The great curved faces of *Lima's* courses crumpled as they were gathered up from below by the tightening clewlines, drawn up in loose folds against the main lower yards to clear the air immediately above the deck for the free-wheeling action of a sea fight.

"God. She *is* huge!" said O'Farrell, through his teeth.

Gallant nodded. "Richard, I think we're in for a fight," he said briskly. "And a bloody serious one. I'd suggest you go to Quarters. Immediately!"

O'Farrell turned to him. "I'd be pleased," he said quietly, "if you would command us in this, capitaine!"

Gallant looked sharply at him. "*Diane* is your ship, Richard."

"And this is a fight that means the most to you."

Gallant paused. All around him, he could sense that the talk and tumult on deck had ceased altogether. Their conversation had been heard. And in the silence, the men of *Diane* were waiting to hear Gallant's reply.

Gallant flicked his eyes briefly at *Lima's* looming shape, at O'Farrell's ready, willing expression. And for an instant, into the watchful eyes of Marianne, standing with Béssac and Aki-woya across the deck. And he saw the message there.

"Very well," he said, lifting his chin. "I assume command. Thank you, Richard! Béssac! You'll assist M. O'Farrell's second! Akiwoya!"

"M'sieu'?" boomed the African.

"Get below to the gundeck. *Diane's* gunner knows you, hein? Good! Take charge of the batteries, starboard and larboard! I want double shot, every gun, and that includes the weatherdeck guns. But don't run out till I give the order! Clear?"

"Oui, m'sieu'!" exulted the African, vaulting for the companionway.

Gallant swung back. "Richard, what have you got in the way of small arms?"

O'Farrell snorted. "Enough to arm a bloody regiment. M. d'Argennes insisted we take the stuff—"

"Then listen carefully! I want you to see it's brought up for ready use, Richard! By each gun position, hein? Make sure *each* man has a cutlass or a half-pike! Pistols if you've got enough!"

"Boarding weapons? God, surely you don't intend—!"

"Bear with me, mon vieux! When you've got the arms ready at hand, divide the lads into two groups. Topmen and fo'c'sle under you, to board for'ard! Waistmen and afterguard, with me aft! Clear?"

"Yes, but—!" Gallant's expression stopped the Irishman in mid-sentence. "Clear, capitaine."

"Bon! Have you a drummer?"

O'Farrell nodded. "And a marine squad of six, in case you'd forgotten."

Gallant grinned. "I had, Richard. Have your lad beat to Quarters, will you?"

Within a few moments the beat of the deep, unsnared drum filled *Diane*. But even before its thrilling rhythm had begun, *Diane's* men, half-wild with sudden excitement, were flinging themselves into the readying of the little ship. The squeal of blocks aloft told that the great courses were being clewed up out of the way, and the agile topmen were already hanking staysail halyards on to the snakelike roll of the damage net they would haul up to hang spread over the decks to catch gear falling from above. Crashes and the pounding of feet mingled with orders and yells from below meant that Akiwoya was having the gun crews knock down and clear away the gundeck partitions and mess furniture, opening up space in which the frantic business of serving the long guns could take place.

Now on *Diane's* weatherdeck, the gun crews were arriving at their posts, casting off the seizings on the side and trail tackles, slacking off the heavy breeching lines, throwing their weight into the tackles to heave the guns back for loading, their trucks squealing on the deck planking as they rumbled back.

Pacing the quarterdeck, still clad in nothing but his ragged trousers, the ancient cutlass still thrust in his belt, Gallant nodded at O'Farrell.

"Damned good gun drill, Richard! You've been working these lads hard!"

O'Farrell's expression was grim. "By the look of *Lima*, capitaine, they'll need it," he said quietly.

Gallant squinted. The Spaniard was about a mile off now, punching in ponderous majesty out to meet them. It was time to put *Diane* under way.

Béssac halted, puffing, before the two men. "She's . . . at Quarters, capitaine! Gun crews and sailhandlers at their posts. Aki says he's double-shotted the whole gundeck battery. And I've put the marines in the tops, three to a mast."

"Bon," Gallant nodded. "Catch your breath, mon ami. You're wheezing like a beached manatee."

Béssac puffed out his cheeks. "Abuse. Always abuse. Just wait'll you're my age, capitaine. — M. O'Farrell's coxswain is on the way to the helm."

Gallant grinned, hearing O'Farrell laugh beside him. "Good, Théo. Stand ready for some quick sail handling!"

"Oui, m'sieu'," said the Mate, and shambled off down the waistdeck ladder, bellowing at his sailhandlers.

Gallant looked aloft, watching the play of the wind across the face of the mizzen topsail, and then at *Lima*. The humour vanished from his mind like vapour in sunlight, and he noticed that his legs were trembling. He hoped it was not visible to any of the men about him on the quarterdeck.

"Stand by your helm," he said through tight lips to the burly senior seaman who was arriving at the wheel. "We'll be turning off the wind in a clock's tick."

"Oui, m'sieu'!" said the coxswain. He was a thickset man with wisps of white hair wind-whipped by the wind around an otherwise bald head. His arms were like the limbs of a young tree. He spat a stream of tobacco juice accurately over the rail to leeward and winked at Gallant.

"What's your name?" asked the marine.

"Carty, m'sieu'."

"Another heathen Irishman. See you steer small and true, Carty!"

Carty grinned, a gap-toothed grimace. "You'll have it, m'sieu'!"

Gallant moved to the waistdeck rail, cupping his hands, conscious of the eyes of the waiting gunners on him.

"For'ard, there! Béssac! Back the headsails to starboard! Man the foremast braces, there!'' He turned to Carty. ''Down helm. Hold her there while she makes sternway!''

''Down helm, m'sieu'!'' grunted Carty, his hands slapping on the brass-capped oaken spokes of the great wheel.

Slowly, dipping gently, *Diane* fell off the wind, her bows swinging off to larboard. Gallant watched aloft, eyes keen for the ripple in the backed foretopsail.

''Now!'' he cried. ''Let go, starboard braces! Haul away, larboard! Lively, now!''

Diane swung on, and as the wind came behind her foremast canvas, the forces of her sails ceased battling one another, and the ship began to foot through the sea.

''Set headsails! Midships, Carty! Steady as she goes!''

Gallant heard footsteps on the deck behind him, and turned expecting to find O'Farrell. But instead he was looking into the green eyes of Marianne de Poitrincourt.

''Marianne, what are you doing here?'' he burst out. ''It won't be sa—!''

The girl was still in the tattered chemise, against the thin front of which her breasts were pushing in teasing firmness. But she was hauling up over her hips a rough pair of seaman's breeches, tucking her shift down into them and briskly buttoning the front. As Gallant stared, she picked up a heavy pistol from the deck, thrust it into her waistband, and then began tying her hair back in imitation of a seaman's queue. From a few of the beaming gunners nearby several claps of applause sounded.

''Damn you, Paul Gallant, don't give me any more orders!'' said the girl spiritedly, and at the expression on Gallant's face the grins on the watching gunners' faces widened even further. ''I'm up to see what's happening. And what I can do!''

''Lisette. How—?''

''Sleeping in Richard's bunk. The old seaman used some kind of salve that seemed to take the pain away. She doesn't need me now.''

Gallant ran his fingers through his hair. ''Look, Marianne. *Lima* is beating up for us. I'm trying to figure out a way to fight her without turning us all into mangled gull-meat. But the greatest risk is up here!''

''So?'' She shrugged her slim shoulders.

''So will you please go below where you will at least have *some* protection—!''

Gallant stopped in mid-sentence as Marianne's hand came up. But not to strike him, as it had at Martinique. To lie, cool and delicate, against his cheek. Her eyes looked deep into his: open, exquisite, alight with emotion and disarmingly direct.

196

"I'll stand with *you*, Paul, thank you very much," she whispered. "Not below there. And what happens to you happens to me!"

For a second Gallant could not speak. Then he found his voice, if at first only in a whisper.

"Marianne — !" he managed, and then, oblivious to all, he swept her against him in a deep embrace.

He was suddenly conscious of the roar of cheers that had burst from the throats of the watching gunners, and he lifted his head to see Marianne's eyes twinkling up at him, O'Farrell grinning like an ape, and the gun crews waving their hats at him as they burst into new cheers.

O'Farrell was shaking his head, the grin widening as he saw Gallant turn beet red.

"Jesus, capitaine!" he laughed. "Now you *have* to give us some kind of victory, after *that*!"

Gallant swung to look at the onrushing *Lima*, Marianne's hand still in his own. He thought wildly that they should all be cowering in fear at what was bearing down on them. Why was he shaking instead with joy, and why were these poor doomed rats in *Diane* cheering him like fools?

He cupped his hands, feeling a bubble of recklessness surge up within him, all caution gone. "We'll keep to windward of him lads! Make him fight on our terms! And remember! It won't be the first time a sloop has taken on a sixty-gunner and won! And, by God, it won't be the last!" He spat to clear his dry throat. "Remember to stand ready to board, if we have to!"

Again the *Diane*s were cheering, eyes wild.

God, thought Gallant. The spirit is there. But will it be enough? *Diane* forged on, tacking now at right angles to *Lima's* course. Working up to windward this way, Gallant was prolonging the moments before the sixty-gunner would be in accurate range. But that would not be long in coming.

He peered through narrowed eyes at the mass of the Spanish ship, looking for something that might give him some clue, however small, about . . .

"Richard!" he barked, suddenly.

"Capitaine?"

Gallant held his arm, pointing with his free arm at *Lima*. "Look carefully at her! See anything odd? Anything peculiar?"

"What? Ah — no. Nothing, m'sieu'."

"Aloft? In the rigging?"

O'Farrell shook his head. "No, m'sieu'. What — ?"

"The topmen, Richard! Sailhandlers. Sharpshooters. The usual lot you'd find aloft in a ship that size."

"Why, they're — you're right! There aren't any! Hardly a soul aloft in her!"

"Exactly!" said Gallant. "Remember the mutiny in her, when we boarded? Half the Dons against the other half? Hell, she's short-handed!"

"And that means — ?"

"I'd bet on only one broadside manned at a time! Starboard or larboard, but not both, hein?" Gallant swung on Carty. "Up helm, Carty! Fall off to a run! Make to pass down *Lima's* larboard side! Béssac! Mind your braces and sheets!"

O'Farrell gaped. "Have you lost your senses, capitaine? That'll —"

"Set us up for a point-blank broadside from him! Yes!" He looked for Béssac among the men hauling with frantic energy at *Diane's* sheets and braces as the ship dipped round. "Let her fill clean full, Théo! We're running down on her!"

O'Farrell glanced at Marianne and grasped Gallant's arm. "Paul! For God's sake — !"

"Look, Richard! We pass him — or act as if we intend to pass him — to his larboard side. He puts his gun crews on those batteries, enh? But if at the last minute — !" He did not finish.

"Ah," said O'Farrell, a light dawning in his eyes. "I — I'm sorry, Paul."

Gallant gave him a grin. "No matter. Let's just pray it works!" He moved to the waistdeck rail again, cupping his hands. "Gun captains, stand ready for a broadside to starboard! You, drummer! Pass the word below to M. Akiwoya!"

He turned back to O'Farrell and Marianne. "Our only hope is to outsail him. Duck under or avoid his punches and try and strike him as fast as we can. And then hope we can cripple him or disable him somehow!" He looked at O'Farrell. "Those boarding weapons issued out?"

"Done."

Marianne touched the tanned and muscled hardness of Gallant's arm. "But if we can't avoid him, Paul? What — ?"

Gallant touched her cheek. "Then we may not have much longer to live, ma petite." He felt a pang in his chest as he saw the girl's face pale, but her chin came up in a lift of courage and determination. On impulse he reached for the great telescope in its leather sheath by the helm and gave it to the girl.

"Here. Clap an eye, as the hands say, on *Lima*. Keep watching her. And tell me anything out of the ordinary you notice!"

The girl nodded. Her hands trembled as she opened the long brass instrument.

"About extreme range now for those chasers of his, capitaine!" came Béssac's bellow from forward.

Gallant stepped to the binnacle, eyed the card, looked aloft quickly and then at *Lima*. "Starboard a point. Another. Good! Hold her steady on nor'nor'west. For God's sake tell me if you sense the wind backing!"

Gallant noted Carty's nod, the helmsman's face a study in concentration.

It was time to show *Diane's* teeth. Gallant moved to the rail, hands cupped.

"Run out!" he bellowed. "Starboard and larboard batteries!"

There was a deep rumbling and squeal as the gun crews threw their weight against the falls of the side tackles, snouting the guns out through the red-lidded gunports.

"Prime and ready your match, captains!"

Gallant turned to O'Farrell. "He'll see both batteries run out. Still won't know what we're up to!" he said, raising his voice over the wind and sea noise. "Larboard battery!" he bellowed in the next instant. "When we pass along *Lima's* side, you're to lie flat on the deck! Spring up on my command!"

He moved quickly to the larboard rail. *Lima* loomed ahead, towering over the *Diane* as the two ships rushed together. He could see *Lima's* figurehead now above the boiling bow wave: a berobed, cherub-supported image of the Virgin.

"Eight hundred yards!" bellowed Béssac. "He's holding his fire, capitaine!"

Gallant nodded. The swine would do that. Waiting to inflict the greatest pain, the greatest hurt.

"Paul?" called Marianne, her voice high and strained. "I'm seeing the men on her decks. He's—there. Castelar. He's waving a sword and most of the men are running over to the guns on the side toward us!"

Gallant slapped the rail. "By Christ, that's what I wanted! Now if only we can turn in time—!"

In *Diane* rushed, running down to meet the great mass of the *Lima* that towered over her, pitching over the swells.

"Steady now, lads!" Gallant cried. "Not a man makes a move till I order! Ready at those sheets and braces, Béssac?"

"Ready, m'sieu'!" boomed the Mate.

Five hundred yards. Then three hundred. Two. Then one. Then—

"Now, Carty!" roared Gallant. "Hard a-larboard! Sheets and braces, Béssac! Damn your eyes, get her around!"

Heeling hard over to the sudden thrust of her helm, blocks

squealing aloft and canvas thundering as Béssac's men hauled with frenzied energy, *Diane* swung dramatically across the bows of the towering *Lima*, her yardarms seemingly inches from the Spaniard's stretching jib-boom. Shouts and cries rang down from *Lima's* foredeck, and several muskets popped, the balls thwacking here and there into *Diane's* deck.

A second more. *Diane* hurtled past *Lima's* undefended starboard bow, too low a shape to depress the chase guns down to, the great red and gilt wall of the Spanish ship's side rising like a heaving fortress above the hurrying little ship.

"Now!" cried Gallant. "Fire, lads! *Fire!*"

In ragged succession from the bows, *Diane's* battery of heavy guns and the lighter weatherdeck guns banged out, fifteen-foot tongues of pink flame framed in billows of grey, acrid smoke lancing out at *Lima* as she slid by. The concussions, reflected by the oaken walls of the Spanish ship, were ear-splitting. Again and again the linstocks arced down, the pink-flamed "huff" jetting head-high from each vent, and then the gun banging with a hard, metallic ring, leaping back against its breeching as a huge cloud of smoke boiled up over the side. Even before the violent recoil ended, the crews were leaping to sponge out and reload.

Gripping the rail, Gallant watched in wild excitement as the shot from *Diane's* guns struck home in splintering impacts on *Lima's* side, punching open great rents in the planking, arcing showers of fragments into the smoke-filled air between the two hulls. Here a gunport smashed crazily agape, there a ball lodged, smoking, embedded in the hull, the paint breaking into flames around it.

Diane sped on. Now cries of rage were echoing down from the big Spanish vessel. Muskets barked from the rail overhead, and several men fell in *Diane*. Beside Gallant's hand, a ball struck inches away, carrying off a cartwheeling splinter the size of a boot.

"Reload!" Gallant roared. "Béssac! Tend your sheets and braces! We're turning to starboard! Carty, bring her round! Hard a-starboard!"

"Crossing her stern?" cried O'Farrell, who had lost his hat.

"Yes! *Turn* her, Carty!"

Diane swung hard over, heeling as she turned, lifting and plunging into *Lima's* wake. A hail of musket shot burst from *Lima's* transomrail, pinging down over *Diane*, and Carty swore, clutching at his arm. He fell back, calling.

"Capitaine!" he gasped. "I'm — I can't — !"

Gallant spun. "Richard! Take the helm!" He swung back. "As you bear, starboard battery! *Fire!*"

200

The guns roared out again, the fire more ragged this time. Bang after bang sounded, the smoke whipped, acrid and blinding, up over the rail and into the gunners' faces. The humming iron shot smashed *Lima's* gilded, elaborately carved stern galleries, glass fragments and bits of woodwork splintering and cart-wheeling up and out over the sea surface. Several shot missed, bracketing the tall stern, leaping to the height of the mizzen spankeryard.

And then, as Gallant watched, a ball struck dead on the rudder post of the great ship. A halo of wood fragments and bits of ironwork leapt into the air. With a groan that was audible over the bark of the guns, *Lima's* broad rudder began to move oddly. It twisted, gleaming in the sun. And then it tore away from the high stern, trailing half-submerged on its chains.

"Jesus! The rudder! *We got her rudder*!" O'Farrell was bellowing.

"Hard down, Richard!" Gallant barked. "We'll board her! Béssac!"

"Here, capitaine!" came the bellow in the smoke.

"Brace her round, hard! We'll board her, starboard side to! Grapnels, fore and aft!" On this last order he could see out of the corner of his eye several men at the quarterdeck guns drop their gun tools and leap for the carefully coiled grapnels and their lines, neatly laid out on the deck.

Gallant spun on O'Farrell. "Turn her, Richard! For God's sake—!"

But O'Farrell had. Pitching as she swung, her canvas slatting as she came into the wind, *Diane* nosed in alongside *Lima's* massive hull, the water between the two ships suddenly a leaping mass of white foam. There was a grinding crash, and the two hulls met with a jarring impact that threw Gallant to one knee, with Marianne clutching at him for support. Aloft, *Diane's* yards buckled and whiplashed as they fouled in *Lima's* shrouds and braces. The canvas of both ships rippled in deep gunshot booms, and rudderless and dragged by *Diane's* hull, *Lima* slewed off the wind.

Grapnels flashed in the air from *Diane*, hooking high in *Lima's* rigging and instantly heaved taut. Gallant was suddenly on the rail, his ancient cutlass in one hand, bellowing behind him for the aft boarding party. And then they were rushing in behind him, eyes wild, hands filled with cutlasses, pikes and here and there a brandished pistol. The air was foul with smoke, and from above muskets began to flash in the gloom. Here and there, a *Diane's* man pitched back out of sight as a ball smashed him down.

"Now, lads!" shrieked Gallant. "*At 'em!*"

Gallant leaped wildly for *Lima's* side. He was airborne for a moment over the horrid, hissing abyss, and then he was banging down hard on the red, salt-gritty wood, clawing for a fingerhold. A line trailed a foot away to one side, and he clutched at it, giving it a savage tug. It held. Gallant thrust his cutlass into his belt behind him and clung on the line, monkeying up it with a fierce energy. He was conscious only that he seemed lost in a cloud of smoke that was filled with an appalling tumult of noise: oathes, screams, the clash of steel, running feet, the light bark of pistols and the heavier thump of muskets. Where in the name of God was he?

Abruptly, the line gave way, and he was falling, a scream choked off in his throat as he hit, hard and painfully, into a sprawl on wide deck planking, the cutlass clattering out on to the deck beside him as he hit.

Wild-eyed, he clutched at the cutlass, seeing himself surrounded by dark, struggling shapes. Suddenly he realized he was on *Lima's* deck, pressed round by a mob of men who were fighting in a desperate, brutal struggle. Screams rang in his ears, and he was momentarily blinded by the flash of a pistol inches before his eyes.

"*Diane! Diane!*" he cried, and lunged recklessly into the mob. He was shouldered by a tall, half-naked Spaniard. As he reeled back, the man bared yellowed, rotting teeth in a hideous grin below a drooping moustache and lunged at him with a vicious half-pike. With grunting force Gallant struck down at the pike, sending the severed point clanging to the deck. As the man stared incredulously at the shattered shaft, Gallant caught him with a whistling backhand cut across the head. With a bubbling scream the man put hands to the dissolving red mask of his face and fell away.

In the next split-second, the air hummed near Gallant's ear as a cut from a cutlass missed his head by inches. He ducked low as the backhand return cut whistled through the space where his head had been, and then lunged with the cutlass point toward his shadowy assailant. The blade plunged with a foul sound to the hilt in the muscular belly of a red-shirted black, who dropped his own weapon and, mouth open in a soundless scream, clutched his hands around Gallant's blade. Nausea swept over Gallant. Sobbing with effort, he fought to wrench his blade free, smashing at the man's face with his free fist until suddenly the man released his grip. The black fell heavily to the deck, mouth still gaping, as Gallant finally pulled his blade out with one last effort.

In the next instant, a blaze of incongruous sunlight washed over him, dazzling and unreal. The enormous pall of smoke from the guns had been whipped away by the wind. Gallant was standing in the waist of *Lima*, his breath coming in gasps, staring round him. All over the bloody and littered deck, men with wilted red ribbons in their hats or knotted in their queues were flinging down weapons, backing against bulkheads and fiferails, hands raised in surrender. Everywhere, men from *Diane* were swarming about the Spanish vessel, disarming her crewmen and thrusting them into small knots of miserable, squatting prisoners.

It was over.

O'Farrell, his hanger blade bloody and one sleeve of his blue coat ripped, was grinning at him from a few feet away.

"You've done it, Paul! We've *taken* the bastard!"

Gallant was without words for a moment, feeling his arms and legs trembling, his mouth dry. God, was it over? Had they—?

A pistol shot rang out, high and thin. With a gasp, Richard O'Farrell put his hand to his side, and then fell to the deck heavily.

"Richard!" burst out Gallant, in anguish. He spun round, a wild anger in his eyes.

And then he stopped, staring at the tall, dark figure that stood at the top of the quarterdeck ladder, a long, gleaming blade in one hand and a smoking pistol in the other.

"*Castelar!*" breathed Gallant.

"A pity," smirked the cruel, handsome face. "A ball meant to end your tedious life takes that of your noble little Irish bucko. How unfortunate."

Gallant's lips tightened to a hard, white line. "You contemptible bastard!" he whispered.

A Compagnies Franches marine from *Diane* stepped forward, hefting his musket and looking questioningly at Gallant.

"M'sieu'? Shall I—?"

Gallant shook his head violently, his eyes never leaving Castelar's.

"No!" he barked. "He's mine!"

He began to move toward the ladder, eyes still on the languid, handsome features.

"Ragged-looking, aren't you," hissed Castelar, motionless. "Tarry breeches and a dirty face. Much more appropriate to upstart colony filth, hein?"

Gallant was nearing the bottom of the ladder now. There was silence in the ship, as all eyes were locked on the drama.

"I should have killed you when I had the opportunity," said Castelar. "As we villains always say in such situations. But no

203

matter. I shall enjoy doing it — *now!*'' With snakelike speed, Castelar's arm cocked back, and he threw the pistol at Gallant's head.

But an instinct moved Gallant, and the pistol whirred past his ear, to splash overboard far below.

"You crow̃ too early, Castelar. Far too early!" he murmured. And then he leaped for the ladder.

Castelar turned and retired several steps with the grace of a fencing master as Gallant's bare feet slapped on to the quarter-deck. He saluted Gallant with the gleaming blade and then fell into a classic fencing position.

"Ready at last, are we?" he said smoothly. "Then we'd best begin!"

With lightning quickness he lunged forward. Gallant barely saw the flicker of Castelar's blade before he was reeling back, a hot lancet of pain burning in his shoulder. As Castelar slid away with low, mocking laughter, the marine looked down to see a broad gash in his left shoulder welling up with dark blood.

"Ah, first blood to me!" cried Castelar smoothly. He circled his blade, centring it on Gallant's chest.

Gallant shook his head to clear it of the fatigue and pain, ignoring the hot blood running down his arm. He circled Castelar, cautious, ignoring the mocking smirk, watching the eyes. And this time he saw the strike coming.

Castelar lunged, the blade licking out cobralike. But Gallant parried it with a ring of steel on steel, and then was in on Castelar, smashing in with furious blows at head and neck, driving through the Spaniard's defence, forcing him back with sheer force, a wild and uncaring anger alive in him.

"You'll die — ," he raged, " — like all — your kind — deserve to die — !" Again he swung, this time the final blow, the one which should have split Alfonso Castelar to his belt.

But the Spaniard had seen. His shoulders and hips twisted with a dancer's ease, and Gallant's blade hummed down, inches from Castelar's face, to impact against the iron of one of *Lima's* quarterdeck guns. The pain shot through Gallant's hands, and he gasped. And in the next instant his head had snapped back with the paralyzing force of Castelar's punch, and he sprawled back on the deck, the cutlass spinning from his fingers, a black blur of pain clouding his vision.

He could see the tall red figure moving over him; saw the blade lifting. He fought to sit up, to move, sobbing with the effort, trying to make his suddenly weak body act.

"Rats must die like rats, Gallant!" sneered the blurred red figure. "*Like this!*"

204

Gallant saw the silver blade flash in the air. He half rose to meet it. . . .

The pistol report rang in his ears, sharp and painful. Suddenly his vision cleared. And he was staring up at Don Alfonso Castelar, who was standing motionless, gazing down at him with an expression of astonishment. In the centre of his forehead was a neat blue hole.

And then the sword clattered from his fingers, and with a horrid sound the body fell stiffly backward to the deck.

As if at a great distance, Gallant saw the girlish figure at the top of the quarterdeck ladder, her eyes welling up with tears, the smoking pistol held stiffly before her with both hands, behind her the pale but alert form of Richard O'Farrell clutching a bloody bandage, supported by Béssac, both men's faces full of relief.

Then the pistol was falling to the deck, and he was rising to meet her as her feet flew across the planking to him. Their arms clasped shut around each other, and as he heard her sobs, Paul Gallant closed his eyes against the sweet pain and buried his face in the perfume of her hair.

"Oh, Marianne," he said simply.

Sir Aubrey Cathcart cupped his hands to shout to *Saracen's* maintop lookout. From where she lay anchored off the smoking ruins of Jacob Ten Haaf's stronghold, the British forty-four's main truck was high enough to glimpse a portion of the open sea. And his lookout had reported a most extraordinary thing.

"*Fight*, you say? The Frenchman *took* that bloody great Spanish vessel?"

"Aye, sir! Quick an' dirty it was too, sir!"

Cathcart turned to Sebastien Rye. "Got your prize crew aboard that other Dutch sloop, Rye?"

"Yes, sir," said Rye. "Pity about the other one."

"Mmm. Yes. What the deuce d'you make of that Froggy vessel taking the Spaniard? Not that I mind, eh? Thought we had a deuce of a chase on our hands."

"Sir," said Rye. "I have a feeling, sir. If you'll indulge me."

"Eh? What's that?"

"The Frenchman, sir. I have a feeling that he knows what he's about. And that he's done us a favour."

"Yes. So?"

Rye smiled. "I'd—leave him be, sir. Let him get on with his business. And we'll get on with ours."

Cathcart raised his eyebrows. "What? And let him get away with that bloody great prize?"

"I — ah — think she might prove more trouble than she is worth, sir."

Cathcart looked at him keenly. "You suspect that Portugee — or whatever — is behind something?"

"I do, sir. And perhaps to our advantage. And I'd hate to spoil it for him. After all, bringing his boat in perilous seas all the way in here —"

"Eh? He survived? But you said —"

"My telescope observed many things as we sailed in, sir. And since."

Cathcart nodded. After a moment he said, "Very well, Mr. Rye. Your advice will carry the day. But I hope you know what you're doing." He stalked off.

"I believe I do, sir," said Rye. And he looked up at the lookout, and then eastward as if his eyes could see what the lookout could see.

"And I believe so did he!" he murmured.

EPILOGUE

Versailles
the 6th August
1748

His Excellency the Comte de Maurepas
Minister of the Marine

Excellency:

You will be apprised, My Lord, of the sensation and perfect uproar the Court is in over the Valigny affair, and of the joy of His Majesty over the safe deliverance of the delicious Marianne de Poitrincourt, Marquise de Bézy; that a general Peace cannot come too soon, and is in fact imminent, I regard as a singular blessing, for one can only stand so much excitement. The Court is captivated by the Marquise, and of course not enough can be said about young M. Gallant, who is the rage *ad nauseam*. Not content with Your Excellency's promotion of M. Gallant to capitaine de vaisseau, he has settled another knighthood on him, in consequence of which the Marquise has declared she intends that they should marry. Her prodigious dowry which it was feared had been lost was in fact recovered virtually intact in the holds of that treacherous Spaniard's vessel when the Marquise was rescued, her sanguine young cavalier boarding and taking the vessel itself and duelling with the villain, and the Marquise, if it can be believed, pistolling the fiend to come to the aid of her beloved! His Majesty, with some deductions, has settled virtually the full amount upon them. The gallant fellow, if you will excuse a weak jest, has asked if you can believe to be given lands in Canada, and as His Majesty has granted him an enormous seigneurie among the snows and savages below Québec, and the Marquise has made it clear she will go with him, they are bound to travel there as soon as the Peace is concluded. There is much exclamation and sighs over this prodigious success of Cupid and of course no soul would deny the idyllic couple any reward, so charmed is the Court; but as to why they have chosen *Canada* it is beyond the capacity of your humble servant to say . . .

BESTSELLING BOOKS FROM TOR

☐ 58725-1 *Gardens of Stone* by Nicholas Proffitt $3.95
   58726-X   Canada $4.50

☐ 51650-8 *Incarnate* by Ramsey Campbell $3.95
   51651-6   Canada $4.50

☐ 51050-X *Kahawa* by Donald E. Westlake $3.95
   51051-8   Canada $4.50

☐ 52750-X *A Manhattan Ghost Story* by T.M. Wright
                                                 $3.95
   52751-8   Canada $4.50

☐ 52191-9 *Ikon* by Graham Masterton $3.95
   52192-7   Canada $4.50

☐ 54550-8 *Prince Ombra* by Roderick MacLeish $3.50
   54551-6   Canada $3.95

☐ 50284-1 *The Vietnam Legacy* by Brian Freemantle
                                                 $3.50
   50285-X   Canada $3.95

☐ 50487-9 *Siskiyou* by Richard Hoyt $3.50
   50488-7   Canada $3.95

Buy them at your local bookstore or use this handy coupon:
Clip and mail this page with your order

TOR BOOKS—Reader Service Dept.
49 W. 24 Street, 9th Floor, New York, NY 10010

Please send me the book(s) I have checked above. I am enclosing
$_____ (please add $1.00 to cover postage and handling).
Send check or money order only—no cash or C.O.D.'s.

Mr./Mrs./Miss _____

Address _____.

City _____ State/Zip _____

Please allow six weeks for delivery. Prices subject to change without
notice.

MORE BESTSELLERS FROM TOR

SOLDIER OF FORTUNE

MAGAZINE PRESENTS:

☐ 51202-2   DOORGUNNER $3.50
     51203-0   by Michael Williams   Canada $4.50

☐ 51206-5   MISSING BY CHOICE $3.50
     51207-3   by Roger Victor   Canada $4.50

Available in May

☐ 51204-9   THE CULT CRUSHERS $3.95
     51205-7   by Carl H. Yaeger   Canada $4.95

Available in June

☐ 51213-8   VALLEY OF PERIL $3.50
     51214-6   by Alex McCall   Canada $4.50

Available in July

☐ 51208-1   THE COUNTERFEIT HOSTAGE $3.95
     51209-X   by Carl H. Yaeger   Canada $4.95

Buy them at your local bookstore or use this handy coupon:
Clip and mail this page with your order

TOR BOOKS—Reader Service Dept.
49 W. 24 Street, 9th Floor, New York, NY 10010

Please send me the book(s) I have checked above. I am enclosing
$_____ (please add $1.00 to cover postage and handling).
Send check or money order only—no cash or C.O.D.'s.

Mr./Mrs./Miss _____

Address _____

City _____ State/Zip _____

Please allow six weeks for delivery. Prices subject to change without
notice.

RICHARD HOYT

"Richard Hoyt is an expert writer."
—*The New York Times*

THE SNOWBLIND MOON
JOHN BYRNE COOKE

"An epic canvas created with sure, masterful strokes. Bravo!"
—John Jakes

"*The Snowblind Moon* is an intensely readable story."
—*The Washington Post*

"An epic tale . . . lyrically beautiful."
—*Los Angeles Times Book Review*

THE BEST IN HORROR